THE DIGNITY OF SILENCE

THE
DIGNITY
OF
SILENCE

A NOVEL

JUNE
FELTON

The Book Guild Ltd

First published in Great Britain in 2022 by
The Book Guild Ltd
9 Priory Business Park
Wistow Road, Kibworth
Leicestershire, LE8 0RX
Freephone: 0800 999 2982
www.bookguild.co.uk
Email: info@bookguild.co.uk
Twitter: @bookguild

This work is entirely fictitious and bears no resemblance to any persons living or dead.

Typeset in 11pt Minion Pro

Printed on FSC accredited paper
Printed and bound in Great Britain by 4edge Limited

ISBN 978 1910508 527

British Library Cataloguing in Publication Data.
A catalogue record for this book is available from the British Library.

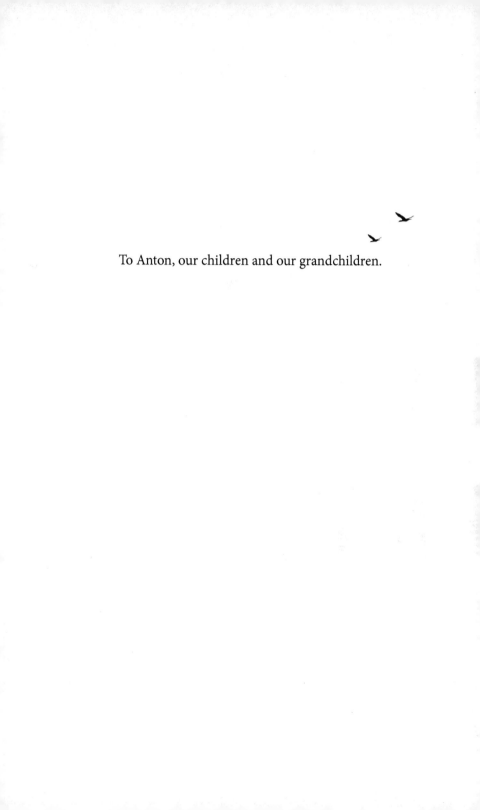

To Anton, our children and our grandchildren.

PART ONE

SEPARATION

ONE

THE ESCAPE

'Why did Lotte have to marry a Jew?' Frau Hoffmann sobbed, looking out through the window and waiting anxiously for Ernst, her son-in-law, and her granddaughter to arrive.

'You are being irrational.'

Hans could almost taste his wife's bitter tone.

'When you live in irrational times, you say irrational things,' barked Inge.

It was 1941. What was left of Czechoslovakia was under Nazi rule. Few were safe. Subterfuge had replaced trust.

Inge heard the car pull up outside in the narrow street. She rushed to open the front door and, sweeping her two-year-old granddaughter Sophie into her arms, led Ernst into the lounge. 'Thank God!' she sighed, brushing Sophie's head of soft curls against her cheek. In a fleeting moment she captured the stark reality that Lotte, her only daughter, was dead.

Ernst – in a trancelike state, his watery blue eyes staring out into the middle distance, then suddenly catching his mother-in-law's accusatory gaze – felt totally out of place, quite unable to think beyond the loss of his wife and how he would cope with Sophie and Oska, his and Lotte's newborn son. When Frau Hoffmann begged him to leave the baby with her, he was too distraught to do anything other than agree, seeing it as a temporary arrangement.

Frau Hoffmann had urged him to stay in Pilsen with his parents. Three long weeks had passed when their letter arrived with the news that, in giving birth to his son, Lotte had died. Frau Hoffmann had insisted that he and his family not attend Lotte's funeral in Prague. His world fell into an abyss. Jews were being rounded up, and his life, like those of most Czech Jews, hung in the balance.

Hans Hoffmann, a senior civil servant, had arranged for Ernst and Sophie to escape from Czechoslovakia. Ernst, devastated, had acceded. He had had no choice. His in-laws had sent their driver to bring him and Sophie to their home in Prague, where they would spend the day before leaving for England. It would be the first time Ernst saw his three-week-old son – only to say goodbye.

Confined in the Hoffmann's elegant home by the Charles Bridge, Sophie screamed to go into the back garden.

'Sophie, darling,' her grandmother pleaded, 'let Papa read you this lovely book, or would you like to see the baby?'

Screaming and kicking, Sophie fell to the floor.

Ernst appealed to Frau Hoffmann. 'Can't I take her out for five minutes?'

'Absolutely not. Ernst, I don't want to upset Sophie, but surely you understand the risk? We can't trust our neighbours. Sophie is going to have to learn to do as she's told, otherwise you won't get further than Prague Station.' Frau Hoffmann was desperate.

Sophie lifted herself off the floor and buried her head in Ernst's lap. He tried to distract her. 'Dearest, we're going on a holiday and you must listen to everything Papa tells you.'

'Mama! Mama! Mama! Mama! Mama!' she screamed, throwing herself onto the floor again.

'Mama has gone to heaven and you are going with Papa.'

Sophie's screaming reached a crescendo.

Ernst knew his mother-in-law was right. She had organised every detail of their escape. There was no way to help Sophie understand. Perhaps, one day, he would be able to explain, but he knew his love for her couldn't make up for the loss of her mother.

The Hoffmanns watched helplessly.

The day was filled with tears and silences. At last the time came for them to leave. Ernst picked up, hugged, kissed and said goodbye to baby Oska.

'Go, go now!' urged Frau Hoffmann, wanting the unbearable moment to end.

Dr Hoffmann poured a brandy for himself and Ernst. There was no right way to say goodbye, and in the suspended silence. 'You're doing the right thing; it's the only thing you can do.' He stood upright, a commanding figure looking directly at Ernst. 'We'll do what we can,' he continued, in a voice weaker than he'd intended. He bent over to give Ernst a bear hug, then, grasping his hand firmly as if unable to let go, conveyed a fleeting moment of authenticity that enabled Ernst to leave.

Knowing that survival took precedence over suffering, Ernst picked up Sophie, who, moulding her small body into his, wrapped her legs around his waist, one arm clinging to his shoulder while the other held her favourite book and a soft doll. With his left hand Ernst picked up his leather suitcase filled with manuscripts, photographs, clothing, and food and drinks for Sophie. Not looking back, he walked slowly towards the door. Sophie lifted her tiny hand in a hesitant wave, her innocent gesture capturing all of their suffering.

*

In the car to Prague Central Station he recalled how he and Lotte had talked of little else but how to escape to England. He blamed himself for being so easily won over by his in-laws, whose advice had seemed logical at the time. As a senior civil servant, Dr Hoffmann knew and had kept him informed of the latest edicts and prohibitions, and of the number of Jews who were being arrested and sent to Theresienstadt concentration camp. He had assured Ernst that he would get them visas to England in spite of the visa quota and the four-year waiting list.

But then Lotte had been alive. Perhaps they should have left sooner, but Ernst had been persuaded by his father-in-law's promise to get additional visas for his parents and two sisters. Perhaps if he had not considered Frau Hoffmann's plea to let Lotte stay with them in Prague for the last two months of her pregnancy, Lotte would still be alive. At the time he had weighed the risk of staying against the long-term gain of their new life in London. Now, as if governed by robotic force, he gazed mindlessly at the passing scenes of Prague. Sophie, oblivious then, would later relive the anxiety of that time.

Ernst's thoughts turned to his family in Pilsen. His father had encouraged him to leave Czechoslovakia, and even his mother, who knew but didn't talk of the imminent threat, had urged, 'Go! Go! You have no choice.'

Those last weeks in Pilsen had been the worst, anxiously awaiting news of Lotte. For the rest of his life not a day would pass without his reliving the day the letter arrived. Nothing could have prepared him as he read and reread it. His legs gave way and he flopped onto the nearest chair, the blood draining from his face. Trembling, he felt himself descending into an abyss. It was unthinkable that Lotte could die.

In the days that followed, while waiting for their exit visas, he'd lived in a trance. As he kept Sophie entertained and tried to be supportive to his parents and sisters, he did what he could to suppress his own grief. In the long, painful nights, he'd tried to contemplate a life without Lotte, and had been sustained by the hope that, as soon as Dr Hoffmann had got their visas, his family would join him in London. But nothing could be certain in this rapidly disintegrating world. The descending sun cast a rosy glow across a seamless sky on their last warm August evening. Ironically, he was leaving Prague in style as Dr Hoffmann's limousine moved slowly through the traffic. The passing scenes of people going about their business gave no hint of the tragedy that had befallen his beloved city; nor could he ever have imagined this day, fleeing the family he loved for an unknown life in London. He tried to repress his self-pity and despair by repeating one of his many maxims: 'I will make the best of things.'

At the station, dressed in a three-piece suit with his gold fob watch hung across his stocky figure, no one questioned him. The trick was to appear confident, as if entitled and authorised to go about his business. But he was terrified of being stopped and searched at any one of the checkpoints. The SS guards were everywhere; some in ordinary clothes, blending in with the crowd. Variably, at random, people were being stopped and searched, and Ernst deliberately kept his hands away from the few gold coins sewn into the seams of his suit. Posing as a Sudeten-German businessman travelling to Paris, he had indoctrinated himself to play the part. He had the papers to prove it, and the names and addresses at the ready, and kept reminding himself that it takes two people to believe a lie. He had to believe that he was the man he was pretending to be if he was to convince the Nazi police. He would have felt more confident if it hadn't been for Sophie clinging to him. It was past her bedtime and he hoped the movement of the train would lull her to sleep, but she whimpered fearfully as Ernst, in trying to calm her, quelled some of his own anxiety.

*

Their harrowing journey across Europe, scrutinised at every checkpoint, shaped the way Sophie would view her father. Over time her memories faded, but she retained an impression of a darkened room with figures looming over her; and then of being wrenched into Ernst's arms, infused with his panic and an archaic feeling of clinging to and being part of him; of men shouting, stamping through corridors; of the train's seemingly perpetual rhythm then of suddenly stopping and starting with her father's heartbeat as, while she was tightly clinging to him, SS guards marched up the carriage and seized the man sitting next to him and took him away; then of a wide expanse of emptiness and Ernst forever holding her, turning the pages of her picture books.

She never ceased to sense, but could never share, her father's pain, and had learned not to ask questions. Often it was on the tip of her tongue to ask, 'Tell me about my mother', but she dared not intrude into his grief. The silence had become encrusted and buried between them, hovering without shape or form, but permeating and dominating the rest of their lives.

TWO

LONDON

Ernst marvelled at how Sophie had adapted to their new life in London, how speedily she had acquired English at nursery school, and how she had excelled at the local primary school. She appeared to be an undemanding child, and Ernst may not have realised why his shy and anxious little girl did not invite any friends home. Nor, for her part, could she tell him that she was embarrassed by their sombre apartment with its continental furniture filled with books, and by her father's foreign accent. But most of all, when other children talked or boasted or complained about their mothers, she couldn't explain why she did not have one, for she did not know the reason herself. You could lose your book or your favourite doll, but how could you lose your mother?

School holidays proved difficult. Sophie filled her days with reading, finding comfort in those characters that echoed her own hopes and dreams, and Ernst would often interrupt his busy struggles to survive to take her on outings to museums, cinemas and restaurants. Sophie developed a fascination with World War II; it was as if sensing Ernst's avoidance of the subject increased her curiosity. On her fourteenth birthday she asked him why he had left it so late to get out of Prague. Without realising, he reverted to speaking German: 'Aber manchmal ist es nicht. Es war nicht nur um Prague zu verlassen aber auch was man dort verliess "ui iu".' ('Timing is everything, but there are times when it is nothing. It wasn't just leaving Prague, it was who we had to leave behind.')

Sixteen years had passed since the end of the war. Ernst had learned through the refugee organisation that his mother, father and his sisters had died in Theresienstadt, and he had, despite an almost overwhelming urge, adhered to Dr Hoffmann's demand that he neither directly nor indirectly make any contact or enquiry of them, for the Nazis and their Czech collaborators were constantly seeking out Czechs, particularly government officials, who had, or even appeared to have, any contact with the West. After Germany was defeated the Communists became the major party, and the typhus epidemic of 1946 was as nothing to the pandemic of collaborators, their friends and families, Czechs, Germans and many Hungarians. Then, a couple of years later, backed by Russian tanks, a *coup d'etat* gave the communists total power. Now the victims of the purges were new, but the pattern of those purges was the same. One of the numerous crimes that ten government ministers and high officials, the majority Jews, were publicly tried and executed for was their connections to the West. Another hundred were similarly tried and executed. This was no time for Ernst to even try to find out if his son or the Hoffmanns were alive, for to do so might cause their deaths. He had no doubt that the pain he suffered for his enforced silence all those years was not something he should ever put upon or share with Sophie. He had no reason to believe that she wasn't reasonably contented, especially when she gained a scholarship to Oxford. He felt justified in keeping their past from her. 'You don't unravel something that's working,' was another of his mantras that helped guide his behaviour.

*

Sophie, now eighteen, was the image of her mother. It was a deep wrench for both her and Ernst when she went up to Oxford. In spite of her quintessential English persona, feeling herself an outsider, she became one. She made acquaintances, which never developed much beyond her helping them with their academic problems. It was as if she had lost trust when her essential bond with her mother had broken.

It was 1961, and England was flourishing with a new sexual freedom. Sophie listened with amazement to other girls boasting of their exploits and kept her disapproval to herself. In the last week of her final term, she walked to the pub, where other students were celebrating their results. She stood by the door, looking out for familiar faces.

Surprisingly, she saw Marc approach her. 'You look like a classics scholar,' he said facetiously, studying both her unruly head of curls that obscured her classic features and her slim figure beneath an oversized sweater and baggy jeans. Then, seeing her flushed cheeks and pained expression, he stepped back. 'Sorry, I didn't mean to encroach. Anita asked me to bring you over.'

Sophie recalled helping Anita with an essay, after which the other girl had barely made contact. However, she was caught up in the general excitement, with everybody swapping addresses. She chatted mainly with Marc, whose warmth and kindly disposition helped her relax. He told her that he had just finished his final architectural exams at the Oxford Poly, and asked if they might meet when he went down to London. After three lonely years at Oxford it seemed like a godsend.

Back in London, Marc met Ernst, who welcomed his open,

down-to-earth attitude. He trusted Marc, seeing him as a much-needed companion for Sophie. One evening when they were all dining in one of Ernst's favourite restaurants, Marc asked Sophie if she would like to join him in touring around Europe before he started work in September. With a fleeting look at Ernst she said excitedly, 'I'd love to', and was amazed when Ernst encouraged her, considering that she had only known Marc for a few weeks.

Sophie found Marc kind and undemanding, and knew he wasn't surprised when she told him she was still a virgin. Marc was different; she trusted him, and was pleased that he waited.

They wandered around Ravenna with its sixth-century mosaics, then on to Rome. In sharing her enthusiasm for classical architecture, Marc gave the illusory impression of like-mindedness. They had been together for two months when, after a romantic dinner, she succumbed. She didn't know what to expect. Marc was caring and patient.

She spent the rest of the summer in a trance, drinking coffee in pavement cafes and watching the world move around her. They returned to London at the end of September, so that Marc could start his new job in the Local Authority Planning Department. Too alarmed to tell Ernst, when Sophie discovered she was pregnant, she blamed him for encouraging her to go on the trip.

When she told Marc, he didn't hesitate. 'We'll get married.'

'Are you sure we're doing the right thing?' She needed to know.

'I do love you. I know it's a shock. Come here.' Marc swept her up in his arms. 'I know it will be good for both of us,' he murmured in her ear.

His large arms encircled her, and fleetingly, she felt safe. But she realised that a fundamental change had taken place, and as he pressed against her swollen breasts, a sense of depletion and slight nausea took hold.

Ernst hid his dismay and guilt. He liked Marc, who had been quite open with him when asking for his permission to marry Sophie. All he could think of was how to protect his daughter.

Marc's parents took the day off from work to attend the marriage ceremony in the Hampstead Registry Office. Afterwards, they took a taxi to the Dorchester Hotel in Mayfair for a celebratory lunch. Ernst learned that Marc's mother worked as a cleaner and his father was in the building trade. They all got on well, and Ernst admired Marc and his parents for their honesty and kindness. Most of all, he was reassured to see how attentive Marc was to Sophie.

Ernst proposed that they rent a flat while looking for a house to buy. After a couple of months Marc found a run-down Edwardian house in a leafy crescent in Muswell Hill. It was much larger than they needed, but Ernst saw that Marc could improve it and that it would be a good investment. The separate flat in the basement was an added attraction. Marc relished the challenge.

Ernst accepted that Marc's salary couldn't support Sophie and his future grandchild, and readily provided the necessary help. He concealed his irritation at Marc's left-wing dogmatism and contained his doubts, recalling how the Hoffmanns had openly expressed their disapproval when their daughter married a Jew. Knowing Sophie's fragility and solitary nature, her happiness was the priority, and for her to be content was good enough. For Ernst, living with a loss that could not be expressed, life would always be a compromise.

THREE

THE CONFINEMENT

Woken by violent spasms in her abdomen, Sophie squinted against the sunlight streaming through the window. Her dream vanished, leaving her with a faint memory of being pursued. Watching Marc fast asleep, she felt alone, trapped by the irreversible process that had transformed her body but left her unprepared for motherhood. Something more entrenched bothered her, too. All her life she had suppressed any longings for her own mother, and she feared that this may have blunted her maternal instinct. Why else did she feel so detached from the rapture described in books about childbirth? If anything, the more she read the more detached she felt, yet at the same time she feared a painful birth.

She slipped out of bed and went down to the kitchen. While waiting for the coffee to percolate she gazed out at the long, narrow garden with its central stone path overrun by rhubarb and building rubble, and blue wisterias entangled with rose creepers weighing down the wooden shed. The hazy blue sky promised another hot day. Going out onto the terrace abutting the kitchen, she felt obliged to mark her last batch of exam papers. Her work as a part-time external examiner in Latin and Greek A Level served as a quiet distraction. Academia appeared to be the only place she felt comfortable. When the coffee was ready, she got up to pour herself a cup. Surprisingly, the aroma made her feel queasy. She went back upstairs. In the bedroom, she slumped into the Victorian chair by the window and waited for the giddiness to pass.

Marc stirred. 'Are you okay?'

'I feel a little light-headed, but I promised myself I'd post the last batch of exam papers today. I'd better get going.' She dragged herself into the bathroom and splashed handfuls of cold water over her face, whereupon another bout of dizziness forced her to sit on the edge of the bath. Spotting her sandals under a pile of towels, she bent down to retrieve them and the room spun round. Suddenly seeing her feet, she yelled, 'Marc! My feet are huge! Something is wrong!'

Marc jumped out of bed and wrapped his large hands around her balloon-like feet. 'Why don't you lie down? I'll phone the doctor,' he said, helping her onto the bed and hiding his alarm.

'I feel so ill, I don't think I can finish my work,' she mumbled apologetically.

'Relax, you'll soon feel better.' But he didn't believe it.

He phoned the doctor and watched her fall asleep. The sunlight shimmering over her damp forehead surrounded by thick, wavy hair revealed her haunting beauty and palpable fragility. Studying her pale face, high cheekbones and full, sensuous mouth, he realised the weight of his responsibility. He rushed around picking up clothes strewn over the bedroom floor, tidying the bathroom and waiting anxiously for the doctor. He thought of Sophie's incompetence and too of Ernst's overprotection which had contributed to her lack of practicality.

The doctor arrived, examined Sophie, gave her a sedative and called for an ambulance.

Marc knew that he had to phone Ernst. 'Sophie isn't too well.'

He heard Ernst's silent anxiety. Then his voice cracked. 'What's wrong?'

'She has some form of toxaemia and I'm waiting for the ambulance to take us to the clinic.'

There was a deathly silence.

'Ernst!'

'I'm here. Why didn't they see it earlier?' Ernst demanded, weeping.

'Don't worry, I'll phone you from the clinic.' Marc tried to reassure him, but Ernst had unnerved him. He had not considered the possibility of anything going wrong.

In a weak and shaky voice, Ernst pleaded, 'Please, Marc, phone me with any news. I hope they know what they're doing, these doctors. I hope there's enough time.'

Gripped with fear, Ernst's mind slipped back. It couldn't happen again, not after all he had gone through. Not after losing Lotte in the same circumstances. He had always wanted to tell Sophie about her mother, but in waiting for the right moment, no right moment had come. The longer he'd remained silent, the more difficult it had been to speak. Now he promised himself that if Sophie lived, he would tell her about her mother, and Oska, her brother.

Watching Sophie sleep, Marc thought about how she bore no resemblance to Ernst, who was short and rotund while Sophie was tall, slim, shapely and naturally beautiful. Yet she and her father were of the same mind, always distilling and dissecting ideas, which made Marc, who saw life in simpler terms, wonder whether Sophie and he really belonged together.

The wail of an ambulance siren broke his chain of thought, and he took comfort in having acted so speedily. He was reassured that Mr Lewis, the obstetrician, would be waiting for them at the clinic. Filled with gratitude for the privileges of private medicine and for Ernst's generosity in paying for it, Marc forgot his duty as a socialist to the National Health Service.

FOUR

THE CLINIC

Heavily sedated, Sophie was vaguely aware of Ernst pacing up and down the clinic foyer.

'How on earth did he manage to get here before the ambulance?' Marc muttered, not expecting a reply.

'I'm sorry, Marc, I hope he behaves himself,' Sophie mumbled, thankful for her father's presence.

Marc was directed to the artificially lit waiting room where Ernst and two other men were also waiting.

Radiating fear, Ernst peered nervously down the passage in the hope of talking to somebody. 'We're being ignored; the whole place appears chaotic. Why don't they send somebody to tell us what's happening? I must know what's happening to Sophie. I hope this Mr Lewis knows what he's doing. Believe me, you can't trust doctors,' he barked, apparently unaware of the other men in the room.

Marc glared at him. 'I'm sure Mr Lewis has more than enough to do without worrying about us.'

His attempt to calm Ernst had the opposite effect. 'I expect better; this isn't your National Health Service,' the older man shouted.

Marc didn't reply. Time dragged. Ernst walked into the passage and saw a man in a green theatre gown approach. Aubrey Lewis, the obstetrician, went up to Marc, and Ernst edged himself between them.

'This is Mr Graff, Sophie's father,' Marc explained.

Aubrey gave Ernst a cursory glance. 'Although Sophie is stable, her toxaemia isn't responding to treatment. I will operate in the next half-hour.' He turned to leave, obviously in a hurry.

'Why didn't you see it earlier?' Ernst demanded.

Aubrey was taken aback; he would never have associated Sophie's English reserve with her father's temperament and autocratic foreign accent. 'Mr Graff, I understand your concern, but these hidden toxaemias are quite rare. Our main concern is to keep Sophie calm.'

'Can you save my daughter?' Ernst demanded.

'Mr Graff, I have every intention of saving your daughter and delivering her baby.' Aubrey turned to Marc. 'You may go and see Sophie for a few minutes only, but please keep her calm.' Before leaving, he added, 'Try not to worry, Mr Graff.'

A few minutes later Marc returned and gently laid his hand on Ernst's shoulder. 'Can I get you a cup of coffee?'

'How is she?' Ernst asked, thinking of his wife who was almost the same age as Sophie when she died. He thought too of his own mother and the last time he had seen her. 'You go, don't worry; we will be all right,' she had said. 'Don't be sad; you will upset Sophie.' He had promised her that he would get the family out of Czechoslovakia. Lotte's father had promised to get the visas, and now, as he waited for Sophie to come out of the operating theatre, he was too frightened to believe anything.

Suspended in his mistrust, he was too distracted to see the

nurse in charge come into the waiting room, and didn't hear her tell Marc that he had a son.

Excitedly, Marc prodded Ernst. 'It's a boy! Sophie is fine. We can go and see them.'

Ernst wept. 'Thank God! You go; I'll wait here.'

Sophie was drowsy and unresponsive when Marc kissed her. 'Well done, dearest.' He looked in the crib, entranced by the completeness of his pink, velvet-skinned baby with his swathe of brown hair. Marc resisted an overwhelming desire to pick him up and hold him. Sophie had fallen into a deep sleep. He held her hand. 'He's quite beautiful; a miniature replica of you. I'll be back,' he whispered.

Back in the waiting room, he found Ernst more composed.

'You must see your grandson; he's quite gorgeous. Sophie is still drowsy.'

Marc watched Ernst take his white silk handkerchief from his top pocket, wipe his eyes, stand erect and then pause, waiting for Marc to lead him down the corridor. Inside Sophie's room Marc stood back, observing as Ernst kissed her on her forehead and then, seemingly in a daze, looked into the crib.

Ernst thought of Oska. He could picture him as a baby quite vividly, but couldn't imagine him as a grown man. He would never give up hope of seeing his son again one day. His mind slipped back to that nightmare of 1941 when he had been forcibly cut off from one life and thrown into another. He and Sophie had survived, and now he had a grandson.

For the first time he experienced a connection with Marc, and felt indebted to him for helping him to survive the day. He recalled that when he had asked Sophie to tell him about Marc, she'd replied, 'What you see is what you get.' At the time he'd thought she was being flippant, but Sophie was right. He valued Marc's uncomplicated emotions and simple decency that had helped him get through the day. He smiled to himself, thinking of his own difficulty in taking anything at face value. No wonder

Sophie had married a man like Marc. Deep down, she must have known that by taking everything as it was and at its face value, the power of the past over the present would diminish. The more he thought about it, the more he liked the idea and started to mould it into his justification for not telling Sophie about their past.

Outside, despite the oppressive heat, Ernst felt comfortable in his cream three-piece suit. He walked effortlessly amongst the crowds, hoping to hail a passing taxi. He would phone Jane when he got home. Although they didn't live together, Jane had been his loyal companion for the past ten years. He would ask her out for dinner to celebrate.

FIVE

THE MEETING

Drifting in and out of a drug-induced sleep, Sophie slowly opened her eyes. The shimmering sunlight behind the patterned curtains cast eerie shadows across the pink walls of the small room. As she swallowed automatically against the sensation of a sandpapery tongue, unfamiliar aromas filled her nostrils. She turned towards a muffled sound, but was restricted by the plastic tube attached to the needle in her arm. She managed to lift her head to glance at the crib beside her bed and saw her baby swaddled in a white blanket, his tiny hand, with long fingers just like hers, spread out against his cheek. His eyes were closed, and thick lashes defined their almond shape. She waited for some feelings to emerge, but none came. Her detachment was unsettling, compounded by unfamiliar sensations that slowly took hold. Her breasts ached. Sharp pains pulled across her abdomen, and she lifted the sheet to glance at her swollen tummy covered with a strip of gauze dressing. Surrendering now to the seeping stickiness underneath her, she felt trapped, anxious and claustrophobic. It didn't occur to her to ring the bell above her bed. Unable to quell her sense of loss and longing, she burst into tears. Then the door opened and, seeing a nurse approach, she stopped weeping.

'How are you feeling, Sophie?' asked the nurse.

'A little uncomfortable,' she replied, attempting to mask her terror.

'Don't worry; we'll soon get you straightened out. Then you can feed your baby. I'll be back to help you freshen up,' replied the nurse matter-of-factly, and left the room.

Rivulets of hot, salty tears trickled down Sophie's cheeks and into her mouth. She couldn't explain her low spirits and aching loneliness. When the nurse returned Sophie felt disinclined to talk to her. Remaining passive, and letting the nurse take off the theatre gown and gently wash her, she was hardly aware of her arms being lifted and rubbed dry, but grateful for the nurse's light touch on her tender body. She watched the nurse pick up her baby and, before she was ready, place his little body across her chest. His soft crying terrified her.

'I don't think I can manage; I feel too ill,' Sophie pleaded through her tears. She watched him open his eyes. His little arms hung limply at his sides as he turned his head to her breast while the nurse supported his back. 'What do you want me to do?'

'Just guide your nipple into his mouth, and he'll latch on.'

She felt his warmth and breathed in his sweet baby smell. Her body stiffened with pain as he sucked hard and rhythmically. She loathed it.

'There you are – only for a minute on each breast. You'll soon get the hang of it.'

Sophie willed the time to pass until the nurse picked up the baby to wind him and place him back in the cot. After the nurse left, her entire body shuddered with uncontrollable weeping. Trying to compose herself, she peered through the gap in the half-open door. A trolley with neatly piled linen passed by; a man holding a huge bouquet of white flowers talked to a nurse; the grinding noise of a vacuum cleaner and the persistent hum of machinery increased her sense of alienation. She tried to imagine how her life might have been if she had had a mother. The closest she had to a mother figure was Jane, but even now she thought of Ernst and Jane as an odd couple. When she was younger, Sophie remembered being intimidated by Jane, but now she believed that Jane had, in her way, understood her motherless state. She recalled her embarrassment when Ernst had assigned Jane to talk to her on the pretext of her eleventh-birthday outing. Sophie had enjoyed the Pierre Bonnard paintings at the Royal Academy, and especially Jane's enthusiasm for and knowledge of them. Afterwards, they had gone to Fortnum & Mason for tea. In between ordering cakes, Jane, who owned a small art gallery, continued to discuss the Impressionist painters; then abruptly made vague references to girls growing up and their bodies changing, which she clarified by anxiously suggesting that after tea they go to the chemist to buy the necessary items. Jane had told Sophie to let her know when it happened, but the reality had come as a shock; a shock that she now equated with her present predicament. Desperately, she envisaged Marc taking care of their baby, and wanted to see him. She also needed Ernst to restore some stability to what appeared to be her crumbling world. Aware that her mind was flitting at random, she forced herself to focus. She thought of last summer, when she'd been so happy travelling with Marc through Europe.

*

She couldn't tell how long she'd been dozing when Aubrey Lewis and the nurse came into the room. 'Good morning, Sophie, feeling any better?' She watched Aubrey glance at some notes under the pretext of observing her, then fix his heavy-lidded eyes on her, which appeared to pierce her fragility. 'How is the breastfeeding going?'

She hesitated. 'I'm not sure.'

'Try not to worry. You've been through quite an ordeal, and the first few days can often be unsettling. I'm going to prescribe something which should help. I'll call in again tomorrow.'

Hanging on to his every word, she was pleased when he left, and wondered whether she had managed to mask the depth of her shameful despair. Trying to distract herself, she phoned Jane. 'The flowers are beautiful, thank you,' she said, suspecting that Jane recognised her lifeless tone, and appreciating her restraint in not even enquiring about the baby.

'Is there anything I can do?' Jane asked.

'I only have a few creased T-shirts and I need something more practical that buttons down the front.' She wanted to add, 'for feeding my baby', but couldn't.

'I'll gather a few things together and bring them down later. You must rest; it's very early days,' Jane said supportively.

Whilst Sophie had harboured doubts about Ernst's relationship with Jane, for all they appeared to share was a love of art, she now realised how he must be comforted by Jane's unfussy goodness.

A knock on the door, and a porter came in with a large bouquet of white roses. Rereading the card seemed to alleviate her sense of isolation. 'To my courageous daughter and grandson, love Ernst.' She swallowed a lump in her throat to answer the phone, sensing it was Marc.

'Our son is quite beautiful. Are you feeling any better?'

'Not really,' she barely managed to say, wiping the tears from her eyes. It was as if she was drowning in a sorrow which she could neither explain nor dare to display.

'I'm on my way,' he replied.

*

25

Later that day, Sophie heard a knock on her door. She looked at the petite woman, smiling in a cream silk dressing gown, standing at the end of her bed.

'I asked the nurse if it would be all right to visit you. I also had a caesarean yesterday, and so did the woman in the next room. Isn't it extraordinary that we all had boys? By the way, I'm Emma, Emma Bloom.'

Sophie studied Emma's high colour and large, widely set brown eyes. 'You appear very active; I can hardly lift my head off the pillow,' she said, instantly regretting her display of self-pity.

'I should be fit after all the exercising I've done, but I suspect your situation is more complicated. The nurse told me you had toxaemia.' Emma, peering into the crib, enthused, 'Your baby is gorgeous – all that hair, and such beautiful hands. But I'd better go and let you rest.'

'Thank you for coming,' Sophie said, wondering what she had in common with Emma's overbearing liveliness and haughty accent. The fleeting encounter made her conscious of her own despondency.

*

Sophie woke with a start to see Marc standing next to her. He bent over to kiss her, setting her off into muffled sobs. He tried to draw her towards him but was prevented from doing so by the drip.

'Go and look at the baby,' she urged.

Through her tears she watched Marc's softened expression as he stood by the crib. 'Can I hold him?' he asked.

'I suppose so. I just hope he doesn't wake up and want a feed or something.'

Marc gently picked up his baby and cradled him in his large hands. 'He's quite beautiful, isn't he? I think he looks like you...' He bent to lightly brush the baby's head with his lips, as if inhaling nectar.

Profoundly moved by his tenderness, which served only to enhance her sense of failure, Sophie was distracted from her crying by a knock on the door. It was Ernst holding an enormous teddy bear.

'I don't think he's quite ready for that.' She couldn't disguise her flat tone as Ernst kissed her on the cheek.

His first words – 'You look very tired, dear' – set her off again.

'I'm sorry for being so miserable but I can't seem to help it. I know I should be ecstatic, and that makes everything even worse. Ernst, would you like to hold the baby?'

'I'd better not; I've come from the office and I don't want to pass on any germs,' he replied, standing motionless, looking intensely at his grandson.

She found nothing odd about Ernst's introspection. Marc stood by the window, and it wasn't long before he suggested that she should rest. They would come back later. She was relieved to be alone, imagining that they would go down to the coffee bar and share their concerns about her.

*

She couldn't tell how long she'd been sleeping when she woke to see Emma smiling at her, standing at the end of her bed holding a bouquet of roses.

'I don't usually go around delivering flowers but the lady in the next room asked me to give these to you.'

'How extraordinary!' Sophie wanted an explanation, which Emma promptly delivered.

'Don't worry, there isn't an inch of space in her room for another flower. She must be some sort of celebrity. She's quite beautiful and awfully nice. Her name is Angelica Stern; when you're up to it, you can go in and thank her personally. I told her about your ordeal.'

'I suppose I should write a thank-you note.' Sophie looked at the drip in her arm. 'You're so active. I just don't know anything about babies, and I don't know how I'm going to cope.'

'Where do you live?' asked Emma.

'Muswell Hill.'

'I live in Stanmore. That's not so far; if you need any advice, just phone me. I've read that it's best to find a routine and stick to it.' Emma hovered by the bed, waiting for Sophie's reply and not knowing whether she wanted her to stay or not.

'I would be grateful for any advice,' Sophie said.

'I'm happy to help, but I must warn you: most people find me a bit bossy.'

Sophie reproached herself for being so judgemental. Emma's offer of friendship apparently quite genuine, even natural, compared to her own wavering attempts, and she worried that her tardy response might drive Emma away.

Sophie heard a knock on the door. 'May I come in? I'm Angelica Stern. Emma told me you had your caesarean after me, so I wanted to see how you're getting on.'

Sophie took a few seconds to make the connection. It was difficult to think of Angelica as another patient; her fresh complexion, blue eyes and soft features best belonged to a Botticelli painting. Her full lips broke into an engaging smile.

'How is your baby?' Angelica asked.

'He seems fine, although to be honest I don't think I'm the best person to ask. I appear to be the only one still in bed, and I feel too weak to move. How's *your* baby?' Sophie asked, feigning interest.

'Very small but perfect. I would have lost him if it wasn't for Mr Lewis. Isn't it strange the way things work out? Do you mind if I sit down? I suddenly feel exhausted.' Angelica flopped onto the chair by the window, wrapping her silk turquoise dressing gown around her. Sophie couldn't place her accent but felt reassured by her caring and calming manner.

'I suppose I'm still shell-shocked,' Sophie said apologetically.

'You'll feel different tomorrow. I've made a recovery. I was dreading getting up, but I do feel better for it,' Angelica said.

After Angelica left, Sophie felt obliged to make an effort and asked the nurse to help her. Half-heartedly, she walked across the room and looked at her baby. The nurse suggested she sit down, but when she placed the baby in her arms, Sophie felt her body stiffen. She studied his dark eyelashes. His features appeared to imply a most potent image of herself. She turned to look out the window, thankful that he was asleep and oblivious to her sadness. His innocence threatened her.

*

Later, when the time came to discharge his three patients, Aubrey Lewis was intrigued to learn that they had become friends and often gathered together in Emma's room. From the nurses' progress reports, it seemed that Emma was not only doing very well herself, but demonstrating how best to feed, bath, massage and exercise a baby to Angelica and Sophie. The nurse's main concern was Sophie, reporting that she was less tearful when she was with Emma and Angelica but often broke down at other times, particularly when her father visited. She also took so long to bath and feed her baby that she hardly had time to rest in between, so the nurse suggested that Sophie might find it easier to bottle-feed her baby as her husband could then help.

Aubrey Lewis disagreed, concerned that it might reinforce Sophie's sense of failure, and reflected on how he had been stirred by his brief encounter with Ernst Graff's devotion to his daughter. 'I would like to have a word with her husband before she leaves,' he told the nurse. There appeared to be something in Sophie's personality that drew help from others.

SIX

AT HOME

Sophie followed Marc upstairs, her legs still stiff and heavy. Tensing her mouth and blinking to suppress her tears, she felt both fear and relief as she stood in the doorway of the nursery, watching Marc put their baby in his cot. Her mood lightened when saw how Marc had transformed the room. He had painted each strut of the old wooden cot in the primary colours and placed a matching chest of drawers that doubled as a changing table against the opposite wall. Above the chest he had built red, blue and yellow shelves, arranged in a geometric pattern to hold nappies, toiletries, clothes and toys. On the black-and-white tiled floor stood three empty plastic buckets labelled 'Dirty nappies', 'Washing' and 'Rubbish'.

'Marc, it's wonderful; you've thought of everything.'

A diagonal beam of sunlight struck the baby's head, prompting Marc to say, 'I still have to put the blind on the window.'

'I can't believe you did all this in ten days.' Sophie watched

Marc hang a towel over the window to create temporary shade. How could she have been so wrong as to suspect that he would not get it all organised?

'I enjoyed doing it, although I could have done with another week.'

'I couldn't have stayed in the clinic another hour; I feel so much better being at home.'

They heard a taxi pull up outside. 'On cue,' Marc said, but privately thought, *Saved by the bell*, as he went downstairs to let Ernst in.

Overloaded with bags of food from the delicatessen, a huge bunch of roses and a variety of toys, Ernst bustled in. 'How is she?'

'It's early days,' Marc warned as they went up to the nursery.

Ernst kissed Sophie on the cheek, then, noticing the nursery, gasped. 'This is truly wonderful, Marc; he'll become an artist like Lotte.'

Sophie wanted to ask him why, after all these years, he'd spontaneously started mentioning her mother, but knew better than to do so, resigning herself, as she had always done, to his silence. 'I've decided to name him Lucien,' she announced, then noticed Ernst's eyes glaze over. Throughout her childhood she'd become inured to those sad and silent moments that often happened, signalling that she shouldn't ask questions. She recalled Emma telling her that it was a Jewish custom to name a child after a deceased parent, but that too had never been discussed with Ernst.

Marc interrupted the silence. 'I think it's a great name. I'll make some coffee. Sophie, you should have a rest before Lucien wakes up.'

Sophie's eyes met Ernst's in acknowledgement of how Marc made everything seem so simple.

Alone on her bed, waiting for Lucien to wake up, she welcomed the calm, in contrast to the panic she experienced when confronted with Marc or Ernst. Lucien's presence appeared to have unearthed an aching for her mother. She felt tormented by Ernst, who would suddenly come out with remarks like, 'The baby reminds me of your mother. He's a real Hoffmann.' She felt saddened by his odd references. It was as if they were reading each other's minds.

She thought of her new friends from the clinic. She had prejudged Emma as living a boring life, but now she imagined that there was some pinnacle of domestic harmony that Emma had achieved, but would elude her. She had expressed her sadness to Angelica, who appeared unable to grasp the concept of despair, and believed that everything in life was meant to be and there was good in everything.

*

Sophie worried that Marc would tire of her. Time seemed both endless and fleeting. She had been at home for almost a month. Lucien settled into long sleeps in between feeds and was surprisingly undemanding. She welcomed the interruption of the phone and hearing Angelica's warmth and optimism.

'I've decided to have a mum-and-baby lunch on Wednesday. I do hope you will be able to join us.'

Sophie hesitated, which made Angelica more persuasive and suggest that Emma could call for her if she didn't feel up to driving.

'I wouldn't put Emma to so much trouble; I'm sure Marc will bring me,' she said, knowing that she hadn't been out on her own yet.

'Honestly, Sophie, you will feel better, it just takes time.'

'Well, I do have some good moments and I'm probably managing because Lucien is very settled, or maybe he has learned that he just has to cope. I really do want to see you and Emma.'

Marc didn't hesitate. 'I can take you. It will do you good to get out.' He hoped Sophie's lighter mood was the long-expected step forward that Mr Lewis had forecast.

'I know I should be driving by now, but I'm quite nervous with Lucien in the back.' She couldn't tell Marc how even the simplest of tasks seemed to be beyond her.

Marc looked at the breakfast dishes piled up in the sink, with no sign of dinner being prepared. 'I've been thinking – perhaps we should get an au pair. I could clear out the top room and paint it over the weekend.'

'I know you think I can't look after Lucien, and maybe you're right, but I've made up my mind that I must at least try. Don't you understand that I have to try?' she wept.

'I didn't mean that we would get someone to look after Lucien. I thought we should have more help in the house; then you could spend more time with him.' Marc often found himself trying to pacify Sophie.

SEVEN

THE VISIT

Sophie, rummaging through a pile of entangled clothes in the Victorian linen press, pulled out her Liberty print silk blouse and navy slacks that Ernst had bought for her graduation. 'I can't possibly wear these,' she told Marc.

'They just need ironing. I'll take them to the two-hour cleaners and pick them up on my way back from work.'

'Would you?' She bucked up and, catching sight of her navy cashmere cardigan, added it to the pile.

'Relax, have a long bath, and I'll be back by twelve.' Marc rushed off, irritated at the way she neglected to take care of her clothes and wondering if she would ever become more practical.

*

Angelica's white-stuccoed Georgian house was tucked behind a high hedge in a quiet tree-lined road between Regent's Park and St John's Wood High Street. Angelica heard the car arrive

34

and opened the front door to greet them. She kissed Sophie on her cheek, hiding her dismay at the sight of her gaunt face and downcast expression. 'I've been looking forward to seeing you.' Seeing Marc get the carrycot out of the car, Angelica hoped he wouldn't join them, and was relieved when he told her he wouldn't be staying.

He followed them into the house and took a quick look around, impressed by the black granite floor, white walls, and a large, abstract orange, black and ochre painting in the hall. 'What harmony! It's remarkable; I've often thought about the problems of combining contemporary furnishing with period architecture.' He followed them into the sun lounge where he greeted Emma, who was holding her son, Daniel.

Emma couldn't hide her alarm. Sophie's dull eyes portrayed a deep melancholy, and her neatly pressed clothes hung loosely around her bony frame. 'Oh, just look at Lucien; he's so cuddly! He must be feeding well,' Emma enthused, then kissed Sophie on the cheek. 'He definitely looks like you, Sophie, with those hazel almond-shaped eyes, and he's so good and peaceful.'

'He is good. Too good, really,' Sophie replied.

'What do you mean? How can he be *too* good?' Emma replied, giving Angelica a sidelong glance.

'Well, I don't know what I'm doing half the time. That's why Marc brought me here today because I haven't starting driving again yet. He still leaves work early and comes home to help with the evening routine. I should be able to cope on my own by now; it's over a month since we left the clinic.'

Angelica went over to her and put her arm around her. 'It will get better, you'll see, and why shouldn't Marc help if he can? Look at me – I have so much help I'm sure I wouldn't cope without it.'

Emma looked at Sophie's sad expression. 'Sophie, I had no idea you still felt so bad. I would have come over to see you. You should have told us.'

'I didn't feel like telling anybody. It just seems so silly.' Sophie started to sob, worried that Marc would appear.

Emma felt helpless. Whilst she had read about postnatal depression, confronted with Sophie's almost palpable fragility she could do no more than ask, 'Have you spoken to Aubrey Lewis? I'm sure he can help.'

'We do every week; that's why Marc comes home early and helps me with Lucien. Mr Lewis suggested it. I'm even finding coming here a strain, but I wanted to see you both.'

'We want to help,' said Angelica, looking at Emma. 'If you like, I could come over and see you. You shouldn't be on your own. I also get quite lonely at times, with Jonathan.'

Marc came back into the sun lounge and pretended not to notice Sophie's tear-stained face. 'What time do you want me to fetch you?' he said, kissing her on the cheek.

'Any time,' replied Angelica.

'Well, you know where I am; phone when you're ready. Goodbye, all,' he said, and left.

'He seems very nice. I can't see Alan driving me anywhere, or coming home early to help with Dan. He also expects a three-course meal when he gets in,' Emma said.

'Well, that's because you're so capable,' replied Sophie.

'It's probably why he married me. He knew he was on to a cosy life.' Emma sounded almost resentful.

'I have no idea why David married me. I was poor, uneducated and not even Jewish,' Angelica announced.

'He married you for yourself, of course; what more proof do you require?' Sophie interjected. 'Marc married me because I was there and needed to be married.'

EIGHT

FRIENDS

Standing at the sink, washing up the breakfast dishes, Sophie didn't hear Marc come in.

'I see Emma has brought us another casserole, so I won't have to cook tonight,' he remarked.

'Yes, isn't she delightful? She said we needed a break from soup. Marc, this is the first time I feel I have genuine friends.'

'I must admit they've been pretty good to you, but quite frankly I just don't see what you all have in common.' Then, seeing the indignation on Sophie's face, he added, 'I suppose when women have babies, they have a lot in common.'

'It's not just that,' Sophie protested. 'When I was at Oxford everybody appeared so pretentious and competitive. I was desperately lonely. Are you saying that unless people are alike, they can't care about and have relationships with each other?'

'I don't know what I'm saying. I had a tough time at work today,' he replied, escaping upstairs.

It was unlike Marc to complain, and Sophie felt crushed.

Later when Ernst arrived, she bucked up. 'Would you like a cup of tea and some of Emma's almond cake?' she asked, filling the kettle.

'That sounds good,' Ernst said, surprised by her new-found liveliness.

Sophie turned to look at him. 'Marc thinks that Emma's a professional housewife and Angelica's only interested in her appearance. He won't accept that I actually enjoy their company. What do you think, Ernst?'

Ernst put his cup down. 'I can't understand friendship. I thought I had many friends.' He paused, forced to think about something he'd pushed aside, and hesitantly explained, 'When Lotte died, I lost my only true friend. We can expect too much of friends, only to be very disappointed. But then, I will never forget Heida, the woman who cleaned Uncle Joseph's apartment in Prague. Before the Nazis took him away, he gave her his best manuscripts and asked her to send them on to me. I have no doubt that she knew exactly what she was doing, and the risk to her and her family. Without her act of pure kindness, neither of us would have survived. I suppose in those days we measured friendship by different standards.'

Whilst he hadn't answered her question, Sophie thought fleetingly of Jane, who remained Ernst's sole companion, and wondered why he hadn't mentioned her.

As an afterthought, Ernst added, 'I don't know Emma and Angelica but I'm sure they are not as shallow as Marc thinks. It's not easy to make good friends when your family and friends have been taken away from you.'

Sophie noticed how increasingly Ernst referred to the past, and that his German accent seemed to be getting stronger. 'Ernst, I've just had that feeling again. Last week, when you came into the nursery and we were both standing looking at Lucien asleep in his cot, I had the sense of it being somehow familiar, but I couldn't make any connection. It felt so real that I had to go out of the room.'

A cold shiver ran through Ernst. 'Many people experience

déjà vu. It's not surprising you have these feelings. After all, when we came to London, we spent most of our time together in a small flat. We only had each other.'

Marc came into the kitchen.

'I've just made some tea, would you like a cup?' Sophie asked, feeling that Marc also had his limits. 'I could be mistaken, but I think Lucien smiled at me today.'

Marc caught Ernst's cheerful expression, as if indicating Sophie's lighter mood, and recalled Aubrey Lewis saying that she would get better. His routine of coming home early to bath Lucien and help Sophie was paying off. Even his absence from the office had provided an unexpected benefit. The political infighting at some council meetings necessitated a neutral figure in the Planning Department, and perhaps because he had not passed any opinion on a contentious matter, he had been promoted to the position of principal planning officer. Watching Sophie's slender body as she moved around the kitchen, Marc allowed himself the longing which he had suppressed. Controlling his desire to touch her, he thought of Aubrey Lewis's comments: 'She's doing fine, but there could still be pockets of vulnerability.'

'Why don't you go and lie down and I'll bath Lucien, then you can feed him?' Marc suggested.

Sophie looked at him appreciatively. 'Thanks, that would be great. He's still asleep. Do you think we should wake him?'

'No! Why look for trouble? If he takes after me, he'll hate it. If he takes after you, he won't eat unless he's hungry.'

'Well, I don't know who he takes after. He hasn't asserted himself yet; perhaps he doesn't realise that I'm a complete walkover.' Sophie gave a half-smile.

'Wait till he grows up. You'll look back on this time as the golden age of parental control. You'd better go and rest while you can,' Marc urged.

Upstairs, Sophie kicked off her shoes and, flopping onto the bed, covered herself with the duvet and dropped off to sleep.

*

Awakened by Lucien's distinctive noises, she turned to see Marc standing by the bed holding their clean and sweet-smelling son.

'He really is a nice chap; he loved his bath.' Marc had a way of making everything appear so uncomplicated.

She decided, just for once, to take life at face value. 'Thanks, Marc,' she said, taking Lucien in her arms. 'I enjoyed the nap and I'm ready to feed my brilliant baby. I hope he's hungry.'

Lucien, smelling of talcum powder and cream, sucked vigorously. She felt Marc's eyes upon her as he stood by, ready to wind him. His firm hands massaged Lucien, who emitted a loud burp of gratification.

Stirred by Sophie's pensive beauty, Marc strained to control his desire. 'He's getting quite chubby; I'll put him down now. Why don't you have a long bath and I'll pop down to the Indian restaurant and get some nosh?'

Sensing Marc's suggestive tone, she felt uncertain. 'Do you think he'll sleep?' she asked.

'I don't think he can move. I'll go and let the water run.'

Hearing the water gushing into the bath, she went to the bathroom. She heard Marc shout, 'Be back soon,' and the front door slam. Lying in the bath, the water washing over her softened, empty breasts, she felt her now-firm tummy with its fading pink scar and knew she was getting better. She got out of the bath, wrapped a towel around her body and another around her wet hair, and went to check on Lucien. He was lying on his back, spreadeagled, his little arms on either side of his head with the backs of his hands flat against the sheet. A pleasurable ache went through her which she recognised as love. Outside, the darkness wasn't disheartening; nor did she feel apprehensive about the approaching winter. She went to dry her hair, comforted by the thought that Emma had also told her that one day she would wake up and feel different.

The familiar slam of the front door told her Marc was back. The noise of the hairdryer blocked out the sound of him coming into the room. He stood quietly looking at her soft, heat-blown hair fanning out in circles of shiny, springy curls. Sophie felt his eyes upon her, warm and wanting.

'I've put the food in the oven to keep warm; we can have it later.'

It had been a long time since she'd eased herself alongside him. Her consent was located more in her mind and her appreciation for his help over the past six weeks. Marc was gentle, taking his time, waiting for her to relax, but she could not blank her mind. Caressing her breasts, he must have felt her hesitation signalling that they still belonged to Lucien, but he could not stop himself. She was pleased not to have retreated, and, turning on her side, felt his kiss on her back as she fell asleep.

*

Marc stirred. 'Do you fancy an exceedingly overcooked chicken vindaloo, onion and mushroom bhajis, madras vegetables and oven-dried rice?'

'I'm so hungry I'll eat anything.'

'Well, I'd better hurry before Lucien takes you away again,' Marc said, leaping out of bed.

His innocuous remark unsettled her.

'Don't come down; I'm bringing the lot up on a tray,' he shouted from downstairs.

She slipped on her T-shirt and sat up in bed. 'What luxury; I really feel very spoilt. Marc, thank you for everything.'

They ate ravenously. Sophie talked about Lucien, and then, as if in passing, said, 'I think I'll phone the Institute tomorrow and inquire about part-time lecturing for the spring term. And if they haven't got anything, I could do some Latin and Greek home tutoring. What do you think?'

'That would be great. I can always come home early; the office are used to my new working hours.'

For the first time in some time, they laughed.

NINE

THE CONSULTATION

'I wonder if babies think. Do they dream?' Sophie looked lovingly at Lucien, awake in his cot.

Marc chuckled. 'Don't expect too much; he might rebel later.'

'You're far too good-natured to do that,' she said, kissing the top of Lucien's head.

'Are you sure you don't want me to drive you to your postnatal today?' Marc asked.

'Thanks, but Emma insists on taking us. We're having lunch with Angelica and leaving the babies with Angelica's nanny while we go to see Aubrey. I would like to take him a book, but I have no idea of his taste. He's been fantastic. Perhaps it would be better coming from Ernst; he's got loads of art books in stock.'

'Good idea. Aubrey's advice has been pretty sound all along,' Marc said, without admitting that he doubted that they would have got as good and as much attention in the National Health Service.

'Tell me, Marc, do your Labour Party colleagues know we went privately?'

'Well, it never really came up, so it isn't an issue.'

'And if it did?' asked Sophie.

'I'd just tell them the truth: your overprotective father insisted.'

'I think you're wonderful, the way you cope with him.'

'Do I have a choice? In fact, I rather like him.'

Sophie was about to change Lucien when the phone rang. She heard Emma's gushing voice. 'I just want to remind you that we'll probably have to have one of those ghastly examinations, so wear a half-slip.'

'Really, Emma, it never occurred to me. I don't know how I'd manage without you.'

'Well, perhaps you don't find it so embarrassing. My mother left me a legacy of inhibitions, but, I dare say, there isn't anything like childbirth to make you get over it. I find Aubrey something else, I suppose... you know what I mean?'

'Sometimes when I look at Lucien, I spontaneously stop breathing; it just seems so miraculous.' Sophie talked as though she'd fallen in love.

'You're right. Men can't possibly understand, even an obstetrician. Dearest, I'd better stop chatting. I've got to make two more calls and then do my postnatal exercises and have a bath.'

Sophie liked Emma's grasp on life, and confidence that she herself lacked. Before she had Lucien, life had seemed uncertain – she hadn't planned ahead or imagined that she had a choice – but now every day had meaning as she watched the tiny changes in her son.

She was about to dress him when she heard the phone ring. It was Angelica. 'Emma's hilarious; she phoned to tell me not to wear trousers.'

'I know, but I'm more worried that I haven't done any postnatal exercises. Have you?' Sophie asked.

'A few, when my maternity nurse reminds me, but I didn't think it advisable after a caesarean,' Angelica told her.

'Well, Emma appears to think it is.' Sophie enjoyed talking with Angelica and Emma, and was comforted that her years of isolation had ended. Angelica, who seemed so open about her life and often admitted to her shortcomings, made Sophie aware of her own caution.

Knowing that Emma would arrive on time, she rushed to get ready. A feeling of gratitude swept over her as she opened the door to greet her friend.

'Where did you buy that wonderful coat?' Emma noticed the change in Sophie's demeanour.

'Ernst bought it for me when he was at the Bologna Book Fair.'

'He certainly has very good taste; navy cashmere is a classic. Then, of course, Bologna has some exquisite shops. I went there on my way to Venice when I opted out of that ghastly Swiss finishing school. I met Alan in Venice. You could say it was fate.'

'I'm sure Angelica would. She truly believes that life is fated, and if you wait for the right moment, destiny will show you the way.'

'Well, I'm not surprised; her life so far certainly has the makings of a fairy tale. I believe you make your own luck,' Emma replied, suddenly aware that she was having an ordinary conversation with Sophie. She recalled Angelica telling her not to prejudge Sophie until she recovered. She was mesmerised by Sophie's delicate beauty: her eyes that sparkled with hints of green, grey and hazel; her wavy hair knotted in a soft chignon; and most of all, her look of contentment.

*

Later that day, at the clinic, Aubrey greeted them in the waiting room. 'Lovely to see you are all still friends. I'll see you first, Emma.'

Emma followed him, turning to wink at Sophie and Angelica.

'She really is a sport,' said Angelica.

'Even Aubrey seems to think so. I must say, I feel a little nervous.'

'Let's wait and see what Emma says,' Angelica replied.

Emma returned beaming. 'I'm in perfect health; everything has gone back to normal. He's brilliant, but it's a bit embarrassing. You're next, Angelica.'

Angelica returned elated. Aubrey had told her that the laboratory results indicated that it could have been a lot worse and she was exceedingly lucky.

'Good luck,' Emma whispered to Sophie as she headed into the consulting room.

She settled herself in the chair opposite Aubrey.

'Are you feeling any better?' Aubrey asked sympathetically.

'Yes, and I'm coping well with Lucien. I even have some very good days, but the fact that my husband still comes home early to help me probably means that I'm not quite back to normal yet.'

'Don't be so hard on yourself. It was my suggestion that we shouldn't change the routine until I'd seen you. Believe me, I have seen all this before. Having a first baby can be an enormous shock to the system, and not just in social terms. Each woman responds differently. And you also had severe toxaemia. Well, there's one good thing: you've made some friends.'

'And the other good thing is Lucien,' she retorted.

'Well, that's nice to hear.' Aubrey smiled.

'I hope he won't hold his bad start against me when he grows up.'

'I'm sure he will tell you in time. My children certainly do, and believe me, when they reach adolescence it doesn't matter what kind of parenting they've had; they just turn on you,' Aubrey confessed.

Sophie, feeling that she was being treated as an equal, relaxed.

'Well, we'd better get on with the examination, so if you would just get ready?'

Sophie got up and went behind the screen while Aubrey called in his nurse. He completed the internal examination, and asked Sophie to get dressed. Feeling the worst was over, she sat back down and was just about to thank him for all his support when he asked casually, 'Have you had a period yet?'

'No, when am I supposed to?' Sophie asked, quite confused.

Aubrey didn't answer the question, but asked another. 'Have you resumed sexual relations with Marc?'

'Not exactly… well, what I mean is, yes, once.'

'I'm only asking because on examination there are some changes in your cervix.'

'I don't understand. Is there a problem?'

'I don't know for sure, we will have to do a test, but the changes are consistent with a very early pregnancy.'

Sophie put her head in her hands. 'I can't believe it.'

Aubrey spoke gently. 'Did you and your husband use any form of contraception?'

'No! I can't believe this is happening again.' Sophie was distraught.

'A lot of women think that breastfeeding is a form of contraception, but it isn't. Let's wait until we get the test results tomorrow,' Aubrey stated conclusively.

'What shall I do? I can't possibly manage.' Sophie burst into tears.

'Talk to your husband, and whatever the result, I would like to see both of you tomorrow. It's unfortunate that I didn't see you earlier. I usually do the postnatal consultation six weeks after delivery, but I go away every September and this was the earliest I could see the three of you on the same afternoon.'

Sophie looked up. 'Well, I can hardly blame you.'

Aubrey smiled. 'In America, obstetricians can be sued for less. But seriously, Sophie, you would be surprised how often women return pregnant before their postnatal. These things have a way of sorting themselves out. We'll speak tomorrow.' He stood up and walked with Sophie to the door, repeating, 'Whatever the result, I want to see you and your husband.'

With shock written across her face, Sophie walked towards Emma and Angelica.

'Sit down,' Emma said protectively.

'No! Can we get out of here?' Sophie demanded.

They followed Sophie to the car in silence, feeling the weight of her mood, Sophie went to sit in the back.

Emma broke the silence. 'I hope the babies are all right. It was a splendid idea to leave them with your maternity nurse, Angelica, particularly on her last day.'

'I'm really looking forward to having Jonathan to myself, although I must say, at the beginning, I certainly appreciated her,' Angelica said, keeping the conversation going.

As they drove through Regent's Park, Sophie spontaneously blurted out, 'I'm sorry for being so unsociable, but I'm just devastated.'

'Can we help?' Emma asked.

'Darling, you don't have to tell us if it's too difficult,' Angelica coaxed.

'Aubrey thinks I could be pregnant.' Sophie's lifeless tone had returned.

After another silence, Emma asked, 'How can he tell?'

Sophie told them about the examination and the test, and that she would know for certain by five o'clock tomorrow. 'I don't think Marc can go through this again, and I certainly can't.'

'My maternity nurse leaves today and I'll get you her name and address. She's absolutely marvellous; I couldn't have coped without her,' Angelica said.

Emma suppressed a giggle. 'With friends like us, Sophie, you have to be tough.'

'I think we could all do with a cup of tea and some apple strudel,' Angelica suggested as they parked outside her house.

'I still can't believe it,' Sophie repeated.

*

At home, Sophie flitted from one thing to another, while Lucien, as if responding to her plight, was particularly lovable.

At five o'clock the next day, Aubrey Lewis phoned. 'Hello, Sophie, how are you?'

'Very anxious.'

'The test is positive, so I would like to see you and your husband tomorrow at four.'

Sophie felt the weight of the phone in her hand. She sat down at the kitchen table, waiting for Marc to come home.

When he arrived, seeing her stunned expression, he said, 'I take it that we've got the result.'

'It's positive,' she mumbled.

'I'll make some coffee. Is Lucien asleep?' Marc asked, not expecting a reply. He switched on the percolator, walked over to Sophie, kissed her on the cheek and then sat down opposite her. 'Sophie, I know what you've been through, but it's also my responsibility. In fact, more than that, it's my fault. I just didn't think. I'll support you in whatever you want to do.'

Tears trickled down her pale face. 'I know one thing: I could never go through an abortion; not with my background. Poor Lucien, he hasn't had much of a start, and now this!'

Marc gently cupped his hand over hers. 'I'll help. There's plenty of room in the house; perhaps we should get some live-in help.'

Sophie looked up. 'Angelica said I could have her nurse. You know, Marc, sometimes I think Angelica is right. Our lives do seem to be governed by some outside force. I really don't know how I'm going to tell Ernst. He will probably think I'm trying to replace the six million.'

Marc, responding to the lighter atmosphere, said, 'Well, technically you aren't Jewish and neither am I, so our children can't be.'

'Genetically my father is Jewish, so I must be half and our children a quarter, and that was good enough for the Nazis. I suppose sometimes I just feel Jewish.'

'That's probably why you're depressed,' Marc replied.

PART TWO

BEFORE JERUSALEM

TEN

THE IN-BETWEEN YEARS

Sophie quivered with anxiety when Marc phoned Ernst that evening.

'Sophie's pregnant. It wasn't planned but we've both decided to get on with it.'

She was amazed by Marc's courage, wondering what her father would say.

'He said, "Congratulations",' Marc told her afterwards.

She could hardly believe it.

'I don't know why you feel guilty; we've done nothing wrong,' Marc insisted.

'Perhaps Ernst thinks we've been rather careless, considering what I've put everybody through, and I can't blame him.'

Ernst, whilst able to control his shock, felt angry. Marc's matter-of-fact announcement on the phone seemed insensitive. He recalled Sophie's view of her husband: 'What you see is what you get.' Previously he had welcomed Marc's plain-spoken behaviour, but now he felt irritated by it. Then, thinking of Lotte's unplanned pregnancy and its consequences, he calmed down.

*

The following day Ernst left work early and rushed over to see them. Marc was busy making dinner in the kitchen. Sophie was upstairs with Lucien.

'I'm making spaghetti bolognese; will you join us?' Marc asked, as if nothing had changed. Then, seeing Ernst's solemn expression, he added, 'We are going to get live-in help in the house and a maternity nurse. Things will work out.'

Ernst unfolded his arms and sat back from the table, and his face softened into a smile. 'Life is a gift,' he said, seemingly to himself.

'We saw Mr Lewis this afternoon and he will be monitoring Sophie to prevent a recurrence of the toxaemia. He also suggested that she spend the last month of her pregnancy in the clinic,' Marc said with some diffidence, for it was Ernst who paid the clinic's bill.

Sophie heard them chatting about Lucien as she came into the kitchen. She had felt uneasy facing her father, but as usual Marc had smoothed the way. It appeared ridiculous that yesterday she had been horrified at the thought of another baby, yet now suddenly felt delighted. 'What do you think of our news?'

'It's wonderful, and this time I'm sure nothing will go wrong,' Ernst replied.

'Let's open a bottle of wine,' Marc suggested.

Ernst knew he had no choice but to get on with it. He wondered whether Sophie would ever take responsibility or show more initiative. It seemed to him that she was always drifting along in a cloud and letting things happen to her rather than initiating or making decisions. He was reluctant to attribute this to the loss of Lotte and their traumatic start in England. He was grateful to Marc, who seemed caring and content with Sophie, giving him hope that she might have a fulfilled life. He was grateful too that he had done sufficiently well in England to help provide for Sophie and his grandson, and he smiled to himself.

*

Marc found an au pair to help with the housework. Sophie spent more time with Lucien, and more afternoons with Emma and Angelica. Her pregnancy progressed well, and in the last month, under Aubrey's instructions, she was admitted to the clinic for monitoring and rest while the nanny took care of Lucien.

Hannah was delivered without any complications and turned out to be a perfect, happy baby. Lucien, now a year old, started walking. Ernst came around as often as he could, ever on the lookout for any hint of Sophie's previous depression. He couldn't believe that she appeared so relaxed with Hannah, who, he repeatedly claimed, was the very image of his own mother.

ELEVEN

LUCIEN

The years passed as quickly or as slowly as is their wont. Sixteen years later, Sophie's daydream was interrupted by Marc's arrival in their bedroom with their morning coffee. As he placed the tray on the bedside table, Sophie commented, 'Isn't it strange how a chance meeting can lead to a lifelong friendship?'

'If you're referring to Angelica and Emma, I suppose you've adapted to a chance meeting and haven't had or made an opportunity to meet anybody else. Not a day passes without you contacting them; you might as well be on a desert island.'

'Marc, the problem is not what you're trying to say, but what you're trying not to say,' Sophie retorted, then thought it ironic that he never considered their own chance meeting in the pub in Oxford.

'You were always too clever for me, and you are also probably a lot smarter than Angelica and Emma, so I can't understand your dependency on them.'

'Well! How could you understand friendship? After sixteen

years in the Labour Party, you just go along with the party line.' Sophie was more hurt than angry.

Marc, looking at her downcast expression, realised that she was upset because Lucien had announced that he was dropping out of school. 'I suppose there comes a time when loyalty can work against you.' His voice dropped as if losing interest in the conversation.

Sophie's voice rose. 'What exactly are you inferring? Are you warning me off Angelica and Emma?'

'No. I just resent that all the time you're either worrying about Lucien and Hannah or talking to Emma and Angelica, not to mention Ernst. I just feel left out, that's all.'

Sophie considered that nothing Marc had said was untrue, but it felt false. She had to put an end to the discomfort between them. Her voice softened. 'Marc, I think we should at least examine the facts. For the past sixteen years you have spent at least three evenings a week, even weekends away, attending either council or Labour Party meetings. Whether I became more dependent on Angelica and Emma because you weren't around, or you weren't around because I was too preoccupied, we'll never know. But the fact is that Lucien needs you, and maybe he wouldn't be dropping out of school if you had been around more. I know I'm probably responsible for his failure, and I know you were incredibly supportive when he was a baby. But he needs you now, and I don't know how to cope with him. Can't you just forget about us for the moment and focus on Lucien and Hannah? Even as an infant Hannah seemed to realise that Lucien needed the lion's share of attention, and she's still incredibly kind to him.'

Marc knew he had just turned everything around to make it all look like Sophie's fault, and felt an overwhelming desire to tell her about Maureen. Maureen, who openly confessed that if she wanted something, she would act, unlike Sophie, who appeared able only to react; even in bed she held back. Most of all, Marc felt threatened by Sophie's naivety. Whilst his relationship with Maureen remained platonic, he felt culpable, knowing that it was only a matter of time before he succumbed. He didn't want to hurt Sophie, but recognised that they were drifting apart and regretted having embarked on the conversation. It wasn't just her preoccupation with Lucien that irritated him. Increasingly, he saw that Hannah seemed more confident and competent than her mother, and couldn't understand why, with all their help and privileges, Sophie couldn't get on with her life.

'Honestly, Sophie, I don't have anything against Angelica and Emma; they have been nothing but loyal and caring. I don't even know why I criticised your friendship.'

'Well, you must have your reasons,' Sophie said charitably.

'I suppose I'm jealous,' Marc said.

After he left, Sophie thought that it had been just another of those uncomfortable discussions that seemed to be happening more and more frequently. She wondered if she had been selfish – after all, having two children in two years had hardly been the best start to their marriage, and Marc had been very patient.

Her thoughts drifted to Lucien. She was at an impasse. Now seventeen, her son was adamant that he wouldn't go back to school. The new term was starting in two weeks. Desperate to change his mind, she impulsively rushed to the top floor and knocked on his bedroom door. Thundering music ensured that Lucien was unaware of her entry, and her stomach turned at the all-too-familiar wafts of pot and cigarettes and the sight of empty packets from crisps and chocolate bars strewn on the floor. Lucien was lying, half asleep, across his unmade bed. Sophie forced a half-smile.

'What do you want?' Lucien blurted, indifferent to her stepping between full ashtrays, dirty coffee mugs and unwashed clothes.

She sat on the edge of his bed. 'I want to talk to you about going back to school.'

'Now why would I want to do that?' Lucien grunted.

'Because you're bright, and surely you can see that you could wreck your chances in the future?' Having started, she wasn't going to give up.

'You don't listen, do you? I'm not going back to that dump that Dad calls a school.'

'You could go to another school, or a college,' she suggested.

'Oh yes, I can just see Dad accepting that the Labour Party's wonderful comprehensive doesn't do it for me; after all, look how well Hannah's doing. He doesn't listen either. Anyway, it's too late; I've already decided. That's it!'

Lucien's dissenting tone made Sophie plead. 'It's never too late—'

'I hate that dump of a school and everything to do with it!' he shouted.

'So what do you intend doing?'

'I don't know, stop hassling me!'

Sophie went downstairs, anxious to escape further contact. She thought of all the things she could have said to him but hadn't for fear of making it worse: Lucien spending his days, dishevelled and isolated, in his bedroom; or, even worse, going out to meet up with other dropouts, from whom he would receive approval for his aberrant behaviour. Sitting at the kitchen table, she felt the weight of her failure, and was annoyed that Marc seemed to be ignoring the problem. She made herself a mug of tea, went into the drawing room and slumped on the wine-red velvet chaise longue.

The disagreement with her husband had left her powerless. She recalled that their first major disagreement had been over Lucien's education. Marc had been adamant, and far more concerned about Labour's educational policy than his own son's. Distressed, Sophie had rushed round to see Emma and told her that Lucien was far too sensitive to survive at the local comprehensive school, unlike Hannah, who seemed to be a natural academic. Emma had pointed out that if Hannah could achieve good grades then it wouldn't be the fault of the school, which was exactly Marc's argument. His total belief in the need for an equal education for all persuaded him that, even were Lucien to slip into the bottom stream, the system would allow him to recover. After all, Marc himself had done well at his comprehensive school. But he hadn't taken into account that Lucien had made some undesirable friends, and the school couldn't help him. When Sophie suggested that they should find another school, Ernst offered to pay the fees. Marc became incensed, particularly when Sophie compared Lucien to Emma's boys, who were doing well at a private school. Finally, she'd had to admit defeat, and could only think that Marc's intransigence had to do with his position in the Labour council. Now Lucien's dim future could not be ignored, which hurt her more than she would ever admit to Emma. Her thoughts became circular, and her feelings of despair following his birth re-emerged.

On impulse, she phoned Ernst. By the tone of his voice, she knew that she had interrupted him in a meeting. 'I'm sorry for phoning you at work, but I need to speak to you.'

'See you at the Connaught at one.'

Sophie realised that she couldn't drag him out for yet another circular discussion, but hoped that a fresh approach to Lucien's problems would emerge during lunch.

*

Sitting at his table by the window, waiting for Sophie, Ernst assumed that she was having difficulties in her marriage. He blamed himself for being overprotective. He had long since resigned himself to his role of providing unconditional love, and accepted that he could not expect more of Marc, whose modesty and kindness meant few restrictions for Sophie.

He looked up to see her slim frame walking towards him.

Her thick brown hair, hanging in natural curls, surrounded a careworn look. She was the image of her mother, but unlike her in every other way. Ernst sighed, baffled as to why his beautiful and intelligent daughter lacked confidence. He braced himself, decided to let Sophie do all the talking, and was astonished when she never mentioned Marc, and instead spoke compulsively about Lucien. Though irritated by the unnecessary interruption to his work, he managed to give her his full attention.

'Sophie, I think we should let Lucien be, and only hope that he doesn't become a drug addict or get into trouble. He's intelligent. Let him stay in the top of the house if you can't stand his mess or his friends, but whatever happens, make sure he doesn't leave home. That's when things can really go wrong.'

'Really, Ernst, I can't imagine why you think I *want* him to leave home.' Feeling criticised, she added, 'I know you don't mean to upset Lucien, but every time you and Hannah get together and chatter away, I feel for him; he looks so left out.'

'I think you're exaggerating.' Ernst's expression changed. His eyes took on a mournful expression and, fearing Sophie's fragility, he spoke more sympathetically. 'Sophie, dearest, you must be careful not to make Hannah suffer because of Lucien. Hannah is a natural optimist; she's so full of enthusiasm. We can't ask her to stop living while we wait for Lucien to join in.'

'I suppose you're right, but it's damn difficult to see Hannah so full of life, and poor Lucien struggling. It must be genetic. Hannah got even less attention than Lucien.' Sophie took a deep breath, dropping her shoulders in defeat.

Ernst wanted to shake her. 'Sophie, when are you going to stop putting yourself down? Children are all different. Hannah resembles my mother, and she has the same joy of living. You know, even when everybody in Pilsen was worried about the Germans, my mother refused to become depressed. She just said, "It will be all right." His eyes glazed over. 'Perhaps that's why I feel so attached to Hannah, but that doesn't mean I don't love Lucien, and for more reasons than I can talk about.' He took the handkerchief out of his top pocket and wiped his eyes.

'I know, Ernst. I just feel so worried about Lucien. Do you think that he was affected when I stayed at the clinic for the last month of my pregnancy with Hannah? He wasn't even a year old when I brought her home, and I often wonder how he felt at the time.'

'Sophie, if Mr Lewis hadn't put you in the clinic you could have got toxaemia again, and then what good would you have been to either of your children? Besides, Lucien was very well looked after. He'd even started walking on his own by the time you brought Hannah home. If you like, you can blame Marc and me. We insisted that you keep the nanny for six months. I really think we all benefited from her support.'

Sophie's face relaxed in agreement. 'Perhaps Hannah takes after Marc,' she mused, thinking of how her daughter had become an uncomplicated fifteen-year-old.

'You know, I think nature does have an edge over nurture.'

She sounded a little more optimistic. 'Perhaps Lucien will also show his true talent one day.'

'Never, ever give up on anybody, Sophie, not if you have the love and the time to help. Life is a very long business and things can go wrong at any time, but they can also come right. It's a matter of timing. This is probably just the wrong time for Lucien, but I'm sure that he'll come right.'

'I know, and deep down I believe you. I've just become so despairing, especially when Angelica tells me how well Jonathan is doing at school, and Emma seems to have successfully programmed Daniel and Adam on the fast track for the rest of their lives.'

They both laughed.

'I think we'd better get out of here before they kick us out,' Ernst said, looking around at the waiters, who had started laying the tables for dinner.

'I'm sorry for being so depressed, but it seems that every August I go into a decline. I don't know why.'

But Ernst knew, and believed that even though Sophie couldn't remember the facts, she must have remembered the feelings. He couldn't imagine how she must have felt on losing Lotte, and then being dragged across Europe in the nightmare of August 1941, and then their struggle for many years as refugees in England. There was so much he could not speak of. He couldn't risk telling her about the hard choices that he had had to make, or of his worries that might have affected her.

TWELVE

SOPHIE AND ANGELICA

Angelica had a talent for making the best of life. She had become the chair of two Jewish charities, arranging concerts and getting celebrities to speak at functions. She'd converted to Judaism even though it didn't matter to her husband David, to please her in-laws. It seemed to Sophie that Angelica was confident and comfortable with anybody in any situation. But when Angelica confided that she felt like an outsider, Sophie realised that her friend's feelings mirrored her own. Marc had been wrong to say that they had nothing in common. She smiled to herself when she thought of Angelica's belief in fate – how she read her daily horoscope and sought after fortune tellers, and her conviction in the validity of telepathy. Sophie marvelled at the way Angelica would selectively arrange the information gleaned from these sources to guide her judgement and remain convinced that her meeting David, Jonathan's survival, and the three women's meeting in the clinic were all meant to happen. Even with her knowledge of classical Greek culture and the huge value it placed upon fate, Sophie was not to be persuaded, and was surprised when Angelica told her she felt there were some bad omens to govern her life.

One day, Angelica phoned Sophie asking her to come around to see her; it was very urgent. Over coffee, she calmly described how, whilst relaxing in the bath, she had been guided by destiny to move her hands lightly over her breasts, palpating their soft surface. Then, as if she'd known, she had felt a hard lump on the outside of her left breast, about the size of a grape, that pushed against her fingertips. It had seemed separate and self-contained; inside, but not of, her body.

Sophie was alarmed that Angelica sounded so resigned, saying how this had all happened on her birthday and she had decided not to tell David and spoil the family celebration dinner. Sophie phoned Emma, who had spoken to Angelica earlier to wish her a happy birthday and knew about the lump.

'It could be the time of the month.'

Sophie wasn't reassured by that suggestion. 'What if it isn't?'

'Well, in any case, she must have it checked. I know it's not exactly Aubrey Lewis's field but he's a good first port of call, and he'll act quickly. There is absolutely no point in worrying until she has a diagnosis. Women often get lumps and they are usually absolutely harmless but, as I say, the sooner you know the better. I'm going to phone Angelica immediately and ask if she would like me to make an appointment and I'll go with her.'

Emma could be so forceful and unfeelingly practical but, when Sophie compared this to her own feelings of helplessness, she knew that Emma was right. She was reminded of when Angelica had told her that she'd last seen Aubrey Lewis eleven years before when her son was five, because she and David had tried and failed to have another child. Aubrey had concluded that there was nothing wrong, and since then, Angelica had never talked about their disappointment.

'Would you mind if I went with you and Emma for your appointment?' Sophie asked Angelica.

'I didn't want to ask. Thank you, Sophie.' Angelica's words seemed like an omen. Outside, gusts of wind whipped up the autumn leaves, signalling the end of summer.

*

'Right on time as usual,' Angelica said, climbing into the car.

'You know I regard being late as the height of rudeness,' Emma protested.

'If it wasn't for you two coming with me, I don't think I could face this.'

Sophie thought of how she and Angelica had often joked about Emma's controlling behaviour.

'I know I seem a bit tetchy but I'm so angry with Alan. He came in very late last night and hadn't even bothered to phone. I left the casserole in the oven and of course it was ruined. At least I've trained Daniel and Adam! I suppose it's my fault for putting my whole life into my family,' Emma protested.

'You should do something for yourself; start studying and get out more. The boys will be fine,' Angelica advised, pleased to have some distraction.

'You're right, Alan certainly doesn't appreciate me, but for the next two years I want to help the boys through their O and A Levels and then I'll have done my bit.'

Sophie remained quiet, half listening to their conversation.

'Mr Lewis will probably think I'm pregnant after all these years,' Angelica sighed as they found parking in Harley Street.

'Come on; let's get it over with. You remember our postnatal? I'll never forget the expression on your face, Sophie.' Emma seemed determined to keep the conversation going.

'It was fate. Hannah has turned out to be quite extraordinary: confident, kind and clever,' Angelica said.

'I wish I could say the same about Lucien,' Sophie said half-heartedly.

They sat in the familiar waiting room, quietly flipping through magazines, and then looked up to see Aubrey walking towards them, mildly surprised to see them all together. 'It's Angelica who has the appointment,' he confirmed.

Angelica got up and followed him into his consulting room. He sat at his desk opposite her, tilting his head forward, waiting for her to speak; observing that she had hardly aged and appeared even more beautiful than he'd remembered.

'Yesterday I found a lump in my left breast. I know this isn't your field, but Emma suggested that I see you,' she said nervously.

'If you slip behind the curtain, I'll examine you,' he said, calling the nurse to chaperone them.

Angelica undressed and lay on the examination table. Aubrey washed his hands in hot water to warm them and then skilfully palpated the lump, fingertip pressure defining its boundary, before completing the examination in silence.

'Fine – get dressed and we'll have a chat.' His usual response before confronting the patient with bad news. Back at his desk, he spoke calmly. 'I have only done a manual examination and until you have a mammogram it would be foolish to speculate. I could arrange for you to have the mammogram now; it's just a few doors up the road and it would save you coming to Harley Street on another day.'

'You did find it? I wasn't imagining it?' Angelica pressed.

He looked tenderly at her. 'Yes, there is a small lump. It could be anything, so let's wait for the result of the mammogram. It really is impossible to make any conclusive diagnosis on the basis of a manual examination. I know waiting can be very unsettling.'

'I remember your reassurances those years ago. Perhaps I've just used up my share of good fortune. I've been waiting for years to fall pregnant and now I have this problem. Don't you think it's more than a coincidence?'

Aubrey was reminded of her fatalistic view during her confinement. 'From a medical point of view, I can't find a connection,' he said, observing her blue eyes glaze over with unshed tears.

'I just feel that it is destined; that this was all bound to happen.' She looked at him, wanting him to agree.

'Angelica, I promise I will contact you as soon as I know more. Let's get the mammogram done,' he said, pushing back his chair and getting up to signal the end of the consultation. Then he walked into the waiting room. 'It's good to see you both looking so well,' he said, addressing Emma and Sophie.

A gentle heat flooded Emma's cheeks, which she hoped Aubrey and Angelica hadn't noticed.

*

After the mammogram, Emma insisted that they stop at one of the coffee shops in Marylebone High Street. 'Let's just be sinful; I need a sugar fix. Well, that's a bit of luck,' she added, spying an empty parking meter.

'Perhaps it's a good sign.' Angelica sounded flat.

'I can imagine how you feel, Angelica, but you could be worrying for nothing,' Sophie said, with little conviction.

'You're right. Let's see if we're lucky in finding a table,' Angelica said. Scanning the small gold tables and the romantic scenes painted on the wall rather lightened her mood. 'Another good sign – there's one; the last table.' She walked ahead.

'Emma, if I didn't know better, I would think that Aubrey had a thing for you,' Angelica remarked a few minutes later, sipping her tea and pushing her pastry around her plate with her fork.

Emma felt her cheeks prickle. 'Dearest, he's like that with all women, haven't you noticed? He's a gynaecologist, after all.'

THIRTEEN

THE DIAGNOSIS

With a sense of foreboding, Angelica took her afternoon cup of tea into her sun lounge, hoping that no one would invade her privacy. Looking at the leafless trees and the mottled grey sky, she heard the phone ring but did not rush to answer it.

Aubrey's calm voice had no effect on what she already knew. 'Angelica, I have the result of your mammogram. The radiologist recommends that we have a proper look at the lump. The best way to do this will entail you having an anaesthetic so we can do a biopsy. I have spoken to a colleague, Dr Jameson, and he is able to see you tomorrow. As you know, this isn't my field, but if you want to talk to me at any time, I'll be pleased to see you.'

Angelica listened, feeling disconnected. 'Thank you. I would like to see Dr Jameson.'

It was as if she was talking on behalf of someone else. The sky darkened, threatening a storm, and within minutes diagonal sheets of rain beat hard on the sun lounge's glass roof. Aubrey's phone call presaged the end of one life and the beginning of another.

*

Sophie relied on Emma to keep her up to date.

'I hope they've managed to get it all out. Some surgeons believe in doing a radical mastectomy, but fortunately, Angelica has had a lumpectomy and will need radiation therapy,' Emma told her.

'Poor Angelica. At least they've caught it early.'

Emma seemed unstoppable. 'I've found an article about a woman who has confounded doctors by refusing orthodox treatment and reducing her tumour by going on a detox diet with specific vitamins and minerals, and practising meditation.'

'I don't think you should even mention it to Angelica; she has such faith in Dr Jameson, and I doubt David would accept a holistic practitioner,' Sophie warned her.

'I know what you mean, dear. People are so prejudiced. I remember trying to find an obstetrician when I wanted to have a natural childbirth, and today that's almost taken for granted. I bet you in twenty years' time cancer will be treated differently. But of course, that won't help Angelica.'

*

Sophie's preoccupation shifted between Lucien and Angelica, and, fearful of another upset, she avoided sharing her feelings with Marc. However, she noticed that lately he appeared overly attentive. There wasn't anything specific, yet she had the impression that he felt guilty, and was quite surprised when on impulse he suggested that it would be a good idea to convert the loft into a storage room. Her silence impelled him to explain.

'I thought I could get Lucien involved.'

'It's a wonderful idea, but how do you think you will motivate him? He is spending more and more time up in his room. I can't even go and see what he's doing in case he flies into another of his rages.'

'Leave it to me; I'll get started and hope that he'll become involved.'

Whilst conceding that Marc's approach held less risk of failure, she had lost heart in her attempts to rouse Lucien from his indifference. It seemed extraordinary that when it came to Angelica or Emma she remained in full control of her wits, never crossing the unspoken boundaries of friendship, but with Lucien those boundaries were blurred and she appeared unable to separate her feelings from his.

FOURTEEN

TWO YEARS LATER

Sophie could hardly remember Angelica's life before that dreaded autumn of 1982, as she watched her increasing debilitation. She noted that David spent much of his time at home with his wife. She was profoundly moved when Angelica related a dream in which she had wept profusely while people with blank faces stood by. She was deeply affected by Angelica's stoicism, and talked to Emma, who seemed more rational.

'You would think that after two years of gruelling treatment Angelica would look elsewhere. I mean, first she has a lumpectomy, followed by a course of radiation therapy, which didn't appear to help, then within a year she has a hysterectomy, and twelve months later the cancer has spread to the bowel. And now she has to cope with a colostomy and more chemotherapy. I can't believe the way she just gets on with it.'

'It must be agonising for David to watch her rapid decline. Even after losing all that weight, she is still quite beautiful – in a way, *more* beautiful. It's her attitude. She is so dignified,' Sophie noted wistfully.

'Quite frankly, I can't see what more orthodox medicine can offer her,' Emma persisted.

An unnatural silence crept between them, as if Emma's words might tip some fragile balance.

More and more, Angelica turned to her prescient feelings. David told Sophie how, out of the blue, she had reminded him of Jonathan's premature birth, how they'd nearly lost him, and how she had known at the time that something terrible would happen to her.

'What did she mean?' Sophie asked.

'She believes that, whilst she was lucky with Jonathan's survival, it was a sign that the die had been cast and she was destined for another crisis.'

'What did you say?'

'What could I say? I didn't want to upset her, but neither could I go along with it. I told her that I'm too rational to believe in prophecies, although I accept that it would make life a lot easier. I'm not against any belief, if it helps. I still find it amazing that Angelica converted to Judaism. The truth is, she is a much better Jew than me; always observing the holidays. She insisted that Jonathan have a bar mitzvah.'

Sophie recalled Angelica telling her that, when she converted, she hadn't thought beyond memorising a set of rules and stories and promptly forgetting most of them afterwards; but that now she wondered whether her conversion was also part of her destiny.

Later that day, David opened the door to Sophie and took her aside to tell her that, 'With the exception of you and Emma, many of our friends have stopped phoning. I suppose people are afraid of illness. In case I haven't mentioned it before, I want you to know how grateful I am to you both. Emma has hardly missed visiting Angelica every Wednesday, and you have always been there to drive her to her chemotherapy.'

*

The following Wednesday when Emma arrived, Angelica was sitting downstairs in the sun lounge. Emma was surprised to see her fully dressed in dark brown woollen trousers and a pale blue polo-neck sweater that seemed to float over her skeletal body. Her serene expression and compelling beauty were accentuated by her chiselled jawline and high cheekbones, her unlined face and soft blue eyes more vivid against her short crop of curly white hair. A side effect of chemotherapy. Her delicate, long-fingered hands lay loosely in her lap as her unblinking eyes looked directly at Emma.

'Emma, do you think converted Jews are really Jews?' Angelica asked.

'Darling, there are so many different kinds of Jews and I am sure the one thing they all have in common is that they disagree. Just find your own brand of Judaism and enjoy it. That's my approach; that's why I belong to the Reform lot.'

Angelica smiled. 'Emma, you are funny – I ask a serious question and you find a simple solution.'

'Well, I suppose I have never taken religion seriously. I've just had to get on with it: cook for the holidays, get the family together, occasionally go to synagogue once or twice a year, that sort of thing. But don't get me wrong; as soon as I have a problem, I'm as devout as anybody in begging God for help.'

'Now you've really confused me,' Angelica sighed.

'Join the club. If you want an unbiased and logical opinion, you should ask Sophie.'

That evening, Sophie was unprepared when Angelica phoned her and asked her the same question. 'Faith and religion are not necessarily the same thing. You can have one without the other, but I suppose it's probably better to have both,' she told her.

'You make it sound so obvious,' Angelica said thoughtfully.

'You shouldn't be fooled. It's probably my way of copping out. The truth is, I can't really answer your question. Firstly, I've denied my Jewish heritage; Ernst hardly ever talks about his family and so I don't know much about Jewish traditions. But secondly, faith clearly exists, I can understand the reason for its existence, and more importantly, faith changes the people who have it.'

Sophie had unknowingly touched a nerve. Angelica was now gripped by the idea that faith could change a person.

FIFTEEN

ROSALIND COHEN

In her pristine room in the private hospital, Angelica stretched out her arm as the doctor patted and rubbed it to bring her veins to the surface, inserted the needle for the drug infusion, then adjusted the drips per minute falling into the tube.

'There you are. It ought to be a little better this time; I've altered the dose slightly. You should be through by eleven o'clock tonight and then we can give you something to help you sleep.' He left having never once made eye contact.

Being a good patient enabled Angelica to cope as the drugs violated every cell in her body. A curious sensation swept over her; a feeling that she had been freed and wouldn't have to pretend any longer. She resolved that whatever was left of her life she would accept the challenge and hope that David would see it the same way.

Later that day, after succumbing to the pervading waves of nausea, flitting muscle pains, and a throbbing headache, Angelica woke to hear a knock on her door. She turned to see a woman dressed in a denim skirt and white blouse, with a round face mostly hidden by oversized glasses, standing by her bed.

'Hello, I'm Rabbi Rosalind Cohen. I saw on your admission slip that you are Jewish, so I thought you might like a visit. Sometimes it helps to take one's mind off the treatment,' she said in a soft voice.

Momentarily relieved to have some distraction from her headache, Angelica closed her eyes and allowed Rosalind, who knew the soothing power of touch, to hold her frail hand.

'How long have you been ill?' Rosalind asked, her voice conveying the compassion and experience of one used to working with the terminally ill.

With her eyes half closed against the light, Angelica murmured, 'About two years, but who knows how long cancer lies dormant before it erupts?' Mouthing the word 'cancer' released the mounting tension that had built up. She thought of Dr Jameson's veiled references – 'The tumour has spread' or 'It will respond to chemotherapy' – which had supported her denial. Now she understood that her illness had become a part of her. 'I keep thinking about it. After I converted to Judaism, we never went to synagogue more than once a year. Do you think everything that happens in life is fated to happen?' she asked.

'It might be helpful to think about your illness as being part of your life rather than your destiny,' Rosalind said, gently wiping the beads of perspiration gathering on Angelica's forehead. 'You're too ill to talk now. Try to sleep; I'll be back later.'

Lulled by Rosalind's words, Angelica felt less oppressed by the chemotherapy. She slept, and when she woke up again, all she could remember from her curiously comforting dream were the words, 'Ultimately, we are all in God's hands.' She wondered if belief could really be so simple. She thought of the doctors who could do no more for her, and was resigned that this would be her last summer. Then she thought of leaving David and

Jonathan, and lamented, desperately fearful of how they would cope on their own.

*

David was getting ready to leave the house for the hospital, dreading seeing Angelica's drawn face, which appeared to get smaller and more strained after each bout of chemotherapy. He would have felt more alone were it not for Sophie and Emma, who continued to sustain them through the nightmare.

The phone rang.

'Hello, Sophie, I was just thinking of you. I've spoken to Angelica; she seems stronger this time. I can't imagine why, unless they gave her a different cocktail of drugs.'

'Would you like me to come over later?'

'Thanks. I find visiting quite exhausting, and I'm sure Angelica will also appreciate another distraction.'

'Give her my love,' Sophie said, finding it increasingly difficult to prolong their conversations.

David couldn't admit his dependence on Sophie and the comfort he found in her.

The phone rang again, and he picked it up to hear Emma's bubbly voice. 'Hello, how was the treatment?' she asked, oblivious to the fact that David found her manner intrusive.

'Well, you know Angelica; she doesn't complain. She appears rather brighter than last time.' David controlled his irritation.

'You know that if there's anything I can do, you only have to ask.'

'I really can't think of anything at the moment, but I appreciate your caring. It means a lot to Angelica, and also to Jonathan and me.' David felt trapped by his own predictability, wanting to end the conversation without offending Emma.

'The A Level results come out on Monday. I hope there's some good news; it will really help Angelica,' Emma asserted.

'It's an awful responsibility for Jonathan. The last thing he needs is to let us down. Thank goodness he's going to cricket this afternoon. He doesn't say much, but he is deeply affected by Angelica's illness, so if he doesn't come up to expectations, it's understandable,' said David defensively.

'Well, he managed to sit the exams and he has a place at Oxford. Of course, he has your brains.'

'Meaning that Angelica doesn't have any?' David retorted.

'Oh, come on, David,' Emma protested. 'Of course Angelica is intelligent; probably brighter than all of us put together. It's just that she hasn't proved it academically. For that matter, nor have I. That's why I understand her so well.'

'I'm sorry, I don't mean to be so irritable. I just feel so protective when it comes to Angelica that I doubt I listen properly to anybody any more. Please forgive me.'

It sounded to Emma as if David was justifying himself rather than apologising. 'I'm sorry for bringing up the A Levels; I only meant to compliment Jonathan. I'd better let you get on. Give Angelica my love and tell her that I'll phone her after she's had her rest.' Dropping the phone back onto its base, Emma wiped away her tears. She could not be spontaneous with David and had to admit that they had never quite hit it off.

*

While waiting for David, Angelica heard a knock at the door and Rosalind popped her head in.

'How was the treatment?'

'To be honest it was just as bad, but I've got over the worst. Can I tell you about the dream I had last night?' Angelica asked.

Rosalind sat next to the bed, observing Angelica's pasty grey complexion.

'Do you think faith can be so simple?' Angelica asked, convinced that in her dream she had been called to God.

'We can't always know the process that moves us towards faith. There is no reason to say it can't happen in a dream. Perhaps when you converted to Judaism all those years ago, you embarked on a journey which has taken you further than you could foresee.'

'Are you saying my life is predestined?'

'We worry all our lives about why bad things happen to us. Most Jews believe that nothing in life is written in the stars, but unlikely events do give us pause to reflect. Albert Einstein believed that coincidences are God's way of remaining anonymous. We rush through life, and if we have time to look back, we see a pattern emerging. If we were to believe that everything in life is predestined, the Ten Commandments would be meaningless. It's only because we are given the power to make conscious decisions that we can choose between good and evil and have a measure of control over our lives.'

'Sometimes I think my illness is a way of telling me to stop trying so hard and accept what I am. I've always read my horoscope, hoping for some reassurance, and now I just want to be myself and to feel that I'm good enough. I have a lot to be grateful for: a good marriage; a son whom we adore, and who is happy and healthy compared to some of the problems my friends have with their children. Still, if I'm honest, I have found it quite stressful keeping up appearances. Could that have caused my illness? Nobody in my family has ever had cancer.' Angelica wanted to go on talking, as if suddenly she had been freed of the pressure of pretence.

'We don't know whether stress can cause cancer, but it's helpful to understand the past if it makes you see things differently now. We have to accept the good as well as the bad.' Whilst Rosalind realised the conversation wasn't particularly sequential, she felt that they were communicating and it was important to be responsive to Angelica's needs.

'It's extraordinary. Yesterday when I came to the hospital, I felt different, as though something new and exciting was happening, as if I was changing my path. And then you walked in. Perhaps I have been preparing for this for a long time. I have known for many years that I have my own way of believing in God, but now I want something more, although I don't really know what it is.'

Rosalind, moved by Angelica's simplistic insights, realised that she would have to be careful not to undermine Angelica's beliefs, but to support her by incorporating them into a broader context. 'Perhaps it would be best for me to visit you at home when you are feeling better and we can talk in a more relaxed atmosphere. I should leave you now.'

'Will you be here this afternoon? I would like my husband to meet you.'

'Yes, I promise to pop in.' Rosalind knew she couldn't let Angelica down.

*

When David arrived, Angelica was sitting up in bed, her blue eyes more alive than usual as he drew her towards him, feeling the bony contours of her body.

'You look far better than I expected.'

'I feel far better than I expected. David, something extraordinary happened yesterday. A woman rabbi visited me.'

'Is it extraordinary to find a woman rabbi, or did something else happen?' Her animated mood infected him.

'Well, I suppose I was particularly impressed that she's a woman. Her name is Rosalind Cohen, and she's from the Reform synagogue.'

'What did she say?'

Angelica sat forward, adjusting the pillow behind her head. 'Oh, so many things. We spoke about my illness, Judaism, and the family. I just felt that I could ask her questions and she would make sense of them. I feel so much calmer, as if my worries are floating away.'

'If she helped you, it can only be good. I would like to meet her.' Privately, David hoped that Rabbi Cohen didn't represent yet another belief system for Angelica.

'David, I *know* she can help me. I told her about my conversion to Judaism, and that I now feel ready to learn more.'

David hadn't considered the religious aspect. He had hardly been inside a synagogue after Jonathan's bar mitzvah, and found it worrying that Angelica was surrendering their comfortable secular Judaism on the basis of one meeting with some Reform rabbi. Concealing his surprise, and wanting to neither discourage nor enthuse, he replied, 'I suppose the Reform lot are reasonable enough.'

Angelica beamed. 'I knew that something worthwhile was going to happen to me yesterday. Wait till you meet her; she's so natural and warm.'

The nurse came in. 'Good morning, Mr Stern. Doesn't she look brighter this time?'

'Absolutely,' responded David. Then, 'Remind me to send the usual chocolates,' he murmured to Angelica. He wanted to ask if her parents had spoken to her about her illness, but perhaps her deterioration was so visible that it wasn't necessary to state the obvious. But the right time to ask never came, and he didn't know how to begin the conversation.

*

After lunch, while Angelica slept, David read the newspaper. She stirred when there came a knock at the door.

Rosalind came in. 'I'm sorry if I woke you,' she said.

Angelica propped herself up. 'David, this is Rabbi Rosalind Cohen.'

David leapt to his feet, putting his hand forward, and then withdrew it.

Rosalind smiled. 'It can be confusing meeting a woman rabbi. Don't worry, it's the usual reaction. Most women relate to me as a woman as well as a rabbi.'

David laughed sheepishly. 'I can't see why men don't relate to you as a woman.'

'That's exactly my point. Men can't take me seriously, even though there's no fundamental principle in Judaism that states that a woman can't become a rabbi. Women have a very important role in teaching, and that's one of the reasons why I became a rabbi.'

'And the others?' David asked, lightening the interchange.

'Who can answer that? Faith is also a matter of practice. We're all at different stages and I try to help others to decide for themselves.'

'That's reasonable – if there's any reason in faith, that is.'

'Oh, I think there are lots of reasons to make us believe. After all, isn't it reason that saves us from the excesses of fanatical faith?'

'And other reasons?' David asked, now genuinely interested.

'Many. But perhaps the greatest use of reason is that it tells us when it has served its purpose, when it can go no further. Then it tells us either to leap into faith or to stay stuck where we are.' Rosalind stopped spontaneously, realising that she was in the middle of some unresolved feelings between Angelica and David on religion.

'David, you know what I would like to do?' Angelica interjected.

'Just name it.' David couldn't imagine.

'I would like to go to Jerusalem, just for a short holiday, to see it and to understand things.'

Almost accusingly, David looked at Rosalind, who felt obliged to respond.

'That's fine, but you must ask your doctor. I have to see somebody upstairs now, but I'll pop back in later.'

Shortly after Dr Jameson came in, accompanied by a nurse. 'Well, my dear, how are you feeling this time?' he asked in his warm Scottish accent.

'Not too bad, but I really don't want to go through another bout of chemotherapy,' Angelica asserted.

'That's not on the cards at the moment, but I would like you to have a body scan and a blood test. I'll get my secretary to arrange it.'

'Dr Jameson?' Angelica paused. 'Do you think it would be all right for me to go on a short holiday abroad?'

'Where were you thinking of going?' Dr Jameson's tone gave nothing away.

'Jerusalem; only for a week.'

Dr Jameson thought for a moment and then, looking at David, said, 'It's a civilised enough place and they certainly aren't short of doctors there. In fact, I went to an oncology conference there a couple of years ago, and was very impressed. I tell you what, let's get the results of your tests. It should only take a week and, if you feel up to it, I think I could arrange a follow-up there. Let's wait and see, huh?' Then he turned to the nurse. 'Mrs Stern can go home this evening. I'll write up a script for her. I'll see you next week.'

Uncertainty was written all over David's face. It had been so long since they had planned a holiday that the thought of any change provoked panic.

'You see, David? Everything seems to be working out,' Angelica reassured him.

'If that's what you want, we should do it,' he said, masking his alarm.

Later, Rosalind came back. 'Angelica, I'll phone you at home and arrange to come and visit.'

'I appreciate that. I would also like to discuss Jerusalem with you as I think we're going soon.'

'That's absolutely wonderful; it will give you a perspective on Judaism that no amount of reading or synagogue attendance can provide. It is the most spiritual place in the world, and it's a good time of the year to visit. I'll bring some books for you to look at when I visit.'

David was hardly able to take in what was happening, until Rosalind said goodbye and left. 'It looks like we're going to Jerusalem with Rabbi Cohen's blessing,' he said, not wanting to quash Angelica's pleasure.

*

When Sophie arrived, Angelica was bubbling with excitement, while David appeared ill at ease.

'You look much better. What's happening?' Sophie asked, giving David a sidelong glance.

'You tell her,' David suggested, half hoping that Angelica had changed her mind.

'We're going on a short holiday to Jerusalem.' Angelica beamed.

'That's extraordinary, delightful – it's unbelievable. Do you feel up to it? That's the one place I've always wanted to visit. It's sacred to Judaism, Christianity and Islam, and one of the oldest living cities in the world.'

'Why not come with us? I'm sure David will be pleased to have your support. I know my David – look at him.' Angelica smiled sympathetically at her husband. 'Dearest, I don't blame you; I know I'm quite a responsibility. In fact, the more I think about it, the better I would feel if you could join us. Would you, Sophie, please?'

Events seemed to be overtaking David, but Angelica often had a way of knowing what he wanted before he did. 'I agree,' he said. 'I know we're asking a lot of you, Sophie, and of course you would be our guest. It would be wonderful if you could manage it.'

'It sounds wonderful. When do you plan to go?'

'Not for a couple of weeks.' David interrupted himself. 'And nothing is certain yet. Let's wait and see what Dr Jameson has to say.'

Sophie leafed through her pocket diary. 'I would like to be back for the start of Hannah's new term.' Then she thought of leaving Lucien.

'What's Lucien doing?' David interjected, hiding his pleasure at the prospect of Sophie accompanying them.

Sophie looked downcast. 'I despair; he's a talent gone to waste. We'll just have to see what happens in the A Levels, not that he'll achieve much. He decided not to go back to school last September, then turned up in the summer term, a month before the Art A Level, and asked if he could sit it. I went along to the school and begged. Eventually, he was allowed to present his portfolio. I really don't know what more I can do. Marc has tried. Ernst has tried. Poor Lucien, he's such a worry, and I blame myself. I was much better with Hannah, and it shows. She's so capable, and with only eleven months between them, Lucien doesn't need Hannah overtaking him. I'm sure they could all manage without me, particularly if Marc decides to pull his weight. But he appears to be so busy, going to meetings every week.' Then, feeling Angelica and David's silence, she recognised her inappropriate outpouring and added, 'Thank you for inviting me. I'm sure it will be all right.'

Angelica looked doubtful. 'Oh, I hope Marc will stay with the children; I wouldn't want to upset anybody.'

'Don't worry, he will. Everything will be fine, and if there are any problems, you know Ernst; he doesn't even need an excuse to rush over. He adores Lucien and Hannah.'

Angelica's ecstatic expression returned. 'Oh, I just know it's the right thing to do.'

'Well, that leaves me to do some research and make the arrangements,' said David.

'Which takes all of one minute, to instruct his secretary,' Angelica teased.

David's reply was interrupted by the nurse. 'Mrs Stern, you can go home as soon as you're ready. Would you like some tea before you leave?'

'Champagne will do.' Angelica smiled.

SIXTEEN

THE CONSULTATION

Sophie realised that she had been too hasty in acquiescing to Angelica's plea to accompany her to Jerusalem, but how could she have refused her anything? David also seemed eager for her to join them. She had noticed how his initial reluctance had changed to animation when she had agreed to go. But notwithstanding the lifelong burden of her own anxiety, there was the added uncertainty of Angelica's scan.

*

Angelica felt mildly detached as she waited for Dr Jameson to speak. She was determined to refuse further chemotherapy and, most of all, she wanted to know the truth. Focused on his every move, she observed him glancing alternately between her and the file on his desk. Then, making fleeting eye contact, he spoke slowly.

'I'm sorry I don't have better news for you. I had hoped that the chemotherapy would have more impact on the tumour, but the scan shows that this is not so.'

Angelica paused, then looked directly at Dr Jameson and asked, 'Am I going to die?'

Until now, like many of his patients, she had accepted the general inference of her illness without pursuing the fundamental question, and he wasn't sure whether she was ready to accept the inevitable. For the first time he noticed her determined expression.

'I can only make assumptions. As a general rule, if the disease isn't improving or halting, then it could worsen. Of course, there is always the chance that the body will find a way of fighting back.' His warm, melodic voice took her into a stunned silence.

She sat back in her chair, intent on having the conversation that she had rehearsed in her head. 'What is your opinion, Dr Jameson? I need to know because I cannot go on deluding myself, and I have to think of my husband and son. You see, we have never discussed my death, and the fact that we can't discuss it probably means that we haven't prepared ourselves.' Her voice shook but she forced herself to continue, and was surprised to find some relief. 'I need to know how long you think I have left.'

After treating her for two years, Dr Jameson now realised how little he knew her. Only last year he had written an acclaimed paper on *When to Tell the Patient*. But he had omitted the vital question of *How to Tell the Patient*, which he could no longer avoid. Pausing for a moment, he looked directly at Angelica. His expression softened. Then, speaking in a calm voice, he had her full attention. 'If we just focus on the scan for the moment...' Releasing the results of the scan from the file, he placed them on his desk while watching her take a silk handkerchief to dab her eyes. 'It looks as though you have a new tumour just above the area where we operated last time. That is, just above the colostomy. I believe it to be inoperable.'

Succumbing to the full force of her death sentence, it was

as if everything in her life had led, and could only have led, to this moment. There was no purpose; nor did she have the power to abate the flow of tears. Her tight fistful of screwed-up handkerchief failed to mop up the warm, salty rivers that flowed into her mouth. Dr Jameson waited, suspended by his limitations. Neither he nor Angelica could tell whether she wept more through desperation or in relief, but he knew that he had removed all hope.

'Angelica, I'm sorry but I cannot suggest any more treatment, and I wonder whether it is now time for your husband to be involved.'

She looked up and took a deep breath. It was the only time he had addressed her by her first name. She felt a calmness sweep over her. 'No, I really don't think that's possible because he couldn't accept it. I must first prepare myself, and only then can I help my husband and son. I have thought about it, and I'm grateful for the truth. Can you tell me how much longer I've got?'

Dr Jameson diverted his eyes to the scan, giving him time to think. 'We are talking about months.' He stopped himself from saying weeks. 'But there again, that's looking at the gloomiest outcome. I'm not God and would not like to presume.'

Her skin looked translucent after the wash of tears, and he was struck anew by her beauty. How could he be honest, witnessing the progressive attack on her frailty? All he could do was provide different kinds of temporary palliatives.

'Can I still go to Jerusalem?' she asked. 'I really want to. We've almost finalised the arrangements.'

'If you feel up to it, as a matter of fact, I can be of some help. I will phone a colleague, Dr Avram Levi; a first-class chap at the Hadassah Hospital. We will all feel better knowing that if you have any problems, you will be taken care of. Dr Levi and I have worked together before and can ensure continuity of care, which is our main task. Could you please let my secretary know the exact dates you will be in Jerusalem and where you will be staying?'

Angelica began to feel at ease. 'This is my last question. Will it be painful?' Realising that he too hadn't missed the connotation of the word 'last', she felt a shiver go down her spine.

'I really can't be sure, but I will give you a prescription for tablets, with clear instructions. On balance, I do not envisage much discomfort, but please feel free to phone me, and I will be writing to your GP today. I'm sure Dr Levi will monitor any level of discomfort and prescribe for you in Jerusalem. It would be more helpful if you would involve your husband, but of course, that's your choice.'

*

Outside, Angelica felt estranged from the people she saw walking along the pavement. The word 'dying' gnawed at her thoughts. Whilst she could reconcile herself to the fact that everybody has to die, the unacceptable part was leaving David and Jonathan.

The sun was still high when she sank into the warm leather seat in the back of the car as it cruised through Regent's Park. She saw a woman jogging in a bright pink tracksuit; an elderly couple walking arm in arm under the vibrant hues of trees shimmering in the sunlight. The images moved like a film in slow motion, as if time had suddenly slipped or converged. Unbidden, her thoughts came in vestigial flashes and then receded.

In the distance, she heard the driver say, 'Mrs Stern, I'm sorry to disturb you, but we're home now.'

PART THREE

JERUSALEM

SEVENTEEN

ANGELICA'S MISSION

At home, Angelica phoned David. 'It's fine. We can go to Jerusalem.'

'Fantastic. Does the scan actually show an improvement?'

Angelica fudged. 'Not exactly – Dr Jameson says it's difficult to see the exact outcome after chemotherapy – but the important thing is we can go.'

'That must be good news,' David replied.

'Dr Jameson is writing to a colleague there, so we'll even have our private doctor in Jerusalem. Everything appeared to be working out well. I'll phone Sophie and let her know. Oh, and I forgot to mention that Rosalind is coming to see me tomorrow.'

'You're a great organiser; another eight days and we'll be on our way. I'll be home soon,' David said, reassuring himself that his unease was probably due to leaving the safety of their home.

Angelica knew she had fostered in him a belief in her recovery, and felt ashamed of her dishonesty. It wasn't that she'd told a lie; she just hadn't told the truth. Dr Jameson's words had been clear: 'Perhaps it's time to involve your husband.'

*

Sophie was surprised by Marc's enthusiastic response when she told him that the trip was on. He promised to spend more time with Lucien, which he knew would lessen her worry. She said that while the trip might not be a picnic it might also be good for Sophie to get out of the house. Sophie still harboured doubts that seemed more entrenched than usual, and phoned Emma, who warned her that she would have to choose her words carefully because she had found David hypersensitive. Lastly, Sophie phoned Ernst.

'That's good news, the treatment must be working, but who knows for how long?' he replied.

'Did I tell you that Angelica is turning to religion? Well, it appears more a mixture of intuition, prophecy and astrology all blended into Judaism. Even if it's an act of desperation, it's helping her, and David and I are supporting her.'

'I'm pleased that you accepted their invitation. Angelica is a wonderful friend to you, Sophie, and I'm sure you'll be very helpful. As an atheist, I think of belief as an invisible means of support. Don't worry about religion; I also have the occasional yearning for certainty. And don't worry about Lucien, either; I'll be in constant touch with him.'

'The whole trip could turn out a disaster. I don't think anybody really thought it through, especially Angelica, who acted impulsively after meeting a woman rabbi at the hospital.'

'You worry too much, Sophie. Angelica will probably only see what she wants to see. You must also try to get something out of the trip. I think it will do you good,' he reassured her.

*

Back at home, resting on her bed, Angelica watched the darkness settle. Various thoughts, mostly jumbled, disturbed her. She wondered whether her need for God was just a cry for help, and sobbed, only to feel the more unsettled by her self-pity. Perhaps the certainty of her death was too much of a challenge. Perhaps God was presenting her with this final test of faith and her doubts were an essential part of the journey. She recalled standing under the canopy in the synagogue twenty years ago, wondering what on earth she was doing there. She had read the prayer book, and to some extent the text had calmed her and helped her deal with her feelings of alienation. But that was different to believing, and now she sought the meaning she had missed. Perhaps her intuition had been prophetic all along and she needed to have an honest discussion with Rosalind Cohen. She thought of Emma, who usually invited the family on Jewish festival days. There Angelica had learned the forms of observance, but, as with the rest of her life, in conforming to the form she had missed the substance.

She picked up the card Rosalind had given her and phoned her. 'I hope I'm not disturbing you; it's Angelica Stern.'

'I was just about to phone you. I would like to come and see you at about three tomorrow. How are things?' asked Rosalind.

'We're going to Jerusalem, but there are so many things I need to understand. I hope it's not too late.'

'I'll do my best to help, and I look forward to seeing you tomorrow.'

Angelica thanked Rosalind and gave her the address. She was determined to talk openly with her, she prepared a list of questions and told her housekeeper that they were not to be disturbed.

*

Rosalind was surprised by Angelica's height and elegance, for neither had been apparent when she was lying in bed in the hospital. Following her into the drawing room, Rosalind watched her slump into a Charles Eames chair, supporting her long legs on the footstool. She sat opposite her on a leather couch and, noticing the tension around Angelica's eyes, sensed her impatience to begin the conversation.

'I've brought some books on Jerusalem for you to browse through.' Rosalind decided on an indirect approach.

Angelica glanced at the pile of books on the couch and then, as if she'd missed her cue, responded, 'Thank you. We're going in seven days.'

'I'm really pleased for you. Do you feel up to the trip?' Rosalind asked.

'At the moment, I feel very confused.' Angelica's eyes glazed over with tears.

'Has something unexpected occurred?'

'In a way. You see, I've always known that my chances were pretty slim, particularly during this last bout of chemotherapy, but there was always the hope…' She spoke in bursts, unable to hold back the flood of tears. Unstoppable, her words tumbled out. 'Yesterday, I went to see Dr Jameson. In a way, he only confirmed what I already knew, so I suppose when I was with him, it was some relief to know the truth, but now I feel quite desperate. You see, I don't want to leave David and Jonathan alone.'

'Do they know?' Rosalind asked.

'No, that's the problem: I can't tell them because I couldn't bear their pain, and deep down I think they hope I will recover. I don't know how to manage all this. That's why I wanted to see you.'

'I understand, but without talking to them, you might not realise that their feelings are similar to yours. We must work together to help the whole family and find a way for you all to manage. It can be done, you know. It's important for you to feel in control of your life, and through managing it, you will gain strength.'

Rosalind welcomed the interruption when the housekeeper came in to place the tea tray on the table. She moved forward to pour the tea, which Angelica accepted.

'Do help yourself to some cake,' Angelica urged, folding her arms across her abdomen as if holding herself together amongst the cold surfaces of glass and marble. 'There are things I want to understand that I don't even know how to express. I've always believed in God, and at first I wondered whether it was my illness that made me look to Him for help. It's easy to pray when you are desperate. I remember feeling God's presence when Jonathan was born. He was premature and an emergency caesarean, but I just knew that I was being protected, that it would be all right, but it's different now. I feel I am being called.' She stopped for breath, took a sip of tea and continued. 'I often read the Bible. I carry a pocket edition around with me. The habit started when David's mother gave it to me. I thought it so beautiful that I just kept it inside my bag.' She handed Rosalind a small Bible bound in mother-of-pearl.

'It's most unusual, and certainly well fingered,' she said, handing it back.

'I don't know why these feelings take over,' Angelica said, 'but one thing leads to another. Whenever I had an appointment and the other person was late, I never minded because I'd have my Bible to read. Not in any specific order – I would open it at random. Often the words seemed to be speaking directly to me; it happened yesterday while I was waiting to see Dr Jameson. At the top of a page I read, "Call unto me and I will answer thee, and show thee great and mighty things that thou knowest not." It's from Isaiah, and when I went in to see Dr Jameson, I felt that I was being led along a familiar path.

'Last night when we were having dinner, I felt very low and David and Jonathan got involved in one of their political discussions. David was particularly relaxed and happy because Jonathan had done rather well in his A Levels and is going to Oxford in October. They were joking, and Jonathan was teasing David: "Well, Dad, at least I'll be going to Oxford. You only went to the London School of Economics." Then he said something which affected me deeply: "Even Mum knows more about Judaism than you, and you're supposed to be the real Jew here."

'I wanted to answer but could not. I felt choked, as though my own son was closing the last door open to me. I know he meant no harm and hadn't realised what he'd said, but I'm so sensitive that I find meaning in everything.

'David made light of the whole thing. He laughed and said, "You're right. Why do you think we're going to Jerusalem? Your mother has more interest and commitment than both of us put together."

'I felt so unsure of myself that I interrupted and asked Jonathan what he was going to do while we were away.

'He looked at David and smiled. "Well, thanks to you-know-who, I just happen to have tickets for the Test match at Lord's…"

'Their previous taunting melted away. I suddenly saw how their lives would be without me, and I knew I was beginning to leave them.

'After dinner, I went upstairs. I often read in bed, and I picked up my Bible and it fell open at Ecclesiastes. The words appeared to embrace me. It was as though they expressed and gave form to my grief, to my own mourning. And they made everything seem so obvious. "For everything there is a season, and a time for every matter under heaven. A time to be born and a time to die…", and then it describes the different kinds of vanity, and the value of wisdom and the stupidity of anger. I keep reading and rereading this section, and while I am reading, I find that I can accept dying. And it helps. Everything makes sense. Nothing is as natural or as inevitable as dying. I don't feel frightened or alone. It's when I stop reading that I am spontaneously confronted with the world of David and Jonathan. I become so confused. And that's why I want to be with David in Jerusalem.' Angelica was weeping uncontrollably now.

Rosalind noticed how these moments of aching sadness erupted when she talked about her husband and son. 'I can understand how you might feel alone in your faith, not just because David and Jonathan may feel differently, but because you wonder whether it's real and whether it can sustain you. You would also feel more comforted if David believed in God, or at the very least supported your faith.'

She saw the tension in Angelica's eyes lessen in agreement.

'I do need reassurance that my faith isn't just a childish cry for help. I don't feel confident in expressing it, because David would ask how can there be a God if He takes me away from him? And I don't know how to answer.'

Rosalind was uncertain where to start, but was guided by her compassion. 'David knows it isn't that simple,' she replied after some thought. 'Indeed, the notion of reward and punishment is exceedingly complex. We must look for guidance in what wiser rabbis have told us. Maimonides, a great twelfth-century sage, when asked a similar question, replied, "*That no man should make a deal with God, and that only vulgar men are trained to serve God out of fear of punishment or out of greediness for reward.*" That doesn't mean that we don't feel cheated when we are suffering, but we all have to try to make sense of it in our own way. David may not find these ideas useful and you have to respect that his understanding is very different to yours, but clearly you'll make him feel better if he knows that your belief is a comfort to you.'

Angelica listened attentively and then, as if unable to take in any more, stirred and shifted her position in the chair. 'Would you like some more apple strudel?' she said, offering the plate to Rosalind.

'It is quite delicious, but no thank you,' Rosalind said, feeling that it was time to leave. Angelica was deathly white, her heavy eyelids reminding Rosalind of a Greek marble sculpture. 'I want you to know that I will do all I can and you need not be afraid to ask, or feel alone. You mustn't feel defeated. In Judaism there is guidance on every issue. Belief can be a very long and complicated path, but it is there to bring you comfort. I hope I haven't exhausted you,' she added quietly.

With her eyes almost closed, Angelica gave a deep sigh. She felt overwhelmed by her inadequacy, and desperately wanted to relinquish responsibility. How could she involve David and Jonathan as Dr Jameson advised? 'I realise it's difficult to sustain my faith when I understand so little, and you've helped me see that.'

Rosalind moved forward to let Angelica know that she was leaving. 'On the contrary, your belief is probably purer because you have come to it in your own way. Just knowing a lot of words and being able to quote lots of prayers can enhance one's belief, but it isn't divine essence. You are finding in your Bible the words that suit you, and those will be the right ones for you.'

'Yes,' said Angelica, and paused. 'Thank you.'

Rosalind got up to leave, and Angelica, mildly revived, walked with her to the door. Gently, Rosalind put her arms around her. 'I'll be back tomorrow,' she said.

EIGHTEEN

SHOPPING

Angelica noticed the change in her sleep pattern. It was as if nature was informing her and altering her perceptions. Time seemed neither to have slowed down nor to have speeded up, but as if it were suspended in itself. As if guided by an inner force, she would awake with the first light, at times feeling overwhelmed by a penetrating sadness, as if her skin were open to the elements, yearning for harmony in every situation. She would look for and sometimes find solace in the shape and colour of a flower. Her heightened sensitivity, which came in bouts, made her feel bombarded when David and Jonathan talked too loudly. She feared contention, and would almost panic if she thought that their discussion could lead to a disagreement. When they were playfully goading each other, she would make excuses to retire.

She couldn't forget David's shocked expression when unwittingly he glimpsed her colostomy and was traumatised by the sight of the unnatural hole in her side exuding excrement into a transparent plastic bag. He started taking sleeping tablets. Whilst she had learned to manage the dressings and the occasional accident of overflow that stained her clothes, the high-tech dressings couldn't disguise the escaping sanitised odours.

Often, she brooded over one particular line in the Talmudic writings that Rosalind had given her:

We did not choose to be born, nor do we choose to die; we can only choose what to do with the days in between.

Watching the leaves fall from the tree outside, the words of the verses in Ecclesiastes that, seemingly by chance, she had read the previous night echoed within and saturated her very being. One was:

All the rivers run to the sea, yet the sea is not full; unto the place from whence the rivers come, thither they return again. All things are full of labour; man cannot utter it; the eye is not satisfied with seeing, nor the ear filled with hearing.

Another was:

To everything there is a season, and a time for every purpose under heaven. A time to be born and a time to die; a time to plant and a time to pluck up that which is planted.

The wisdom was there for her to make her own – it was time to plant. Through David and Jonathan and Sophie and Emma, she could extend her life beyond winter and on into the spring and beyond.

With a sudden surge of gratitude, she waited for David to bring her morning cup of boiling water, then said, 'David—'

Before she could finish her sentence he replied, 'Of course, delighted to help', and smiled.

Angelica laughed. 'But how do you know what I'm going to say?'

'Well, let's see. Is it to do with Jerusalem?'

'Sort of. I would like to have the car today. I was thinking of buying Sophie a new outfit. It's our way of saying thank you to her, for coming to Israel with us. She also doesn't appear to make the best of herself and I thought it would be fun to find her a new image.'

'Good idea, but have you thought how she might react? She has a lot of pride and I suspect she doesn't think spending money on one's image is that important. After all, anybody can look better depending on how much time and money they dedicate to themselves,' David asserted.

'I agree, but Sophie doesn't seem to have a clue. Look at Emma – most of the time she wears run-of-the-mill outfits, but she knows how to choose colours and put them together; she's always well groomed. I can't imagine her wearing anything ethnic. Sophie seems to find such weird clothes. It must be the shops in Muswell Hill.'

'I look forward to seeing what happens. Buy her something very special; don't worry about the cost.' He had not seen Angelica so happy for months.

'It's extraordinary, the way you read my mind – or do you think that I'm really reading yours?' Angelica sounded serious. Knowing her views on telepathy, David looked at her lovingly.

'Who can tell? I'm not going to own up to my thoughts, otherwise we could get involved in a form of suggestion exchange.'

Angelica gave a hearty laugh. 'Really, David, you can be quite crazy but I love you.'

She couldn't wait to phone Sophie. 'Are you busy today?'

'Not really; just trying to get some shopping in before the trip,' Sophie replied, knowing that she was needed.

'Good, because I want you to come shopping with me at Harrods.'

'I didn't mean that kind of shopping. My list is more like basic household supplies.'

'Then I insist; I'm quite impulsive lately. Our driver will take us so we won't have any parking problems.'

'That sounds a lot more attractive than buying detergent. I'm ready.'

'Sophie, I really don't know how you cope with the house as well as your work, and still have so much time for me.'

'As far as the house goes, I don't cope and never have; it's more a matter of preventing collapse. Fortunately, Marc helps when he can, but that mostly means keeping his study perfectly organised. Hannah appears to have taken over the management. She loves cooking and keeps on telling everybody to tidy up. I suppose incompetent mothers have a way of making their daughters overcompensate. As far as my very part-time work goes, marking exam papers every six months is hardly a burden.'

'I really don't know why you're always putting yourself down. Not everybody could get a double first. I'm so indulged – practically everything is done for me,' replied Angelica.

Saddened, Sophie saw that no amount of indulgence could ever outweigh Angelica's suffering. She had not sought luxury, but had simply adapted to David's lifestyle. 'I suppose I feel a little guilty going off to Jerusalem, so I was trying to play the perfect housewife. I guess they'll all see through it, but I'm hoping to change after Jerusalem,' she said, thinking of Emma and her organised systems.

'I am afraid you're going to change before we go; I am determined to find you a new image. That will be the way I'll have a good time. The car will pick you up in an hour. We're going to have a really fun day, you'll see,' Angelica said, feeling more settled as she prepared for the last phase of her life. She couldn't tell whether it was her daily talks with Rosalind Cohen or something else that had made her sense of purpose return.

*

The Designer Room at Harrods was almost empty, with an in-between-seasons feeling as Angelica studied the display. Selecting a burgundy suit, she beckoned enthusiastically to Sophie, who was standing back. Then she picked out a few other items and watched admiringly as Sophie tried them on, the latter beginning to feel as if she were being indulged by an adoring mother.

'Sophie, you look stunning in everything – we just have to have them. I don't care what you say.'

'I couldn't possibly have *two* designer suits,' Sophie pleaded.

'You did promise that it would be my fun day. Please, it means a lot to me.'

Sophie relented. 'Thank you very much. I'll always treasure them,' she said, wondering how she was going to explain her new image to Marc. She knew that Ernst would be delighted to see her looking so elegant, but he was a proud man and would also be concerned about Angelica's generosity.

In the restaurant, Angelica looked tired but content. 'I've had a wonderful time and you are so gracious in accepting the clothes; I hope you really like them.'

'No one has ever taken such an interest in my appearance, and I love everything you've chosen for me. I just feel so guilty.' Sophie looked tenderly at Angelica's calm expression.

'I know how you feel. I felt the same when David first showered me with gifts. He said it wasn't the amount he spent, which he could easily afford; just that he enjoyed seeing me look so good. Besides, I don't have a daughter and I think I've missed out on all that frivolous stuff.'

'Thank you. What worries me is that Marc will flip when he

sees me in them. Actually, more to the point, he probably won't even notice.'

Feeling mildly uncomfortable about Sophie's disclosure, Angelica added hastily, 'I'm sure Hannah will notice. I think she's stunning, but like you, she doesn't make the best of herself. Perhaps we could have some fun taking her out on our next shopping spree.' She stretched out her arm across the table and placed her hand over Sophie's. 'I won't be here forever, you must accept that, and think of all the pleasure it gives me to see you happy. Well, you know what I mean.' She glanced at her watch. 'The car will be here in five minutes, so we'd better start making our way down.'

*

Back home, whilst Sophie was putting her new clothes away, Hannah came into the bedroom. 'Wow, what gorgeous colours; they must have cost a fortune! These are definitely the genuine thing!' She fingered a fine woollen jacket.

'How can you tell?' asked Sophie.

'The buttons, for one,' said Hannah, transfixed on the gold designer initials.

'I feel terrible; I just couldn't say no. It seemed so important to Angelica. She was quite manic, and could easily have gone on buying me everything in the shop.'

'Do you think you could take me along next time? I need to change my image.'

'Dearest, I promise we'll go shopping as soon as I get back. We couldn't afford these clothes, but there's probably a lot of lovely things out there, and I'm sure Ernst will be delighted to help.'

'Don't be silly, Mum, I was only joking. Try them on; I'd like to see you in them.'

Sophie was pleased to see herself in the clothes again.

'Mum, you look stunning. You have an amazing figure. I've decided, I'm going on a diet,' Hannah proclaimed.

'Well, if you lose some weight, we should find some gorgeous clothes. You have a beautiful face, Hannah, and wonderful hair. Ernst thinks you're the image of his mother; you certainly don't look like Marc or me.'

Hannah smiled appreciatively. 'I really am going to try. What do you think, two stone?'

'Don't put yourself under pressure, just start eating less and see how you feel. With the way you run around, the weight should drop off,' Sophie encouraged her.

Later, knowing Angelica's belief in portents, Sophie phoned her. 'You remember what you said in Harrods about Hannah? You must be telepathic, because she's repeated almost verbatim that she wants to go shopping with us.'

'Sophie, I'm pleased you've some evidence. You see, this sort of thing happens to me quite often. Even David laughs. He calls them my telepathic turns. But I know that sometimes I understand events beyond the point of coincidence.'

'It must be a gift. I certainly believe you,' Sophie said with assurance.

'Thank you; that means a lot to me.'

*

That evening, Sophie spoke to Emma. 'Poor Angelica, she appears to be searching for meaning in every situation.'

'Dearest, with what she's going through, and I'm sure we only know half of it, I certainly wouldn't be so selfless.'

'You're right. Today she said that she won't be here forever. I felt I had to go along with everything she wanted. She even offered me the clothes she no longer wears. I really don't know how to handle it. When I'm with her it all seems rational, but afterwards I feel panicky.'

'I suppose she's grateful that you're going with them to Jerusalem, and guilty that she's taking you away from Marc and the children.'

'I am worried about leaving Marc, although I really don't have any reason to be, beyond the fact that he appears so preoccupied and spends so many evenings at work. Do you think he could be having an affair?'

Emma gasped. 'Darling, all marriages go through a dormant period. Why imagine the worst? Marc strikes me as a rather benign and committed husband. I can assure you, my marriage isn't perfect, but I make the best of it. I hardly see Alan, and he seems so busy nowadays, too.'

Sophie felt confused. Emma sounded more resentful than reassuring. 'I suppose I'm worried because it's the first time I'll be going away alone. I know I'll be with Angelica and David, and I can't help comparing my marriage with theirs. They are so close, and their love for each other seems so natural… I can't explain it.'

'Come on, Sophie, look at their situation. It's hardly surprising that they cling together. Perhaps you've taken on too much going with them to Jerusalem?'

'Probably, but how could I refuse? I suppose that's why I feel unsettled and imagine all these things about Marc.'

'I'll be spending the afternoon with Angelica tomorrow. You'll be leaving on Sunday. How about if I come over for tea on Friday afternoon?'

'Thanks, Emma, I'd like that.'

*

On the terrace, Sophie passed Emma a cup of tea and watched her fiddle with the modern gold necklace she was wearing.

'I agree with you about Angelica; she insisted on giving me this necklace and it's not exactly my taste, but I couldn't refuse,' Emma said.

'It suits you,' Sophie said, looking at the figure-of-eight design.

'It's Cartier. It must have cost a fortune. I usually wear antique but I think I could change my image. There's good design and bad design. Just look at Angelica's house: even after twenty years, it looks marvellous.'

'Emma, I think I'm crazy going to Jerusalem with them. It appears inappropriate and I really don't know how I'm going to manage. I don't want to intrude on their intimacy, particularly at this time.'

'Perhaps they need you to stop them getting too close. I don't know. But we have to prepare ourselves. I don't know what other treatment Angelica can undergo, and how much more David can endure. He goes home every afternoon – I was surprised to find him there when I visited – and I agree with you about their relationship; it's incredible. Do you really think he believes that Angelica will get better?' asked Emma. 'It is impossible to ever know what anybody else really thinks. I suppose we're all living in a conspiracy of silence.'

'Frankly, Emma, you've become rather distracted lately and I wondered whether I've done anything to offend you?' Sophie asked.

'Of course not, it's nothing to do with you. I wish it were; it would probably be easier to sort out. Look, there is no easy way to say this, so I'll come right out with it. I'm having an affair. Please, not a word to Angelica – not yet, anyway. There are very good reasons.'

'What do you mean?' Sophie, thinking it had something to do with David, panicked.

'You might as well know, and believe me, you are the only one who does. I'm involved with Aubrey Lewis,' Emma announced.

'Our obstetrician?!' Sophie exclaimed.

'Yes. I have been for about a year.'

'What about Alan?' Sophie asked, unable to hide her shock.

'Well, darling, two can play the same game,' Emma said emphatically. 'My dear husband has been having an affair with his secretary, on and off, for five years. He would never admit it, and wouldn't even think of it as an affair. He would just think of it as a little bit on the side; you know, a weekly late shift at the office, the odd business trip to Geneva…'

'How did you find out?' Sophie heard herself asking.

'By chance.' Emma, aware of Sophie's alarm, regretted telling her.

Sophie looked down. 'I'm amazed I made so few mistakes. I'm so insecure and naive, it just never occurred to me to do those things. They seemed okay in novels, but that's fiction. I honestly thought of you and Alan as the epitome of domestic bliss.'

'You're absolutely right. When I found out about Alan, I knew I had to keep my head, for the boys' sake. There was no point in throwing away sixteen years of marriage without carefully considering the consequences. That's probably why I was able to get involved with Aubrey without too much of a conscience. In fact, quite easily – maybe it was revenge…'

Sophie sat on the edge of her chair, and turned around as if to make sure that the house was still empty. She wanted to know more, but at the same time felt contaminated by the information. She recalled that Emma had dropped Angelica and her a note saying that she just had to get away for a week to a health farm. 'Did all this happen when you went away to the health farm?'

'Yes. Finding out about Alan was the most traumatic experience of my life. I don't know how I managed to stay sane. In fact, I knew that if I didn't go away, I would destroy the boys and my family. Fortunately, I met a woman there who was going through a similar experience, and she helped me. I didn't come back until I was able to maintain a semblance of normality,' Emma admitted.

'Oh, darling, I'm so sorry. I can't imagine how you managed.

You must be very strong-minded. So how *did* you find out?'

Emma puckered her lips and then half smiled. 'Silence isn't always a strength; in fact, I regard my behaviour as a weakness. My dependence on Alan outweighed my desire to walk out of the marriage. I've survived, so I suppose that's a kind of strength, but at the time I was devastated. Only my pride kept me going.

'Alan and I were supposed to go to the theatre and then out to dinner afterwards. He told me he had to work late and I should meet him at the theatre. I thought I'd see what was on offer at Selfridges, which is just around the corner from his office. You know me, I spontaneously thought poor Alan might be hungry, so I bought some smoked salmon sandwiches and walked round to his office. It was about half past six. I went up in the lift and the office door was closed, but I could see the lights were on through the glass panel above the door. I rang the bell a few times and there was no answer, so I became concerned and went downstairs, found the caretaker and insisted that he let me in. I must have a strong heart. There they were on the carpet in Alan's office: him and that twenty-five-year-old secretary. I think I stopped breathing. I ran out of the building, and just walked. I couldn't go home in my state.

'I must have walked for hours; I remember going through Regent's Park and landing up at Swiss Cottage. I saw a taxi, and eventually got home about eleven o'clock. Alan was sitting in the kitchen. I never said a word to him. Fortunately, the boys were upstairs in bed. I couldn't go upstairs, and slept in my clothes on the settee. I got up early, had a shower and got the boys ready for school. I was determined to protect them. I told them that I had taken up a special offer to go to a health farm and would be back in a week. After they left for school, Alan came down; I couldn't look at him and went up to pack my bag. When he asked me where I was going I said, "Ask your sons."'

'How are you and Alan getting on now?' Sophie asked, concealing her disgust.

'Alan feels very guilty and can't do enough, but the trust has gone. I never thought that I could continue in this sort of situation, and in a way I hate myself for it. But I rationalise it by thinking that in life there is love and there is responsibility. I've worked too hard to let Alan's stupidity make me throw everything away. He's a good father, and the boys are at a vulnerable age.'

'I understand, but what made you get involved with Aubrey Lewis?' Sophie asked.

'You won't believe me if I tell you. I didn't mean to, it just happened. Really, Sophie, I'm not like that; Alan was the only man I ever knew. The whole thing was a chance happening. Do you want the whole story?'

'Only as much as you feel able to tell me.'

'As you know, I was with Angelica when she went to see him for that fated consultation. Well, six months later we received a wedding invitation from Alan's cousin. It turned out his son was marrying Aubrey's daughter. Of course, I was intrigued when I heard that Aubrey and his wife had divorced a few years earlier, and wondered how they would cope at the wedding.

'Everything appeared to be fine at the synagogue, but there was an obvious tension during the reception. Alan's cousin told us that Aubrey's ex-wife was still quite bitter. During the evening Aubrey came up to me and asked me about Angelica and you. We got talking and he asked me to dance. I suppose the medical ethics thing didn't apply in that situation. I really don't know. While we were dancing he asked me how I was getting on. You know how he has that concerned way of talking, and I suppose because of him being a doctor or something, I couldn't lie. I just said, "Fine, except for my marriage." Aubrey didn't say anything, the dance ended, and that was that.

'About a month later, he phoned me. Naturally, I was surprised. I thought it was about Angelica. It seemed a reasonable connection. And when he asked if I would like to meet him for lunch, I don't think I thought too deeply about it. Perhaps I was looking for something, but at the time, I naively thought that lunch meant lunch.' Emma giggled.

Astonished, Sophie waited for her to continue.

'Well, one thing led to another, and one thing is sure: I can't ever be a patient of his again.'

Sophie couldn't think what to say. Then she asked, 'Does Alan know?'

'Of course not. Look, it's not that intense; nor do I want to go through another traumatic time. Believe me, I've learned the art of compromise, and for the moment, that's how I manage. You must remember that I've known Alan since I was eighteen. I suppose we've both just grown up.' Seeing Sophie's shock, Emma exclaimed, 'I shouldn't have told you! You see, you think you have friends but then something like this happens and it cuts deep. Some things are better kept secret. I think I've lost your respect or something; I don't know, I just feel it.'

Emma was right, but Sophie wouldn't admit it. 'Emma, I'm not judging you. I'm just confused, because I thought you'd be the last person to have an affair. I suppose it's partly because I know Aubrey Lewis. I don't think I could go to him again either. I just don't know. You see, it's hard for me to understand your behaviour, because I feel unable to take a stand on so many issues. Of course, I can understand how two people can be attracted to each other, but I wouldn't risk admitting it – maybe after a fleeting recognition of my feelings I would hold myself in check. That's me. No risk, no loss. But you seem able to act. You always have.'

Emma looked wistfully into the distance, and sighed. 'I suppose I don't think as deeply as you do. I grasp the day. I deal with life as it presents itself – no questions, no confusion. We're just different, you and I.'

Sophie was keen that Emma would not leave without repairing the rift. 'Emma, I honestly believe that you've suffered. I cannot understand Aubrey's behaviour and really, I prefer not to think about it for the moment. The fact that you've stayed with Alan and kept your family together is commendable. I don't know whether I would be capable of that, if Marc had an affair. As you say, behaving in a civilised way must mean something. I know I have to adapt to the changing world, but I'm too anxious. I need things to remain the same to feel safe. You're different; that's why we get on. I agree that Angelica must never know. I promise it will go no further.' She got up and put her arm around Emma, kissing her on the cheek. 'Let's get out of here. Let's go up to Hampstead and do something frivolous.'

'Thanks for listening. You're a brick, Sophie,' said Emma, near to tears.

*

The next morning, sprawled across the bed, watching Sophie pack, Hannah asked, 'Has Angelica got long to live?'

Her candour shocked Sophie, anxiously folding her clothes and hurriedly placing them in the suitcase. 'That's not the point. She needs me now, and Angelica often makes momentous decisions which appear to work out. And you? You seem a little subdued – is it because I'm going away?'

'Not at all; I think you need to get away. Can I help you pack?' Hannah asked, but she was more concerned with wanting to tell Sophie that yesterday she'd seen Marc sitting with another woman in her favourite patisserie, but had managed to slip away unnoticed.

'I don't even know where my passport is,' Sophie mumbled childishly.

Hannah leapt off the bed, fumbling through the heap of papers in the bedside cabinet, and took out two passports. 'Why have you kept your old passport? You look so young. Was the photo taken when you were at Oxford?'

Sophie looked over Hannah's shoulder. 'I was nineteen,' she

said, seeing her thin, cheerless face encircled by a mass of unruly hair.

'You haven't changed much, considering that you're almost forty.' Hannah handed her the current passport. 'Put it in your handbag right away, then you'll know it's there. Can I repack your clothes? I love filling in all the spaces.'

As Hannah bent over to fold the clothes, Sophie glanced at her daughter's bulging hips. Only yesterday, she had recognised the paper bag from the local patisserie in the kitchen bin. No doubt Hannah had popped in on her way home for a treat. But she had so many good points that it seemed wrong to nag her about something she herself was only too aware of. Sophie's concerns were more about Marc, who appeared so distant and was spending more time away from home. She was also unnerved by Emma's infidelity.

'What time is Ernst arriving?' Hannah asked, prompting Sophie to assume that she was anticipating her next meal.

'He'll be early as usual, and Marc will probably arrive at the very last moment. I only hope Lucien isn't too bad-tempered.'

'You take Lucien too seriously, Mum – his attitude is only a front.'

'Well, until I can have an honest discussion with him before he walks off in a huff, I have every reason to be worried.'

'Give him time; he'll be fine.' It was typical of Hannah to try to hold the family together.

'I hope you're right.' Whenever Sophie thought of Lucien, she felt a rising panic. When she dared to ask him where he was going his harsh response was inevitably, 'Out.' Her hopes had risen again when he'd got an A* in A Level art, but instead of going to art school, Lucien had decided to take a year off, to no known purpose. Now, all she could hope for was that Marc would spend more time with him while she was in Jerusalem.

NINETEEN

THE JOURNEY

Willing the day to arrive, Sophie watched the sky soften in the first light as vaporous clouds reassembled into streaks of pink and orange. She glanced at Marc sleeping beside her, feeling that she could no longer deny the increasing gulf between them. It was as if they were slipping away from each other, and all they had left in common were their children.

Marc opened his eyes. 'I'll go and make the coffee,' he said, avoiding yet another debate over whether or not Sophie should go to Jerusalem. He couldn't tell her that her trip was serendipitous for him. Over the past year he had become more deeply involved with Maureen, and it was she more than he who had asserted her feelings when they were together at various Labour Party meetings. She had urged him to leave Sophie, but he had resisted. Now, with Sophie about to leave the country, he felt less threatened. He climbed into his jeans and slipped a T-shirt over his still-muscular body.

'Marc, you really have slimmed down. I wish you would

encourage Hannah to go to the gym.' Sophie watched him getting dressed.

'I'll try,' Marc said, aware that his visits to the gym had begun as a way of being with Maureen.

'Thanks. Her overeating is quite worrying; we don't want her to feel left out at school or to be unable to form relationships with boys. She has a lovely face and could actually be very attractive. You must help her,' Sophie said anxiously, reflecting on her own adolescence, although her sense of alienation had been for very different reasons.

She got up and went to say goodbye to Lucien and Hannah. Hesitating outside Lucien's room, she knocked gently on the door, waited a moment and went in. Controlling her revulsion at the nauseating mess, she bent over and kissed him without expecting a response.

'Goodbye, Mum, have a good trip,' he mumbled.

She wanted to hug him but anticipated his objection. 'Look after Hannah,' she said absurdly.

'It's too early for jokes, Mum,' he grunted.

Hannah was sitting up in bed waiting for her. 'Are you ready? You look really good in that beige trouser suit.'

'Angelica gave it to me. I don't know whether to wear her clothes to please her, or if it's in bad taste to do so.'

'I wouldn't worry; she practically forced them on you, so I suppose she gets a kick out of seeing you in them. If I had a friend like that, it would be worth dieting. Don't worry about anything here, Mum,' Hannah said, hugging her.

'I'll phone tonight,' Sophie promised, and went down to the kitchen.

'You look very chic,' Marc commented while pouring the coffee.

'I didn't think you'd notice.'

Silently, he watched her savour her first sip.

'Marc, are you annoyed with me for going to Jerusalem? You

seem to be in some sort of a sulk or something.'

'Don't be silly. I'm just tired and have a lot on at work. You enjoy yourself, although I suppose that might be difficult, but make the best of it anyway. Don't worry about Lucien; I'll try and have a talk with him, but I can't promise a miracle. I think Ernst offering him driving lessons isn't such a bad idea. It might get him going.' Marc knew that talking about Lucien was by far the best way to distract her.

'I know Ernst is as worried as I am, but he doesn't let it show; that's why Lucien responds to him. I bet if you or I had made the same offer, he would have said, "Stop hassling me," or something.'

'Sophie,' Marc said in desperation, 'there's nothing you can do for the next week, so try to relax. I promise to spend time with Lucien.'

Suddenly relishing her forthcoming escape, Sophie sighed. 'I suppose I could find something else to worry about. It would make a change, and they do say a change is as good as a rest.'

They heard the doorbell. 'That's the car,' she said, and got up.

Marc walked with her to the car and kissed her affectionately on the cheek. 'Take care, and phone us this evening.' He waved until the car disappeared around the corner.

The roads were empty as David's driver manoeuvred the Rolls-Royce smoothly up the hill into Hampstead Lane. Sophie touched the electric button and the window slid down, letting a rush of cool air skim her cheeks, and enhancing her sense of liberation. It seemed only minutes later that David, dressed in a navy-blue blazer, white shirt and pearl-grey trousers, opened the front door. Spontaneously, noticing his receding hairline, lined face and weary expression, Sophie began to lose her enthusiasm for the trip.

In the lounge, Angelica was in an armchair, sipping a cup of hot water. Sophie took a moment to adjust to the beatific expression on her shrunken face. She wondered how Angelica still managed to look so stylish, with her silk scarf knotted into a turban to cover her balding head, an ice-blue swagger coat draped over her bony shoulders, and her long matchstick legs, hidden within blue trousers, stretched across a footstool. Holding back her tears, Sophie bent to kiss her.

'Sophie, I'm so excited, I can't believe we're actually going.'

Out of the corner of her eye, Sophie caught David's strained expression, as if he, like her, was trapped in an inescapable folly and couldn't imagine what Angelica expected of the trip. She recognised Angelica's bulging Hermès bag stuffed with an arsenal of fresh dressings for her colostomy, plastic bags in case of nausea, fresheners to wipe herself down, painkillers, sleeping pills, ointments, disinfectant sprays, and perfumes to disguise unpleasant odours. She wondered how her friend would manage to take care of the undignified parts of her illness in the cramped aeroplane toilet.

Angelica half smiled. 'Sophie, David thinks you mind me choosing your clothes.'

'On the contrary, I feel very privileged,' Sophie replied artfully.

'Perhaps because Angelica isn't your mother.' David had learned to keep conversations going and avoid the silences that could so easily descend.

Sophie stopped herself from saying that her mother had died before she had ever got to know her, realising that she had to be on guard for such awkward moments that could unwittingly surface. 'Angelica has natural good taste and her persuasive powers have affected Hannah, who insists I take her shopping when we return from Jerusalem.'

'I'd love to help, perhaps when we get back,' Angelica said, and another silence threatened, but fortunately Jonathan came into the room. Sophie thought him devastatingly handsome, seeing in him David's tall physique and Angelica's high cheekbones, blue eyes and soft mouth.

'Congratulations. I believe you're going up to my old college,' Sophie said.

'Yes, did you enjoy Oxford?' Jonathan asked.

'It's funny, I can hardly remember it; I suppose it was just a phase in my life. I just happened to go to Oxford because Ernst and the school wanted me to. Education is a privilege; it's not always a matter of intelligence.'

'And now?' Jonathan asked.

'I suppose I would really have liked to be a painter. That's why I feel so frustrated with Lucien. It's the one thing he's really good at, but knowing Lucien, he'll do it in his own time.' Suddenly aware of the heat rising in her cheeks, Sophie felt ashamed of her piffling complaint.

'Talking about time, I think we ought to get going,' David reminded them.

Jonathan hugged Angelica before helping her into the car next to Sophie.

'Jonathan is so like you.'

'I know,' Angelica replied, blowing him a kiss as the car glided away.

'Are you two comfortable back there?' David asked.

'Fine,' replied Angelica, aware of how tense David had been before Sophie arrived.

*

At the airport, David confronted the reality of the journey ahead, as he looked around for a porter with a wheelchair. Initially embarrassed at being helped into the wheelchair, Angelica soon realised that she couldn't have walked through the endless passages. Sophie and David quickened their step to catch up with the porter, as he passed pairs of armed policemen and a dog handler before arriving at the El Al check-in at the end of the terminal.

'Is anything wrong?' Angelica asked the porter nervously.

He laughed. 'No. Just El Al security; it's the safest airline in the world.'

'I had no idea that El Al was segregated from the rest.' Sophie followed David and the porter to the security check. A muscular Israeli dressed in faded jeans and a dark green anorak greeted them. She thought him not much older than Lucien as he started his rehearsed questioning.

'Is this your first trip to Israel? Where are you staying? Did you pack your own bags? Did anybody give you a parcel or anything to take with you? Have you been with your bags all the time until now?' He repeated these questions to each of them in turn, studying their faces as they replied. Satisfied, he stuck labels on the bags, wished them a good trip and directed them to the first-class check-in counter.

'It's incredible, considering the repetitious task, how he conveys a sense of purpose,' Sophie remarked.

'They all go into the army and are trained to detect and act on any slight variation in response,' David replied.

'Not that I would want anybody to fight in a war, but after seeing that young Israeli, perhaps we should have conscription in the UK too. You can see how desperate I am about Lucien,' she said lightly.

They found a quiet corner in the El Al club lounge. David looked at his newspaper while Sophie and Angelica sat talking.

'It was good of Emma to phone me early this morning to say goodbye. I know she can be rather pushy, but compared to her mother, she's really quite tame. She swears that her mother sent her off to boarding school to get rid of her; that's why nothing will ever induce her to leave her own children. She once told me that even if she was unhappily married, she would find a way to hold the family together,' Angelica remarked.

Sophie was relieved to hear their flight being called.

Once on board the plane and settled in her seat, Angelica fell asleep. 'She must be exhausted. She's been up since the crack of dawn, and I'm still not sure that this is such a good idea,' David said.

Sophie agreed but, remembering Marc's advice, said, 'We can't turn back, so we'd better make the best of it. I share your concern, but we shouldn't let Angelica sense it.'

'Of course, you're absolutely right, Sophie. I wouldn't be here at all if it weren't for you.'

*

At Ben Gurion Airport, Sophie watched David look around anxiously for a porter while she stayed with Angelica. Standing by Angelica in a wheelchair, Sophie felt cut off from the strong and healthy throng rushing in all directions. At the exit, automatic glass doors opened onto a concourse of intense heat and dazzling sunlight. Men in shorts and T-shirts, young girls colourfully and scantily dressed, Orthodox Jewish men and women, white faces, brown faces, black faces, scruffy soldiers in open-necked khaki shirts and baggy trousers tucked into dirty brown boots, young women soldiers with guns hanging over their shoulders. A cacophony of different languages rose up from the crowd pressed against the barriers, calling out for their friends or relatives and hugging and kissing loved ones as, pushing their luggage trolleys in front of them, they emerged from customs.

Sophie bent down to talk to Angelica. 'I feel as though I want to flick a switch and turn the light down.'

'It will be much cooler in Jerusalem. Tel Aviv is oppressive, especially if there's a *hamsin* heatwave,' David told them.

'You appear to know a lot.' Angelica was encouraged by his interest.

'Just quoting from the El Al magazine.' Then, spotting his name on a board, he announced, 'There's our driver – Plan B confirmed.'

At the hotel, Sophie went to her room and phoned home. Hannah answered immediately. 'Hello, how's Angelica?'

Sophie wanted to know more.

'Dad is out. Lucien is upstairs. Everything is okay.' Hannah pre-empted her question.

'Give them my love; I'll phone tomorrow.'

Although she was exhausted, Sophie couldn't relax. She was annoyed to learn that Marc was out, after he'd promised to spend more time with Lucien. Her thoughts flitted to the confident young Israelis she had seen earlier that day; a sharp contrast with Lucien's lethargy. She blamed herself for acquiescing to his ugly language. His outbursts of 'I don't need this kind of pressure' and 'Don't hassle me' oppressed her. She could no longer deny that her son was lazy and insufferable. Enervated, she eventually fell asleep.

*

In the distance she heard an unfamiliar ring. Taking a moment to orientate herself, she stretched out to pick up the heavy phone.

'Shalom, good morning, are you ready for breakfast?' David sounded happy.

Sophie glanced at her watch. It was nine o'clock – she had slept right through and could have slept on. 'Not exactly; I'll be with you in twenty minutes.'

'Angelica has had her hot water and I thought it would be fun to go downstairs and try out the Israeli breakfast.'

'I'll see you down there. How's Angelica?'

'She's keen to see Jerusalem. Well, you know Angelica. We'll be in the dining room.'

David had hardly put the phone down when it rang again.

'Shalom, Mr Stern, this is Dr Avram Levi. Dr Jameson from London asked me to introduce myself to you and your wife. I am in the hotel lobby if you would like to meet me.'

'Oh, that's wonderful. We will be down in five minutes. How will I recognise you?'

'Don't worry, I'll find you.'

David looked at what was left of Angelica's hair as she knotted the silk scarf around her head, recalling how luxuriously thick and soft it had once been. 'You won't believe this, but Dr Levi is waiting in the lobby.'

'I told you everything would work out. Why don't you have more faith? Dr Jameson said he's a good chap, and you see, he's turned up. But I must admit I didn't expect to see him on our first morning. David, aren't you pleased we came?' Angelica pleaded.

'Yes, I like it here. It feels good. We'd better hurry; I don't want to miss him.'

In the grand foyer, a man of about fifty with bright blue eyes, a tanned face and a mop of curly grey hair, dressed in jeans and a white open-necked shirt, walked towards them. 'Shalom, I'm Avram Levi. How was the journey?'

Angelica looked worse than he'd anticipated. 'I managed very well, and El Al was wonderful,' she said, responding to the unexpected informality.

David stretched out his hand. 'It's very good of you to see us on our first morning.'

'Well, to be honest, it wasn't entirely planned. After I spoke to Dr Jameson, I realised your trip coincided with my vacation, so you see, it's also my first day.'

'Would you join us for breakfast?' David asked.

'I never say no to a breakfast at the King David, if only for the cheese blintzes.'

'Excuse me,' David said, moving towards the lift as he spotted Sophie.

'Sophie is one of the best friends a person could have,' Angelica said, taking the opportunity to talk to Avram. 'I don't think my husband would have agreed to this trip if she hadn't agreed to join us.'

'I've had a long talk with Dr Jameson,' Avram said, scrutinising Angelica.

David returned. 'Dr Levi, I'd like you to meet Mrs Thomas.'

'Just call me Avram; I'm on holiday. You look like an Israeli,' Avram said to Sophie, who was also wearing blue jeans and a white shirt.

'It's my hair; it has that international quality,' she replied, standing next to Angelica.

They followed David and Avram to the dining room. Angelica nudged Sophie, then raised her eyebrows, making Sophie stop short of a giggle.

In the grand dining room, they were shown to a table with a view of the Old City. 'Now for the serious business of the breakfast buffet.' Avram stood up to lead the way, and they followed him to an abundance and variety of platters filled with exotic fruits, vegetables, salads, cheeses, eggs, fish, breads, pastries and more, all displayed like trophies at an agricultural show. 'Can I get you some coffee? I can't think before I've had my coffee,' he said, studying Sophie.

'Thanks, and a pot of very weak Earl Grey tea for Angelica.'

'You must be quite a friend to her.' Avram beckoned the waiter.

Before Sophie could reply, David returned with three platters of food which he placed on the table. 'That was quite a challenge,' he said, helping Angelica.

'Enjoy! Now it's my turn. I'll show you the Israeli way,' said Avram, getting up.

'I feel guilty already.' David mimicked an Eastern European accent, and Angelica laughed with relief at seeing him more like his old self.

Avram returned with a platter of food. 'I've ordered some extra cheese blintzes, just in case you're hungry.'

Sophie smiled. 'If this is breakfast, what can lunch be like?!'

'It's a custom started on the kibbutz, where work starts very early before it gets too hot. Then at eight o'clock, the workers need a large breakfast, and the rest of us just eat for fun. So now I start my holiday. If you like, I can show you a little of Jerusalem.'

'That would be delightful, if it isn't too much trouble,' Angelica enthused.

'The English amuse me. When we offer our services in Israel, people enjoy it more when they know that it's trouble, but I can assure you it is no trouble at all, unless other people make trouble for us.'

'Thank you very much. I've arranged for a car and a driver,' David said cheerfully.

Avram waved to someone at another table and went over to them.

'It seems quite an imposition – he's a doctor, not a tour guide,' David said, relishing his cucumber and yogurt salad. 'On the other hand, why not?' He gestured theatrically with his hands and shoulders as he looked up towards the ceiling.

Angelica nudged his arm. 'Seriously, David, I really like him.'

'It's a marvellous opportunity. I believe Israelis are like that: they're so proud of their achievements and have a compulsion to convert everybody into supporters,' Sophie said, checking that Avram was out of earshot.

David sighed. 'I get confused between pride and arrogance. It's quite something to have our own doctor and guide. It couldn't be better.'

Angelica touched his hand. 'You see, it *was* right to come here. You can't deny that there's something quite special about this place. I can't explain it.'

Sophie liked the feeling of authenticity. People here appeared to have no airs or graces, and the very behaviour that tourists found unpolished, she valued. There was a need to confront reality, to say it as it is.

Avram came back to the table just as the waiter arrived with hot cheese blintzes. 'Until you've tasted one of these, you haven't arrived at the King David,' Avram insisted, cutting one up and placing a portion on each of their plates.

Angelica had a taste. 'They're even better than Emma's.'

'I agree, but she wouldn't like to hear you say that,' David suggested weakly.

Sophie had just been thinking of Emma and was astounded that Angelica might have intuited it.

'We'd better go soon if we don't want to be out in the midday sun, which doesn't discriminate between natives and tourists. Angelica, you must let us know when you've had enough; we've had more than enough heroes in Israel already,' Avram warned.

'We're in your hands,' David replied.

'Well, you never know – one day I might be in yours.'

*

In the car, Sophie opened the window, savouring the scent of eucalyptus, sunlight enhancing its bluish leaves against the pinky-silver walls of the hotel.

'The Old City will always have special meaning to me,' Avram remarked. 'I first entered it with the IDF paratroopers in 1967.'

'You were actually here!' exclaimed Sophie, reflecting on how, twenty years later, so little had been resolved between the Arabs and the Jews, and imagining a thirty-year-old Avram dressed in full military gear. She felt torn between her left-wing anti-Zionism and her pride in Jewish survival.

The car stopped as they entered the Jaffa Gate and were approached by two armed soldiers.

'Is it dangerous to go in?' David asked.

'The army is carrying out routine checks on Arab cars. In this country, every line can be a front line. We can't really tell whether all this security makes us feel better or worse. We've just got used to it.'

'Can we please stop for a moment and get out?' Sophie

demanded spontaneously. She felt claustrophobic and had an overwhelming need to deal with her anxiety about the narrow road ahead.

Avram asked the driver to pull up and they all got out and walked into the centre of the open courtyard. King David's Tower was to their right. Avram looked at Sophie. 'If you want to go in, I suggest you do it another time.'

'Of course, I wouldn't think of walking up the tower now. I thought Angelica might enjoy knowing about it. It's so inspiring to see something that I have only read about.' Sophie proceeded to give an account of its history.

'I'm very impressed with your knowledge,' Avram said.

'Well, Sophie is a classics scholar,' Angelica boasted.

'I find it quite amazing to be walking in a place that's been here for three thousand years,' Sophie told them.

Angelica beamed. 'You see, it was right to come here. Sophie, you must come back later when I am having my rest, to have a proper look at David's Tower.'

'Perhaps I could join you; I could learn a lot,' Avram suggested, then sensed that he had embarrassed Sophie. Seeing the beads of perspiration on Angelica's forehead, he hurried everybody back to the car.

Moving slowly through low arches and closed-in passageways, Sophie again began to feel oppressed, and tried to distract herself. Her disorientation intensified into panic when she saw Armenian priests dressed in black gowns and tall black hats disappearing through narrow blind passages. 'Where are we going?' she asked, hoping that she hadn't conveyed her disquiet.

'There is nothing to worry about; we'll be in the Jewish Quarter soon,' Avram explained.

How much longer is 'soon'? she wanted to ask, but she held back.

David also felt uneasy, and to distract himself asked, 'How many people live in the Old City?'

'About twenty thousand, and that includes me,' Avram replied.

'You actually live here!' Angelica exclaimed.

'Yes, I was lucky enough to buy an apartment. Perhaps you would like to spend Shabbat with me? The real attraction is seeing the Wall at night, with the ultra-Orthodox Chassidim constantly at prayer. In Jerusalem we are surrounded by the sounds of God. The muezzin calls the Muslims to prayer, the bells of the Holy Sepulchre ring, and the constant humming from the ultra-Orthodox at prayer and all the tears and prayers of thousands of years saturated in these stones make this a very spiritual place.'

Sophie felt caught between curiosity and fear, and worried that they would notice her anxiety, until the car moved into an open space where she was able to look down across tiers of arched and sculptured stone buildings and gleaming cupolas under a serene sky. Whether it was the unexpected beauty of sunlight striking the pink-and-gold Jerusalem stone, or just relief at looking at the views beyond, she was awestruck.

Angelica, gazing wistfully into the distance, muttered to herself, 'There's just so much to take in.'

The car moved at a snail's pace through the three right angles of the Zion Gate. 'It's quite unnerving going through all these blind turns. Are you very tired, Angelica?'

'I really want to see the Western Wall.' Angelica touched Sophie's hand reassuringly as the driver parked the car.

Walking in the rising heat, they arrived at the vast stone courtyard. At the far end towered the Western Wall. Angelica was overwhelmed. The devout at prayer, the Wall, the courtyard, the sky and the light all came together as one, speaking to her innermost being – each part was merged into a whole, a complete, united one. Subdued, David put his arm across her back to support her, and Sophie scrutinised the Wall and then looked down to see Angelica's shrinking frame with its shadow cast on the stones below, and went to her.

'Let's go right up to the Wall,' she said, linking her arm in Angelica's to guide her.

Angelica nodded, and slowly they walked to the women's section and watched women kiss and clutch and press themselves against the sacred stones. Angelica placed her hands against the stones and sobbed. 'I don't want David to see me crying, but I just can't help it.' As they turned to leave, they noticed that other women were walking backwards, and did likewise. 'It's incredible to think that a wall can make one feel like just one tiny part of the infinite. I could never have imagined this,' Angelica whispered, more to herself than to Sophie.

In the men's section, David and Avram saw men in prayer shawls kissing the wall, rocking backwards and forwards in prayer, and placing little notes of their prayers in the crevices between the massive stones. They joined them, and when they reunited with the women Avram, noting Angelica's pasty complexion, said, 'It's enough for your first morning in Jerusalem. And it's also time for hardened Israelis to get out of the midday sun.'

*

Back in the hotel, they sank into the now-familiar armchairs in the cool, dark lounge. David stretched out to hold Angelica's hand, and beckoned a waiter. 'We could all do with a drink. You must rest this afternoon.'

'The coffee bar serves light snacks, if you don't feel hungry,' Avram suggested. Finishing his drink, he got up to go. 'I'll come back at four o'clock. If you like, we can go on a cool, relaxed drive.'

'That sounds inviting. Thank you for such an inspiring time.' David stood up, stopping short of shaking Avram's hand.

Sophie felt uncomfortable knowing that they had all conspired to avoid mentioning Angelica's obvious exhaustion.

TWENTY

TRUTH

During lunch, Angelica broke the silence. 'Sophie, I've got a great idea: while we take our rest, why don't you go downstairs and have one of those smart Israeli haircuts? Everything closes between one and three in these hot countries.'

Nothing had been further from Sophie's mind. She had intended taking a taxi back to the Old City and going to one of the museums, but acquiesced.

Afterwards she met David and Angelica in the foyer.

'You look wonderful,' Angelica enthused. 'You see, David, I was right to make her do it. Turn around, let me see the back. You couldn't do better in London.'

'Thanks, Angelica; you seem to know what's good for me. I would never have dared to make such a radical change, let alone in a foreign country.'

'David appears to think that I'm interfering in your life. He doesn't quite understand how much fun women can have dressing up. That's how little girls have always played.'

'I quite agree. As a child, I spent most of my time reading; now, thanks to you, I'm catching up on girlie things,' Sophie said appreciatively.

'Play as much as you like. It's a good thing men don't have to understand women to love them. Here comes Avram.' David walked ahead to greet him.

'Shalom, I hope you feel refreshed. I have a plan to suit all of us,' Avram said, glancing at Angelica.

'What do you have in mind?' Angelica asked eagerly.

'Firstly, I would like to have a chat with you, Angelica, in my room at the Hadassah Hospital. It's a lovely drive through the valley of Ein Kerem, and the hospital's Chagall windows are high on the list for tourists. So you see, everybody can get something out of the trip.'

'I would very much appreciate your opinion too, Avram,' David said, hoping that Angelica would let him join her during the consultation.

'So, let's go,' Avram said, turning around to talk to Sophie. 'I see that you've had a good rest at the hairdresser.'

Sophie felt herself blush. 'Actually, I had an uncanny experience. The hairdresser had a concentration camp number tattooed on her arm. I was filled with humility knowing that my father and I might have shared the same fate, had we not escaped from Prague just before my third birthday. I have always known that most of my family perished in the death camps, but meeting that woman made it only too real, especially because she also came from Czechoslovakia. I feel unnerved, even ashamed... I can't explain it.'

'It's known as survivor's guilt. In Israel we're all survivors. I think you should pay a visit to Yad Vashem. It will give you another perspective on our own petty lives.'

'Yes, I probably need to,' Sophie said, knowing that she wouldn't have chosen to go, just as David wouldn't have chosen to come to Jerusalem. She mulled over the powerful influence

Angelica had always had on their lives, and how they had failed to notice it because of her beguiling nature and beauty.

*

It was much cooler driving down into the leafy valley. Avram pointed towards the huge modern buildings on the ridge above the ancient town. Inside the Hadassah Ein Kerem Hospital, they followed him through the noisy, crowded corridors. Doctors and nurses greeted him. Arab women with their heads covered, surrounded by their families, stood or sat around, waiting to be seen.

'I'm surprised to see so many Arabs here,' Sophie commented.

'We also treat Arabs from neighbouring states here, as well as our Israeli Arabs,' Avram told them, pushing through the narrow spaces. 'I'm sorry we are in such a rush but I didn't want you to miss the talk on the Chagall windows.'

They arrived at the small, round synagogue as the door was being closed. Avram found them seats. 'I will be back in fifteen minutes. Enjoy,' he said.

They listened to the guide analysing the meaning of some of the symbols in the windows and relaying how, in 1959, the artist Marc Chagall had responded to a request to decorate the hospital's synagogue. Afterwards, they sat there in silence as the crowd departed.

Avram suddenly reappeared. 'How was it?'

'Uplifting,' Angelica replied.

'An unexpected marvel, thank you,' David added. 'I found it quite inspirational; I never realised stained glass could be so moving. I really could appreciate the detail, which is quite different to seeing stained-glass windows high up in badly lit cathedrals.'

Sophie, still gazing at the windows, heard Avram say, 'We can go now.'

'Do you mind if I see Avram alone?' Angelica looked guilty. 'Then later we can all talk.'

Obviously upset, David sat down next to Sophie.

'We'll be back soon. In the meantime, enjoy the windows,' Avram said gently, guiding Angelica towards the corridor.

Sophie felt hurt for David, but said nothing.

*

In his small consulting room, Avram turned the pages of Angelica's file. 'Dr Jameson has been very thorough. How are you feeling in Jerusalem?'

'Surprisingly well. I'm very pleased I came, and sorry I never came before.'

Avram considered her response, which didn't fully answer the question. It never failed to amaze him how some terminal patients could deny their discomfort. Struck by her extraordinary sense of purpose, he sought neither to undermine her spirit, nor to give her false hope.

As if reading his mind, Angelica asked, 'Could you do me a favour? It isn't exactly medical.'

'Sometimes the distinctions are blurred.'

'I believe that I don't have much time left. I know David will be devastated, and my son Jonathan too, and I want to try to help them after I'm gone.' Angelica seemed to gain strength from talking, but worried about keeping David and Sophie waiting.

'It's important that you feel in control of your life, whatever the quality. Are you having any pain?'

'No. Do you expect me to?'

'Pain is a very personal matter; it's good if you're not experiencing it. Who can tell why some people feel pain even when we can't find any medical reason for it, and others never complain when we assume they should? It is important that you make the best of your stay here, and if you agree, I would like

136

to examine you another time to see if I can suggest anything to help. How would you like me to involve your husband?'

'The truth is that we haven't really discussed my dying, and perhaps I've left it too late. It's difficult because we are so close that sometimes talking appears to get in the way.'

Observing her distress, and suspecting that she wanted him to provide the answer, Avram sought to make her take responsibility herself. 'Doctors know so little. Some keep bad news from their patients, others rush to tell them the worst, but the patient's wishes must be respected whatever their attitude. That's my belief, anyway.' Then, softening his voice without losing its insistence, he went on. 'But you must know that David and your son have the need – and, you could also say, the right – to know the truth. I know it is difficult, but is your silence due to your concern for their emotions, because you don't believe they are capable of dealing with it? I believe it is possible to find a way to help, rather than any conviction that you alone can decide what is good for your husband and son.'

Angelica felt ashamed. 'I would like to involve David now.'

Avram put his hand to his chin. 'We should meet again with David and the three of us can explore the problem. I have some experience in such matters, and you have my respect and concern.'

'Thank you, I would like your help.' It seemed as if a cloud had lifted, and Angelica felt an urgency to involve David.

'They must be getting quite tired of Chagall,' Avram said, disguising his alarm at her exclusion of her husband, and stood up to signal the end of the consultation.

*

David was relieved to see Angelica looking so much more relaxed, and took it to be a hopeful sign. He glared at Avram, wanting to know what had happened, and talked to hide his anger. 'I'm so pleased we saw the Chagall windows. It must be wonderful for patients to come here.'

Angelica rushed to his side. 'We've had a helpful consultation, and Avram can see both of us tomorrow.'

'I'd appreciate that,' he said ungraciously, and instantly regretted it on seeing Angelica's downcast expression.

On the way back to the car, David caught up with Avram. 'You must invoice me for all consultations, otherwise I won't feel free to ask your advice,' he said, in a tone intended to warn the doctor that he wasn't accustomed to being ignored.

'I understand. You will not be excluded next time,' Avram reassured him. 'I would like to see you with Angelica. I'm sure that she is more than ready to participate in any discussion.'

'The sooner the better,' David replied.

'I'll try to book a scan for tomorrow and then we can all meet afterwards. Even though I have Dr Jameson's files, there's no harm in seeing if our scan shows up anything different.'

'Thank you, I totally agree,' David said, softening his stance.

On the drive back, the setting sun cast pink, red and gold tints across the stone-faced buildings. Not a leaf moved on the trees. David felt Angelica's damp, flaccid hand tucked into his and the balance between them shift; it was as if she was relinquishing control.

Back in the hotel's cool foyer, Angelica and Sophie went to refresh themselves. Avram wanted to leave, but David insisted he stay and have a drink. Once they were alone, David asked the question he had not dared to ask before.

'What do you think of Angelica's chances?'

'In Israel, we often answer a question with another question, until we are sure of the exact meaning of the question. Perhaps you can tell me how much you know already?'

Impatiently, David asserted, 'I know, or at least I feel, that Angelica is keeping quite a bit back from me. I also feel that she didn't want to involve me in her talks with Dr Jameson. I need to know what her chances are and how I can help.' He took out his folded handkerchief and wiped his eyes.

Avram looked directly at him. 'Firstly, you must understand that it's difficult for a doctor to talk to the husband without the patient's permission. But I understand your position. According to Dr Jameson's report, the chemotherapy hasn't reduced the tumour and further surgery isn't appropriate. I believe he discussed this with Angelica. The problem is what we can do at this stage. I can give you a more conclusive opinion after the scan. I didn't examine Angelica straight away as I wanted to get to know you both first. This is not a usual referral situation, but Dr Jameson and I have worked together before and I know he would be pleased to have my opinion.'

David pressed on. 'Are you telling me there's no hope?' The weight of his desperation commanded honesty.

'I can say there's little hope for a remission,' Avram replied.

David looked down at his drink, tightening his grip on the glass. 'I suppose, deep down, I knew, but I always hoped. But I won't accept that nothing can be done until I've explored every option. You understand?'

'I understand your predicament. Believe me, I've been through it myself.' Avram looked directly into David's eyes.

'What do you mean?'

'I shouldn't be telling you this, but I feel I must. You see, my wife died two years ago of cancer.'

David looked up to see Angelica and Sophie walking towards them, Angelica half of Sophie's size. Why hadn't he seen her like this before? Her gaunt face frightened him. The few minutes alone with Avram had shaken him.

Angelica saw David looking intently at his glass, obviously shocked. 'Well, what have you two been up to?' she asked.

'David and I think it would be useful for me to examine you tomorrow to give you a second opinion,' Avram said. 'If you agree, I will arrange a scan at the hospital. It shouldn't take long and we can drop Sophie at Yad Vashem on the way.'

'Good. That should be very helpful, don't you agree, David?' Angelica said, desperate to placate her husband. Turning to Sophie, she asked, 'Do you want to go to Yad Vashem tomorrow?'

'I need to go, which is different to wanting to,' Sophie replied.

'That's the way I feel about the scan. Then it's settled,' Angelica said in a tone that put an end to any further discussion. 'Now, can we order a drink?'

Avram got up. 'I'll phone you tomorrow morning.'

Impulsively, Angelica suggested, 'I wonder if Sophie would like to go out this evening? We'll be quite happy relaxing in our room.'

'Really, Angelica, I'm sure Avram has done more than enough escorting for one day,' Sophie protested.

'Well, I do know of a wonderful, authentic restaurant.' Avram appeared to welcome the opportunity.

'If Sophie wants to go, that would be splendid,' David said.

Sophie looked embarrassed. 'Well, if I'm not needed, thank you.'

Avram handed David his card. 'I'll be back at eight. Please, if you need me for anything, here is my home phone number.' He smiled gently and left.

The foyer began to get noisy with people coming in after their day's outings.

'Isn't Avram a strange man? He seems unusually helpful,' Angelica said.

David didn't respond, so Sophie did. 'Did he say he was born here? I can't remember. We don't appear to know much about him, do we?'

'I must say, he's the first doctor I feel I can really talk to,' Angelica asserted.

David got up to help Angelica out of her chair. 'We'd better go up now; you need to rest. I can look at the room service menu and you can advise Sophie what to wear for her date.' He sounded flat.

'That's my very thought. Come on, Sophie, let's go and play our dressing-up game,' Angelica said, as if to avoid reality.

'David, do you think I would dare to go anywhere without Angelica's special touch?' Then, realising a possible deeper significance in her remark, Sophie fell silent.

In the crowded lift, David found himself looking at Sophie. She had changed. Perhaps Angelica did have an extraordinary ability to transform people and situations, or perhaps it was being away from London that had helped to release Sophie's graceful beauty.

*

Once in her room, Sophie phoned home. Hannah answered as if expecting her call. 'Hello, Mum.'

Sophie heard her bubbly voice. 'How did you know it was me?'

'By the ring.'

'Oh, really?! How is everything?'

'Fine. No problems that I know of. The house is intact. I'm enjoying my cookery course, Lucien hasn't had a party, and Dad was away last night.'

'Where?' Sophie exclaimed.

'I really don't know. He said he had to go out of town for the night, but he didn't say where. Is everything okay? How's Angelica?' Hannah asked, redirecting their conversation.

'So far she is fine. I am pleased I came. Jerusalem is fascinating; there's so much to see and do. We've been very fortunate, and have met a wonderful Israeli doctor who is looking after Angelica. Give Lucien, Marc and Ernst my love. I'll phone tomorrow.' She hung up, feeling unsettled by Hannah's garbled report.

In the bath, she thought of Marc. He would have approved of the way the hotel had used the space and lighting to make the small bathroom feel so comfortable. He could have been a very good architect, but his involvement in local politics weakened his aesthetic vision and passion, the very qualities that had attracted her to him. Why was he spending a night away from home when he'd promised to be there for Lucien and Hannah? She had hoped he'd use the opportunity to influence Lucien to study, but realised that she could no more motivate Marc than she could Lucien. Wrapping herself in a towelling gown, she went to lie down on the bed. It seemed wrong to feel released from family obligation, but being in Jerusalem provided a fresh perspective.

The phone rang. 'Just checking what you're wearing for your date.' Angelica giggled.

'I suppose it'll be quite informal, but I can't resist one of your classics. What do you think of the cream skirt and the olive-green silk T-shirt?'

'Perfect. Please come in and show me how you look before you go out.' Angelica's insistence appeared unnatural.

'Of course, see you in a few minutes,' Sophie replied.

Angelica, pale and drawn, was lying propped up in bed. 'You know he's a widower, so be careful.' She winked.

'No, I didn't. Are you trying to set me up?'

'Don't be silly. I genuinely thought it would be a good opportunity for you to see something of Jerusalem at night. Honestly, Sophie, do you think I would encourage you to have an affair? Although in this case, I'm sure even Emma would approve.'

Sophie was astonished; it seemed more than coincidental that she would mention Emma in this context. Possibly Angelica had intuited her feelings which she wasn't yet ready to admit, although she was intrigued by Avram, whose personality seemed to be the antithesis of Marc's. It wasn't the first time that Angelica's response to events had seemed prophetic.

TWENTY-ONE

SOPHIE AND AVRAM

Waiting in the crowded foyer, Sophie watched as Avram came through the revolving door. His athletic deportment and determined stride made her conscious of her tendency to slouch.

'You know, you look more like an Israeli tonight.'

'It must be my new haircut,' she replied, feeling the heat rise in her cheeks.

'I'm taking you to a good restaurant. When I say, "good", I don't mean fancy, I mean authentic. But first I want to ring David and Angelica to see if they are all right.'

'Of course; David looked so despondent tonight. I feel bad about going out and leaving them.'

He looked at her with an expression that implied, Are you surprised?

While she waited for Avram, she watched people milling around and enjoying life and tried to remember the last time she and Marc had done anything enjoyable together. Deep in thought, she didn't notice Avram return.

'We can go now,' she heard him say.

'How's Angelica?'

'Probably a lot worse than she lets on.' He lowered his voice, signalling the end of that conversation.

Avram's battered Ford was parked, badly, in the forecourt. Sophie turned to look at the back seat piled high with journals, newspapers and odd boxes.

'That's nothing; wait till you see the boot. I spend my time schlepping things back and forth. What you really need if you live in the Old City is a donkey; it's impossible to carry everything at once, so every day you make a choice. Sometimes food, other times books – it's a constant battle between romanticism and realism, and I obviously haven't settled on either.'

'I would have thought that in Jerusalem they were one and the same thing.'

'You could be right.'

As they drove down the hill, Sophie opened the window. The dense night air made her blouse cling to her skin. In the distance, illuminated against the skyline, she recognised David's Tower. 'I must go back to the Old City. There are so many layers to understand, I'm sure I could spend a week there,' she said.

'We can go there if you like, after dinner.'

'I'd love to, but it's wrong for me to be enjoying myself.'

'I understand,' Avram said, driving into and stopping in a narrow street. 'Here is our famous restaurant,' he announced.

'I hope you like spicy food.' He raised his voice as they pushed past closely spaced green-plastic-covered tables spilling over with food, arriving at a far corner table with a reserved notice on it. They had barely sat down when a waiter arrived with multiple plates of food balanced along his outstretched arm. With his other hand he arranged the warm pitta bread and small plates of eggplant, hummus, tahini, pickled vegetables, falafel, chopped tomatoes, and cucumber salad on their table.

'That's pretty good service,' commented Sophie.

'Not always, but I'm practically family, I eat here so often. This is just the *voorschspizer*.' Avram smiled, seeing her surprise at how each dish was filled to the brim.

Sophie smiled too.

'That's an expression my father uses; I wouldn't have guessed you speak German. At home, my parents spoke Czech, Yiddish and German. I was born in Pilsen and came to Israel as a child.'

She wanted to know more but, not feeling free to probe, turned to the dishes. 'This is wonderful – so delicate.' Copying Avram, and aware of his scrutiny, she dipped her pitta into the eggplant.

'Enjoy, enjoy,' he urged.

'If I eat the entire *voorschspizer*, I won't be able to eat the main course,' she replied, observing the faint laughter lines etched across his tanned face.

The waiter arrived with a steaming plate of scented lamb knuckle surrounded by saffron rice. 'It's the house speciality. I told you I would take you to a typical Israeli restaurant,' Avram said. 'The food is excellent, just too much for me. Everything here is a set price, so you can eat as much as you like.'

'How do they make a profit?' Sophie asked, seeing the queues outside.

'Food in Israel is not expensive, and this is a family business. They all work in the kitchen, and luckily have the magic formula in that families who work together, stay together. Do you have a large family?' Avram asked.

'I'm an only child. My father and I got out of Prague in 1941, after my second birthday. I have a son of eighteen and a daughter of seventeen, and my husband is an architect. And what about you?'

Assuming she was reserved rather than evasive, Avram replied, 'I have a son and a daughter in the army.' He paused. 'My wife died two years ago.' He poured himself another glass of wine. 'Whose idea was it to come to Jerusalem, considering the extreme circumstances?' He appeared to want an explanation, and his unblinking eyes looked right through her.

'Angelica wanted to see Jerusalem. She converted to Judaism when she got married but I think she wanted to understand more, and how could we refuse? She's incredibly brave and unselfish, which makes it all the more difficult to know how to help her.'

'I understand,' said Avram.

'I believe you do. You talk and behave not quite like the usual doctor, or maybe not like an English doctor.'

'To tell you the truth, I had no intention to get involved, but when I saw Angelica, I couldn't help myself. It's not too difficult to understand.'

'What do you mean?'

'Well, you see, my wife died on the 15th August, two years ago. It seemed an incredible coincidence when Dr Jameson sent me Angelica's case notes; it was like going through my wife's medical history all over again. I felt compelled. Perhaps I could have done more for her. So, it's not surprising that I forgot my vacation and stayed. I think Freud refers to it as repetitive compulsion; a need to repeat what you haven't resolved.'

'Have you had analysis?'

'No, Israel isn't a country that can afford such luxuries. We are still trying to survive, and then we feel guilty because we have survived. Anyway, survival here is a deep question. It is hard to find a family that hasn't suffered a loss in one of our wars. But that's different to losing my wife to cancer, especially as an oncologist.'

Sophie absorbed every word, feeling the excitement of a transformative moment. 'That's incredible. This must be very difficult for you. I'm sorry.'

Captivated by her Slavonic looks combined with her very English behaviour, Avram stopped himself from touching her delicate, long-fingered hand in front of him. 'Life has a way of playing tricks. Believe me, I've never behaved like this before with a patient; it's as if I've been given another opportunity to heal myself.'

'I'm sure your involvement is invaluable. I know that something is changing in Angelica and David. They've always been close, but now they appear to have entered a new dimension of togetherness. I can't describe it, but they are different.'

'I know; I've experienced it myself. Perhaps it's a bit like a mother and her newborn baby; a preoccupation with each moment. I know. I remember. I felt that just being with my wife could keep her alive. It's a very intimate time.'

Sophie recalled her painful time with Lucien. 'That's a very sensitive way of describing it. It's so hard to know what goes on between two people, but whatever is happening to Angelica and David is both wonderful and frightening.'

'Now you understand how I got sucked in.'

'Did you know that Angelica has become quite religious? Not in a ritualistic or traditional sense, but she has a deep belief in divine providence.'

'I didn't know that, but she does seem to have a spiritual quality about her.'

'She probably sees your arrival in their life as some God-given gift.'

Avram smiled. 'Well, who can tell? When you live in the Old City, it's difficult to resist God. It must be a consolation to her, and a help in leaving David.'

Sophie felt a shiver run through her. 'Are you saying that there's no hope?'

Avram tried to backtrack. 'What I'm saying is that Angelica feels that her illness is separating her from others. It's a slow process, but she could be thinking about it. Each person reacts differently. I have seen some patients angry until their last breath, and others begin to let go long before we could prognosticate with certainty.'

Sophie knew he was avoiding the issue, and did not persist. Avram would only let her know as much he wanted to.

The intrusion of the waiter asking whether they wanted coffee provided some relief. 'Would you like some Turkish coffee?' Avram asked.

Seeing the small cups of thick, black, syrupy mixture on the table next to her, she said, 'I'd better not; I won't sleep if I drink that brew.'

Avram spoke to the waiter in Hebrew and paid the bill; then they pushed through the queue of chattering people outside.

*

It was past eleven when they got out of the sticky night air and into the air-conditioned hotel.

'Perhaps I should phone to see if everything is all right,' Avram said.

'At this hour?!' exclaimed Sophie.

'In Israel, it's still quite early,' he assured her.

When she picked up her key at the desk, there was a note saying, 'Pop in for a late-night drink.' The message had been taken only fifteen minutes earlier. Sophie turned to Avram. 'You're quite right,' she said, handing him the note.

'The note is to you; I'll phone first,' he said, going to find a guest phone.

He appeared preoccupied as they went up in the lift, and Sophie let him be. David was still at the dining table, surrounded by bowls of fruit, salads, and a pot of Earl Grey tea. He told them that he and Angelica had fallen asleep early and had only just ordered room service.

Angelica rushed to explain. 'Probably the effect of the tablets you gave me. As you suggested, I took them to alleviate any discomfort before it built up, and they completely knocked me out.' She was sprawled across the settee in a pale grey dressing gown which was, it seemed, not a dissimilar shade to her complexion.

'Darling, you were probably very tired; I know I was,' David added.

Avram wanted to tell them that he had used the same combination of drugs during his wife's illness, but instead said, 'I'm pleased; I believe good management helps everybody.' He had a way of making his point which was not lost on David or Sophie. 'I'd better let Sophie tell you about her evening. I'll phone in the morning and let you know about the scan.' He said goodnight and left.

'So, tell us about Israeli night life. David and I have had no end of fun with our fantasies about you and Avram.' Angelica's lively manner did not correspond to her dull, watery eyes, but Sophie wanted to please her.

'Really, Angelica, I'm a married woman with a drop-out son, a very smart daughter and an overly solicitous father.'

'So what! A little fling will only serve to make Marc realise that he could lose you,' Angelica teased.

David marvelled at his wife's brio, and had to admit that she was right. Sophie looked particularly radiant, and hardly mentioned Marc these days.

Sophie told them about her evening and, seeing Angelica's pleasure when she spoke positively of Avram, concluded, 'All I can say is, I believe he is genuinely a good person, and that I trust him as a person as well as a doctor. We are extremely lucky, and I know that he really does want to help.'

'I believe we were sent here, it's all worked out so well,' Angelica said with conviction.

'It's really quite remarkable the way things happen, but then Angelica always appears to surround herself with excellent people.' David looked at her lovingly.

'You're right,' Sophie said. 'I would never have come here, or imagined that I could be so drawn into this place.' She kissed

Angelica goodnight. 'We've got a long day tomorrow, so I'd better let you have some rest.'

The next morning, Sophie was in bed sipping a cup of coffee when the phone rang.

'I hope I didn't wake you,' David said. 'Avram has just phoned to say that they can't do the scan today. Angelica wants to stay in and write a letter, and I'll catch up with some office problems. Why don't you have a day off and see some sights?'

Sophie hesitated. 'If you really don't need me, I'll be back for lunch.'

'Angelica sends her love and suggests you ask Avram to join you,' David added.

'It's really hard to tell when you're joking,' Sophie retaliated, thinking that it would be nice, but that she would never make any such proposal.

TWENTY-TWO

THE SCAN

Avram phoned the next day to say that he had arranged the scan and would pick them up after breakfast.

Angelica and David were in the dining room when Sophie joined them. Feeling that she had interrupted some crucial silence, she said, 'I'll go and help myself at the buffet. Can I get you anything?'

'No thanks, David and I were just saying that you look stunning in those colours, Sophie,' Angelica replied.

'I feel a bit like the Israeli Army,' said Sophie, referring to her khaki trousers and olive-green silk blouse.

Increasingly their conversations moved to trivia, with David mostly maintaining a morbid silence. Sophie observed Angelica, gently squeezing his hand while looking at her.

'Sophie, do you also feel that some change is taking place in you? I do; it's just everything about this trip. There are too many coincidences.'

Sophie caught David's resigned expression. 'You could be

right, dearest,' was as much as he felt able to communicate.

They saw Avram coming towards them. 'Shalom,' David said, as if hope had returned.

Sophie felt Avram's eyes on her, and hoped that the sudden rush of heat to her face wasn't noticed as he sat down, gesturing to the waiter for coffee.

'Have you recovered from the Yemenite restaurant?' Avram asked.

'The food was excellent.' Sophie stopped just short of saying, 'And it was buzzing with life'.

Avram turned to Angelica. 'Sorry about the confusion. I've got an excellent person to do the scan and we can go to my room and talk while we wait for the result.'

'Thank you.' David sounded defeated.

'If you're ready, we can leave. I'll have to go without the cheese blintzes today, which is really doing myself a great favour,' said Avram, patting his stomach.

'Come on, Avram, you look quite gorgeous,' Angelica said mischievously.

*

In the car, Sophie gazed out at the mists of heat above the western ridge of Jerusalem and the church steeples rising above the new geometric architecture faced with pinky-gold sandstone. She thought of the city's layer upon layer of turbulent history, and its architecture seemed to symbolise the tensions between the spiritual and the secular, the ancient and the modern.

Angelica cut across her thoughts. 'Sophie, I really believe that you are meant to go to Yad Vashem. Isn't it strange how everything just works out – I mean, it being on the way to the Hadassah Hospital and all that? I know that it may be hard for you, but you should go for Ernst.'

A sensation like an electric current shot through Sophie, for at that very moment, she was thinking of Ernst.

Avram interrupted. 'Yad Vashem is about fifteen minutes away from the Hadassah, so it's quite convenient to drop Sophie off here and then pick her up on the way back.' Looking in the rear-view mirror, he caught a glimpse of Angelica and David holding hands. The car stopped.

'What does *Yad Vashem* mean?' Sophie asked Avram.

'The phrase comes from the Book of Isaiah and means "an everlasting memorial". There's a lot to see, but there's also a place to rest and have coffee. We should be about an hour and a half, and we'll meet you at the cafeteria,' he told her.

Getting out of the car, Sophie leaned down to kiss Angelica on the cheek. The sensation of burnt air brushing against her face threatened another stiflingly hot day. She stopped under a tree along the narrow path to read a notice:

The Avenue of the Righteous
Each of the six thousand trees planted honours a Gentile
who risked their life for the Jews during the Holocaust.

Looking beyond into the shaded forest, Sophie thought of her Christian grandparents who had saved her and her father's lives. She had understood the historical facts but now, in the quiet of this dignified forest with its message somehow echoing Ernst's silence, as she walked amongst the memorial to those who had suffered in her place, she felt implicated. A spontaneous surge of melancholy reminded her to think of how fate had played a part in her survival, and how Angelica, who governed her life by fate, had brought her here.

Exhausted, she sat in the garden of the cafeteria, watching people reading pamphlets. Their tired expressions told her that she was not alone. There appeared to be no escape from the suffocating heat but to go inside one of the air-conditioned buildings. She followed a group of people into the cool Hall of

Names to read beautiful gold lettering recording the names of many of the six million who had been murdered in the camps. She was astonished by the number of Graffs, her family's name, and wished Ernst had told her about them; then she might at least have been able to identify them on the memorial. *There but for the grace of God am I.* Automatically she followed the slow-moving group into the Hall of Remembrance. The long stone building closed in on her, and she looked down at the mosaic floor to calm herself. Although she felt like she needed to get out, the solemnity of the tribute forced her to stay.

She squinted as she came back outside into the dazzling sun, feeling the moisture evaporating from her skin. In the cafeteria garden, perspiration ran down the inside of her blouse, and her skin prickled in the intense heat. She drank a glass of mineral water, then poured the rest of the bottle over her face and hands. Looking beyond at the gardens with their laid-out stones, she saw Avram walking vigorously towards her, his full head of silver hair glistening in the sun.

'Are you all right, Sophie? I'm sorry we were so long.' He spoke with some urgency.

'How is Angelica?' she asked, hurrying after him.

'Not too good,' he said abruptly.

'I came to help them, but I don't know how.'

'You are allowing David and Angelica to be together, and that's important. David told me a part of him has been denying the reality and I have helped him understand. The truth is, he has also helped *me* understand. You are their friend, Sophie, and I'm their doctor, and we can only wait until we are needed,' he said faintly.

'Is there any hope?' Sophie thought at first that he hadn't heard, but then realised that he wouldn't answer. 'Poor David – perhaps we should go home so that they can get back to Jonathan.'

'I think that would be wise. It's very difficult not to interfere, and it's important not to take away Angelica's dignity.'

'I agree,' Sophie replied, still not fully registering the gravity of his comments.

When they got to the car, Angelica and David were holding hands, deep in conversation. Then Angelica looked up. 'Was it bearable?'

'Overpowering,' Sophie said, noticing David's tortured expression.

The journey back to the hotel seemed endless. No one spoke; even Angelica didn't attempt her usual light chatter. The oppressive midday heat combined with the blinding prisms of white and gold light bouncing in front of the windscreen made Avram break the silence. 'We're having a heatwave, a *hamsin*.'

'Is that what it is? I can hardly breathe,' said Sophie.

*

Back in the cool of the hotel, Angelica suggested that they all sit down and that she would join them in a few minutes. Sophie wanted to go with her but knew Angelica probably wanted to go alone to change her colostomy dressing. They sat in the corner, away from the crowd.

'I need a drink,' David mumbled. Avram ordered him a brandy.

Sophie touched his arm. 'David, do you think we should go back to London?'

David seemed unable to speak, so Avram responded. 'I think it would be better. I'm very impressed with Angelica's tenacity and courage. To tell the truth, anybody else would never have undertaken this trip.'

David took out his silk handkerchief and wiped his eyes.

Sophie leaned over with her hand on his forearm. 'David, we have to be brave for Angelica's sake. Let's put it to her that we've had a very full time here and the heat is becoming unbearable.

Avram, I'm sure that if you suggest that the heat is too much for her, she'll agree,' she urged.

'My professional opinion is that the sooner you go home the better,' Avram said with authority.

Sophie stood up. 'I'll go to the front desk and find out about flights. It's important to be equipped with the information,' she said, wanting David's agreement.

'Thanks, Sophie. We'll have to go very gently with Angelica; I don't want her to feel defeated. After all, this trip was her idea.'

Angelica returned, looking drawn and ill. 'Where's Sophie?'

'She's gone to find out about flights. Apparently, the *hamsin* may last a few days, and I really think you should go home. There's no point in struggling. The heat is too much for a healthy person, and it's not good for you, Angelica,' Avram answered.

Angelica remained serene, her blue eyes dull and knowing. 'Won't David and Sophie be disappointed?'

Avram was astounded by her denial and her selflessness, and became insistent. 'We'll all be relieved to see you out of this extreme heat and in the comfort of your own home.'

When Sophie returned, it was obvious that some discussion had taken place. David's voice was flat but determined. 'Sophie, we have talked it over and I think we should go home immediately.'

'I agree,' she said, and another silence ensued.

David turned to Avram. 'I know I'm asking a lot, but I would be extremely grateful if you would accompany us on our journey home and stay with us in London for a few days.'

'When did you think of this?' Angelica looked directly at him.

'Right now,' David said blankly.

Avram moved his hand up to his chin in a thoughtful gesture, relaxed his forehead and spoke as if to himself. 'Why not?'

'That's wonderful!' Angelica exclaimed.

'And as I'm so impulsive, I invite you all to have dinner with me this evening at my flat in the Old City.'

'That's wonderful,' Angelica said, feeling that the downward spiral had been miraculously broken. She couldn't bear to see David so collapsed. She needed him to be strong. It had been right to bring Sophie along to help, and now Avram would also be with them, it would be all right, she told herself.

Responding to Angelica's determination to bring out the best in everybody, Sophie asked, 'Would you like me to help you, Avram?'

'We've known Sophie for eighteen years and she's never volunteered to cook!' David interjected.

'In that case, I think we should give her every encouragement,' said Avram.

'I said help, not cook,' she asserted. 'But only if I'm not needed here. Do you need me to sort out the tickets, David?'

'One step at a time,' David said, sending out a signal not to upset Angelica. He stood up purposefully to move away from the discussion. 'Would you like to join us for a light snack in the coffee bar, Avram?'

'I would love to, but I must go back and tidy my flat, make a few phone calls, and then get back to fetch Sophie at four o'clock. We'll do the shopping at the Jaffa Market and then come back to fetch you and Angelica.'

In the coffee bar, they had hardly sat down when David sank back into a depression. Angelica tried to distract him, and held his hand while looking at the menu. 'Darling, they have your favourites.'

'I'm really not hungry.' He spoke as if swallowing his words. 'I feel so ashamed. Here am I being miserable and you, with all your pain, are trying to cheer me up.'

A knot tightened in Sophie's stomach. It was obvious that something terrible had transpired at the hospital; something which had radically affected David. 'I am sure it's right to go home. Jonathan will be pleased, and I think it was a stroke of genius to invite Avram,' she said, looking at Angelica.

'Oh, Sophie, I'm pleased you said that – I was feeling worried about cutting your trip so short.'

Sophie was mildly irritated. Either Angelica was unable to think of her own needs, or she didn't dare to. 'It may have been short but it's been quite intense for all of us, and perhaps that's all we need for now.'

David looked up. 'You're right; if we hadn't come here, I wouldn't have known how ill Angelica is, and we wouldn't have met Avram, even though I can't wait to go home. Perhaps it was meant to be.'

'That's exactly what I believe; it says that no one can enter Jerusalem and go away unchanged,' whispered Angelica, cupping her hand over his.

'I'll arrange our tickets after lunch while you rest,' David instructed. The food felt like warm, damp cotton wool in his mouth, but he ate to please Angelica.

'Are you sure you don't need me this afternoon?' Sophie checked.

'Not as much as Avram,' Angelica teased.

Sophie blushed, but wouldn't admit, even to herself, that she found Avram attractive. 'How long do you think he'll stay in London?' she asked.

'Apparently, he has the rest of his two-week holiday,' David said.

The porter came to tell David he had a phone call, and he went to the reception desk.

'You'll look after David for me? He seems so lost,' Angelica said.

The knot in Sophie's stomach tightened again. 'Angelica, what happened at the hospital?'

'I suppose, nothing new from my point of view. Avram told us more or less what Dr Jameson predicted. The only difference is that this time we were together. Avram had a way of putting things which allowed David to question him, but when it came to it, he just couldn't speak. I think he expected Avram to tell him that he had a new treatment which would turn everything around. But instead he said I shouldn't hesitate to tell him if I felt any discomfort and he would monitor my situation. David was very good at the time, but appears to have collapsed since. That's probably why he asked Avram to accompany us home.' Angelica spoke as if she had been set free. She told Sophie that she was desperate to see Jonathan, and this more than anything was on her mind.

Sophie was disconsolate. Angelica had told her in so many words that nothing could be done, but she still did not want to believe it. 'What can I do to help?'

'Just being with me is a help, because you can be with David too, and support him. He has always needed a woman to take an interest in him, and it's becoming difficult to cope with my own needs as well as his. So, if you could just be with him, let him talk and not leave him alone too much, I won't have to worry so much about him.' Spotting David coming towards them, she added, 'You know what I mean,' and stopped abruptly.

'That was Jonathan on the phone. I told him we're coming home. I've also booked four seats on tomorrow evening's flight. Let's go upstairs and have a rest,' he said anxiously, as if rationing Angelica's energy could extend her life.

Angelica put her arm through David's and they walked towards the lift. 'Darling, I'm feeling fine, and I'm really looking forward to going out this evening. I'll take one of Avram's special pills and have a little sleep. Those tablets are really effective.'

TWENTY-THREE

SHOCK

'I want to look in on Angelica before we go,' Avram said, leaving Sophie to wait in the foyer.

She wondered whether Angelica had suddenly deteriorated. Surely David would have phoned her? Being excluded made the time drag; fifteen minutes passed and she decided to go up to see what was going on.

She was about to get into the lift when Avram came out. 'David wants you to go up,' he said.

'What's wrong?'

'Nothing new, except that your friend is quite a woman. She wants to come with us to the market.' Avram sounded bewildered.

Angelica was sitting in an armchair and David was pacing the floor nervously. He seemed furious, his brown eyes noticeably swollen.

'Angelica wants to go to the market. What do you think, Sophie?'

'I think we have to let Angelica do what she wants, and in any case, there would be no point in trying to stop her.'

'Profoundly accurate.' David relented, thinking only of the hours he had to get through before going home.

*

The afternoon light cast bluish tints on the Jerusalem stone. They parked as near as they could to Mahane Yehuda Market. Thankfully, the hot winds were abating as they walked into narrow passages alive with cries of salesmen and sounds of haggling at the crowded stalls. Sophie and Angelica walked slowly, arm in arm, behind David and Avram, who were busy buying food.

'I can't take the smell of raw fish; let's go to the flower stall.' Angelica hung on to Sophie as they walked, breathing in the scent of arum lilies. Buckets of roses, gypsophila, orchids and exotic blooms in abundance brought tears to her eyes. 'I'm so pleased I came.'

They watched David and Avram pass counters dripping with chocolates, sweets, dried fruits, dates and nuts, all attracting wasps. At the bakery stall, Avram bought a large challah, and an apple tart which was still warm. 'Let's go,' he said, glancing at Angelica.

Back in the Old City, Avram parked his car and they walked slowly through a maze of terraces, arches and stairways, ascending and descending. Angelica stopped every now and again and stood still, seemingly in a trance, almost physically ingesting the spirit emanating from every stone.

Avram, hardly believing her determination, asked her, 'Can you manage? It's another few minutes to my flat.'

'Oh yes, I feel privileged to be in this special place.'

Sophie caught David's expression, which barely masked his anguish. Passing a heavy wooden door, they heard the sounds of prayer. Thin men dressed in black coats, with stick-like legs in black socks, dashed in and out of the doors of their religious schools. Pregnant women wearing wigs or headscarves pushed and pulled prams up and down stone stairs. In the narrow cobbled roads, artists displayed their work. Going through a covered arch, they arrived on another level into an open space.

'We're here,' Avram announced, unlocking a wrought-iron door. 'These stone terraces are beautiful to look at but not so easy on the legs, but I can assure you that you will soon see how the beauty lasts long after the schlep is forgotten.' He led them through the kitchen onto a large terrace. 'Now you can understand why I live here.'

They stood in silence, looking down onto the Western Wall and across to the Temple Mount. The golden Dome of the Rock sparkled in the sunset and the silver dome of the Al-Aqsa Mosque completed the ornate and sacred skyline.

'What a sight,' exclaimed David, wanting to please Angelica.

'I think we all deserve a drink,' Avram suggested, aware of David's fragility.

The flat was small but well designed, giving a feeling of spaciousness. A mellow Bezalel carpet rested on the pink Jerusalem stone floor. A glass-domed window encircling the bay opened to extend the lounge onto a small terrace.

Avram addressed Angelica. 'Why don't you put your feet up in the lounge while my assistant and I organise the food?'

David sat next to Angelica on the couch. She appeared at peace with herself, calm and content, sipping a glass of iced water. David, on a constant lookout for signs of deterioration, saw how she was fading. Her beauty took on a deeper quality as he looked at her thinning blonde hair pulled back into a chignon, her skin almost transparent around her watery blue eyes. Part of him still hoped for a miracle. He caught his breath and swallowed hard.

In the small, modern kitchen, Sophie watched Avram

emptying cartons of food into bowls. He handed her some cutlery and glasses. 'If you set the table, then we're done,' he said. 'Well, after all that fuss about cooking...' Sophie mocked, taking the food over to the round glass table in the bay window. 'I wonder what Marc would make of this architecture?' asked David, trying to make amends for his moody behaviour.

'He would probably love it, and would start making a fuss about the economic and political background of every stone.' Sophie too felt on edge.

'You certainly have a grasp of his political philosophy,' David said.

'David, perhaps you're jealous because Marc's a real socialist,' Angelica teased.

Avram listened keenly, eager to get information about Sophie's husband.

Angelica bent over and kissed David on the cheek. 'Darling, I know it was crazy to come here, but isn't this worth it?'

'Who knows?' he said.

Angelica wanted to hold him in her arms, but couldn't risk it. Sensitive to the moment, Avram thought it best to leave them alone.

He turned to Sophie. 'We have a bit of time; I could show you some more of the Old City.'

'That's a great idea. Sophie, why don't you and Avram go out? David and I will be fine here,' Angelica encouraged.

'Are you sure?' Sophie asked, looking at Avram.

'We'll be back in twenty minutes.'

Sophie turned to see Angelica touching David's hand like a mother reassuring her child.

*

Sophie followed Avram up the stone stairs, frequently looking back, needing to memorise the way. From the level above, she looked out over terraced buildings and down to the vast paved area in front of the Western Wall. Blinding shafts of white, ochre and gold bounced off the rock-faced walls.

'I feel so guilty leaving them like that.'

'You shouldn't; they need to be alone, it's very important. Bonding is the most primal function. That's what a mother does instinctively with her newborn baby, and when we are dying we also need to bond, not to feel alone, to feel safe—'

Sophie couldn't let him finish. 'You make it sound so inevitable, so natural. I can't bear it.' Unwittingly, he had also stirred up her guilt about Lucien.

Avram put his hand on her shoulder, sending a quiver through her. 'I'm sorry, Sophie, but I have to deal with this every day; it's an inevitable and natural part of my life, and of everybody else's too.'

Squinting against the sun, she saw his body as firm as the surrounding rock. She waited for him to speak, and when he did, the words resonated through her.

'I must tell you, Sophie, that for the first time I am beginning to understand my loss. I can accept it. I suddenly feel free of the guilt, the anger and the fear that have oppressed me for the past two years. I have Angelica to thank for that. Perhaps you can understand why I feel obligated to go with them to London.'

'I understand what you're saying but I have yet to experience it,' Sophie replied.

'I can only explain what I know to be true for me. The rest is up to you. Now, let me show you a little of the Old City, and let Angelica and David have their time together.' He sounded mildly irritated, and hurried ahead, turning right and then down a slope towards the Arab Souk.

Sophie peered into the entrance and hesitated. The thought of going through the narrow covered passages and the labyrinth of alleyways brought on her claustrophobia. But she couldn't refuse, nor let Avram know her weaknesses. Bracing herself, she stepped through the ancient arch into the crowded, noisy souk. Endless stalls of bead jewellery made her momentarily consider buying necklaces for Hannah and Emma, but she lost heart. Kilim carpets, brassware, leather goods, fake Roman glass, fake antiques and embroideries, and keffiyehs hung from the entrances of poky stalls. The carved olive-wood pens and pencils would also make nice gifts for Ernst, Marc and Lucien, but she couldn't bear to linger and haggle. She was just wondering if Avram was aware of her unyielding panic when she heard him say, 'Let's go.'

They pushed past bearded men smoking hubble-bubble pipes and back through the archway into the spacious Jewish Quarter. How could she complain, how could she compare her anxiety to the reality of dying? Yet her fear *was* like the fear of dying and, as Avram had said, she could only explain what was true for her. Her mouth felt dry, but the hot air felt fresh.

'I just wanted you to see how close we are to the Arab Quarter,' Avram said.

'Isn't it dangerous?' She took another deep breath.

'It's getting dangerous. Each night residents take it in turn to do guard duty. It's part of the price we pay for living here.'

The contrast between the affluent Jewish Quarter and the old Muslim Quarter made her think about Marc and his left-wing dogma, but it was different to experiencing the perpetual struggle of daily life. Marc's temperament had been shaped by England and its gentle weather and people. She wondered whether Avram noticed the raw tension she was feeling. She looked back to get her bearings and saw the setting sun casting pink and mauve shadows across the buildings.

Avram turned round to see her panting a few steps behind. 'I'm sorry it's such a rush, but I just want to give you a small appetiser in the hope that you will come back.'

'I find it difficult to take it all in; I keep thinking of Angelica and David.'

'I understand, but if the Old City teaches us one lesson, it is that life goes on. In addition, it provides enforced exercise.'

He never misses a thing, she thought, stopping to catch her breath.

They arrived at the Cardo and stood on one of the platforms built across the excavations, with a view of the original Roman street. Avram pointed down to the large, wide floor. 'By chance we found this road that was part of Roman Jerusalem. After the Crusaders were expelled it was buried under thirteen feet of rubble. The historians knew that the road existed because it's recorded on a sixth-century mosaic map. In the Old City, we have a rule that before we build up, we must dig down. I thought you would enjoy seeing it, with your enthusiasm for ancient history.'

'Isn't it amazing? I've only read about all these layers of civilisation.'

'We must get back to Angelica and David now,' Avram reminded her.

TWENTY-FOUR

GOING HOME

David and Angelica were sitting on the terrace, holding hands and listening to the muezzin calling the Muslims to prayer.

'Isn't this proof of the existence of God?' Angelica said.

'It certainly makes you wonder why so many people have prayed for so long to get so little,' David whispered, but they all heard him.

'Darling! You do have a funny way of seeing things.' Angelica kissed him affectionately on his cheek.

'Sorry we were so long; it's impossible to know this place or understand it,' Sophie said.

'I think I understand less and less. Perhaps I should live here; it makes my confusion commonplace.' David seemed to be taking everything personally.

'Oh, David, even when you're depressed, you're funny.' Sophie wondered how much longer Angelica could tolerate David's collapse.

'David does have a point, but this is Jerusalem, where

everybody appears to have a point. Time to try our market feast,' Avram said light-heartedly, and they all stood up to go inside as the bells of the Church of the Holy Sepulchre rang out.

Sitting under the domed ceiling, they inspected the spread on the round glass table, but nobody was hungry.

'I'll have some of this lovely fresh challah,' said Angelica, putting a few crumbs in her mouth and sipping her water.

David looked at Avram as if to say, *She's getting worse.*

'It's amazing how Avram managed to produce all this in a few minutes,' Sophie teased, scooping oriental aubergine onto her pitta.

'Now for some excellent Israeli wine.' Avram handed David a glass.

Aware of the effort being made by everybody else, David raised his glass. 'I'd like to propose a toast to our doctor, friend and guide, Avram.'

Angelica gave Sophie a nudge under the table.

'I second that,' said Sophie.

'Avram, we really appreciate you coming back to London with us,' Angelica added.

'The wine is surprisingly good,' David said.

Sophie went to join Angelica on the settee, leaving the men to finish the bottle.

It was just after seven when Avram announced, 'We all need an early night before our trip tomorrow.'

*

Back in their suite at the hotel, Sophie helped Angelica to undress and settle in bed after she had taken her pain-relief cocktail. Then Sophie and Avram sat in the other room with David, who seemed calmer and engaged them in talk, as if not wanting to be left alone.

'Although this trip has been quite an ordeal, I'm pleased we came. Until today I hadn't realised – I mean, I realised, but didn't want to know – that Angelica was so critically ill.' He stopped, unable to go on, then in a quavering voice said, 'It must be this place that makes me feel so defenceless; that's why I want to go home. It's the history… it's just everything. People appear to have always suffered here. I find Israelis a bit hard and too direct. It's not a criticism, Avram; it's just that it seems impossible to deny anything in Israel. In England we are more closed in and have learned how to hide our feelings. Everything here is so real and so open. The wars, the struggle, the political and religious tensions… I don't suppose I needed it at this moment.' He paused as if gathering his thoughts. His face looked pinched and strained; his voice was lifeless. 'But Angelica is right; her judgement is always so acute. She probably knew that we both needed to come here because we were avoiding the issues in London,' he said, as if releasing some internal pressure.

Sophie could hardly bear to see David so low. Touching his arm, she said, 'Angelica appears to be able to face it; we mustn't let her feel our distress.'

Avram looked thoughtful, as if she had touched a nerve. 'I think that's most important. We will just have to suspend our anguish because we have to allow Angelica the dignity of accomplishing her mission. I might have failed in this with my wife, and now I feel privileged to help all of you.'

David began to cry, and Avram went to the bar to pour him a drink.

Sophie spoke softly. 'David, I really believe that Angelica knows what she has to do, and if she believes in God, we must help her. We must get her back to be with Jonathan; that's what's worrying her most.'

It was ten o'clock when Avram gave David a sleeping tablet and said he would be back in the morning. Sophie kissed David on the cheek and reminded him that she would do all the packing.

Sophie had been dreaming all night, but couldn't remember any details, only the associated confusion and sadness. She ordered her morning coffee and then phoned home.

Hannah answered and was surprised to hear that she was coming home. 'What's wrong?' she asked, getting to the point.

When Sophie explained, Hannah's response was reassuring. 'You're doing the right thing,' she said in her matter-of-fact way.

Sophie thought it remarkable that Hannah was so naturally mature and supportive. Perhaps it was innate. She couldn't think of another explanation.

She dressed and went to see Angelica. David had ordered room service and was sitting alone at the table, having his breakfast. 'Angelica is having her hot water in bed; would you like some breakfast? There's enough here for six.'

Avram arrived and went in to see Angelica before joining them at the table. 'She seems less tired than yesterday. We definitely overdid it with that walk to my flat, but it's difficult to find the balance between taking away her autonomy and dealing with the reality. I believe she did get something out of the visit, and now she wants to get up later and have one last look at the Old City. So, I agreed we could go for a little drive before lunch, and then return and rest before we go to the airport. I told her no walking.'

'If that's what Angelica wants.' David's acquiescence cut deep. *He too has given up*, Sophie thought.

'I'll go and sit with her. It's much cooler today,' she said, and went to see Angelica.

Avram looked at his watch. 'It's 9.30. So, if we leave in an hour, we can go for a short drive and get back before midday and have a rest. Then we can go to the airport about four.'

The car moved slowly uphill towards the Mount of Olives.

'I don't think we should be out long,' David asserted, then fell silent.

Only Angelica talked and Avram replied, knowing that his patient was hovering between life and death, and at this moment he had to respond to her life force. 'You could be a tour guide,' Angelica said appreciatively.

'Every Israeli is a guide. I think we get our information from the stones. The rest we invent depending on whether you're a Jew, a Muslim or a Christian.'

The sound of his voice seemed to facilitate her serenity. 'It's strange but I don't feel the heat at all today,' she told them.

'Perhaps we should go back,' David urged, fearful of her decline.

'We'll drive up the hill to where you can see the most spectacular view of the Old City, then we will go back,' Avram suggested.

The car stopped on the ridge. 'What a spectacular view,' David commented.

'Can I get out for a moment?' Angelica asked. She walked a few steps, holding on to David, and looked out across the Kidron Valley illuminated in the sun and felt at peace. 'It's time to go home, David; I want to see Jonathan.'

David held her hand. It was like a child's without a grasp reflex. He held on to her, but could feel that she was letting go.

Avram walked a short distance away with Sophie. 'I know that this trip is a heroic attempt, but I don't understand why Angelica felt compelled to make it,' he said.

'Perhaps it's a spiritual journey, I don't know. But we have to accept that some things don't need to be understood. That's what Angelica taught me. She can be extraordinarily prescient without questioning how or why. That's what makes her so special.' Sophie knew she wasn't being rational, and wasn't surprised when Avram said nothing.

Back in the car, Angelica and David sat holding hands, rapt in their bonding. Sophie looked out of the window at the passing scenes of Jerusalem. People, buildings and trees merged into the distance. In the deathly silence, she could hear the sound of her own breathing.

PART FOUR

AFTER JERUSALEM

TWENTY-FIVE

SHOCK

Dark clouds descending over autumnal trees reminded Sophie she was back in England. Marc's affectionate hug as she walked through the door made her think that her disquiet was groundless. Although tired from the journey, she couldn't fall asleep, her mind filled with images of Avram in Jerusalem. As dawn broke, she woke with her last dream seeping into her consciousness. In it, Lucien stood in the kitchen. A black-and-white checked keffiyeh covered part of his face. He offered her a minute cup of syrupy coffee scented with cardamom. She was scared to refuse, but said she would wait for Marc. Lucien said he had gone. Hannah and Angelica called to her. They were shopping in Harrods. She went to them, but they vanished in a labyrinth of covered passages. An Arab man told her that she must leave immediately; it was dangerous. She panicked, and then saw Ernst walking towards her. The memory of the dream faded and she roused herself.

She left Marc sleeping and went down to the kitchen. An unexpected surge of energy presenting her with a fresh outlook led her to walk around the house while waiting for the coffee to drip through the filter. As if seeing her home for the first time, she wanted to rearrange the furniture. She thought of Ernst's open offer to join his publishing house, and felt ready to do so. Back in the kitchen she decided to cook a meal for the family, and made a list of Israeli vegetarian dishes, including cheese blintzes. She would get the recipe from Emma, who wouldn't be surprised that they'd returned early. She thought of Angelica, who had appeared so calm, and decided to go and see her later. Sipping her coffee, she thought again of Avram, who'd taken responsibility for Angelica on their journey and enabled her and David to relax.

She heard the phone ring, and Marc pick it up in the bedroom. Then he came down the stairs and stood in the doorway.

'Would you like a cup of coffee?' Sophie asked.

Marc looked at her and then came right out with it. 'David phoned. Angelica died at eight o'clock this morning.'

'No! It can't be; she was fine on the journey. Even Avram said that she had coped well. Something terrible must have happened after we came back from the airport.' Sophie gasped for air and strained to speak. Her voice caught in her throat. 'What happened? What did David say?'

'I didn't know how to ask him.'

She was offended by Marc's lack of clarity. He should have called her to the phone. Staring into space, she forced her words through her dry throat. 'I must go to David immediately.'

'Do you think that's wise? It might be too soon.'

'Of course! It's the right thing to do,' Sophie shouted. 'I don't understand your instincts. I'll phone Emma; she always knows what to do.' She calmed herself. 'I feel at such a loss. I must know what happened. We were all together yesterday and now David's alone.'

'The Israeli doctor and Jonathan are with him,' Marc said, watching her face pucker and give way to grief. 'I'll get dressed and drive you there.'

'Thank you, I can't face going on my own,' Sophie sobbed.

Unable to marshal her thoughts, she sat, immobilised, at the kitchen table.

Marc came down. 'I'm ready. Don't you think you ought to get dressed?'

'I haven't phoned Emma,' she said.

'I'll phone her and ask if she wants us to pick her up,' Marc suggested.

'That's a good idea. Marc, it's unbelievable that she died so soon. Of course I knew she was very ill, but I expected her to live longer.'

Sophie rushed upstairs and slipped on her jeans and T-shirt, and then worried that it was disrespectful to dress so casually. She looked at the unpacked suitcase on the floor and went to her cupboard and took out a skirt and blouse that Angelica had chosen for her. Downstairs, she grabbed her raincoat from the hall cupboard. 'Are we fetching Emma?' she asked, looking away from Marc.

'No. I just missed her – she had gone to do her weekly shopping – so I left a message saying that you were back from Jerusalem and she should ring immediately she got in.'

Sophie was annoyed with herself for not phoning earlier. Sitting silently in the car, she stared at the autumn leaves floating to the ground and couldn't imagine winter without Angelica. She was consumed by guilt for not realising the situation, even after Avram had told her that there was no hope. Whilst she had been mourning Angelica's dying for some time, it was the possibility she had mourned. It was unthinkable that Angelica was no longer there, especially now that Sophie had come to know her so differently. Angelica's fortitude and faith had made it easier for others to deny her suffering. Sophie tried not to cry in front of Marc, and kept telling herself she must be strong when she saw David and Jonathan.

They were the first to arrive. The housekeeper opened the door and Sophie went to David in the drawing room. She wanted to ask him what had happened, but her instincts prevented her from doing so. Hugging him, she felt his warm, quivering body mould into hers. Silently, they comforted each other. Marc watched, not knowing what to make of their desperate embrace except that he was not part of it. Jonathan came in and touched David's shoulder. David instantly turned towards him, nestling his tear-stained face on his son's shoulder. Then Jonathan moved away and embraced Sophie. He seemed more in control.

'Jonathan, tell me what happened?' Sophie asked tearfully.

'Mother was so happy when she came home last night. All she said was, "It's wonderful to see you, Jonathan, and we'll speak in the morning." Then Maria helped her into bed and brought her her usual cup of hot water. She must have only had a sip, because the cup was full on the bedside table. It seemed perfectly reasonable to let her rest, and we never thought of waking her. We had no idea that she was going down so fast. She just slipped into a deeper and deeper sleep, and it only occurred to Dad to get Avram when her breathing changed at three o'clock this morning. Avram examined her and told us that she was sinking, and that her courage had made her hide her discomfort. We stayed with her and watched her breathing become more irregular as she sank into a deeper coma. She didn't appear to suffer. Avram stayed with us all night, and at eight o'clock this morning she just stopped breathing.' Jonathan made it sound so natural, almost acceptable, especially with his declaration that she hadn't suffered.

'Where's Avram?' Sophie asked, looking around the room.

'Dad insisted he take a rest. I don't know how we would have coped without him.'

In the elegant drawing room, the air was heavy with silence. It was as if Angelica had left her legacy of little complaint, yet every fibre in Sophie's body protested against the raw injustice. She couldn't imagine how David would cope. She had always thought him strong, but in Jerusalem she had witnessed his dependence on Angelica, and she too had relied on her. Angelica could have been so angry at everything that was happening to her, but instead she'd seemed to have found a way to accept it.

Jonathan went to talk to David, who appeared to be visibly shrinking in his grief. His dark-ringed eyes peered vacantly across the mournful gathering and caught Sophie's.

Then she felt Marc's eyes upon her too, and saw him standing alone. She went to him. 'I'm ready to leave.'

Marc went up to David. 'I'm very sorry.'

'Thank you for coming, Marc, and for letting Sophie come to Jerusalem. She was really wonderful to us.' David glanced at Sophie.

'I'll be back later.' She kissed him on the cheek.

*

On the way home Marc said, 'You seem to be quite at home there.'

Sophie felt a twinge of guilt. 'Yes, it's strange how people bring out different things in each other. I suppose being so close to them in Jerusalem has made me feel like part of the family, whatever that means,' she sobbed. 'And now Angelica's gone and I shall never have a friend like her again.'

'What about Emma? You're pretty close to her,' Marc said, not knowing how to cope with her grief.

'I must phone her; she'll be heartbroken. What's the time? I hope she's at home. Emma will know what to do; she always knows what to do.'

Marc listened, but said nothing.

'Thanks for taking me. I couldn't have gone alone,' Sophie said as they pulled up by the house.

'I know it's a shock, but you can hardly say it's a surprise. Angelica must have been suffering more than we knew, and it's a release for her.' Marc parked the car outside their house.

'I suppose you're right. You make everything sound so simple. My own feelings are too complicated.' Dabbing her face, she followed Marc into the house, then rushed to answer the phone.

'I've just heard; Jonathan phoned, and he said I should phone you.'

Hearing Emma's voice set Sophie off crying again.

'What happened? I can't believe it. What happened?' Emma repeated, not knowing if Sophie was still on the line. 'I'm coming round now – is there anything I can do?'

Sophie hesitated. 'Well, I haven't had time to go out and shop and I wanted to cook the family a special meal tonight. I don't suppose they've eaten properly since I left.'

'I've got a vegetable lasagne in the deep freeze. I'll bring it round,' Emma offered.

'Thanks, I just can't think.'

'I'll be round in a jiff,' Emma said, putting the phone down.

Sophie considered how Emma so readily transformed devotion into action. She hardly ever missed her Wednesday-afternoon visit with Angelica. She regretted being so judgemental about Emma's affair with Aubrey. It was obvious that she was on the rebound after discovering Alan's betrayal. She admired Emma for keeping her family together and protecting her sons. She owed her an apology. 'Emma's on her way,' she told Marc, who was standing at the open fridge.

'Good, then I'll grab a sandwich and go to work. Will you be alright?'

'Yes, I'll go out later. I want to cook a special meal for Lucien and Hannah tonight. It's probably good to do something practical. Please come home in time for dinner.'

After Marc left, she composed herself and phoned Ernst. 'What's wrong?' he asked on hearing her voice.

'Angelica died this morning,' she wept.

Ernst paused. 'Maybe it's a release.'

'I know she suffered, but now she's gone. I can't bear it, don't you understand?' protested Sophie.

'Sophie dear, of course I understand, but my understanding can't bring her back. I was amazed that she wanted to go to Jerusalem. It was incredibly brave of her, and marvellous of you to go with her.'

'We were more like sisters. I always longed for a sister or a brother, and Angelica was there for me.'

Ernst remained quiet, pained both by her pain and by his own overwhelming shame that he had never told her she had a brother who, all those years ago, he'd had to leave behind in Prague. 'When is the funeral? I would like to go.'

'I'll let you know,' she said through her sobbing.

'I'll come over this evening,' Ernst said.

'Thanks.'

Ernst felt the shock filter through him. How could he console Sophie? He knew that part of her grief belonged to another time and, as time passed, her loss was compounding. He thought of himself as a man of integrity, but then why had he never told her the truth? He hadn't actually lied to her, but not telling the truth was itself a lie. Losing Angelica had brought the pain of Sophie's past to the surface. He couldn't be sure what she remembered from those harrowing times after fleeing Prague. He'd been grateful that she'd been such an easy child to manage when they'd first arrived in London and he'd had to find a flat, a job and a nursery school. When the war was over, he had learned that his father, mother and sisters had died in Auschwitz.

Ernst had been warned that he should under no circumstances contact Lotte's parents and his son, Oska. It was dangerous for any Czech, particularly a senior civil servant like Dr Hoffmann, to have any contact with the West. The communist hold on Czechoslovakia had never been secure and Ernst knew that if his son and the Hoffmanns had survived the war, any attempt to contact them would put an end to whatever peace and security they might be enjoying. This seemingly unresolvable conflict had immobilised him.

TWENTY-SIX

SOPHIE AND EMMA

Sophie answered the door to find Emma crying.

'I've brought a load of stuff for you. Can you help bring it in?'

She followed Emma and helped fetch the various dishes from the car. 'This is delightful, Emma; I feel I should have made the effort to cook.'

'You always feel so guilty about everything, Sophie. You went to Jerusalem; I couldn't possibly have done that. We all land up doing what we can do best, so let me do the cooking, but first I'd love a cup of strong coffee. I know I shouldn't, but I really need a boost today. Then you must tell me everything that happened in Jerusalem.'

Sophie recounted their time in Jerusalem and what Jonathan had told her, emphasising that Angelica hadn't suffered.

'What does it mean to be obstructed? She must have shown signs of it. Did you notice any change in her in Jerusalem?' Emma sounded almost accusatory.

'Really, Emma, I can't be sure of anything; Angelica never complained. Perhaps the tumour had grown so large that even the colostomy didn't help. I don't know. Perhaps she had become so deeply religious that she was capable of hiding pain even from herself. Perhaps I shouldn't have supported her when she insisted on going sightseeing and David protested. I just don't know. It was a miracle that Avram came back with us. I now realise that he must have known.' Sophie sobbed.

'He sounds amazing. Surely, he would have stopped the sightseeing. You can hardly blame yourself, Sophie.' Emma sighed. 'Do you think Angelica believed that she had a special line to God? She really changed during her illness. I don't mean physically, because in a way she looked even more beautiful; I mean her whole personality. At times it appeared that she would live forever – her quietness, her intense interest in us and our children. She told me I'm a wonderful mother but will be lost when the boys go to university, so I should do something with my life. You know, I think I will. To think that she was busy planning our lives while she was dying… I feel so bad, but what can I do?' Emma dissolved into tears.

'I suppose you could go out and do something as a tribute to her. Perhaps we should both make some personal effort.'

'You're right, I will; as soon as Daniel settles into university life and I am sure that Ben will manage his A Levels without my nagging. Angelica gave us something special, but why did she have to die for us to know that?'

Sophie liked this side of Emma. Perhaps losing Angelica was making them more open with each other. She thought of Ernst and how he seemed to idealise his mother, usually referring to her as an angel. It was true that she had encouraged him to leave Czechoslovakia, knowing that he would be safe in England, and if she had thought, as she must have, of not seeing him again, she'd never said anything. Even now he could not say that she had died in the Holocaust, but he must know. 'I suppose when someone dies it's easier to focus on their good points because their faults can't do you any harm.'

Emma wouldn't let her finish. 'That's not always the case. I can assure you my mother's behaviour will be with me whether she's dead or alive. The very fact that she sent me to boarding school when I begged her to let me stay at home has affected me all my life. You know what she asked me when Daniel was four and Ben just eighteen months? "When are you sending them away, dear?" Well! I kept quiet. Don't tell me that when she dies, I'll suddenly start believing she was an angel or something.'

Sophie was taken aback by Emma's outburst. 'Honestly, though, Emma, you have to admit that if Angelica had faults, they weren't evident.' She recalled that when she'd first met Angelica she'd thought her rather superficial, but in her last few years she'd appeared to grow and develop, often asking Sophie to recommend books and wanting to discuss them with her. 'She was a very intelligent woman – look how she adapted to David's culture.'

'You're right; she knew more about Judaism than I do, or care to, and certainly took it much more seriously,' Emma admitted.

'Poor David, he's devastated. The strongest image I have is of them surrounded by a kind of golden halo. I don't think they were aware of it, but I felt it. I don't know what to do – perhaps we should go back to the house?'

'Let's go in half an hour; it's customary among Jews to come and go to pay their respects, even if only for a few minutes. I definitely must go,' Emma said.

'I'll drive,' insisted Sophie.

'Where's your lot?' Emma asked, noticing the quiet house.

'Lucien went to a music festival and stayed over with friends. At least, that's what he says. He'll be back this evening. Hannah left early this morning. She's doing a cookery course; a present from Ernst. That's why I wanted to have something special for them tonight. I couldn't disappoint Hannah; she is so enthusiastic about cooking. She'd be delighted if you wrote down the recipe for the lasagne. Knowing her, she may even attempt one tomorrow.'

'I wish I had a daughter. My boys are both so scientific.'

'That's what Angelica said when we went shopping at Harrods. I can't believe it was only ten days ago.'

'Sophie, life must go on; I'm sure that's what Angelica would have wanted,' Emma lamented.

'That's what I told Jonathan this morning. He's so much like Angelica, you know; I'm sure he'll do something unusual with his life.'

As if to change the subject, Emma looked around the bedroom. 'I do like this house – it has so much character, and you've done a lot to it. I remember when I first came here and things were all over the place. Do you remember how you left your clothes on chairs and in piles on the floor? I was shocked then, but now I don't think such things are important. I guess we've all changed.' She flopped onto one of the Victorian chairs. 'Marc certainly did a good job of designing your wardrobes.'

'Yes, he found the antique pine doors at a junk shop and adapted them to the DIY carcasses. I won't tell you how long that took. Marc is a perfectionist. He takes forever to do something. Just look at the doors – he stripped each one, and then waxed them to show the grain in the wood. Each door took about three weekends, so you can imagine, the lot took months and months. Now, he's flooring the loft for storage. I hear this constant hammering but can't be bothered to climb up the stepladder to see what's going on. When I suggested that the basement would be more practical, he said it would only involve moving things out when he converts the basement into a separate flat. And so it goes on. I've been living in an architectural happening for the past nineteen years.'

'You don't know how lucky you are. Alan can't even change an electric light.'

Sophie told Emma about Avram's flat in the Old City, how she shared his history as his parents had also escaped from war-torn Europe, and how she'd spontaneously felt released from the silence of her false identity. She was now ready to confront Ernst, and felt compelled to know everything about their family. Her experience in Jerusalem had opened up a new reality that had given her a new sense of pride. She realised that those few days with Angelica and David had made her want more from her own marriage. She knew, too, that the model Angelica had provided of dignity and courage would sustain her for the rest of her life.

She reminded Emma that they needed to go to visit David, and opened the wardrobe to reveal some of the clothes Angelica had insisted on buying for her. 'I can't believe that she won't even see me in them. She took such an interest in how I looked. She practically forced me to go to the hairdresser in Jerusalem.'

'It's a wonderful cut; I've never seen you look so lovely,' Emma told her.

Sophie glanced at herself in the mirror, suddenly realising that Marc had not noticed her new hairstyle or, if he had, had never mentioned it.

*

The house was already crowded by the time they arrived. People sat around talking quietly, supporting David in his benumbed state. Sophie and Emma recognised Angelica's and David's parents, and when David walked up to them Emma kissed him but was unable to bring herself to say anything, and was relieved when he took the initiative.

'Thank you so much for coming; the three of you were so close. Rosalind Cohen will be along later. I am grateful that Angelica turned to her, if only during her last week. I'm sure it gave her the strength to face what we couldn't.' He choked.

Emma reverted to ritual. 'I'll go and say hello to your parents and Jonathan and help Maria serve the tea and cake,' she said. 'Well, you know it's a Jewish custom that you wish the mourners a long life and then you feed them. When you think of it, there are very few Jewish customs that don't involve food. I should have brought a cake or something; I will tomorrow.'

Jonathan told them that the cremation had been arranged for two o'clock the following day.

'Don't worry, I'll tell Maria what to prepare for afterwards,' Emma responded.

'Thanks, it will take a load off my dad. By the way, I expect I'll be seeing Daniel at Oxford,' he said to please her.

'Fortunately, the term doesn't begin for another month, but I'm sure they'll understand if you delay your start,' Emma told him.

'I'm not looking forward to it, but I know Dad expects me to go and I suppose that's what Mother would have wanted.'

After an hour Sophie and Emma left. 'Jonathan seems to be coping well,' Emma remarked. 'I don't think it's hit him yet.'

'I find him a bit unreal, too,' Sophie replied.

They stopped at a greengrocer and Sophie set about buying everything in sight. She was eager to return home to be with her family.

TWENTY-SEVEN

THE CREMATION

Driving to the Golders Green Crematorium as the rain pelted down across the windscreen, Marc was irritated by Sophie's silence. 'Do you think there'll be a huge crowd?'

'I don't know.'

'I envied your friendship with Angelica,' he told her.

She took her time to answer, making Marc wonder if she had heard him above the rhythmical noise of the windscreen wipers. 'I suppose Angelica was someone who really respected me.'

'I've always tried to encourage you and to give you space,' Marc objected.

'I didn't mean it like that… I could feel her interest in me. You didn't even notice my new haircut. I feel I bore you. I never felt that with Angelica. She needed me and never took me for granted.'

'No, Sophie, that's not true. If anything, it's the other way round. Your relationship with Angelica and Emma – all your outings, all those endless phone calls – I don't know why you never ran out of things to say to each other. Sometimes I think women invented their own language to exclude men. They neither consider guiding principles, nor place anything into any social, political or economic framework. Conversation is all about what happens; it's all about feelings and nothing about thought. I've noticed how much time is wasted at staff meetings because the women take over and change the direction of the discussion. Men approach life differently; I think it's probably because we can't have babies.'

'Really, Marc, I hardly think this is the time. If you're jealous of my friendship with Angelica, I think you could have chosen a better moment.' Sophie was weeping uncontrollably and opened the window to let in some air, before hurriedly closing it against the rain.

'I'm sorry, I didn't mean it that way. You had a wonderful friendship with Angelica.'

'Perhaps if men bothered to learn our illogical language there would be fewer wars.' Sophie calmed herself. 'I'm sorry, Marc, but I feel too upset. You never appreciated Angelica. She was totally without envy; she could never have threatened anybody.'

'That doesn't always work; just because Angelica never envied anybody it doesn't mean that others didn't envy her. I remember when I met David – obviously a very successful businessman, and Angelica looking like a film star, in their magnificent house – I envied them.'

'I agree. Angelica may have been envied because of her beauty but we can't do anything about other people's envy. Appeasement doesn't help, either. Angelica could never have changed her innate beauty, which probably peeved those women on her charity committee. But I'm sure if you had said to her, "I envy you," she would have tried to put you at ease by explaining her own shortcomings. She had to pretend with David's business associates and often admitted that it was a strain, but at the end of her life, she was completely true to herself. She'd never had the kind of education I had, but she had a yearning for knowledge, which is one of the reasons we got on so well. She approached life as though she was forever on the point of discovery, and that generated a wonderful feeling. She wasn't materialistic because she perceived acquisitions as a form of enhancing her understanding, not her status. Maybe at the beginning she didn't make that distinction, but certainly in this last year she was more concerned about her spiritual development.'

'I find it quite amazing how she coped in that environment. It must have taken some guts, converting to Judaism. It seems such a demanding religion.' Marc relaxed.

'Not really; I suppose there are many levels and Angelica just found hers. But she did have courage, or perhaps she just had the knack of ignoring the dark side of life. Probably not being Jewish in the first place helped.'

Marc laughed. 'That's a funny thing to say.'

'Not if you experienced what I saw in Jerusalem. I was brought up in a secular environment. I've never been to a synagogue and Ernst is an atheist, so if Judaism is a culture as well as a religion, I have missed out on both.'

'I sometimes wonder whether you ever think about being Jewish?' Mark asked.

'I do now.'

'Is Angelica having a Jewish funeral?'

'Yes, that lovely Rabbi Rosalind Cohen is officiating. We are on time, aren't we?'

Marc looked at his watch. 'We're here; all we have to do is find parking. It looks like quite a crowd.' Seeing groups of smartly dressed people standing around in the forecourt, he added, 'They all look like David's people: your typical right-wing, middle-class mob.'

Sophie didn't answer. She saw the sombre crowd as a backdrop to her own grief. Nervously looking around, she spotted Ernst standing on the edge of the crowd and went to him. He'd never seen her so distraught, and put his arm round her.

'It's a terrible shock for you, but real friends remain with you in your memory even after they've gone. Sophie, you know what? I would like to go back to Prague. Would you come with me? I don't mean immediately, but sometime soon.'

Her father's deeply felt plea augmented Sophie's grief. 'Yes,' she replied. 'That's exactly what we need to do. We need to go to Prague, and you can tell me all about it.'

She stopped sobbing and looked around. Rosalind Cohen, dressed in her clerical gown, was talking with David and Jonathan. Avram stood next to them, but appeared apart from them somehow. She couldn't see Emma, and asked Marc if he had seen her.

'I'll go and find her,' he offered, pleased to have something to do.

'Thanks; I don't want to sit next to strangers or go in first.'

Seeing the large crowd, Marc wondered if they would find a seat in the chapel of rest. He thought of Sophie's unrealistic approach to life, and now even to death.

Sophie turned to Ernst. 'Would you like to meet the Israeli doctor, Avram Levi?'

Ernst shook Avram's hand. 'You know, I have never been to Israel.'

'There's still time,' Avram replied in a way that was neither reassuring nor questioning.

'Sophie and I are thinking of going to Prague. We left nearly forty years ago; I was only twenty-four. Isn't it strange how life moves on without one doing anything about it?' Ernst asked.

'Perhaps after you've visited Prague you'll come to Israel. I think Sophie got a lot out of her short trip,' Avram said, looking tenderly at her.

'It was overwhelming. I just didn't expect it to end like this,' she said.

'I think it's time to go into the chapel.' Ernst gently put his arm around Sophie.

'I must wait for Emma; we must be together,' she insisted.

Seeing Marc, Alan and Emma walking towards them, Sophie introduced them to Avram. Then she put her arm through Emma's and they walked into the chapel. The sight of David and Jonathan sitting in the front row without Angelica drove home the devastating reality. Sophie made no attempt to hold back the hot tears flowing copiously down her cheeks. She looked at the mahogany coffin covered in white arum lilies that scented the air, and shuddered at the sound of the heavy mahogany doors of the crowded chapel closing. She reached out to Emma, who held her hand and whispered, 'It will be all right.'

Seeing Sophie's pallor and distress, Avram whispered to Ernst, 'Perhaps you should take her out.'

But Sophie heard him, and shook her head. She would never walk out on Angelica.

Rosalind Cohen spoke about the purity of Angelica's faith, about her last wish to see Jerusalem, and about her courage in making the journey because she wanted it to be not just a place in her mind, but a real place inhabited by people in the struggle of everyday life. She told everyone that Angelica had known she was dying and, determined to spare her loved ones pain, saw Jerusalem as part of her spiritual journey. In the last few days of her life she had prepared herself and her family, David and Jonathan, and her friends, Sophie and Emma. As the coffin moved slowly and silently towards the open door, Rosalind recited, 'The Lord is my shepherd, I shall not want; He leadeth me into green pastures...', timing the Twenty-Third Psalm to end as the coffin disappeared and the door closed.

The chapel doors opened onto extensive, peaceful gardens. Sophie and Emma, with hands clasped together, joined the crowd walking behind David and Jonathan. Moving rapidly, the dark clouds gave way to a sky streaked with light. Sophie breathed deeply as she waited for her turn to speak to David and Jonathan.

David took her hand. 'Will you be coming back to the house?'

'Of course,' Sophie replied.

TWENTY-EIGHT

MOURNING

'I can't believe she's gone,' Sophie said to Emma during their daily phone call.

'I know it sounds odd, but Angelica feels more alive to me now; I think of her all the time. She was never ashamed of her background. She often spoke about helping her parents in the pub. She was grateful for advice and had no qualms asking for it. She would probably have gone on to do much more if she'd lived.' Emma choked up. 'I'm sorry for rambling on, but it's just one of those days. I feel so low and unsettled, Sophie. I don't know what it is, but I am so fed up. I know I have to do something to get out of this rut, but I can't think what.'

'I think you should go and lie in a hot bath, then make yourself a nice cup of tea and spend the afternoon resting on your bed,' Sophie said tenderly. She was exhausted herself.

'Perhaps that's just what I need,' said Emma. 'Thanks, you're a brick.'

In her bath, Emma thought about Sophie – her intelligence

and loyalty, and the fact that she had never complained about not having a mother. It was odd that Sophie, who was quite open about most things, had never, ever mentioned her mother.

*

The next morning, she phoned her. 'I've decided I want to study something. What do you think? After all, you're an academic yet you've never urged me to study.'

Sophie was amused by Emma's accusatory tone. 'I'm sorry if I've neglected to encourage you, but I suppose I wasn't all that happy at Oxford. I felt uncomfortable with the rarefied atmosphere and the elitism. If you want my advice, you have to decide yourself *why* you want to study. Do you have a specific interest or do you want to do some vocational training?'

'I suppose, being practical, I would like to study something vocational. I've thought about law,' said Emma, having only just thought of it.

'Good idea; probably the best choice.'

'Do you really think I can do it at my age?' Emma said excitedly.

'Of course you can. You could be qualified by the time you're forty-five, even with the odd retake, and that would still give you a worthwhile career.'

'You make it sound so easy.'

'No, I never said that. In fact, it's quite difficult, but I think you can do it, and I promise to help, if I can. You have got A Levels or something like that, haven't you?'

Emma replied. 'Yes, but I don't know whether they're relevant.'

'What are they?'

'French, Italian and English.' Emma sounded apologetic.

'That should be all right; after all, you'll be enrolled as a mature student. What grades did you get?'

Emma hesitated. 'I suppose I could have done better, but as head girl I had a lot of responsibility. And you know me; I get quite distracted expanding my role beyond the call of duty.'

Sophie waited.

'Well, in the end, I didn't do enough work and I only got Cs for French and Italian and a B for English.'

'I'm impressed.'

'Sophie, your confidence means a lot to me. Do you really think I can do it?'

'Emma, you have a natural grasp on detail and an analytical approach to most matters. You also probably have the academic requirements for the course. It's just a matter of believing in yourself, and you certainly have a lot of confidence.'

Emma laughed. 'Oh, Sophie, with your lack of confidence everybody else must seem to have an awful lot.'

'There you are; that's probably why we get on so well. All you need is intelligence, commitment and motivation. You are certainly intelligent and I know all about your staying power and discipline, so all you have to sort out is your motivation. There again, it helps enormously if the subject interests you, and I think you would make a very good solicitor. You love sorting out people's lives. I should know,' said Sophie.

'You are a brick; I really appreciate it.'

'Not as much as I appreciate your cheesecakes.'

'Well, in that case, there'll be one with me when I come over tomorrow,' Emma replied.

TWENTY-NINE

SOPHIE AND JONATHAN

Struggling with her habitual vacillation, Sophie phoned David at home and was surprised to learn that he'd gone to the office. She phoned him there. 'I hope I'm not disturbing you; I didn't expect you to be at work,' she said apologetically.

'I'm trying. I came back more for Jonathan's sake than mine. I need to speak to you and wondered whether we could meet for dinner this evening?' David asked.

'I really should be here for Lucien and Hannah. Marc is away. I would prefer lunch tomorrow.'

'That's fine; you're right. I should also be home for Jonathan. I wasn't thinking. Would you meet me at one in the Savoy Lounge?'

'I'll be there. You sound quite well, David.'

'I'm doing my best.'

*

As she ambled through the Savoy's crowded foyer, Sophie was surprised by a frisson of excitement at the prospect of seeing David. She slipped into the cloakroom for a final grooming and caught herself admiring her new outfit in the mirror. When she saw him standing in the far corner of the lounge, it took her a moment to adjust to his strained expression as he walked towards her and kissed her on the cheek.

'You look wonderful, Sophie.'

'Angelica chose this outfit for me.' Then she worried that she might have been insensitive.

'She did well. I don't think we can ever forget how generous and considerate Angelica was.' David led her to a couch in a quiet corner, away from the waiters who were milling around offering canapés and drinks to chattering and laughing guests.

'We have to move on, David,' she said, then felt uncomfortable about her predictable cliché.

'You're right but I don't know how I'm going to manage without her. Angelica's unconditional acknowledgement was like a drug. When I think of all the people I know, it was Angelica who helped me build my confidence. Her casual remarks transformed my ideas into actions. She seemed to put me in the right frame of mind to make decisions by creating a feeling of well-being which I recognise as love. I thought I had prepared myself during her last few days; I rehearsed in my mind this time without her, but this is different. She was with me then, but now she's gone. I feel as though I'm spinning in space. If Avram hadn't been with us when she died, I would have joined her. I just feel so weak, so bruised.'

The head waiter came up to them, greeted David, and escorted them to a table overlooking the river. Sophie looked out at the large boats moving slowly through the murky water. A soft light filtered through the autumn sky over a timeless London scene along the Embankment.

David sighed, turning his heavy eyes towards the river,

then looked down at the table as if gathering strength to speak. 'Thank you for coming all this way to see me; I just couldn't talk to you at home. It's Jonathan. I don't know what's happened to him. He has become uncommunicative. It could be a delayed reaction. I don't know what to do. He's got it into his head that he shouldn't go to Oxford. I suspect he doesn't want to leave me alone. That's why I went back to the office to show him that I can manage. Sophie, you're the only one who can help sort it out.' He was aware of her unusual beauty, of which she seemed oblivious. 'Perhaps you'll be able to persuade him. Jonathan respects you, and after all, you also went to Oxford so you can speak from experience. It may help; I just don't know.'

She was pleased to be needed. 'Perhaps he's right. You can't bluff him; he's too much like Angelica.' She found herself mentioning Angelica at every opportunity. She looked at David's drawn face and dull eyes; without his wife he seemed half the man. 'David, don't worry; it could be quite simple.'

'How do you mean, simple?'

'I didn't mean that his problems are simple; I mean that, after I leave here, I will pop in to see him on my way home. I think it's more important that I find out what's on his mind before I state the obvious, don't you?'

'The term doesn't start for another month. I wouldn't want him to lose out for the wrong reasons. It's such early days. I try to convince myself, but I feel so damned lonely. It's so physical, as if I'm missing a part of my body.' David's eyes glazed over again. 'It feels as though I've lost more than Angelica, a witness to my life. She was so involved with everything I did.'

Sophie stretched across and touched his arm. 'It's going to take time. We can't get over such a loss, but we can get used to it. It seemed so sudden, after Jerusalem. Do you think we should have gone?'

'Yes. We were so happy, and you were so supportive. We couldn't have done it without you. We also met Avram, and he's been wonderful. He phones me from Israel and always asks after you.'

'I think he's a very special person. But you know I can't sort out my poor Lucien's problems, yet you believe I can help Jonathan?'

David looked into the distance. 'We feel so implicated in our children's failings, probably because they remind us of our worst traits. You do know that if there's any way I can help Lucien, you only have to ask.' He put his hand over Sophie's, which was resting on the table, then suddenly withdrew it.

She pretended not to notice. 'I know Lucien isn't ready to be helped. I have to believe he won't waste too much of his life before he decides what to do with what's left of it.'

'I won't lose you as a friend now that Angelica has gone, will I?' David pleaded, his eyes sorrowful.

'David, you know that I'm here whenever you need me.' She felt confused, and welcomed the waiter's interruption, offering to refill their coffee cups.

'I really appreciate you coming here today. I have to know what's happening with Jonathan, and you didn't hesitate,' David said politely, as if embarrassed.

'You've caught me at the right time,' Sophie said. 'I've decided I should be more active. I used to spend hours thinking about something instead of just getting on with it. When I think of how Angelica remained active till the last...' She found herself unable to go on. After a pause, she added, 'Isn't this food delicious?'

'Yes, everything is cooked absolutely fresh. Excellent ingredients beautifully prepared. Marvellous service. Angelica loved coming here,' David said.

Sophie moved her empty coffee cup away, indicating the end of their lunch. 'I'd better get going and hope that Jonathan is at home. I'll phone you as soon as I get home.'

David walked with her to her car, kissing her lightly on the cheek.

It was almost four when Sophie arrived and Maria opened the door.

'Is Jonathan at home?'

Maria nodded. 'He's still in bed.'

'No, I'm not,' Jonathan, barefoot and dressed in a black tracksuit, shouted from the top of the stairs. He had grown a beard, and his uncombed hair hung in curls around his strikingly handsome face. He had Angelica's blue eyes and bone structure, and David's dark brown hair and height, but his resemblance to Angelica appeared more pronounced.

'I've just popped in for a cup of coffee. Is that all right?' Sophie tried to sound casual.

'Did Dad send you?' asked Jonathan.

'Yes, but I was looking for an excuse to pop in,' she said, following him into the kitchen.

'You know the last thing I want to do is worry Dad,' he said, preparing the coffee. 'I want to show you something.'

His lifeless tone made her look out the window at the fading light. Something was going on; she could feel it. Jonathan ran upstairs, returned and sat opposite her. He gave her a well-fingered envelope and waited as she opened it. A shiver ran through her when she recognised Angelica's writing.

'Read it,' he urged.

To my darling son, Jonathan.

Sophie read the letter slowly. Her train of thought was interrupted by such strong feelings that the words slipped away and she had to return to them.

The King David Hotel, Jerusalem

My darling Jonathan,

This letter is to you in the event of my death. I am writing it in Jerusalem, because at this moment I am thinking of you. David is reading in the next room and I am resting after a morning at the Hadassah Hospital. I do not know how much longer I will live – a few months, but perhaps less. It is only within the past month that I have become totally aware of the absolute finality of death. I am not afraid, nor unhappy for myself. But I am concerned that I may not have left enough time to discuss this with you and David. My life is not my own; it belongs to the two of you.

Some feelings are so deep they are beyond words. Some remind me of how I felt when you were born. You came early – I was eight months pregnant – and you were born by caesarean. You were small, precious and perfect. There were no words then to describe the joy I felt when I held you. My life was then further enriched by knowing Sophie and Emma. There are few gaps between us because each of us needs the others. It is a coincidence that we are all only children. You are also an only child, and I hope that you will find friendship and, most important, the right partner. I met David by chance, and now I see it was meant to be. When I was your age, I was very confused. My parents loved me, but at first David's parents were not happy with me. But as time went on, they got used to me, and now I really believe we love each other. It was my struggle to be accepted that led me to Judaism, and through my belief I've been rewarded. I couldn't understand what being a Jew meant until I came to Jerusalem. I know others may have thought that my conversion was a way of making life comfortable for David, and at the time this was so, but sometimes the real reason for doing something doesn't emerge for a very long time. I have always felt sensitive to conditions, and had prophetic and intuitive ways of dealing with life.

My cancer was meant to be. Perhaps that is why I know that my faith will see me through. David deals with life differently. He is not guided by faith, but by reason. He has sustained me in the practical world. You are blessed with both reason and intuition; you are more balanced, and I know you will find your way. This thought comforts me. My desire to come to Jerusalem was impulsive. I did not consider whether my health could take it, because I knew it would make little difference to the outcome, but a lot of difference to my need to understand.

Rosalind Cohen helped me to understand that I can find my own level and place in Judaism. She said it's the journey that matters. These thoughts have comforted me, and coming to Jerusalem has also brought David and me closer together. After our meeting with Dr Avram Levi, we know that we must and can be more open about my illness. I wanted to protect David and you, but I now see that it is not possible to keep reality from those you love. They know without knowing. Being here has convinced me that somewhere God is showing me, beyond all the rituals and religious knowledge, that He is with me. I'm much happier.

I must get back to you, my dear Jonathan. You have a lot of David in you, and that's your intellectual ability, but you also have a lot of me in you, and that's your emotional strength. You are loved, educated and socially advantaged. But you have lost me, and what this will do to you I cannot predict. But remember: 'There is wisdom in the house of mourning.' You have judgement and you must assert it. You must be yourself. You must do in life what you feel is right for you, without hurting your father or others. Jonathan, you are young, and now you must

become prematurely wise. My leaving you is the first
challenge. Take care of David; he is not as resilient as you.
He's been so busy building his empire that he never took
the time to think deeply about these matters. I've had a
very happy life with him; he's a wonderful husband, and
you can judge him as a father. But he is also a man who
will be desperately lonely without me. Later I hope he will
find happiness with another woman. You may find that
difficult, but you must not resent her. David must find
a way to live his life, and you must help each other. My
illness gave me the opportunity to accept the unacceptable;
it forced me to stop and think, and that has enriched me.
I have learned so much from my illness, and you too will
learn from your loss. As I write this letter, know that I feel
a deep joy in my love for you. And from the moment you
were born, you have returned that love.

God bless you.
Your loving mother,
Angelica

Sophie wiped her tears, feeling Jonathan's expectant eyes upon her. 'David obviously doesn't know about this letter.'

'No.' Jonathan looked down awkwardly.

'Why didn't you show it to him?'

'I don't know, and now I feel worried.'

She touched his arm. 'Jonathan, there's nothing to be ashamed of.'

'I suppose I do feel ashamed because I hadn't realised that Mother was so ill. I somehow denied those last weeks of her life. When I remember how I enjoyed the three-day cricket event while you were in Jerusalem, I don't know what I was thinking. And now I feel so guilty. I could've done more. Mum and I never really had the kind of conversation that's in this letter, and now it's too late. She can't come back.' He burst into tears.

'Jonathan, I also feel I could have done more, and poor David probably feels even worse. But Angelica never let on. She probably wanted to spare us the pain of losing her. Of course, we all knew in our own way, but she allowed us to deny it. We know now that we can never be spared loss. It has to be faced. It's only a matter of when.'

Jonathan looked up from the table. 'Avram said something like that but I couldn't take it in. And now I don't quite know how to face Dad.'

'Would you like me to tell him about the letter?' she suggested.

'Dad and I were so close and now I feel I can't talk to him. It doesn't make sense.'

'What about Oxford?' Sophie asked, remembering David's concern.

Haltingly, Jonathan explained that it seemed to be the very worst time for his father and him to be separated, and that it would be better if he postponed going up to Oxford until the following year. In any case, he didn't really want to study economics – he wanted to be a doctor but did not have the right A Levels.

'I'm sure that David will understand. Would you like me to talk to him? This whole thing has got out of proportion.'

'I would be grateful.' Jonathan perked up.

'I must go now. I'll phone him as soon as I get home.' She got up and kissed Jonathan goodbye.

*

'I've been waiting for your call. What happened?' David asked anxiously.

'It's not quite so straightforward. Well, it is to you and me, but not to Jonathan.'

'How do you mean?'

'Jonathan has a letter from Angelica to be read in the event of her death.'

'What letter?'

'It was the last letter she wrote. She must have known when we were in Jerusalem that she was dying.'

'Why haven't I seen this letter?' David sounded desperate and angry.

'Jonathan is so raw and shattered. Perhaps he wanted to protect you. He is going to show it to you tonight,' Sophie assured him.

'I should hope so. The sooner the better,' David replied.

'It's a beautiful letter—'

Before she could finish, David interrupted. 'I remember Angelica writing in Jerusalem; she was writing something all week in the bedroom. She was quite cagey about it then. Are you sure he will show it to me?'

'Yes, but try to stay calm. Don't say anything you'll regret later.'

'What about Oxford? I don't suppose you got anywhere with that?'

'It appears that he has had a total rethink about his career. I told him that you'll feel differently after you've read the letter.'

'I knew it wasn't just a passing phase...' He seemed distraught.

'David, stop worrying, it's not all bad. The gist of it is, he doesn't want to read economics at Oxford, he wants to study medicine – quite understandably, in the circumstances.' Sophie sounded firm.

'Well, he could have told me. I'm not against it. I can't see the problem.'

'It's not that simple. He hasn't any of the right A Levels and doesn't know how to proceed. He would need three sciences; English, history and economics aren't acceptable. I promised him that I would contact someone at Oxford and get some advice. If he genuinely wants to study medicine, then he must do it,' she persisted.

'I agree. But can't he go to Oxford first?' David asked.

'Honestly, David, I think he's in quite a state and it would be better for him to defer. The first term at Oxford can be demanding and alienating. He really does need time to decide what he wants to do. You know, losing Angelica has affected all of us in different ways, and if handled well, some good might even come of it.'

'Sophie, you're delightful!' David sounded more like his old self. 'This is crazy; I can't talk to you on the phone. I'll ring again and arrange something. I'm anxious to get home to Jonathan. Thanks a million.'

THIRTY

SOPHIE AND LUCIEN

'Sophie, you're a genius,' David said over the phone. 'Jonathan is so much calmer and quite open to reason. We had some painful silences before your chat with him. I don't know why you feel you can't help Lucien. I'm sure you can.'

'I suspect Lucien's problems are rather more complicated. Even taking Jonathan's shock into account, he still has motivation. I have yet to observe a hint of ambition in my dear Lucien.'

'I'm sorry, that was insensitive of me,' David said.

'Well, in a way, you're not entirely wrong. I could make more effort with Lucien. Ernst feels there's hope, but I don't think Marc sees how bad things are, or if he does, he doesn't seem to do anything. So, thanks for your encouragement, and for the lovely lunch.'

After she put the phone down, Sophie thought of Lucien's angry moods and her fear of fuelling his hostility. She couldn't continue to accept his aberrant behaviour as if she deserved punishment from which Marc was magically exempt. She couldn't forgive Marc for insisting that their children go to the local comprehensive when she had wanted to send them to a small private school where they would have had more individual attention. Ernst had been only too happy to help out but Marc had intimidated her with his socialist dogma, blaming the Tories for everything, and particularly for their socially divisive educational policies. Even when Lucien had failed hopelessly in every subject except art, Marc just kept quiet.

Suddenly, she was overwhelmed by a strong urge to be with Lucien. Angelica would have called it a sign. She wasn't imagining it: since she'd returned from Jerusalem, Lucien appeared more amenable and spent more time at home, which seemed odd because Marc was constantly out. She went to the top of the house and stood outside his room. Her heart sank at the familiar cacophonous thumping of his record player. But she had to try. She didn't know how much pot he smoked or whether it was the cause of his inertia. Confused between cause and effect, but resolute, she knocked on the door and went in. Looking away from the mess, she inhaled the musty air, thick with the smell of tobacco and pot, and the sight of Lucien lying on his unmade bed staring up at the ceiling completed her revulsion.

'I thought I would make a nice meal this evening and wondered if you'll be here?' she asked, not expecting a reply.

'Great. Do you need any help?' he replied, turning down the music.

Astonished that her small effort had brought a positive response, she measured her expectation. 'Thanks; I'll get started. Come down when you're ready.'

Sophie was dicing cucumber, tomatoes and peppers for an Israeli salad when Lucien came into the kitchen.

'I'll do that,' he offered.

'I've just realised why this Israeli salad doesn't quite work in England,' Sophie said, keeping the conversation neutral.

He looked at her suspiciously. 'It was fine the other night.'

'I suppose the taste depends on the quality of the vegetables, and they always taste so fresh in Israel.'

'You know, Mum, since you've been back, it's been "Israel this" and "Jerusalem that". You were only there a week, and you seem totally indoctrinated.'

Sophie was amused that Lucien had used one of Marc's buzzwords, and laughed. 'I remember reading somewhere in the guidebook, "When you go to Jerusalem you come away different," or something like that.'

'Well, of all the excuses, as if I don't know that you're trying to get me to go to Israel,' retorted Lucien.

'That's very perceptive of you. Would you like to take some time off and go and work on a kibbutz for six months?'

Lucien smirked. 'So, tell me – what's so wonderful about Israel?'

Sophie described life there, trying to tempt him. A stint on a kibbutz might motivate him, as well as being a respectable reason for opting out.

'Sorry, Mum, it's not my scene.'

Thankful that he hadn't rushed out of the room and slammed the door, she continued. 'Lucien, I am concerned about what you're going to do. I know I've woken up a bit late, but I want to help now if I can.' Her voice was near to breaking. 'I know I've been preoccupied, but I'm worried about you.'

'Well, I'm pleased somebody is!' he responded.

'I'm sorry, Lucien. I didn't know Angelica would die so soon after we got back, and what with the funeral and everything else, I've been out a lot.'

'It's not just you. We hardly saw Dad when you were away. I don't even know if he slept here.' Lucien suddenly stopped himself telling Sophie about Marc. Maureen had been in the house while Sophie had been away, and Marc's implied reliance that he would say nothing had made him feel split and disloyal.

Even though Maureen had only spent the evening working with Marc in his study, seeing them together, it had been obvious. Hannah agreed with him: she too thought that Marc was having an affair with Maureen. Knowing his mother's naivety and wanting to protect her, Lucien changed the subject. 'Look, going to a kibbutz isn't such a bad idea. But I thought you would have preferred me to continue with my education,' he said ingenuously.

Sophie thought rapidly, careful not to make any suggestions. 'What I prefer isn't really the point. What really matters is what *you* want to do with your life, and you appear to be lost at the moment. I just want to help. If you need to take a year off, you know that Ernst will support you. But I thought that you might get something valuable from being away from home and living in another country. Marc would probably approve, if you were to choose a left-wing kibbutz. Maybe you need to get away from education for a while. You can always come back to it when you're ready. I know it won't be easy, because once you have a break from one thing, other things crop up. But you have a good mind. I don't need exam results to know that.'

Her last remark made Lucien look up, and she could feel him listening.

'Well, I never did a stroke of work for French. I couldn't go for maths because of that fascist teacher. I enjoyed art, but what can I do with that?' he said.

'Lucien, you're eighteen. There's no rush, particularly if you don't know what you want to do. The main thing is to go forward and not stagnate.'

'I'll think about it,' he said, indicating that the conversation was over. But he knew that if he stayed at home and didn't go to Israel, it would be because he didn't want to leave Sophie to find out about Marc on her own.

Sophie was heartened by the fact that Lucien had not stormed out of the room, and decided not to put any more pressure on him. 'What time does Hannah get home?' she asked, redirecting the conversation.

Lucien looked at his gold watch, a present from Ernst. This was the first time Sophie had seen it on him, and she recalled his excuse not to wear it, after Marc had made some disparaging remark about capitalist gold. 'About twenty minutes,' he said as he went to answer the phone. On returning, he explained, 'That was Dad; he won't be in till much later. Apparently, they're preparing a report for a conference in Holland, and he'll be working late every evening.' He felt her disappointment, and was furious with Marc, but said nothing more.

'Just when I'm taking an interest in cooking wholesome food,' Sophie said. 'I suppose he can eat when he gets in. I've hardly seen him in the last week. If he's going to be late tomorrow night, why don't we go out for dinner with Ernst?'

Hannah came in and put a bowl on the table. 'My first cold lemon soufflé and my last day of the course. I'm pleased it's over; it's too much like hard work. School is painless compared to a hot kitchen,' she said, uncovering the soufflé.

'That's amazing,' Lucien exclaimed.

'A soufflé is just what we need to complete our meal. It's a pity Marc isn't coming home,' Sophie said, oblivious to Lucien and Hannah's exchange of looks.

'Is there anything I can do to help? I could make a mushroom risotto. Shall I get a bottle of Marc's plonk and we can put some in the risotto and drink the rest?' suggested Hannah.

'Hannah, I didn't know you drank wine.' Sophie sounded worried.

'Oh, yes, I'm an incurable alcoholic, aren't I, Lucien? What have you done to us, Mum?' Hannah's eyes glazed over with tears. 'Really, after a month on a cordon bleu course, I can assure you that wine is a mega ingredient.'

They watched Sophie energetically putting dishes in the sink to distract herself. 'Who feels like some tea?' asked Lucien.

The next day, Sophie phoned Ernst. 'I need to see you,' she said desperately.

Ernst, assuming that she was going to tell him that her marriage was over, responded to the panic in her voice. 'I have to rearrange my meetings; I'll phone you back.'

She felt guilty about intruding on him but knew that if she compromised now, she would lose the impetus to help Lucien. Perhaps that was what she had missed when he was born. She knew that she could not advance her own life without Lucien also moving forward. Their passivity was somehow bound together, and it was up to her to effect a change; to become proactive, not reactive. For too long – from the beginning – she had left it to Marc to be involved with Lucien, and now it was up to her.

*

In the restaurant, Ernst looked put out. 'So, what's so important to call me away from a vital meeting?'

'I need your help with Lucien,' she said with new-found determination.

'I'm listening, but I suspect this is the easy part,' Ernst said.

'I'd like you to ask Jane if Lucien could have a small job in her gallery.'

Concealing his surprise, Ernst took his time to answer, making Sophie lose heart although only minutes ago she had been fired with enthusiasm.

'We have to do something practical, Ernst. We've done enough talking, and believe me, I've done enough thinking.'

She had touched a nerve. He had spent the past forty years ruminating, agonising over all his unfinished business in Prague. In some way Lucien represented Ernst's sin of omission, his failure. And now Sophie was asking that her child be rescued, just as he had rescued his own when he left Prague. It wasn't the least bit ludicrous that Sophie thought of Jane as family. After all, she had been his companion for twenty-five years. Jane had introduced Sophie to art, and now Sophie wanted her to do the same for Lucien. Forgetting the pressing problems at his office, Ernst answered. 'It's not a bad idea, except I can't imagine what he would do. He is completely unskilled. It's also important for him to feel that he is earning something, and I really don't see why Jane should give him charity.'

'Well, can't you arrange something with her?' Sophie was adamant.

'Like what?'

'Tell her you'll pay Lucien's salary – but, of course, he must never know. Look upon it as some sort of training.'

Ernst was surprised by Sophie's doggedness, even to the extent of concealing the truth. He sat in silence for a few minutes before answering. 'Well, I suppose he could dust pictures, make coffee, help hang new exhibitions… I just don't know. Let me speak to Jane. Of course, I would be responsible if Lucien did something diabolical.'

'Don't even think like that. We have to have confidence in him; I just know it's a good idea and you must agree. Thanks, Ernst, I feel so much better. I can't rely on Marc; he just doesn't see the problem.'

*

Sophie couldn't help but face the fact that she and Marc had drifted apart. Whilst there was no overt resentment, neither was there any real affection – just a slow adaptation with the mutual kindness needed for two people to live together in the same house. She recalled how different she had felt being with Avram; how even in their brief encounter she had felt his warmth. She had also felt closer to David. Either she had changed and wanted more from their relationship than Marc was capable of offering, or worse, he had simply lost interest in her. Perhaps they were both to blame. Marc wanted an easy life and she had always been undemanding, but now, after being with Avram and David, perhaps she was beginning to see men in a different light. She'd never sought male company, nor seemed to have need of it – why, then, was she suddenly feeling unsettled, wanting more than mere kindness? But she couldn't expect Marc to change. His life appeared bland, without ambition or complaint, and it appeared that working for the Local Authority for eighteen years had robbed him of his passion for architecture. She recalled meeting the slightly drunk chief planning officer at a Christmas party, who had accurately professed, 'The trouble with Marc is he suffers from too much integrity. He also has a power phobia.'

She had laughed heartily then, had thought it a compliment, but now realised that his reference might have described Marc's limitations. Why else had he only risen to second in command of the Planning Department? It wasn't surprising that he was the most popular member of the department, because he epitomised the soul of local government. He wasn't expected to do more than provide fireproof cladding schemes for crumbling concrete council blocks; plans that looked good on paper but, without money to back them, stayed there. He had found himself a comfortable niche doing research, with the widest brief which allowed him to work at home and visit parks, nurseries and libraries. His work had taken him to Sweden, Germany and France, and his slim volume on *Social Housing in the Inner City* had made him something of an expert. He appeared quite content going to the gym twice a week, to Labour Party meetings once or twice a week, and to the odd departmental meeting. He had slowly transformed the house, and found a comfortable slot in their marriage. He could do as he pleased as long as she didn't complain, and she had hardly done that.

Sophie now saw their marriage as a sham. Their sexual relationship was non-existent; nor could she remember when she had last felt stirred by him. It was as if a mist was clearing and she could see and understand more. While she wanted to confront Marc, she had to weigh her own needs against those of Lucien, who was settling into working at Jane's art gallery. It wasn't just that Marc was slipping away – for some time she'd had the nagging feeling that he was concealing something. Somewhere in the silence between them, she resolved to find the truth.

PART FIVE

PRAGUE

THIRTY-ONE

DOUBT

Sophie stared up at the slate-coloured sky. It wasn't just the thought of spending a week with Ernst that was unsettling. It was her old fear of the unknown. Ever since she had agreed to go to Prague, he seemed unable to resist various intimations. His characteristic maxim 'Timing is everything' now took on an air of appeasement, as if to forewarn some much-belated confession. 'It would be better to wait until we are in Prague, then you will understand,' he told her. His indirect references would be neatly woven into conversations without giving her an opportunity to respond.

She felt indebted to Jane, who unexpectedly had gained Lucien's admiration. Jane had told Ernst that Lucien was a natural at appreciating a painting. He never missed a day's work, and, in addition to hanging paintings, checking deliveries, dusting, and making coffee, was expanding his role. Sophie laughed when Ernst reported that on one occasion Jane had found Lucien discussing a painting with a prospective customer. His progress had encouraged Sophie to work for Ernst, and she was now spending three days a week reading manuscripts. Marc had encouraged her to go back to work, and Hannah had announced that she would also like to work in publishing.

Reluctantly, she examined the travel documents on her desk, and phoned Ernst. 'I've checked the tickets and everything is in order. The flight leaves Thursday at two, and we should be at Heathrow two hours before,' she said, doodling on the brochure.

'*Wunderbar!* If I had left the arrangements to my secretary, she would have got it wrong. That's why I wanted you to do everything; you understand.'

Sophie sighed. 'Really, Ernst, I think she would have managed.'

'I'll pick you up at ten; that will give us plenty of time for lunch. I can't believe it – another two days. I've been checking the weather for the past week and it seems the same as here. But you can't trust them, I know. Prague can be very cold, so take your warm coat and boots. It's forty years since I last walked on the Charles Bridge. Prague probably hasn't changed much, but I have. The architecture is the same – the Nazis spared the buildings, but I can't imagine what the communists have built. I hope they spared the Old Town. It's incomprehensible.' His voice broke. 'I will never understand it. And for what? All those good people; what was there to gain by murdering them? No one can understand. We must go and see. *You* must see, it's important now. Since last week, I've begun to dream in German. The mind plays many tricks. It's taken a long time, but sometimes it knows best what we are ready for.'

'Ernst, I've got to rush to an appointment.'

Ernst stopped. 'I'm sorry. I didn't mean to keep you. I'll pick you up on Thursday.'

Sophie felt bad about making such an obvious excuse, but was uncomfortable listening to Ernst. Moreover, her lingering disquiet had surfaced because of Marc's behaviour, which was alternating between excessive attentiveness and mild detachment.

She decided to talk to him while Lucien and Hannah were out. 'Marc, I know something is wrong, and it can't all be work,' she ventured, determined not to be sidetracked.

Marc was taken aback. He had relied on Sophie's obedience and naivety, and wondered whether she knew about Maureen. 'You're right. Maybe it's a midlife crisis. I have been feeling depressed for some time.'

'Is it work? After all, the family has never been more settled. I should have joined Ernst's firm years ago; I'm really enjoying it. Perhaps you need a change; you've been doing the same job for years. When I get back, let's have a family holiday. I'd like to go back to Israel. We could stay at a kibbutz guest house, and you would enjoy experiencing a socialist system at work.'

'Let's talk about it after Prague. I'm really sorry, Sophie.' He almost broke down.

She had never seen him like this before, and went to hug him. 'Try not to worry, you'll feel better in time. I know; I know what depression is like.'

'I don't want you to go to Prague worrying. I've been unsettled for some time and I've got to sort out my life in a radical way. I'm just not ready at the moment for a long talk.'

Marc felt that he'd at least paved the way to telling Sophie about Maureen, but her trust and caring amplified his guilt. Sophie, blaming herself for not talking to him earlier, decided that she really must stop ruminating and be more proactive. Nonetheless, she was struck by a lingering feeling that he hadn't been entirely honest.

*

She phoned David, knowing that the following day would be the first anniversary of Angelica's death. They arranged to meet at the Savoy, which had become a neutral place for them; it was as if the formality of the setting forced them to keep their feelings in check. Their luncheons were usually last-minute arrangements, giving credence to her reasons for not mentioning them to Marc or even talking about them with Emma.

That evening, Sophie phoned Emma. 'Do you know what tomorrow is?'

'How could I forget? Let's do something in the evening,' Emma suggested.

'Emma, I'm so rushed and I'm leaving in two days. I really have to spend time with Marc and the children.'

'I agree. Since starting college I haven't any time during the day. I feel so guilty about enjoying my course, and although the family don't complain, they must notice the fast-food service. But I'm sure Angelica would have supported our efforts, and probably would have branched out herself. In a way, our careers are a tribute to her.'

'Emma, you have a knack for finding logic in everything, which makes you most suited to studying law. I'll contact you as soon as I get back.'

Feeling anxious, Sophie went to the kitchen and found the remains of Hannah's apple strudel, which she wolfed down while waiting for the coffee to percolate. 'Making the best of things' was another of Ernst's maxims in which she sought comfort, and which propelled her to pack her suitcases. She would then be free for her luncheon with David the next day.

THIRTY-TWO

JOURNEY

As Sophie waited for Ernst to arrive, she looked out at a veil of mist suspended across a watery sky.

Lucien came into the kitchen, laughing. 'I think Ernst has finally flipped; he's arrived in a hearse.'

She opened the front door and saw a large black limousine with a driver dressed in a navy-blue uniform parked outside.

Ernst, radiating childish excitement, appeared to have reverted to his German accent, which he had spent years eradicating. 'It's *gut*, ha? I left in fear and now I'm returning without reservation.'

'And this is Day One; I've got another five to go,' she whispered to Lucien, who winked at her as the driver helped her into the back of the limousine.

'Say goodbye to Hannah for me,' Ernst shouted.

The autumn sun broke through the mist as the car moved smoothly up the hill. Sophie opened the window to feel the crisp air skim her cheeks. *I'll just have to make the best of it*, she thought.

'A nice day for travelling, ha?' Ernst said, then lowered his voice. 'Sophie, you coming on this trip means a lot to me. I would never have dreamt it possible; but then life is full of tricks. I want you to know your past, and I want to show it to you before it's too late.'

Sophie said, 'I understand,' and fell silent.

Later, driving through Knightsbridge, they passed Harrods. 'You know, the last time I was in Harrods was when Angelica took me shopping,' she said wistfully.

'Angelica had a very good influence on you. You seem to be taking much more interest in your appearance and wearing such elegant clothes.'

'I'm pleased you've noticed; David insisted that I have Angelica's clothes. I was very embarrassed at first, and refused, but he told me that if he was sure of anything, it was that there was no better way of fulfilling Angelica's wishes. And, in a way, it's helped me bear the loss. When I get dressed for work, I know that Angelica would approve of my appearance, and that makes me constantly mindful of her. She often encouraged me to work at the firm. It's odd that I only felt ready after she died and once Lucien had settled at Jane's gallery.'

'You have become much more independent since losing Angelica.' Ernst looked at his watch. 'There's plenty of time for lunch. I booked first class because I really want us to feel good.'

'The last time I went first class was to Jerusalem. It's quite wonderful. I think I could easily adapt to a life of privilege.'

'Maybe you inherited it. Your Grandfather Hoffmann held a high position in the Czechoslovakian Civil Service and enjoyed many privileges. Your Grandmother Hoffmann had remarkable taste. She was a devout Christian, you know, and of course she didn't like me being Jewish. But she wasn't going to lose her only child, and stuck by us to the end. We owe our lives to her. Of course, there are a lot of terrible memories to face, but we are going to have to find a way.' Ernst's voice trembled and he coughed, slowly and deliberately.

His attempts at breaking down the taboo of years didn't escape Sophie. 'What happened to them?' she tried to ask casually.

'I don't know. I hope we'll find out.'

Controlling her frustration, she decided to let him struggle to make amends for all the years of silence.

*

At the airport, after receiving their boarding cards, they went to the restaurant.

'Isn't it amazing?' said Sophie, reading the menu aloud. 'Cream of crab soup, fillet of sole with fennel, or roast duck or navarin of lamb with roasted vegetables. It's probably the last decent meal we'll get.'

'Since when have you become a gourmet?'

Sophie, stopping herself from telling him about her lunches with David at the Savoy, replied, 'We have all raised our standards since Hannah did her cordon bleu course.'

Ernst ordered a fine wine that enlisted the waiter's approval. 'Nothing is too good for us. It's important to know when to give oneself a treat. Life is too short, and by the time we find out, we have saved nothing, only wasted it by not living to the full.'

'When did you make this discovery?' Sophie asked with a hint of irony.

'Too late,' he answered.

The waiter placed an overdressed plate of food in front of her.

'It looks good, and whatever it tastes like, I won't complain. I can't imagine what communist Prague is like.'

'You're right. I think we should buy a few chocolates and biscuits to take with us, just in case,' Ernst suggested.

'It's a good idea, particularly chocolates; we can always give them away,' she said.

In the duty-free shop, they bought boxes of Swiss chocolates, tea, biscuits, and brandy. Finally, their flight was called. They walked slowly and silently down the long corridor towards their plane, knowing that something was about to happen that would change their lives.

*

Two and a half hours later, on arriving in Prague, they saw a man with a board displaying their name.

'So far so good,' Sophie remarked, following Ernst and the driver to the car.

Ernst noted that although the driver understood German, he insisted on speaking to them in Czech. As the car moved slowly through the traffic, Ernst withdrew into his memories.

Sophie looked out at the wide boulevards flanked with handsome buildings of different periods. Prague appeared like any other European city, except for the general neglect and drably dressed people pouring onto the streets in the early evening rush. Anxious and vigilant in unfamiliar surroundings, she saw the entrance to a tunnel ahead and shouted, 'Ernst, I don't want to go through a tunnel!'

Her panic alarmed Ernst, who, speaking to the driver in Czech, then translated to Sophie that it wasn't a tunnel, it was only an underpass, and there was no need to worry as they were a minute away from the hotel.

The car pulled up in Wenceslas Square outside their hotel. 'This is one of the few deluxe hotels in the city,' Ernst told her as they walked through the revolving door.

She looked at its dark, austere foyer and worn brown leather furniture. They were shown to their rooms on the same floor. Sophie felt uneasy at the sight of her shabby room with its faded carpet and high wooden bed, and was ill-prepared for the en-suite bathroom, with its lino floor; massive, stained bath; cracked tiles; large handbasin that almost overhung the toilet; and little space to unpack her toiletries. While she certainly did not want Marc to be here with her, she did wish that, after all his talk about the ideal socialist society, he could see the reality of a crumbling economy in a cheerless country.

At the entrance to the large, badly lit dining room, they waited to be seated. Sophie turned to Ernst. 'You'd think they would be pleased to see us, considering we are the only people here.' She looked at her watch. It was half past seven and she was quite hungry.

'People here don't eat until much later – even nine o'clock is early in Prague. It's amazing; nothing in this room has changed, except the staff, who used to be welcoming,' Ernst remarked.

After the watery soup with its lone dumpling not quite floating on the top, followed by a forty-minute wait for the main course, Sophie prepared herself for the thin, tasteless goulash with bits of stringy meat tinted with tomato puree. Seeing Ernst's excitement, she felt unable to complain. He insisted she try the apple strudel, which was surprisingly very good, despite taking half an hour to arrive.

'Tomorrow I'll take you to a wonderful coffee shop; you will love the cakes,' he assured her.

The next morning, Ernst couldn't wait to show Sophie the Prague of his youth. They walked down the hill away from Wenceslas Square, passing empty shops and a concrete box of a department store with poorly displayed windows of drab clothing and kitchen utensils. Sophie kept close to Ernst as he rushed along the narrow pavement to join the crowd waiting at the traffic lights. She watched him talking confidently in Czech to the man next to him. She did not feel his excitement or enthusiasm, only her own alienation from these ghostlike people who seemed as much out of place in communist Prague as she did. She looked back at Wenceslas Square – the skyline of steeples, the domes, and the dominating castle on top of the hill – then turned away from the cold wind and rushed to catch up with Ernst, who was already turning the corner.

He stopped suddenly – 'This is what I want you to see!' – pointing up to the clock on a medieval tower on a whole array of colourful mechanical figures appeared, rotated and disappeared.

Like an impatient child, he wanted to see everything at the same time. They walked around the Old Town Square, gazing at the delicate, pastel-coloured terraced buildings, graceful Renaissance structures, Baroque buildings, and seventeenth- and eighteenth-century houses, all surrounding the square as if waiting for the overture of a Mozart opera to strike up. Whilst she could appreciate the charm, her heart wasn't in it as she waited for some revelation.

'*Sehr schön, ha?*' ('Very beautiful, eh?') Ernst appeared to be addressing the buildings.

Standing in the narrow street listening to him, she felt the cold cut through her.

'This is the old Jewish Quarter. I'll show you Tante Hannah's house – Mutti's sister. When I got my scholarship to the Charles University, I stayed with Tante Hannah and Uncle Joseph for three years. Every day, I walked over the bridge and often stopped for coffee in one of the coffee houses. That's where I met Lotte, who was studying fine arts.' He feigned a cough to conceal that he was choking with emotion. 'They're all gone.' He wiped his eyes. 'Tante Hannah, Ziggy, Herbert, Leopold and Uncle Joseph. I learned publishing through helping Uncle Joseph in the evenings and in the short holidays. It helped pay my keep. In the long holidays I always went home to Pilsen.'

Sophie couldn't distinguish between the few facts she knew and Ernst's perceptions now. As they retraced his steps she too felt choked with emotion, although outwardly she remained passive, as she had always done. She waited for Ernst to talk, and avoided looking into his sad eyes. She followed him as he meandered along, seeming to resist the route the narrow street was leading them down.

'You see, it's just as I told you – the Germans never destroyed any of the buildings. Everything is just the same as it was.'

'Where exactly are we going?' she demanded, exhausted as much by the icy wind as by the uncertainty of what lay ahead.

'To the Hoffmanns'; your grandparents' home. Lotte and I used to walk across this bridge every day.'

Ernst's reminiscences were getting irksome, but Sophie remained quiet, believing it best for him to talk. The road inclined, then twisted into a small cobbled lane. She ambled along, taking in the theatrical setting of pastel-coloured, terraced eighteenth-century houses.

Then Ernst stopped abruptly outside a large, rather shabby house with a green front door, and announced, 'This is it.'

'Are they alive?' Sophie felt her heart beating.

'Who knows what's possible? I'm sorry, Sophie; believe me, I'm surprised by my stupidity. I've been a coward. There is so much… God knows why, at this moment in my life, I have come back. Perhaps I should have left it alone, buried it for good, but I couldn't. Something in me drove me back here. I've never given up hope.' Ernst trembled.

Sophie took his arm. 'Come on, Ernst, let's go and have that cup of coffee. I'm freezing and I also hate surprises. Let's go where we can talk.'

'I know just the place.' His voice was barely audible.

She followed him as he quickened his pace down cobbled streets with old gas lamps, passing open doors revealing vaulted ceilings and stone floors. The fairyland quality of their surroundings increased her mounting sense of unreality. Then he stopped outside a coffee house.

'This is where Lotte and I often went in the evenings,' he told her.

She pushed past him, letting him follow her. The scents of sweet pastry and coffee filled the warm, crowded cafe. Passing the marble counter with its plates piled high with pastries and croissants, Sophie turned to Ernst. 'This looks fine. I'm starving; I'll have one of those enormous croissants and a black coffee.'

They found a small table in the corner.

'Ernst, I'm sure it was right to come to Prague, but I can see that you are upset, so you'd better tell me what is bothering you. I want to understand what happened.'

He kept his head down. 'You are quite right: it's time enough. You deserve better,' he said, but didn't go on.

'I want to know about my mother; I want to know what happened to her.'

His silences used up large amounts of her energy as she waited for him to talk. She watched him fix his eyes on the table, and strained to listen to his taut voice.

'You must understand, they weren't normal times. There was not much time to think things through. I was young and inexperienced; a bit like you in a way. Probably your brother became more like a Hoffmann.'

The word 'brother' startled her, but she didn't interrupt him.

'You were eighteen months old when Lotte fell pregnant again. At first we were delighted, but attacks against the Jews here and in Germany were becoming routine and very serious. The Nazis took back the Sudetenland, and talk of war took the joy out of everything. Lotte's parents struggled to get over the fact that their only daughter had married a Jew. He was a senior civil servant and had some idea of what was going to happen. It seemed the safe option when he said that Lotte should stay with them in Prague to have the baby and I should take you to my parents in Pilsen. He promised to get us all the papers we'd need to go to England once Lotte had our baby. It appeared to be the best arrangement, especially as they'd eventually come round to accepting our marriage and genuinely wanted to help. You see, to be fair, it wasn't so straightforward for them. Attitudes towards Jews had changed, and Dr Hoffmann could not risk being caught up in the purges of conservatives and Jews.' Ernst paused. 'He needed all his influence to get us out of the country. We should be grateful.'

He began to look very tired, as if he had talked himself out, but Sophie had to know more. 'You said, "your brother". What do you mean?'

He looked away. 'To be honest, I really don't know; I've heard nothing, but I feel something. We must go back to the Hoffmanns' house. I'm ready. Let's go.'

*

Soon they were standing once again in front of the pale green door. 'Don't you think you should have phoned or written?' Sophie asked nervously.

'Yes, but when there is so much to say, it's impossible to know where to start. I know this is not the best way, but it's the only way I can go.'

Ernst lifted his hand to the brass knocker. Impatiently, Sophie grasped it, banged it three times, waited a moment and repeated. With excitement and fear she pressed her ear to the door as icy channels of wind pricked her face. A muffled clumping of footsteps and then the clicks of locks opening made her glance anxiously at Ernst, then step back to stand next to him. The door opened. A younger, slimmer edition of Ernst, dressed in faded corduroy trousers and a bulky beige hand-knitted sweater, sent a rush of heat through her as she experienced an instant connection. Accusingly, she looked at Ernst, who was silent and still.

For barely a second Oska looked hard at his father's face before taking the initiative. '*Wollen sie bitte herein kommen?*' ('Would you please come in?')

Sophie nudged Ernst, but his hesitation forced her to push past him into an ill-lit hall. She watched him as if in slow motion. He stepped inside, resistant but absorbing the shock. The large, sombre drawing room was just as he had left it forty years earlier. He slumped into one of the delicately carved wood-framed chairs; the maroon velvet, now shiny and worn, still retained some of its former elegance. A rush of painful memories induced a throbbing in his chest and a tightening of his throat as he relived the time the Hoffmanns had sat on the identical chairs opposite him, and their shock and anger when he had told them that he wanted to marry Lotte. He knew that they had brought her up to marry a fellow Christian of wealth, rank and reputation. The old house held so many unhappy memories, yet Oska's greeting seemed curiously appropriate, as if he had long rehearsed their meeting.

'The old folk have died,' he said, without Ernst's asking. 'I live here alone. Please excuse me!' Oska's voice faltered. 'I am very confused; I will be back in a moment.'

He left Sophie and Ernst to look round. Ernst recognised the old, intricately patterned beige wallpaper, barely visible beneath the large, gold-framed landscape paintings which gave the room a luxuriant feel. He studied the layers of delicately applied oil paint that captured the glistening light across the river. Each picture depicted evocative views from and of the Charles Bridge set against a dark sky. Ernst was struck by the absence of figures in a painting of Prague's mauve-and-beige cobbled streets winding between elegant houses, reminding him that Lotte's talent had been in portraiture. Sophie recognised the picture of the coffee house around the corner with its half-lit interior and bowls of red apples and wine bottles on the tables. She sat uncomfortably in the upright chair opposite Ernst, but avoided looking at him.

He was undeniably distressed but, she thought, deservedly so. How could he never have spoken of her mother, let alone told her that she had a brother?! Amongst the worn furnishings with their faint scent of furniture polish, she struggled to make sense of it all.

Oska returned with a bottle of wine and three elegant glasses on a silver tray, which he placed carefully on an inlaid mahogany table. His meticulous actions seemed out of place as Sophie, impatient to forgo formality, looked to Ernst, hoping he would take responsibility, but, covering his face with his handkerchief, all he could do was cry uncontrollably.

'You are alive. I knew it, but did nothing all these years, absolutely nothing. Forgive me! Please forgive me!' he stuttered. His face sagged into his double chin; his body spread, like a soft, lumpy cushion, into the armchair.

Sophie, caught up in a mixture of panic and anger, had to hold herself back from shouting at him to pull himself together.

Oska took control. 'This is very difficult… for all of us, I'm sure.'

Sophie snapped at Ernst. 'I think we should celebrate, considering I've just discovered that I have a brother.'

Ernst straightened. 'It's my fault; I should have tried to make contact. I could have; I do not know what prevented me. I do not know how… I should have… I should have… Oh, the shame of it all.'

'I also felt guilty,' Oska admitted.

'Why?' Ernst protested. 'You've done nothing wrong.'

'What the hell! Enough! It's not every day you meet your father and your sister after forty years. We just have to make the best of it.' Oska spoke with assurance, and then left the room and returned almost immediately. He handed Sophie a heavily embossed silver frame with a photo of a young woman dressed in a graduation gown.

Sophie studied her own image in her mother, then passed

it to Ernst, who took it with trembling hands, wiping the tears from his eyes. His face was almost purple, and veins pulsated on his forehead.

'I think you need a drink, Ernst,' Oska suggested.

'*Bitte*,' Ernst muttered.

Oska poured him some wine. 'I've been waiting all my life for you to turn up, so I am not entirely surprised. I would have tried to find you, but then there's all the political problems here. I suppose you wonder how I've managed to stay on in the house. Oupa saw to everything. He remained in government service until the end, you know. And the house has been protected from requisition. I don't know how they did it, but Oupa was a senior civil servant. They adapted to the times. Originally conservatives, they changed to appear to be supporters of the fascists, and then of the anti-fascists, and then the communists. That is what so many of us did. Can you blame us? For the past forty years we've lived in an unreal world without friends for anybody to promote or save themselves will say anything, true or false to the police. I've learned to lie low. I keep to myself. Communism has few friends outside the government and the security services. My grandparents were survivors. I suppose you realise I have their name. They saw to everything; all the papers. I even have a current passport and exit visa. The only truth for us is survival and a hope for better times. They mastered the art of using gaps in the system. So, I have remained here – as an artist working at home, I hardly come into contact with bureaucracy. Ouma and Oupa left everything to me, but there's a clause in their will which is relevant to Sophie, but that's for later.'

Sophie's mind, like a ship in a storm that has lost its anchors, spun with so many questions of how and why and when that spontaneously, hearing her name mentioned, she felt a part of herself revealed and a deepening new connection. Here, surrounded by what she realised was her brother's art, she felt in touch with the deeper meaning of the bold detail and sombre colours reflecting the sad realism of communist Prague. She looked straight at Oska. 'I'm impressed with your English considering your sheltered life.'

'I have my grandparents to thank for that.' Then, correcting himself, '*Our* grandparents. I had a private tutor. They thought they were preparing me for the diplomatic service. I also speak French, Russian and German, and earn a living as a translator. It has its advantages, but not for my profession,' he said, looking at his paintings. 'I've lived here all my life. Even during the war, we did not suffer many deprivations – material ones, I mean. We were lucky. But we were always frightened.'

'Frightened?' asked Sophie.

'Yes, very frightened that they would find out.'

'Find out what?' she asked, noticing a chink in his confidence.

'That my father is a Jew,' he said defensively. 'You must understand the times. It was not easy, and even today, there is enormous confusion. Nothing much has changed, whatever you may think.'

'But according to Jewish law, I'm not considered a Jew, and nor are you. You have to have a Jewish mother to be Jewish.'

'Fascists aren't too concerned about Jewish laws. They made their own,' Oska replied with gentle irony. 'I just wanted to explain that fear and suspicion don't die. I try to get on with my life as a painter. I'm fortunate; I can manage.'

'But why didn't you come to England as well?' Sophie asked, glaring at Ernst.

'Don't you know anything?' Oska looked at Ernst.

Ernst sat with his head down. A sudden longing for his own long-gone parents had brought on another flood of guilt. Then, as if his mind had slipped forward in time again, he looked up to see Oska. Ernst's heart fluttered like butterfly wings in his chest; the tension between his distress and his joy had drained the colour from his face.

'I think I'd better get you a vodka.' Oska left hastily.

'*Danke.*' Ernst didn't look up.

Sophie imagined living in this house, growing up with her brother and a family, but it all made no sense. Oska returned and handed Ernst the vodka. Holding the heavy cut glass in the palm of his hand set off a memory Ernst would never forget: forty years ago, the day he had left Prague with two-year-old Sophie, he had sat in the same chair. Dr Hoffmann had also offered him a vodka, then, touching him on the shoulder, said, 'These are hard times and we cannot know what lies ahead.' Neither could bring himself to say more, but Sophie had sensed that something was going on. Throwing herself on the floor in her very first tantrum, he could still hear her desperate screaming as he and the Hoffmanns stood there, none of them knowing how to comfort her or explain the enormity of their decision.

Now, as Ernst looked up at his children, feelings of deep gratitude washed over him. 'Oska, I've brought you some very good brandy from England.'

'That is most thoughtful; you couldn't have chosen a better present. I'll see what I can find for lunch. I don't think we should go out.'

Sophie followed Oska out of the room. She took her time walking through the long hall with its high ceilings and patterned tile floor, its narrowness emphasised by the enormous oil paintings that covered the walls. She admired scenes of the Vltava River glistening with streaks of orange against a dark sky, landscapes looking across the slate-coloured medieval Charles Bridge, and painted interiors in sombre black, terracotta, aubergine and dark green, relieved occasionally by crimson and yellow ochre blended sparingly to highlight perspective. Repeated scenes told her that Oska had not travelled far from his home. At the end of the hall she found the kitchen, realising that she had just passed a painting of it on the wall. And like the painting, it was impressive. A large black ceramic stove stood in the corner, old copper pots were stacked neatly on a tall iron pot holder, and above it, black iron frying pans hung from brass hooks. Against the opposite wall, fitting into the recess on either side of the stove, stood a rich brown mahogany cupboard with white china handles, displaying blue-and-white china behind its glass doors. In the centre of the room, a large mahogany table and eight chairs stood on the terracotta-tiled floor.

Oska was busy in a passageway on the other side of the alcove. Standing in front of an open fridge, the only noticeable modern appliance, he took out a blue bowl. 'Would pasta with tomato sauce be all right?' he asked, lifting a packet off the nearly empty shelf.

'That's much more than we expected.'

With his back to Sophie, Oska filled a pot with water.

'Honestly, before today, I didn't know anything about you or this house. All I knew was that I was two when my mother died and Ernst took me to England.'

'Do you know the cause of her death?' Oska asked, emptying the sauce into a pot.

'No, Ernst really never spoke about her and I was afraid to ask. I knew that she'd died and that her parents helped us, otherwise we would have died in one of the death camps with the rest of his family. He feels so guilty about his parents and sisters that only lately has he told me anything about them.'

'Well, I can understand guilt,' Oska said. He paused and then went on to say forcefully, 'You see, I was the cause of our mother's death.'

'What do you mean?'

'She had severe toxaemia and went into a coma. In those days, they didn't have the drugs they have today. I was born by caesarean and I'm lucky to be alive.'

Sophie shivered. 'That's extraordinary, and it explains a lot.'

'What does it explain?'

'I have two children. My first, Lucien, was a caesarean because I also had toxaemia. At the time, I couldn't understand why Ernst was in such a panic. Nor could I cope with his anxiety when I was pregnant with my daughter, Hannah. Ernst has always been overly involved with Lucien and I must say Lucien has given us quite a few headaches, but Ernst will see no wrong in him. It's quite a revelation. Tell me about yourself – have you always painted?' Sophie spoke freely, encouraged by Oska's warm smile.

'Yes, I graduated from the same college as my mother – *our* mother,' he corrected himself. 'It has been my way of coping.'

'I've seen landscapes and still life – do you ever paint portraits?'

'That's very perceptive of you. You see, when you have no memory – no visual memory – of your parents, it's difficult to paint portraits. It is for me, anyhow.'

Sophie felt ashamed. At least she'd had Ernst. Oska had had neither a mother nor a father. 'It makes sense. What were our grandparents like?'

Oska got out the china, talking rapidly as if accustomed to being on his own. 'They were typical upper-class Czechs; rather rigid, but growing up before the war in a democratic Czechoslovakia they survived under fascism and then communism only by being discreet and alert at all times, I suppose. Almost everybody here looks over their shoulder, and my presence wasn't so easy to explain.'

'What do you mean? They were entitled to have a grandchild, weren't they?'

Oska turned to look at Sophie, controlling his impatience at her naivety. 'Yes, of course, but if there had been any hint that my father was a Jew, they would have been sent to a camp. I remember my shock, years later, when I learnt that they had suicide pills ready.' He paused. 'You see, it was not only Jews who perished in the camps. Many Christians and democrats today have numbers tattooed on their arms and cannot remember why they were sent to Theresienstadt or how they managed to survive there. People are still suspicious. In fact, I think it must be a Czech disease that will always surface in some form or other. I can't imagine a life free from fear and suspicion. By the way, did you notice if anybody saw you come to the house? I just mention it because you both look so obviously like tourists in your elegant Western clothes.'

Sophie suddenly felt cold. She moved to the warm stove and looked at the bubbles forming on the surface of the boiling water. 'Is it really that bad or are you still deeply affected by our grandparents' fears?'

Oska threw her a reproachful glance before tipping some pasta into the pot. 'They took a very big risk helping you both to get out. I suppose, if our mother hadn't died, she and I would have gone to England and joined our father and you.'

Standing with her back to the stove, folding her arms as she gathered warmth, Sophie looked into the distance. 'It's so difficult for me to think of our mother or our grandparents' lives in Prague.'

Oska, mindful of her protected upbringing, tried to enlighten her. 'When our mother died, our grandparents registered me as a Hoffmann. Who you knew and who you were mattered. The Nazis were paper crazy. The communists today are no different. They kept and checked records on everybody and everything. I can assure you, I'm not imagining these things.'

Momentarily ashamed, Sophie walked towards the large arched window overlooking a small stone courtyard surrounded by high walls. She looked up to the pallid, cloudless sky; a weak sun cast pale shadows over the courtyard. A feeling of déjà vu swept over her, and she shuddered. 'I'm sorry, Oska, if I'm giving the wrong impression. It's just that I find everything so overwhelming, but I want to understand.'

Oska looked at her straight, narrow back. The light caught strands of her soft, springy hair, reminding him of Ouma, except that Sophie appeared fragile. 'I can't imagine what it's like living in a free world. I was born in Prague; Ernst, his family and you stayed in Pilsen because Prague was too dangerous for Jews. You probably don't remember, but you and Ernst stayed here for a day before you left for England. I was three weeks old and it wasn't practical for him to take me across Europe, and perhaps our grandparents needed me after losing their daughter. It was never meant to be forever, but that's what happened and we have to accept it. They did all they could for me, but always kept me at home. I had an excellent education with private tutors, but a very lonely childhood, and just when I've got used to it, you turn up.' He winked at her while continuing to stir the pot of tomato sauce. 'You'd better go and see whether Ernst is all right. Lunch will be ready in five minutes.'

A shiver went through her as if suppressing an archaic memory, as Oska set the table with the blue-and-white china.

In the drawing room, Ernst seemed engrossed in Oska's paintings. 'They're very good, especially if you know Prague,' he said proudly.

'Oska has made us lunch.' Noticing his swollen, red-rimmed eyes, Sophie watched Ernst slowly lift himself out of the chair. He appeared much older, smaller.

'He lives alone, ha? It's sad.'

'Aren't you being a little presumptuous?' she said, hurriedly gathering the empty wine glasses onto the silver tray. 'We hardly know anything about him. You can't assume anything; nor must we be intrusive.'

She returned to the kitchen, Ernst trailing behind her. The mahogany table with its rich patina set off the willow-tree china and silver cutlery, and antique wine goblets completed the elegant setting. She watched Oska toss green salad in a cut-glass bowl and place it on the table.

'I'm sorry the food doesn't quite match the tableware, but I thought we should celebrate our meeting and I've brought up a wonderful bottle of Liebfraumilch from the cellar.' Oska opened the wine. 'You are quite lucky to find me here; I spend a lot of my time in the country where I am preparing a series of landscapes.'

'For an exhibition?' Sophie asked.

'Perhaps one day, when it's the right time. I still keep a low profile, but I believe there will be changes in Czechoslovakia, and then I will be ready to exhibit. I've learned to be patient. I take a long-term view. Look how long I've waited for you to show up,' he said, smiling.

Ernst took another mouthful of pasta. 'You're a good cook. We can't get good food in our hotel. Everything takes so long to come up from the kitchen.'

'And even Ernst realises that it would be futile to complain. Besides, we have no right to,' Sophie said, feeling that Ernst had at last relaxed.

'Where are you staying?' asked Oska.

'Just across the river at the Grand Hotel,' Sophie answered.

'The loyalty is deserved, but you can't have everything.' Oska looked at Ernst.

'What's that supposed to mean?' Sophie asked.

'Oska is referring to the fact that, under the Nazis' policy of restricted areas, the Grand Hotel was one of only two hotels in Prague that accepted Jews,' Ernst explained.

'I'm sorry I can't ask you to stay here; it would attract too much attention,' Oska added hurriedly.

'Of course, we totally understand.' Sophie resigned herself to the frustration of not understanding the tensions in past or present Czechoslovakia.

Rocking a silver fork in the palm of his hand, Ernst reflected on its weight and familiarity. 'Good German, nineteenth century. I recognise it.'

'I'm sure you do. It belonged to your parents, and is now yours. As soon as your father knew that Czechoslovakia was about to fall, he packed all his valuables and sent them here, hoping that after the war he would get them back. Oupa and

Ouma hid them and told me that in the event of not finding you, they belonged to me. I knew that I would never sell such a tangible connection to my family, and I decided to use them, especially today.'

Ernst wept into his linen serviette. 'You should have seen the joy on my mother's face when she prepared for a family celebration. Everything had to be perfect. She would only use her hand-embroidered tablecloths. The maid would spend days cleaning all the silver and washing our best china and glass. Mutti prepared all the food for the Jewish festivals. She was famous for her apple strudel. What a wonderful woman, and they took her. For what?' He gripped his damp, crumpled serviette, unable to stop the flow of tears.

'Ernst, you can't go on torturing yourself,' Sophie said, touching his arm gently.

'You're right,' he mumbled, and sank into a haunting silence for the rest of the meal.

THIRTY-THREE

THE NECKLACE

'Why don't you and Ernst relax in the drawing room and I'll bring in some coffee?' Oska suggested, clearing the table.

Ernst stepped into the hall to look at Oska's painting of the Charles Bridge in the mist. The faceless crowd hunched in frozen postures seemed trapped in time and place. The landscape captured echoes of the despair that had preceded the collapse of his world. He shuddered, recalling the afternoon of the 15th March 1939 on his way home from university. The Charles Bridge had been crowded with people watching and a few cheering as the German tanks rolled into the city followed by the goose-stepping army. He turned to Sophie. 'He understands light, ha?' Then, retreating into his thoughts, he went and sat on his chair in the drawing room and wept.

He had almost drifted off to sleep when Oska returned, accompanied by the aroma of percolating coffee. Sophie saw a square black velvet box on the silver tray which Oska placed on the table, saying, 'Let Ernst sleep. Let's take our coffee upstairs; I want to show you something.'

She followed him up the worn, carpeted stairs onto the landing. Oska pulled out a long wooden pole hidden in the corner behind a door. Balancing against its weight, he hooked it into a latch on a trapdoor in the ceiling. With a slight tug, a ladder descended and unfolded down to the landing. The loft was much larger than she expected, filled with dusty shelves of books and brown cardboard boxes. Oska handed her a box. Her heart quickened when she recognised Ernst's handwriting. Hurriedly she took it, and the lid and a top layer of sepia-tinted photographs slid off, fanning out onto the floor. There was her parents' wedding photo. Sophie gazed in disbelief at a much younger Ernst with a full head of hair, thin and handsome, standing confidently next to Lotte, who wore a cream lace wedding gown with a scalloped ankle-length hem falling delicately above buckled satin shoes. The likeness was uncanny. She could have been looking at a picture of herself. After studying her mother's graceful features and her thick, wavy hair pulled into a chignon, Sophie turned the photograph over. On the back, in Ernst's handwriting, she read, 'Ernst and Lotte after their marriage. Prague, 1938.' Her arms felt like jelly and her chest heavy with anger. Why had Ernst withheld these crucial images from her? What had she done to deserve being deprived of any sense of who her mother was? How could he justify depriving her – no, *robbing* her – of the very source of her life?

She took out another photo and examined an unfamiliar couple. Turning it over, she read, 'Gertrude and Leopold Graff, Pilsen, 1938.' These were her elegantly dressed, gentle-eyed grandparents, standing proudly in front of a grand piano bearing a vase of flowers. Sophie saw Hannah's features in Ernst's mother, and recalled his phrase 'incomprehensible loss', as the images fell into place in her mind. His obsession with Hannah 'being an angel', like his mother, were not as fanciful as she had thought. She hadn't realised that she was holding her breath, and sighed as if expelling some entrenched obstacle. An imagined nostalgia swept over her as she studied an early photograph of her mother and her parents. Her Grandmother Hoffmann was wearing an embroidered blouse, half hidden by a three-quarter-length damask silk coat. Her wavy hair was pulled back into a chignon off her angular face, accentuating the serenity of her warm features. A beautiful necklace made up of small flower rosettes lay delicately around her long neck, the jewel setting discerned through the tinted sepia. The tall, erect man with a serious and commanding presence in his dark three-piece suit was her grandfather. The young girl standing in front of her self-assured parents was unmistakably Lotte, wearing an enchanting party dress with a high neckline. Her slim waist was accentuated by the fitted bodice, and a wide ribbon-sash gathering in the sinuous fabric encircled her buttoned shoes. Her long, wavy brown hair, parted in the middle, hung to her shoulders, and her enigmatic smile and contemplative gaze into the distance completed the ethereal image.

Oska had remained quiet, studying Sophie, suppressing an overwhelming desire to rush downstairs to grab paper and pencil to capture her poignant expression. Sophie picked out another photo from the pile. Neatly written in Ernst's handwriting on the back, she read, 'Lotte, with Sophie aged 15 months.' She stared at her mother holding a plump little girl. Her gentle face with its look of reverie gazing at her smiling baby was beyond Sophie's recall. She trembled with relief and sadness. The thought of that intimacy would have been a comfort to her during her years of deep loneliness. Tears burned her eyes. She wanted the relief of crying aloud, but her throat constricted. Seeing herself as a toddler opened up a wound that must have haunted her infant mind even before she'd had words to shape its meaning. She now associated her recurring feelings of loss and loneliness with that unspoken time. So often she had felt oppressed by the power of Ernst's silence and, not having the courage to question him, had colluded with it. Her anger mounted as she closed the box and gave it back to Oska.

'It's enough for one day. Let's go back to the drawing room; Ernst will wonder where we are,' he suggested.

Descending the ladder in silence, the images fresh in her mind, she felt an eerie sensation sweep over the surface of her skin.

In the lounge, Oska offered to make some fresh coffee, but, unsure of her feelings, Sophie didn't want to be left alone with Ernst. As they listened to his snoring, they drank the lukewarm coffee in silence.

Oska handed Sophie the black velvet box. 'I believe these were meant for you. Go on, open it,' he prompted.

She recognised the flowered necklace and matching earrings from the photo of her grandmother. She gasped. 'How beautiful – are they garnets or rubies?'

'Rubies set in gold – quite something, and they ought to look magnificent on you. Let me help you,' he said, securing the necklace around her neck. 'How you get them back to London is another question; one of many. But that's for later. We have so much to talk about.'

She picked up the inference but didn't know what to say. Admiring the necklace in the mirror above the marble mantelpiece, she saw her flushed neck and face in the fading afternoon light. Oska stretched out to switch on a Vaseline glass lamp, its gentle green light casting shadows across the room, triggering yet another feeling of déjà vu.

'I think we ought to get back to the hotel,' she urged, wanting to escape from what appeared to be a succession of overpowering feelings.

'Let Ernst sleep; I'm sure he will feel better for it,' suggested Oska.

She spoke openly. 'We've lived such different lives, yet I feel close to you. I can only think that I must have known of you and repressed the memory.'

Oska smiled. 'Perhaps it's because I've always known about you. Tell me about your life in London and your family.'

They chatted against the background of Ernst's snoring. It was dark outside when he finally woke up and shifted himself into an upright position. Sophie felt exhausted and asked if they could get a taxi back to the hotel as it had been quite a day and she wanted to phone her family.

'It's best not to phone from here,' Oska advised, helping Ernst out of the chair. 'And don't forget not to mention my existence; you never know who's listening, especially to calls abroad. You can get a taxi near the bridge; just turn right and walk about a hundred metres. Come on, Ernst, let's get you back.' He helped Ernst on with his coat and went to open the bolted front door. 'Can we meet tomorrow?'

Ernst nodded, then hugged him.

'Here?' asked Sophie, yawning, her eyes smarting in the cold.

'I want to take you out to my country cottage; I have some important papers to show you.' He kissed Sophie on each cheek and gave Ernst a bear hug, saying, 'We'll talk tomorrow.'

*

They walked uphill against a tunnel of icy wind and arrived at the taxi rank. Sophie squashed beside Ernst in the back of the small, shabby Škoda. 'Do you remember the limousine?' she said, wanting to shake him out of his brooding retreat, but he remained unresponsive. She looked out the window at the crowds huddled at the traffic lights.

The journey to the hotel took less than fifteen minutes. After an uncomfortable silence, Ernst spoke. 'I'm so sorry, Sophie. I feel so ashamed, but I'm so happy to have found Oska. All these years I thought about him every day. I was scared he would reject me, and instead he made us so welcome. The Hoffmanns did a good job raising him. I owe it to them. They were fine people.'

He walked slowly into the hotel, following Sophie, who went ahead to get their room keys. The concierge handed her a note that read, 'Hannah phoned.' She walked with Ernst to his room and, opening the door for him, gave him a peck on the cheek.

'I think you should order room service and get into bed. I'll see you in the morning.'

In her room, she flopped onto the bed and picked up the old-fashioned telephone. It seemed ages before the operator connected her to London.

Hannah answered. 'Hello, Mum, how are you getting on with Ernst?'

'Everything is good, and most interesting. What's happening at home?' Sophie was relieved to have it confirmed that Lucien was still happily working in Jane's gallery. 'Is Marc at home?' she asked.

'Dad's hardly here, as usual; he's supposedly at the office,' Hannah said evasively, then rapidly changed the subject. It was clear she was covering up for Marc, and Sophie did not take it further.

'I'll phone tomorrow. Love to Lucien.'

She replaced the heavy mouthpiece. Despite the signs coming from all directions, not least from Lucien and Hannah, she was sure that if Marc was involved with another woman, he would have told her.

THIRTY-FOUR

SHOCK

Hoping for a hot bath, Sophie summoned up the courage to face the large tub with its corroded taps discharging a dribble of brownish water. Surmising that it would take at least twenty minutes before the modest flow provided a reasonable soak, and probably an hour for room service, she ordered a plate of sandwiches, apple strudel, and a pot of tea. Communist Prague filled her with humility. She had thought Oska's home dowdy, almost shabby, but now saw its faded display as a monument to his survival. Warning herself about making hasty judgements, she recalled how wrong she had been in her first impressions of Emma and Angelica. *Timing is everything.* Ernst's maxim was rooted in a truth that no amount of silence could disguise. For him and for her, the past had never passed and had been always present.

In the bath, half filled with murky water, she thought of Oska's life, which hadn't made him bitter, and compared it, in spite of Ernst's love and dedication, with her own lack of confidence. The sensation of warmth when Oska fastened her necklace had echoed her feelings when she saw the photo of herself as a baby with her mother. Perhaps in some primitive way she had retained that memory. Her tears fell as the water got cold. She got out of the bath, wrapping herself in the thin towels, before hurriedly putting on her nightdress and dressing gown and climbing into bed, hoping that the food, which she needed more for comfort than to sate hunger, would arrive soon.

*

It seemed like the middle of the night when she heard a persistent ring and, answering the phone, identified Oska's voice. 'Good morning. I've obviously woken you; I'm sorry.'

'What's the time?'

'It's 8.30. I was hoping to meet around ten, but if you are both too tired, we can make it later.'

'No, we must meet, thanks for waking me.' She noted the formality in Oska's tone and, acknowledging his veiled caution, added, 'Where?'

Aware of the probable tapping of foreigners' phone calls, she simply said, 'We'll be there.'

When Ernst didn't answer the phone she asked the operator for help, and was alarmed to be told that there was no answer. Fearing the worst, she rushed along the corridor and, seeing the untouched breakfast tray outside his room, gestured to a maid delivering breakfasts to open his door with her master key. They found Ernst in a deep sleep, breathing heavily. After some prodding and shouting, he stirred.

'*Ja*, what's wrong?' he mumbled.

'What do you mean, "what's wrong?"? I've been phoning you and banging on the door. I thought you were ill,' Sophie cried in relief and annoyance. 'It's quarter to nine, and we're meeting Oska at ten.'

'I couldn't sleep, so I took another two tablets early this morning.' Ernst propped himself up against the pillows.

'I know you had a shock yesterday, but you have to be careful. You can't just take sleeping tablets.'

'Believe me, with what's on my mind, I need a general anaesthetic. Give me some black coffee, please.'

'The coffee is ice cold. We'd better get ready,' Sophie demanded.

'Please order some more; I can't go without first drinking a hot cup of coffee,' he pleaded.

'Give me some dollars!' Sophie replied, aware of the maid standing next to the cold breakfast tray.

Ernst retrieved his wallet from under his pillow and handed it to her. She extracted a five-dollar bill and handed it to the maid.

'Would you get us a large pot of black coffee, and some rolls and cheese?'

The maid looked around, then furtively took the dollars and nodded. Noting Sophie's uncharacteristic resourcefulness, Ernst remarked, 'Five dollars is a lot of money here; she'll get the wrong idea. Let's see if she brings the coffee. When are we meeting Oska?' he asked, as though it was the most natural thing in the world.

'At ten. I know where to go, and you can sit in the foyer until I get back.' She didn't know what to make of his relaxed behaviour, and noticed that the tension appeared to have left his face. It was as if Ernst had reverted to a time before tragedy had struck.

'I must ask him to recommend a decent coffee house.' Ernst chattered as if Oska had always been an integral part of their lives.

Back in her room, she looked out the window at a leaden sky that reminded her of the bone-chilling wind. She dressed in layers of cashmere, and put on her coat with its padded lining, a silk scarf, and fur-lined boots. Wearing Angelica's clothes reminded her of her friend's certainty of predestination, which contrasted with hern own uncertainty and insecurity.

*

She left Ernst in the dingy foyer reading a Czech newspaper and walked towards the monument. Oska appeared next to her in a dark brown three-piece corduroy suit.

'You're very punctual,' she said, reviving their connection.

'Of course,' he replied, implying that good manners were beyond question. 'It's impossible to park near, so let's go to the car and then you will know where to bring Ernst. How is he?'

'Actually, he seems remarkably well, considering,' Sophie said, keeping up with Oska's purposeful stride, which appeared to give him the height and confidence that Ernst lacked.

Oska laughed. 'I was really worried about him yesterday. He was so shocked, and also at a disadvantage. On balance, I knew more than he did.' Then, in a hushed tone, he went on, 'I'm not saying I knew for certain that I would meet both of you, but I was sure you were both alive, and the possibility was always with me. Throughout my childhood Oupa and Ouma spoke about Ernst and you, reassuring me that we would meet again, but that I must wait for the right time. So, I have always held this moment in my mind. When you see the papers, you will understand. I want to take you to our country cottage where we can talk freely. Tell me, when do you intend leaving Prague?'

They arrived at his car. 'On Friday.'

'Good, then we have time, but I will have to move fast.'

'What do you mean?' she asked, realising that she had missed something.

'I want to get out of Czechoslovakia.' Oska watched for her reaction, but Sophie waited, as she had always done, for more information. 'By Friday!' Unable to imagine the depth of his decision, she perceived it as impulsive. 'It's easier to do it quickly and casually.' He looked for her approval.

'But how do you intend to do it?' she asked.

'Leave it to me. My main concern is that you and Ernst accept me in London.'

'Of course, there is no doubt.'

'I want to believe that, but it would be wrong to take anything for granted. After all, I know very little of your personal circumstances.'

'I hadn't realised the urgency. Of course we want to help, but what can we do?' She wanted Oska to come to London; it would be wonderful for Lucien, and he'd also help heal her loss of Angelica.

Pushed back by a flurry of wind, she heard Oska say, 'Ernst will be waiting, you'd better go. Will he manage the walk?'

'I think he'll probably be blown here,' she said light-heartedly.

Oska ran after her. 'I would appreciate it if you would speak to Ernst about my idea. I can't take his response for granted; nor do we want him to have any more shocks.'

*

Ernst was sitting comfortably on one of the faded leather armchairs. He seemed to have lost the ten years he had aged yesterday, and smiled when he saw her. 'Back so soon. Did you find him?'

'He's just round the corner; we'd better go.'

Ernst got up quickly. 'I feel so much better, as though a big weight has lifted off my shoulders.' He followed Sophie through the revolving doors and out into the cold street.

'You should know that Oska is hoping to leave Prague,' she told him.

'Well, he likes the countryside and it must be quite depressing living in that mausoleum.'

'No, I mean he wants to leave Czechoslovakia. He wants to come to London,' explained Sophie.

'*Wunderbar!* I know it's very sudden, but it's strange how things work out, ha? I've waited so long for this moment and now that it's happening, I have no emotions left for it.'

'Are you sure?'

He walked briskly, trying to catch up with her. Oska gave Ernst a bear hug, which brought tears to his eyes, then helped him into the front seat of the car and opened the back door for Sophie. The pristine ten-year-old Škoda started up with a rumble, chugged around the back of the hotel and slipped into the one-way system leading out of the city. As they passed the Smetana Theatre, Ernst announced, 'Oska, we must take Sophie to the opera. I remember how Lotte and I used to stand waiting for cheap tickets. We were so busy discussing politics that we never noticed the cold. You can't imagine the liveliness before the war, and now the fascists and the communists have robbed Prague of its past.'

The old car left the city and joined the motorway. Sophie watched the passing scenery, half listening to Ernst talking continuously about Lotte, finding it confusing after being conditioned to accept his silences.

'We're driving about two hours north.' Oska had something of Ernst's impulsive quality in his voice. 'You must understand I take nothing for granted – even though we're family, we hardly know each other – but your arrival has created an opportunity. I have for a long time wanted to leave, particularly with Oupa and Ouma gone. I no longer have their protection and see nothing but difficulties ahead. I must get out of Czechoslovakia.'

Ernst interjected, 'Please, Oska, there's no question of us not helping you. Just tell us what you want us to do.'

'Your response means a lot to me. My passport needs renewing soon and then I will have to apply to various bureaucrats who may not give me a new one.'

Sophie gazed at the passing fields with their sparsely scattered houses, wondering who lived in them. She couldn't see any evidence of agriculture; just empty valleys between the hills. Oska and Ernst talked away in Czech, without realising that they were alienating her.

As if reading her thoughts, Oska turned to her. 'Are you all right, Sophie?'

'Just thinking.' She welcomed his attention.

'Ernst and I were filling in the gaps. We're almost at our cottage.'

The car turned off the main road, slowing down to negotiate a sandy road that twisted, then sank below the level of the land on both sides of the rocky landscape. Oska, manoeuvring the car, avoided the potholes on the narrow path descending alongside an ever-rising cliff face. Unnerved by the sides of the ravine closing in on her, Sophie turned to look for the road, which had disappeared behind a bend in the valley.

Seeing her discomfort in the rear-view mirror, Oska said, 'Don't worry; I can go through this ravine with my eyes closed. We're quite safe. The cottage is in the valley by the river. It's a wonderful spot, and until you see it, you can't appreciate it.'

'Appreciate what?!' Sophie blurted, as she felt her throat tighten. She ripped off her silk scarf. Gasping for air, she realised that the car had stopped. 'Where are we going and how much longer will we be in this ravine?'

Neither of the men realised the extent of her agitation. Oska talked casually. 'This is as far as we go by car, and now we have to walk. It isn't too difficult; the path winds but it's quite flat. It's impassable in the winter when the water gushes down the ravine. The cottage is purposely secluded and quite difficult to find. In fact, Oupa and Ouma discovered the entrance to the valley by chance. They built the cottage at the bottom as a secret getaway. During the war they had to live very discreetly. They learned to live with the Germans, then briefly with the Social Democrats, and finally with the communists. They lived a double life and the summer cottage was part of our survival.'

Reluctantly, Sophie followed. The cold wind didn't diminish the heat that ran through her veins. Beads of perspiration settled on her upper lip. Her panic worsened upon hearing their voices echo in the narrowing ravine. 'Please, Oska, I must get out now! I can't go on!'

'It is about another thirty metres, that's all.'

His reassurance didn't calm her. 'Can't you be more specific? When I say I want details, I mean precisely that – not "abouts" and "almosts",' she screamed.

Ernst spoke in Czech to Oska, which infuriated her.

'What the hell are you saying?'

Oska, shocked by her clammy grey pallor, held her hand, guiding her through the narrowest part of the ravine. Breathing in short gasps, she screamed again, 'I have to get out of here, Oska!'

When she saw the bulging rock face just above her head, she collapsed. Oska held her under the armpits, dragging her backwards along the narrowest part of the gorge. Reaching a wider area, he lifted her up, carrying her sideways with her head resting against his chest. Moving fast, occasionally balancing himself against the rock face, he panted, 'Don't worry, Sophie, in one minute we'll be in a wide open space. You're quite safe; I know this area well. Please believe me, I had no idea that this would be such an ordeal for you.'

With her eyes shut tight, Sophie pleaded, 'Please, Oska, take me out.'

'You'll be out in thirty seconds; look up and you'll see the sky. We're here.'

Sophie took in gulps of fresh air. On the plain she saw a stone cottage. 'How the hell am I going to get out of here? I'm not going through that ravine again; there must be another way out,' she protested.

'We will face that one later. If we'd all walked at a normal pace, we could have been through the ravine in three minutes.'

Ernst caught up with them. 'Sophie, what's wrong? Are you ill?'

'No! I just don't appreciate being shunted along on some mystery tour, negotiating dead ends and ravines. You know I'm claustrophobic, and you and Oska went on talking in Czech as though I didn't exist. You expected me to fit in as always. Didn't you?'

Ernst looked guilty and remained silent.

'Sophie, I'm so sorry. I won't be a minute; I'm going to get the picnic basket. Will you be all right?' Oska asked contritely.

'As if you care,' she mumbled, looking at Ernst, who appeared more engrossed in the small stone cottage standing in the middle of a small, flat plain scattered with lavender bushes and chestnut trees. She felt abandoned.

Oska hadn't envisaged this setback, and was worried, knowing what they had to confront at the cottage. 'Sophie, you need a hot drink. Honestly, the ravine is no more than thirty metres; the twists and turns make it seem much longer.'

Angry, Sophie walked ahead towards the cottage. 'I know it's a little late, but after forty years I'm entitled to an explanation. I can't take any more surprises.'

Oska reverted to formality. 'I must apologise for causing you such discomfort. I will most certainly tell you everything. The cottage belonged to our grandparents.'

'Does anybody else know about this place?' Ernst asked.

'I don't think so; it was Oupa's greatest secret. There's only one way in and out, and we've never noticed any disturbance.'

'You mean I have to go back through the ravine again?!' Sophie exclaimed.

'Really, Sophie, it's quite straightforward. The narrowest part of the ravine is only two metres, and now that you know about it, you could walk through in three seconds. You'll see why it's worth it,' Oska pleaded.

Sophie looked accusingly at Ernst.

'During the war the cottage was the perfect hideout,' Oska continued anxiously. 'There are important papers hidden there; that's why I brought you here. I've been coming here since I was a child; I know all the surrounding hills and caves. I promise you there's nothing to worry about.'

He opened the wooden door set in the rock walls tucked behind a large chestnut tree. Light and air flooded into the enclosed space, which smelled slightly of turpentine and oil paint. Ernst and Sophie followed him into a the central room with three areas leading off it. Sophie walked towards the bright kitchen. Light came from Oska's studio beyond. The pine kitchen contained a small ceramic wood-burning stove in the corner, and a fridge and cooker connected to a large gas cylinder.

'This is truly remarkable,' Ernst enthused.

'This is what I have been trying to tell you. It is not possible to explain it; you just have to experience it for yourself. Come into the sitting room – we all need a hot drink, and I have some fresh rolls.'

The charming sitting room with its small settee and two armchairs, scattered with cushions embroidered in petit point with flowers in reds, russets, mauves and greens, added to the intimacy.

'Ouma embroidered the cushion covers. They came down most weekends in the summer and relaxed with their hobbies. Oupa had great fun building the cottage.'

'It's remarkable,' Ernst repeated, looking out of the square window onto lavender and hawthorn.

Her panic receding, Sophie felt ashamed of her previous behaviour. She sat silently admiring a wooden chest with five drawers and the delicate initials 'E. H.' carved on the top. Oska returned, and placed the basket on top of the chest.

'Oupa made the chest using dried wood from the local chestnut tree. It doesn't have one nail in it.' He poured the coffee.

It all sounds too simple, too idyllic, Sophie thought.

'I knew nothing of this; I never credited Hoffmann with such imagination,' Ernst said, relishing his ham roll.

Oska seized the moment to tell them, 'Oupa risked his life time and time again.'

'What do you mean?' Ernst asked.

'He lived a double life. As a senior civil servant he had access to special information. He had to make finely balanced judgements between helping others and destroying his and Ouma's life. He knew that he was in danger of being discovered, and then it wouldn't only be him and Ouma who would be tortured and killed; others in the Resistance would be too. He lived with his secrets and only told me about them after he retired.'

'I can't believe it; I always thought he was an anti-Semite. A Jewish son-in-law was no asset in those times, and that's why I felt he was pleased to be rid of Sophie and me.' Ernst's stomach turned over. How could he forgive himself for being so wrong?

Oska looked at his father and saw his face full of remorse. 'He even fooled you. He had enormous discipline and integrity. Believe me, he worked hard. You remember I mentioned that only a few people knew about this place? They were working together with Oupa. They hid many Jews in caves and places like this in the mountains.'

'I can't believe I've been so wrong. It was such a frightening time; no one knew who to trust.'

'Until Oupa died, he lived in the shadow of betrayal, disgrace, imprisonment, torture and execution. Whether it was the Nazis' suspicion and surveillance of the Czech civil servants or the purging by the communists, many of whom had served the Nazis, it was all the same. This cottage is a monument to Oupa's survival in the system. Ernst, believe me, I have lived my life under a cloud of secrecy and deceit.'

'Oska, I truly regret never really knowing Dr Hoffmann, and I certainly never imagined him carrying out these heroic acts. I have wronged him all these years.'

Oska looked at Sophie, who, although listening, didn't appear to be affected. He felt determined to involve her. 'You must know, in 1939 when the Germans invaded Czechoslovakia there were 350,000 Czech Jews. Six years later there were fifty thousand. Then in 1948 the communists took over, and by 1951 there were sixteen thousand Jews living in Czechoslovakia. There might be three thousand in Prague today, most of them elderly, but only a few hundred can be identified. The Czech secret police usually stand outside the synagogue, and Jews are afraid to communicate with any relatives in the West. There are many Jews from mixed marriages, and many who are dedicated party members and now high officials. In Prague the Nazis created a museum of Jewish artefacts, and it contains many objects and books and papers of a people they wanted to make extinct. Oupa managed to get some papers, which I want to show you.' Oska turned about nervously, then said, 'Wait a minute; I must get something.'

He rushed out of the room, returning hastily with a silver box embossed with coloured enamel birds and flowers. Sophie watched expectantly as he gently placed it on the seat beside her, and turned the key.

THIRTY-FIVE

THE SILVER BOX

She was aware of his apprehension as he shuffled through the pile of papers, then handed her a document which she vaguely recognised as a passport with a photo of him as a young man. All she could make out was his name, Oska Hoffmann, and his place and year of birth, Prague 1941. 'I don't understand,' she said, passing it to Ernst.

'I'm showing you my 1968 passport so you can see that leaving Prague and going to London isn't a new idea for me. It's important that you believe that I'm not impulsive. In 1968, I was twenty-seven. Individual freedom had been lost under communism, and my art could be seen as sentimental. Oupa wanted me to leave Czechoslovakia, and managed to arrange a visa for me to England. All I need is for you to vouch for me.'

'Oska, this is truly wonderful news!'

Oska knew that Ernst's joy would soon vanish when he handed him another envelope. 'I know this will shock you, but it's important for you to have these,' he said, half looking away.

Ernst looked at the official brown envelope stamped 'Theresienstadt and Auschwitz'. Slowly taking out the various documents, he became aware of their significance. He went pale when he saw the photo of his mother in a short overall, with cropped hair and a skeletal face, captioned, *'Nahmen: Graff Gertrude. Geboren: 6.6.1889. Ort: Pilsen, Bohemia.'* He waved the papers at Oska, weeping, shouting, accusing. 'Why do you give me this? What does this mean? How did you get these documents? What was Hoffmann up to?'

Oska looked annoyed, and in a trembling voice replied, 'After all I've told you, how dare you even think that Oupa was guilty of something? It's absurd. They got them for you and Sophie at considerable risk to themselves. They wanted proof so that your family would not go unnoticed, and so that you would have some form of identification for your ownership of their property. That was their intention. And now you behave as though I'm the villain, not a victim. Perhaps my survival implicates me, but then so do yours and Sophie's. We're all survivors.'

Oska's stern expression and bright red face made Ernst sit up and wipe his eyes contritely. 'You're right,' he said. 'I didn't think; I apologise. I just can't bear to think of Mutti like that. I am truly sorry. You can see how the Nazis made even good people bad. How can we ever recover from such a thing?'

Still visibly upset, Oska tried to redress the balance. 'It's understandable that when so many Jews were betrayed by their lifelong friends and neighbours, there'd be nobody to fight for you. But believe me, Oupa and Ouma were more my father and mother to me than grandparents.' He interrupted himself and left the room, saying, 'I'll get us a drink.'

'I need some fresh air,' Sophie said, and found her way round the side of the cottage to the garden and sat on a wooden bench sheltered by a stone wall with the warmth of the sun on her face, reflecting that it was perhaps on a day like this that her paternal grandparents had walked into the gas chamber. Gripped by a constellation of anger, shame and confusion, she found herself shaking. How could the Nazis have murdered innocent people? It was like having a terrible nightmare, only to wake up and find out that it was real.

She looked at the chestnut tree and the lavender bushes, and heard footsteps as Oska came to sit next to her. 'I've given Ernst a drink and left him to go through all the papers. Sophie, we're both damaged, but this is truly traumatic for him,' he said, wanting to draw her into a conversation. 'I know I can't remember life before, when I didn't have a sister.'

'Yes, I feel the same. It is strange how I instantly felt comfortable with you.'

'Ouma never got over the loss of our mother, and I don't think she ever realised how guilty she made me feel, as if I was responsible for her death. But being with you, even for this short time, has made me aware of how much I miss her.'

'Have you ever been married? I ask only because you seem so ready to leave Prague,' she enquired.

'That's very astute of you. I'm recently separated after a very long relationship, so there's little to keep me in Prague. I'm still very fond of her but it was too complicated. I felt disloyal to Ouma and Oupa; they would never have approved of me marrying a German. We think we are open-minded, but when it comes down to it, our prejudices or our parents' prejudices take over. Love is not enough when you've lived through so much injustice. Helga and I separated two months ago, so I'll have to see how I get on. I think we should keep this to ourselves,' Oska said.

'Don't worry about Ernst. I think he feels so guilty that all he wants to do is make everything right. His expectations for happiness must be very different to ours.'

They heard Ernst's heavy footsteps on the stone path, and Oska stood up. 'I'll go and pack some things.'

Ernst dropped his full weight onto the bench and sighed. 'It's like a kaleidoscope.'

'What is?' asked Sophie.

'It's like somebody has come along and shaken up all the pieces of my life, and a new pattern should have settled in front of me, but I can't see it. I just feel very confused, guilty and frightened.'

Sophie remained silent.

'I know it's been very hard for you, Sophie, but believe me, I know now that it doesn't do any good to deny your past. I have tried for forty years and it has all come back like an explosion, only it's inside me.'

'Ernst, you should have told me about Oska and my grandparents long before yesterday. Why didn't you?'

'Sophie, I've spent your whole life protecting you. I wanted you to have a fresh start in London and not to have to bear the debris of my fractured life.' Tears trickled down his cheeks which, when he saw Oska coming towards them holding a roll of drawings, he quickly wiped away.

'I'll have to come back and fetch some more things.' Then, sensing that something had happened between them, Oska looked cautiously at Sophie. 'Are you absolutely sure about me coming to London?' he asked.

'Absolutely. My only concern is getting you out of here; all this talk of secret police has unnerved me. Although, to tell the truth, I'm more worried about going back through the ravine.' She managed a half-smile.

'I promise it will be fine.' Oska gently put his hand on her shoulder.

'Oska, I want to pay my respects and visit Theresienstadt. Can you arrange it?' Ernst asked.

Oska responded with the caution he had learned from his grandparents. 'I have contacts and will arrange it, but I can't join you. It would be dangerous to be seen with you, especially at Theresienstadt.' He looked at Sophie sitting with her arms folded, her grim expression telling them that they should let her be. 'Sophie, you'll manage. I'll help you through the ravine. But I have a few things to carry, so we must go.'

Sophie did not look at Oska or Ernst. Slowly and reluctantly, she stood up and saw three large packages propped against the wall by the front door.

'I'll carry the paintings; Ernst, could you carry the silver box with the documents? Sophie, can you manage Ouma's knitted blanket and the embroidered cushion covers? I know that she would have wanted you to have them.' Slipping his arm through hers, Oska spoke calmly. 'I'm going to take you through the ravine very quickly, then come back to fetch Ernst and all the parcels.'

They arrived at the rock and she turned to look at the open space. Her legs felt heavy, as if walking through wet cement. Trying to distract herself, she thought of being at home with Lucien and Hannah, but her claustrophobia pushed through doggedly. She would be trapped in the ravine like Angelica in her coffin in the crematorium. Her face broke out in perspiration.

Oska took her wet hand and said, 'Listen to every word I say and don't think of anything. It will take less than two minutes. Keep holding my hand and look down at your feet.'

Her heart thumped in her chest and perspiration covered her face as she surrendered to his will.

'Just up here; now another five metres. Look at the ground, don't trip. Now we turn the corner; we are coming to the narrowest part.'

When she heard the word 'narrowest' she wanted to scream. If only he hadn't said that word.

Oska could hardly hold on to her slippery palm as he pulled her along. Raising his voice, he said, 'You're doing fine. Another few seconds – keep looking at your feet and watch the rocks. Good, we are almost at the end. Another ten steps. Walk faster, good – there you are, we are in a wider part. Now another twenty steps and we will be at the car.'

Drained but safe, she said, 'Thank you, Oska; go get Ernst.'

He kissed her on the cheek and rushed off. She looked across the rocky landscape and green hills stretching as far as she could see. There wasn't a person or a car in sight; the emptiness of the place made her shiver. Pulling up the collar of her coat, she took in deep breaths of cold air. Her sense of isolation lasted a few minutes before she heard voices and saw Ernst and Oska coming towards her.

'Sophie, you must sit in the front,' Ernst said, also kissing her on the cheek.

*

The car gathered speed along the motorway.

'Oska, I could do with a good cup of coffee and some real strudel,' Ernst suggested, thinking of Sophie's sweet tooth.

'I know just the place; the pastries are the best in the world.'

'Really, Oska, you've hardly been out of Prague,' rejoined Sophie.

They came off the motorway and caught up with the city traffic.

'I can't believe we're here; it appears to have taken half the time to get back,' she said.

'It depends which way you go. The anxious route is never-ending,' teased Oska.

'You're right. I've never been like that before, and I don't ever want to have another anxiety attack,' she said with a hint of apology.

'It was very severe; perhaps you should see a doctor when we get back to London,' Ernst suggested.

'I don't think any doctor could magically wipe away our past,' she replied.

Perceiving it as an accusation, Ernst simply said, 'You're so right, Sophie.'

Another silence ensued. Oska parked the car and they

followed him round the corner to the coffee shop. 'I promised you the best pastries in the world and I'll let Sophie be the judge,' he said.

The inviting interior with its Bohemian glass chandelier belonged to a bygone era. They sat in a corner on a velvet-covered bench by a small marble table. 'Now, let's relax and enjoy,' Oska said, regaining his composure. 'I have a lot to arrange before Friday.'

'Is there anything I can do?' Ernst asked.

Oska's mind raced ahead. 'If you know someone who could send me a telegram inviting me to give an exhibition in London, it would make my trip look genuine. I also want to take some paintings with me. I know it's short notice, but I've only just thought of it.'

'We're in luck; I know just the person.' Ernst thought of Jane. 'Leave it to me.'

'Oska, I think you're right; these are the best pastries I've ever tasted,' Sophie admitted.

Back at the hotel, Oska parked the car around the corner. 'I'll phone you tomorrow morning about getting to Theresienstadt.' He got out of the car, opened the door for Sophie and helped Ernst out.

In the hotel, the concierge handed Sophie a message from Hannah.

'Is everything all right at home?' asked Ernst.

'I hope so. Hannah phoned. Should we have dinner in the dining room later? I don't think I could stand room service and I'm too tired to go out,' she suggested.

'That's a good idea; I'll book a table for eight o'clock.'

In her room, Sophie took off her coat and boots, flopped onto the bed, and picked up the heavy telephone mouthpiece to call Hannah.

'Hello, Mum, how are things in Prague?' Hannah sounded too bubbly, as if she were hiding something.

'Fine – well, not exactly.'

Her remark had just slipped out, but Hannah caught the inference. 'What do you mean, "not exactly"? Is Ernst being difficult? What's going on?' she urged.

Sophie couldn't lie. 'Darling, there's nothing wrong; it's just that coming back to Prague has stirred up a lot for Ernst. We'll be home in three days and then we can have a long chat. How is everything?'

'Fine. Lucien is in his room; he doesn't seem to go out much.'

'I would like to talk to him,' Sophie insisted, sensing Hannah's evasion.

When she attempted to engage Lucien, his voice seemed lifeless. 'So much has happened in Prague! We'll have a proper chat when I come home.'

'You mean you've decided to go for a divorce?' Lucien blurted out.

'Darling, I really don't know what you're talking about. I was referring to finding out about my mother's family, which has caused me to rethink a lot of things. It has also affected Ernst. Please don't worry about Marc and me.'

'Whatever you say,' Lucien mumbled.

'Lucien, we all have to try and make the best of things.'

'Whatever.'

Despair descended. Her first thought was to get back to London. Lucien had left her in no doubt that something fundamental hung in the balance. What had Marc been saying? What was this about a divorce? She had been so intimidated by Lucien's tiresome anger that she had failed to see how insightful he could be. Clearly something had happened to make him feel so low. She wondered if he was still working with Jane. Unable to face another two days in Prague without knowing, she phoned again.

'Hannah, I must talk to Marc, where is he?'

Hannah was taken aback by Sophie's tone. 'I wish I knew; some conference or other.' She wondered what Lucien had told their mother.

'Well, tell him to phone me. I'm worried about Lucien. I'll phone tomorrow. Goodbye.'

Sophie considered her stupidity. It was wrong to take out her frustration on Hannah. It wasn't up to Hannah to confront Marc. She needed to speak to Ernst. Lying in the bath, she thought of how her father had always been so devoted to her. Perhaps he hadn't chosen to hide the facts; perhaps he had suffered a mental block, a reaction to extreme trauma of the kind she'd read about. Once dressed, she examined herself in the mirror approvingly, confident in Angelica's elegant clothes. She phoned Ernst to tell him she was going downstairs.

In the bar, she felt people looking at her and realised that she was probably wearing the equivalent of an annual Czech salary on her back. The evening was pleasant enough. Neither she nor Ernst mentioned the deeper issues.

'To think we've been waiting for over an hour for this minute portion of chicken,' said Sophie. 'I think I'll just order three helpings of apple strudel.'

Ernst smiled in agreement. 'Perhaps if you hadn't got so dressed up we might have received better service, but I don't believe they deliberately didn't rinse the rice.'

It was midnight when Sophie got into bed. She wanted to go home. Something was definitely wrong; it had been obvious from Lucien's voice. Then, needing a distraction, her mind shifted from Oska to Marc until she fell asleep.

*

Her jumbled dream disappeared when she heard the phone ring. 'Good morning; I'm sorry about yesterday. I hope you're feeling better today,' said Oska.

'Much better, thank you.' She was thankful that she had got through another night.

'I have some good news. Can we meet in about an hour? If you turn right as you come out of the hotel and walk about thirty metres, there's a cafe with glass doors etched with roses. I'll wait for you inside.'

'We'll be there,' she said decisively. *At least the morning is accounted for*, she thought, willing each hour to pass.

THIRTY-SIX

LEAVING PRAGUE

They pushed through the crowded coffee shop to find Oska sitting in the far corner.

'It's a nice place,' Sophie said.

'Now it's all right,' replied Ernst, dropping his voice.

'What do you mean?' asked Sophie.

Ernst spoke as if slowly releasing steam from a pressure cooker. 'I often used to come here with Lotte and our friends. Then when the Germans occupied Prague, they banned Jews from most coffee shops and other public places. Then things got worse.'

'But how did we get out?' asked Sophie, committed to knowing.

Ernst looked over his shoulder and Oska leaned towards him. 'I have only heard my grandparents' version, so I would also like to know what happened.'

Ernst put down his cup of coffee, then bent over the table and spoke faintly. 'You must understand what was going on in

Europe at that time. The Germans were gaining strength by the hour. After they seized Prague in 1939, they went on to occupy most of Europe. Of course, Jews were trying to get out, but there was a four-year waiting list and a visa quota. We were only allowed to go shopping for food at eleven o'clock in the morning and again at three o'clock in the afternoon. You can imagine the queues. Of course, there was the black market and some Czechs made fortunes as families like ours stripped their homes in exchange for food. The restrictions affected every aspect of life. As we adapted to them, they got worse, and we were confined to smaller and smaller areas. Our telephones were disconnected, unless you were a doctor, a lawyer or a midwife. At the time I was working in Uncle Joseph's publishing house and living in an apartment with Lotte. Sophie was two years old.' He looked at her affectionately, patting her hand. 'Lotte was six months pregnant with you, Oska.' He wiped his eyes, swallowed, was silent for a moment and then took a mouthful of coffee. 'Do you want me to go on?'

'Yes,' said Sophie, riveted to each word.

'Well, there were lots of discussions with the Hoffmanns and they decided that Lotte should live with them until our baby was born and Sophie and I should go to Pilsen to be with my parents and wait for our visas. Dr Hoffmann promised to get visas for my whole family. Then things happened very quickly. Lotte developed toxaemia and went into premature labour. Oska was born by caesarean, but we lost Lotte.' Ernst stopped, his chest heaving.

'How devastating!' exclaimed Sophie.

'I was a broken man and in no position to think. The Hoffmanns grieved and agonised over the best solution. They convinced me that it was too dangerous to travel with a new and sickly baby, and that they could look after Oska. As soon as our visa came through, I left Pilsen and came to Prague with Sophie. We stayed with them and saw Oska for the first time, but we couldn't go out of the house, even into the back garden, in case we were seen. I was heartbroken, knowing that we had to leave him.'

'But how did we get out?' asked Sophie.

'The Hoffmanns got us papers through his contacts in Slovakia, which still had a treaty with England even after the Germans had split Czechoslovakia. I posed as a German businessman travelling to Paris, which was also occupied. From there we got into Switzerland, and then on to England. By the time we reached London, Jews were being rounded up, and I am quite sure Dr Hoffmann was unable to help my family.' Ernst wiped the tears from his eyes and addressed Oska. 'According to the documents you showed me, my entire family was deported to Theresienstadt in July and sent on to Auschwitz in October 1942. I feel so ashamed. I spent so much energy hiding the truth, and for what?'

Sophie spoke clearly and sadly. 'Perhaps you tried too hard to protect me, but I wasn't really spared. Your pain hovered over us like a dark cloud. Perhaps you can understand how your silence has made a lie out of much of my life. If I had known what had happened, I could have helped you. I don't know how, but I would have done something.'

'Who knows, perhaps I was protecting myself as well,' said Ernst, as if resolving something.

Oska gave Sophie a warning look. 'Really, Sophie, you can't say that you have lived a lie. As long as you behave honestly in the situation you find yourself in, you can do no more. There comes a point when we have to stop blaming each other, or politics, or the weather – otherwise, why not go back to Adam and Eve? We each have to take responsibility for our actions, and I think Ernst is trying to do that. The least you can do is acknowledge his effort and consider that his life hasn't been much fun either.' Oska paused, worrying that he had gone too far, before adding, 'Perhaps we have all had enough.'

Ernst watched Sophie peering into her empty coffee cup. 'You're right,' she said. 'It's time to say enough is enough.'

'Sophie, would you like to go to the opera tonight?' Oska offered.

She looked up. 'That would be wonderful. I'd really like to do something normal.'

'I'll get tickets and see you outside the Opera House at seven. It's my favourite Mozart, *Così fan tutte*; a diabolical libretto and music straight from heaven. Now I really must go.' Then he asked, as if in an afterthought, 'Do you think you ought to go to Theresienstadt tomorrow? I have arranged for a friend to take you to Pilsen as well. I only have another day to get everything ready.' Oska got up from the table.

'I don't want to, but I think Ernst does,' Sophie replied.

'Perhaps you're right; it's been too much. There will be another time,' Ernst replied.

'Why not walk around the Old Town? There's a lot to see, then you could go to the castle.'

*

It was a ten-minute walk to Maiselova Street. Underfoot, the damp leaves added to Sophie's discomfort. They passed an empty delicatessen with nothing but a bunch of garlic in the window. Further on, a crystal shop appeared promising with its window display of decorative wine glasses and dinner services.

'Let's have a look,' Sophie suggested, wanting to get out of the cold.

Inside, she strained to see the empty shelves in the dim light, and was disheartened when the assistant told them that they were waiting for stock. 'It's not as though I wanted to buy anything, but how can they entice people into their shop and then brazenly tell us there isn't anything to buy?' Sophie asked.

'That poor woman probably gets paid the same even if she doesn't sell a glass all week. You must understand that under communism there is little incentive to be a charming shop assistant,' Ernst said.

'I don't think I could live under communism. No wonder Oska can't wait to get out.'

'Forty years ago, the shops were full. Let's try the jeweller around the corner.' Ernst quickened his pace, determined to give Sophie some pleasure.

'I can't afford jewellery,' she protested, walking against the wind.

'I thought you wanted some Bohemian glass. They do some lovely earrings, brooches and necklaces in glass; really beautiful colours. I would also like to buy Hannah something.'

'That's a wonderful idea. What can I get Lucien?' she said, regaining interest.

They found the shop with the delicate Bohemian glass jewellery. 'This looks just the thing. I hope they've got stock,' Sophie said, eyeing a small flowered brooch in the window.

In the warmth of the partly stocked shop, she found a garnet-flowered ring for Hannah, and Ernst insisted on buying the matching earrings. With the pleasure of a frivolous activity, she found a small brooch for Emma, and deliberately bought nothing for Marc. Ernst, too, didn't mention him. She put the precious packages into her shoulder bag, determined to find something for Lucien. Then she spotted an art shop. 'Let's try in there; they must have something for him.' She walked briskly towards it, followed by Ernst.

'Surely you can get better art materials in London?'

'I'm sure, but I must get something that interests him; perhaps I can find something unusual.' Sophie quickened her pace as if the shop might suddenly close.

'Who knows, maybe Oska could help him?'

'I've already thought of that,' she replied.

The austere shop was immediately disappointing, but Sophie scoured each sparsely filled metal shelf tenaciously. 'This is perfect,' she said, picking up a canvas shoulder bag. 'Lucien will enjoy the fact that from the outside it looks like an ordinary bag, and that it will acquire a patina of shoddiness. And nobody would know it's an art bag, so he can continue to hide his talent.'

Ernst smiled. 'We mustn't be too cynical, Sophie. I know he's difficult, but he'll come right.' He filled every one of the bag's pockets with pastel crayons, drawing pencils, charcoal, tubes of paint, and brushes, then, weighed down by his bulging purchases, insisted on carrying the shoulder bag himself.

'We'd better be very low-key about this one, or I think he'll feel threatened,' Sophie warned him as they ambled along.

'Nonsense,' said Ernst convincingly. 'You are too frightened of the boy; leave him to me.'

'Maybe you're right. But he'll soon be nineteen and I just wish he'd get on.'

'Life is full of surprises, Sophie. We can but try, and we must never give up hope.' As usual, Ernst's words seemed to have a way of implying much more than he'd said.

'I haven't. I have moments when I think Lucien will spontaneously blossom, but he sounded really down when I spoke to him last night. I desperately want to go home, and I don't know how I'll get through another two days.'

'I know it has been too much for you. It seems like we've been here for a very long time. Let's try and relax. You mustn't go back to the children in a state of exhaustion. If you like, we can walk to the clock tower; I know a charming coffee house where we can get some fresh croissants.'

The coffee house was pleasant-looking and full of lively conversation. Ernst stuffed the art bag between his feet, and looked around. 'By the look of the crowd, it will be a long wait for service.'

'I'm pleased we're not going out of Prague again,' she told Ernst, who assumed she was referring to their cancelled trip to Theresienstadt.

'I agree; one can only take so much. How are you going to explain Oska to the children?' he asked to change the subject.

'Well, if we've learned anything from our experience, it's that it's always best to tell things the way they are, instead of waiting, hiding, and disguising the facts. By not telling the truth, one is in fact telling lies.' She paused. 'And talking about hiding, I'm worried about my marriage.'

'Is it another woman?'

'Why do you say that?'

Not wanting to upset Sophie, Ernst remained impassive. 'Last year, when you were in Jerusalem, I phoned to ask Hannah out for lunch and a woman answered. She told me that Hannah had spent the night at a friend's and would be back later. So, I wondered what was going on.'

'What?!' Sophie's face registered shock and fury. Oblivious to the people at the next table looking at them, she persisted. 'What are you saying – that you and everybody else have known something and once again decided to protect me, as you put it?'

Ernst tried to calm her. 'Dearest, don't you think that you have also been aware of something for a long time, but tried to deny it? It's perfectly understandable. I know; I've done it all these years.'

She paused, releasing a sigh. 'I suppose you're right, but what hurts me is how much the children know, and that everybody has been so afraid of telling me. It also explains the change in Lucien's behaviour. Would you now tell me everything you know, please?'

'I think the children know something is going on, because when you were in Jerusalem, I asked Hannah if there was a new cleaning lady in the house. She seemed a little hesitant, then told me she was Marc's colleague from work and they were doing some special research at home.'

'It's probably been going on for some time but Marc hasn't had the decency to tell me. That's Marc: so worried about my feelings that he can't face me.'

'Darling, if it's got to be, end it agreeably for the sake of the children. You know I will help you all I can.'

'I suppose I must have known for some time but kept quiet, thinking it would right itself.' Then she added, 'I think Oska might be a light relief; a distraction for the children.'

Ernst looked at her caringly, placing his hand on her arm. 'Sophie, you are still young, and if I may say so, you are looking very good since Angelica took you in hand. I am sure things will work out for you. One thing at a time, *ja*?'

Near to tears, she replied, 'You know, what I really find upsetting is the effect it's having on Lucien. I can't believe that Marc thinks too deeply about his actions. He has always been very kind, but I can't say I understand him.'

A silence fell between them. Then Ernst spoke tenderly. 'In time you might; sometimes our actions precede our thoughts and we catch up later, but believe me, nobody gets away with anything.'

'Honestly, Ernst, I don't think I've taken it in; it feels quite surreal. At the moment I don't feel up to going to a museum. What about an art gallery, or a walk in a park?'

'I absolutely agree, and I'll take you to both places.'

Sophie had never seen Ernst so calm. The warmth of his concern felt like a protecting shield against Marc's betrayal.

*

In the gallery, she stood mesmerised in front of a painting by Vermeer: a woman in blue, standing alone reading a letter in a room filled with filtered silvery light. The power and beauty in the woman's contemplative expression moved Sophie to tears. In the late autumn sun, they strolled through the park, and sat on a bench, silently watching the last of the brown, red and yellow leaves float to the ground. She tried to imagine a future without Marc.

In the evening, they went to a production of *Così fan tutte* at the Opera House. Ironically, the story of faithlessness, deception and retribution, accompanied by heavenly music, appeared somehow to settle her emotions. Sophie felt more hurt than shocked by Marc's dishonesty. Ernst warned her not to upset Lucien and Hannah.

With the prospect of going home the following day, Sophie found that time, which had stood still, suddenly moved on again. She dressed hurriedly for dinner. Oska had chosen a small restaurant in the Old Town that was popular with tourists, and had arranged for Ernst to book the table in order to preserve his own anonymity. When they were seated at a corner table, Sophie said, 'I can't believe we're off tomorrow. I think I'll need one of your sleeping tablets tonight, Ernst.'

'You don't want to start that. I can tell you that since we've found Oska, I sleep like a baby. But I mustn't tempt fate. We still have to get through tomorrow.'

They didn't notice Oska until he sat down beside them. 'I've thought of every contingency plan, so that we will have the best chance of success,' he whispered nervously.

'I am sure everything will be all right,' Ernst encouraged his son.

'What could go wrong?' Sophie asked, but Oska chose not to answer her and instead told them his plan.

'I'm confident that my passport, exit visa, paintings and return ticket should get me out of Czechoslovakia. But I'm not sure of being allowed into England. You may have to vouch for me.'

'Should we meet at the airport?' asked Sophie, deeply concerned that the success of the venture was far from certain.

'I think it would be wise for us to have no contact until we are on the other side of passport control in London,' said Oska.

Ernst, aware that Sophie was becoming unsettled, intervened rapidly. 'Let's order, otherwise we won't get out of here until tomorrow.'

'Well, let me see what I can recommend,' said Oska, reading the menu.

'I'll have anything except fish, meat or vegetables,' Sophie quipped.

Oska looked at her affectionately. 'I'm sure we can oblige; after all, this is communist Prague.'

Ernst chuckled heartily.

*

The following morning, as they went through passport control, Sophie barely managed to avoid looking at Oska, who was standing in the other queue. Ernst, contriving to look at ease, scrutinised a newspaper. At last, the flight was called. Sophie and Ernst, with their first-class tickets, walked ahead, conscious of Oska behind them. When the aircraft door closed, Sophie couldn't resist turning around to look for him, and was alarmed to find that he was directly behind her. Oska pretended to read a newspaper and managed to project such a sense of alienation that Sophie became suspicious of his intentions.

He continued to ignore them when they arrived at Heathrow and walked ahead to passport control. Ernst and Sophie waited anxiously. 'Do you think he'll get through?' she asked as they tried to spot Oska.

'He inspires confidence, and his papers are in order. This isn't Nazi Germany, and we're not in the middle of a war,' Ernst said.

Sophie watched Oska present his papers, talk to the officer and then casually walk through. Still avoiding them, he looked around and went on to baggage collection. They followed him into the arrivals lounge. Still aloof, he positioned himself behind them as if indicating to them to walk ahead. Ernst found his driver, who took his and Sophie's luggage, but Oska carried his, still keeping his distance while following them to the car. Ernst got in first, followed by Sophie, and Oska sat next to her with an air of disinterest. Only when they went into the tunnel did he spontaneously hug her.

'Thank you! I can't believe it; after all these years I feel safe.'

PART SIX

LONDON

THIRTY-SEVEN

AT HOME

The last vestiges of her mistrust subsided, and Sophie prodded Oska playfully, feeling close to him again. 'Don't worry about the tunnel, Oska, we'll be out in a few hours,' she teased.

Oska laughed, but Ernst seemed subdued. 'Oska, I have been wondering how to explain your arrival to Lucien and Hannah.'

Sophie giggled. 'Perhaps I could tell them you escaped through a tunnel.'

'Not really, I was a caesarean; I suppose that's why I'm not claustrophobic.'

They both dissolved into raucous laughter.

'It's truly remarkable that we've all come through this ordeal.' Ernst sounded flat.

Sophia gave Oska a cautionary nudge, aware that Ernst disapproved of her behaviour.

They settled into watching the passing scenes as the car joined the motorway. Oska talked as if thinking aloud. 'The tones are much softer, the greens bluer. The grey sky has an illusive quality; I don't think it's going to be easy to paint. I'm used to a much darker palette. Perhaps Prague isn't as sombre as I painted it, but it shows how the eyes are influenced by emotion.'

Sophie responded to his contemplative mood. 'It must be enriching to be constantly in touch with colour and light. Most of us just walk around half blind, seeing only fleeting images.'

'Well, we all do our own thing at the price of something else,' he replied.

Wedged between Ernst and Oska, Sophie could feel their warmth and a sense of belonging. For the first time, she felt proud of her family's past. It wasn't enough just to be a survivor; her family had lost their lives, and she therefore had an obligation to make something better of hers. She thought of Emma. Previously she had regarded her pragmatism as unfeeling, but now she saw the sense in it. Her words rang in her ears: 'Darling, I just get on with things. It's a simple choice: either you look at the good things in life and say to yourself, *I want them*, or you always find bad, and believe me, there's plenty of it about.' In the final analysis, Emma had triumphed. Her priorities were in a different order, but everything was on the list. She had repaired the rift between her and Alan, and proved that she could think as well as act. Sophie had no doubt that Emma would be a successful lawyer.

It was two o'clock when they arrived at Ernst's flat. Sophie kissed Ernst and Oska goodbye, promising to phone later. Back in the limousine, she inhaled the familiar damp air, pleased to be home and determined to deal with Marc.

A strong smell of bleach greeted her in an oddly empty hall without the usual array of bags, books and coats draped over the oak chair. The black-and-white tiled floor looked too clean. Then, seeing the kitchen door closed, she guessed that Lucien and Hannah were up to something; surely they knew by now that she disliked surprises? She opened the door gingerly and, seeing the kitchen table set with her antique cups, a platter of sandwiches and a home-made cake decorated with 'Welcome Home', waited.

Lucien and Hannah came out from behind the kitchen door, hugging and kissing her in turn, lightening her mood. 'I thought you'd all left home, the house is so clean,' Sophie said, and noticed Hannah glance at Lucien. 'It's a wonderful surprise, thank you.'

Talking compulsively while making the tea, Hannah asked, 'Tell us about Prague, did you have a good time? Your phone calls sounded bizarre, as though you were being overheard by the secret police.'

'Actually, you're not far wrong.' Sophie laughed.

'Tell us about it. How was Ernst stomping about on his old territory?'

Hannah's obvious attempt to keep the conversation going, combined with there having been no sign or mention of Marc, compelled Sophie to ask, 'First, tell me what's been happening here?'

'Dad's left; he couldn't even wait until you got home,' Lucien interjected.

Hannah panicked. 'It's not his fault! It's that Maureen. I told him he must wait and talk to you, but she insisted that he move to her flat before you came back. It was really awful, Mum, seeing him pack up his study with Maureen standing over him. She even asked Lucien to help carry some boxes downstairs.'

'I never helped!' Lucien shouted, watching Sophie.

'What are you saying?' Sophie was distressed, almost in tears, but she remembered Ernst's warning. Numbed and outraged, she heard her own voice, from which she felt disconnected. 'I'm mortified that Marc left it to both of you to tell me. It's not your responsibility. The sooner I find out what's going on the better. This is the first I've heard of this Maureen. How long have you both known? How dare Marc bring her to our home behind my back? I credited him with more sensitivity.'

'I've met her a few times, but I genuinely thought she was a work colleague,' Hannah protested.

In a voice devoid of emotion, Sophie said quietly, 'None of this is your fault, Hannah.' Inside, she felt a murderous rage towards Marc.

The phone rang and she went to answer it. 'I'm sorry I had to do it this way, but I think it's the only way I could have left. Can we meet? You say when.' Marc's naive candour disarmed her.

'I've just walked in. Phone me tomorrow morning.' She spoke quietly, and put the phone down. It all appeared unreal. She could do no more than push events aside and hope they'd go away. 'I really want a large piece of that wonderful cake,' she said.

Hannah rushed to cut it, amazed by Sophie's self-control, assuming that her tea party idea had worked.

'It's delicious,' said Sophie, taking a mouthful.

'Flour, grated carrot, lemon and honey, and cream cheese to decorate,' Hannah gushed.

'You must keep some for Ernst. He would really appreciate it,' said Sophie, then thought of Oska.

'No chance.' Lucien helped himself to a second piece.

Nothing could have prepared her for this abandonment. Ernst's hints, and even her instinct that all was not well, hadn't lessened the shock. Somewhere in the distance she could hear Hannah say, 'Now tell us about Prague.'

'Do you want the abridged version? Actually, I think I will have to tell it as it happened, then you will understand. But I must have another piece of cake and a cup of Earl Grey.' Forcing herself to remain calm, she reflected that she was still in her home with her children. Ernst would come round, and now she also had Oska. She enthralled Hannah and Lucien with her experiences in Prague.

'It's unbelievable!' gasped Hannah.

'Good old Ernst. It's bloody wonderful – is he a good painter? When can we meet him?' Lucien demanded.

Their unexpected enthusiasm was comforting. 'I thought you would be as shocked as I was. Ernst will be pleased you've both taken it so well.'

'I'll phone him and congratulate him. By the way, David phoned and asked you to contact him as soon as you get back,' Lucien told her.

'Is anything wrong? I'd better phone now.' Sophie got up from the table.

David's secretary told her that he was at home, which added to her sense of urgency. Sophie was surprised when he answered the phone. 'David, I've just come home, is anything wrong?' she asked nervously.

'No, nothing wrong, just a surprise. Did you have a good time?'

'I'll tell you all about it, but please tell me first, what's your surprise?'

'I know you've just come in, but I'm having a dinner party tonight and I really want you to come,' David pleaded.

She hesitated, feeling a mixture of shame and relief.

'I know you must be tired, but Avram is here from Israel and he wants to see you again. He's leaving tomorrow.'

Sophie took a deep breath – 'I'll phone you later; I can't think now' – and went to finish her tea.

'What's happened to David?' Hannah asked.

'Nothing, it's just that Avram Levi, the Israeli doctor, is in London, and David expects me to leave my family on my first night home and go to a dinner party.'

'Go,' urged Hannah. 'It will do you good, and anyway, it's later this evening.'

'I'll drive you there,' Lucien offered, 'and I can pop into Ernst's and meet my new uncle.'

'Well, I don't know whether that's such a good idea, but we could invite them for dinner tomorrow night,' Sophie suggested, feeling compelled to respond to their efforts.

'Terrific, I'll cook,' said Hannah eagerly.

Moved by their generous concern, it occurred to Sophie that they too must be suffering. Perhaps they even felt guilty for not making Marc stay. Thankfully, she hadn't made a scene when he'd phoned. 'Are you sure it's a good idea, me going out on my first night home?' she asked.

'Brilliant,' Lucien asserted; a word that encompassed every worthwhile happening.

'Well, then I'd better sink into a hot bath, have a rest and phone David.'

On her way upstairs she looked into Marc's empty study. The walls had been cleared of all his plans and charts, the shelves were without books, his desk and chairs were gone. She panicked when she suddenly couldn't remember his face, and went into the bedroom. Looking in the mirror, she saw again her resemblance to her mother and grandmother, imagining or recalling an intimacy between them. She'd opened her handbag, feeling for the soft velvet box, when Lucien appeared carrying her suitcase. Releasing her grip on the necklace, she saw her mother's likeness in him and warmed to his hazel eyes.

'I've decided to go to art school. What do you think?' Lucien announced casually.

'I think that's wonderful.' Having waited so long for those words, their arrival, like so much else, didn't seem to sink in.

'I have to prepare a portfolio. Do you think my new uncle will help me?'

'He's very talented. Please open my suitcase. I want to show you what I bought for you in Prague.' She gave him the canvas art bag.

'Wow! How could you have guessed?! It's bloody wonderful.' He examined the tubes of paint, touched each brush, explored the other pockets, opened and closed the bag, and finally hung it on his shoulder. 'It's brilliant. Thanks, I really love it.'

'You must also thank Ernst; he bought most of the extra bits and dragged it around Prague all afternoon.'

'You're too right, I will.'

Basking in the joy and gratitude in Lucien's face, Sophie suddenly saw Hannah standing next to her. 'What's going on?' she asked, seeing Lucien parading in front of the mirror with his art bag slung over his shoulder.

'Ernst and I bought these for you.' Sophie handed her the blue velvet box with the Bohemian glass earrings and matching ring.

'They're beautiful, Mum. I've always wanted to have my ears pierced but I'm so scared; now I must.'

'I've got the same problem. We can go together,' said Sophie, knowing that, having spontaneously said it, she couldn't back out. 'I'll unpack later. I must get some rest before I go out. Please take all the phone messages and wake me by six. I'd better phone David.'

Alone at last, she pulled the duvet over herself and sobbed. In her dream she saw Marc vividly; she couldn't discern whether he was coming towards her or walking away, but she felt unable to make an effort. A vague sense of her life changing – or perhaps it was the light changing as she sat in a cafe drinking coffee somewhere in Italy. They were on holiday; the waning sun cast shadows on the burnt sienna and terracotta buildings. Marc waved.

She was startled when Hannah came into the room. 'It's six o'clock. What time are you going to David's? What are you going to wear? Can I get it out?'

'Thanks, Hannah. You and Lucien are being quite marvellous.' Hannah's silence prompted Sophie to ask, 'Do you think I should wear my dark brown crêpe skirt and dove-grey silk blouse? I can't wear anything Angelica gave me.'

'Sounds all right to me, but then, the only skirt I've ever worn is my school uniform.' Hannah went to take the clothes out of the wardrobe.

Sophie poured some scented oil into the bath before sinking into the soothing water. Suddenly the uncertainty of her future paled against the miracle of finding Oska and now knowing about her mother and history and the fate of her family in Czechoslovakia. She also had to let David know, and, wrapping two towels round herself, lay down on the bed to make her calls.

Lucien walked in. 'It's all arranged; I'm taking you to David's, and Hannah and I will pop in to see Ernst and our new uncle. David will bring you back.'

'You've been busy,' Sophie said.

'I'm not one for wasting time,' Lucien replied.

She phoned Ernst. 'Thank you for the trip; it has enriched both our lives.'

After a moment's silence, she heard him say, '*Ja.*'

Swallowing a lump in her throat, she added, 'Did you know that Hannah is cooking a special dinner for us tomorrow?'

'I know everything,' Ernst replied.

'We'll talk later; everything feels a little raw at the moment.'

'*Ja*, I understand,' Ernst replied.

When she phoned David, he responded to her news as if he hadn't quite processed it. 'I hope you'll still be able to come to dinner.'

Wondering whether he had understood, she continued to talk in a hushed tone. 'Marc didn't even have the courage to face me. He moved out to live with someone called Maureen while I was in Prague and left the children to tell me.'

'I'm shocked. All I can say is that you deserve better.'

'You're right! The children are wonderful. The affair appears to have brought out a sense of responsibility in them, so I'm determined to keep the good things going. I know our relationship wasn't great, but there was never any animosity. It's the deceit that hurts.'

'Sophie, if it's too much for you to come to dinner tonight, I'll understand.'

'No, I think it will do me good to get out. After all, I have to make my own life now,' she said defiantly.

'Do you mind if I tell Avram?'

'Why not? It's another way of making it real. I don't know where I've been for the past twenty years. I thought I had a marriage, but now I don't know what I was expecting. Certainly not to be abandoned,' she said resentfully.

'Sophie, try not to let this ruin your life.'

'Well, I can tell you, after what happened in Prague I feel as if my life is completely turned upside down.'

'I don't understand. What happened?' David asked.

'Everything! A long time ago, but I've only just found out about it.' In a rush, she told him about her trip.

'What?' David exclaimed.

'Of course, I couldn't remember anything – I was only two, and Ernst never spoke about our past – so you can imagine my amazement.'

There was no response.

'David?' She wondered if they had been cut off.

'Sorry, I'm still here. It's incredible. It's as if our lives have taken a bizarre twist. These are the kind of events that Angelica would have described as "meant to be". I can't wait to see you. I hope you're not too tired.'

'I'm practically out the door; I need to be with adults who can think. My mind is swimming; I only hope I don't make an idiot of myself. Perhaps I have already done so.' Her voice faded into another silence.

'Please let me fetch you. I don't suppose much more could happen.'

They both laughed. 'Thanks, David, but Lucien would be disappointed. He and Hannah want to see Ernst and meet Oska. Lucien is behaving so responsibly, and insists on driving me. It was their idea that I go out tonight, and they are making such an effort. I'll see you soon. I know you care, and that's what counts.'

'I do.' There was a shade of truth in his tone which they both chose to overlook.

She sensed rather than heard Lucien's quiet steps outside her door. 'You'd better hurry,' he said, coming into her bedroom.

'I'll be dressed and ready in fifteen minutes.'

Slipping into her brown crêpe ankle-length skirt and grey silk blouse, she pondered on Lucien's transformation. Perhaps he now felt that he was the man of the house. Then she thought of Marc again, and couldn't believe that he had left her. She caught sight of her soft, shiny hair in the mirror and, feeling mildly removed from the image, was inspired to wear the ruby necklace. It sat perfectly around her long neck, emanating warmth. She thought of her family, who hereto had only existed through Ernst's vague and limited reminiscences. All her life his silence had made it clear that it was a taboo to talk about her mother, and now he couldn't stop mentioning her at every opportunity.

From downstairs, Lucien called her.

'I'll be down in a minute,' she said, and grabbed her silky knit jacket, taking a last look in the mirror at the ruby necklace.

'You look great, Mum,' Lucien remarked.

'Gosh, you look so slim,' Hannah added.

Sitting next to Lucien in the Volvo estate, she recalled how Ernst had insisted on their buying a family car. Marc had bought himself a Citroën 2CV, which he believed to be some sort of design icon. It was so uncomfortable that nobody liked travelling in it, and it was quite obvious that he would never let Lucien learn to drive in it. Ernst had again come to the rescue and paid for driving lessons.

'The car looks wonderfully clean,' she commented.

'I'm pleased you noticed,' said Lucien.

Gazing at the tree-lined avenue with its clusters of fallen leaves gathering under the bright street lamps, she thought of David and hoped he didn't think less of her. Even though she considered Marc's behaviour despicable, her anger was tempered by her own sense of shame. It all seemed so undignified, the way in which Maureen had snatched him behind her back and in front of her children. Perhaps it was her fault? Should she have done more? And what more *could* she have done?

'We must be early; there aren't any other cars,' Lucien said, driving up to the front door.

Sophie took a deep breath. 'Remember not to stay too long with Ernst. He must be tired after the trip.'

'Have a nice time,' Lucien called after her.

And Hannah added, 'Don't worry, we won't embarrass you in front of our new uncle.'

THIRTY-EIGHT

SOPHIE AND AVRAM

David greeted her with a warm hug. 'You look radiant. I expected to see a worn-out waif. I'm so pleased you've made the effort.'

'Thank you, David. I'm trying, but then so are you,' she said, feeling the reassurance of his hands lightly across her back as he guided her into the lounge. Instantly, she felt Avram's eyes looking at her. She hardly recognised him in a formal grey suit.

'Shalom, Sophie, I thought I'd miss seeing you as I have to go back to Israel tomorrow.' It was obvious by his manner that David had told him about Marc.

'Do you know anything about the other guests?' she asked when David went to answer the doorbell.

'I don't know anybody; it was arranged before I came here. Do you think it would be wrong if the two of us went out for dinner? After all, I'd much rather be with you than all these strangers.'

'It would be exceedingly rude. I wouldn't dream of hurting David's feelings,' Sophie said indignantly, although flattered by Avram's presumption.

'You're right, but wrong.' He smiled.

'What do you mean?'

David came back into the room with two couples. Avram's blue eyes darted over Sophie's shoulder as he craned his neck to attract David's attention. 'You'll see,' he said. After a cursory 'Shalom' to the other guests, he went up to David. 'Would you help me to make a phone call in the study? I never quite understand these English dialling codes.'

David excused himself and followed Avram out of the room. After a few minutes he came back and caught Sophie's attention without interrupting the group's conversation. 'Could you do me a favour?' he asked persuasively.

'Of course,' she replied, assuming he wanted her to help with the guests.

'Avram has an urgent call to make and I wondered whether you wouldn't mind driving him.'

'Can't he take a taxi? It doesn't seem right to leave your dinner party.'

'I'm expecting five more people, so you'll probably be back in time. But don't worry. It's rather complicated. Take the Saab; I'll get the keys.' David thought he was being manipulated by Avram but feeling so indebted to him he couldn't refuse.

Sophie made her apologies to the other guests and followed David into the hall, where Avram was waiting. 'This is all very surprising, isn't it?' she said, sensing tension between the two men.

Avram was silent, then, as if making a point, said, 'I must go and make my apologies to your guests.'

David busily engaged Sophie in a conversation about the central locking on the Saab, and the automatic gears, and something about the patient being in the vicinity of Hyde Park.

'Have you got the address?' she asked Avram, turning her head to reverse the car out of the drive.

He looked at her lean jaw angled over her graceful neck adorned with the ruby necklace. The delicate scent of her perfume wafted towards him as she straightened up. 'I must apologise,' he said nervously.

'Not at all; I suppose David feels he wants to help after all you did for Angelica, and I feel the same.'

Under the street lamps, he glanced at the streaks of light bouncing off her soft hair. 'You see, it's not quite the emergency you think it is, and believe me, I'm not proud of my behaviour, but I had no choice. I can't say David approved, but he cooperated.'

'What on earth are you talking about?'

Her naivety and confusion made it more difficult for him. Avram sighed. 'Well, how can I put it? You see, I desperately wanted to see you again. It was just my bad luck that you were in Prague when I was at a conference here. Tonight, when David told me that your marriage was breaking up, I felt I had a chance to get to know you better. Firstly, I must say that we were not needed at the dinner party. The fact that I was staying with David made it difficult for him to exclude me. I asked that he ask you, and I knew that there was a good chance that you wouldn't refuse his invitation. This part of the plan was not premeditated, but I grabbed the opportunity. When I actually saw you again, I thought, *Why go through a dinner with people I don't know?* Quite impulsively, I devised this exit and David cooperated. Now I have told you everything, I hope you aren't too annoyed.'

Sophie turned off the engine and sat back. 'Avram, I really don't know what to say!' Then she erupted. 'Even if my life was stable, I would be exceedingly angry at being set up, but considering my husband's deceit, well, I no longer know if I can trust anybody. In the last few days, I've discovered the truth about some exceedingly painful events. My own father, who has always been a model of integrity, kept some vital truths from me. It's not that he told me any direct lies; he just didn't tell me the truth, and not telling the truth is the same as lying. Life has a way of either excluding me or including me without my consent. It appears that I don't have to do much. The whole world can go spinning around me while I remain still. You know, sometimes I wonder how I escaped a major catastrophe. I'm obviously so naive. Maybe my inactivity is a sort of bait for others to use. I just don't know.'

She took a deep breath to release tension. Her silk blouse fell invitingly over her shapely body. Avram was moved by her honesty and aroused by her enigmatic beauty.

'I'm very sorry; I should have realised how vulnerable you are. I've been very selfish.'

'No, you haven't. You couldn't have known what has been going on with me. I shouldn't have come out tonight, but I'm pleased to see you again, Avram. And to be honest, I probably couldn't have coped with the other guests.'

'Believe me, I am truly sorry, but there's a funny side to it. I've never done anything like this before. It was sort of adolescent, the way I concocted this excuse, but it did work. Look, we're together, and, in fact, I'm quite hungry. Do you know a good restaurant?'

Sophie succumbed to his humour and assurance. 'I'll drive towards Hyde Park. That's where we were meant to go. At least we can salvage some truth from the situation,' she said, starting the engine. Neither spoke until she added, 'If you look straight ahead, that commanding building in the distance is the Dorchester.' She remembered Marc sardonically pointing it out to her as 'a cafe for the wealthy'.

'Let's go there. Hotels can always find a table, and if they haven't got one immediately, we can sit in the bar and talk,' Avram suggested.

'Good idea,' Sophie replied. Perhaps it was his candour that eased her reticence, shifting her thoughts from what was to what might be.

'You seem deep in thought,' she heard him say, feeling his eyes over her.

'I'm fine,' Sophie said, feeling anything but thoughtful.

Manoeuvring through the traffic down Park Lane, she pulled up in front of the Dorchester and handed the car keys to the doorman; a tactic she had learned from Ernst. They found a comfortable settee in the corner of the cocktail lounge.

'I'm sure we could both do with a drink.' Avram looked at her tenderly.

'I'm so confused, it might be dangerous to drink alcohol. My trip to Prague was an absolute revelation. Finding out about my past was like being reborn. I've always felt like an outsider, and I realise now that, in my marriage, Marc was a link to my Englishness, which Ernst never was.' She knew she was rambling on a bit, but her inner turmoil, combined with Avram's presence, made it impossible for her to relax.

'Perhaps you should live in Israel; everybody is an outsider striving to belong.' Avram looked up at the maître d' walking towards them. 'I'm actually quite hungry. I wonder what David's having for dinner?' he teased.

'Probably a lot better than here, but then forbidden food might taste better.'

'Sophie, you mustn't feel guilty. Try and relax. We're here, so let's enjoy it.'

As usual, Avram was right. Sophie hardly noticed what she was eating. They talked about Prague, Israel, London, books, music and their families. In spite of her chaotic feelings, she felt the relevance of their conversation not only in the content but in the feelings; unwittingly, she was investing in him.

'I feel I have talked out all that lonely time after Yael's death,' Avram told her. 'It's like everything was bottled up inside me.

You have such a special way of listening, and when you talk, you appear to be listening to yourself, which gives an extra dimension to the conversation. Do you know what I am saying?' He looked at her and smiled, his eyes wrinkling at the corners, showing the lightly traced lines across his tanned face.

Sophie began to feel more at ease. 'You echo my thoughts. You see, all my life I've had to listen to different voices: the inner voice that is the conversation I have with myself, and then all those outer voices which can be so intrusive. But talking to you, I feel we are in harmony.'

Suffused with an inner contentment, she felt their minds merging. He stretched out across the table, placing his hand over hers.

'I suppose I feel I can be myself and you won't judge me too harshly. Emma says I'm too accepting, and Angelica used to say that she felt good with me because I never judged her. It's easy to confuse tolerance with a failure of confidence. Since my trip to Jerusalem I understand more, and going to Prague quite altered my perception. For the first time, I have a past and I can relate to it. I feel enriched by the heroism of my grandparents and humbled by Ernst's loss and suffering. I can hold my head up and go forward.'

'Let's go back to the cocktail lounge and have our coffee. It's cosier,' Avram suggested.

Walking behind her, he contemplated her upright back and hips swaying innocently inside her skirt. He ordered a cognac, and Sophie ordered sparkling mineral water.

Moving his hand to touch hers, he spoke faintly. 'You know, sometimes there is no logical explanation for what happens to us; we just have to accept it, and as a scientist I am beginning to enjoy that part of life.'

A jelly-like sensation travelled through her arms and legs, as if she were being caressed by his voice.

'You must admit that it was quite a coincidence that I

happened to be on two weeks' vacation when David and Angelica came to Jerusalem. I could argue that there is no such thing as coincidence, just probability. After all, if you consider the number of similar events in life and divide them amongst the number of people there are bound to be many repetitions. So, according to my calculation, I was going to meet another couple who were going through the same fate Yael and I suffered. But as soon as I met the three of you, I felt that we could help each other, but that coincidence alone cannot transform a situation. Being with David and Angelica helped me heal that terrible pain of losing Yael. It seems that Angelica brought all of us together. I feel very close to David. Perhaps we were all destined to meet; that's what I mean by "illogical". I know it sounds crazy, but for a moment, let's be crazy.'

Although Avram hadn't moved, she imagined he was sitting closer to her. It was as if the entire hotel was spinning round, and they were in the eye of the storm.

'Angelica never looked for logic; she relied on pure intuition. She really did move in mysterious ways. I felt that she gave meaning to each situation without really knowing or trying. It was curious – even in her last days in Jerusalem…' Controlling her tears, Sophie continued. 'That evening when you asked me out for dinner, Angelica became excited for me. She urged me to go, and took such interest in what I was going to wear. She appeared to know that I would enjoy being with you. I had no idea then that Marc was having an affair. I think the children knew.'

Then, suddenly reminding herself of Marc's betrayal, she felt unnaturally hot and slipped her hand out of Avram's to push her hair off her face. He noted her long, thin fingers poised in the delicate, feminine gesture, and waited for her to continue.

'Throughout my life everybody has tried to protect me from the truth, as though it was some awful disease. They never realised that "not knowing" was actually doing me harm, because subconsciously, I knew. I can only describe it as a vague shape which clouded my perceptions, making me feel on the edge of life rather than participating in it. Even Angelica tried to protect me. I didn't really think that her life could be almost over when we went to Jerusalem. I was so shocked when she died. All my emotions imploded inside me. I thought it bizarre at the funeral when people wished David and Jonathan a long life; then Ernst explained that it's a Jewish custom. Since coming back from Prague, I see the wisdom of that odd tradition, and realise that those who are left behind have to move forward. Unthinkingly, we are directed to go on, which requires courage. I now want to be more adventurous – in fact, I feel it is my duty.'

He moved closer to her. Feeling his expectation through their touching thighs, she realised that he had misconstrued her words, but acquiesced, relishing the sensation that swept through her and the knowledge that he was in control.

He looked at her intensely, and squeezed her hand lightly. 'You mustn't be afraid of our friendship. If it feels good, it can't be bad.'

Sophie heard herself say, 'It does feel good.'

Avram slipped his arm around her, inhaling her scent. 'What are we going to do? I want to be with you, I live in Jerusalem, you live here, I'm going back tomorrow – the whole thing is so complicated.'

She felt as if she were floating, and just managed to blurt out, 'Do you know what time it is?'

'Our time,' he replied.

'Come on, Avram, there's no need to get metaphysical, it's nearly midnight. We've been sitting on this settee for hours. I'll have to phone the children and let them know I'm all right.'

They both burst into uncontrollable laughter. 'What are you going to tell them?' He chuckled.

'I don't know, what do you think?' asked Sophie, serious for a moment.

'I think you should say you missed the last bus home and you are spending the night with a friend.'

They seized up again, and she shifted away from him slightly. Part of her knew that everything was moving too fast. Wanting to check her own emotions, she got up. 'I must get to a phone. I'd better speak to David first; he was rather keen to drive me home,' she said nervously.

Avram followed her to the phone booth, giving her his loose change. The phone rang a few times before David answered. 'Good timing; I have just seen off the last guests. I'm slightly bemused, especially because Lucien phoned ten minutes ago.'

'What did you say?' Sophie asked anxiously.

'Just that you had driven Avram to see a patient. The problem with lies is you have to remember them, and with a memory like mine you learn not to tell them. Where are you? Even I've become a little concerned, although I can't imagine why.' David seemed to be warning Sophie.

'I'm with Avram at the Dorchester. Do you mind if I take the car home and bring it back tomorrow? I don't want to get you or Lucien out at this hour.'

'Honestly, it's no problem; I can run you home, I still feel wide awake,' David replied.

'I'll see. Avram wants a quick word with you. I'll say goodbye.' She handed Avram the phone.

'I just want to say thanks, I have a front-door key, and I will see you in the morning before I go to the airport.' Avram replaced the phone and turned to Sophie. 'While you were talking to David I had an idea. Before you report to your son,' he winked, 'could we spend the night together? I could get a room here. I know it sounds corny, but I'm not used to thinking on my feet. I'm not a surgeon, I'm more used to the long-term view, but what is stopping us?'

His matter-of-fact tone disarmed her. 'I just don't know. You can be very persuasive. What can I tell the children?'

He put a protective arm around her and smiled. 'Enough already with this permission from the children.'

She felt herself floating towards the unknown, but was conscious of wanting to be with him. She phoned home.

'Hello, Mum, where have you got to? We've all been very worried indeed,' Lucien said with an ironic air.

Sophie laughed nervously. 'To tell the truth, I've been with Avram all evening and I totally lost track of time.'

'Great. Don't worry about us, we're fine,' Lucien said supportively.

'I'll be back in a few hours; it's just that Avram is leaving tomorrow and we've so much to discuss.'

'It's fine by me,' replied Lucien.

She felt embarrassed with Avram listening and gesturing with his shoulders. 'Lucien, what happened with Ernst and Oska?'

'Gosh, it's so interesting, we couldn't believe half the things he told us. They're coming to dinner tomorrow evening, so you'd better show up for that.'

'Don't be silly, Lucien.' She couldn't remember when Lucien had last been in such high spirits. 'Love to Hannah. Goodbye.'

Avram beamed. 'You see, it wasn't so difficult.'

'Now what?' Sophie asked.

'I'll go and check in. I hope they've got a room. How does that sound?'

'Incredibly reckless, but I always wondered how other people do this sort of thing.'

'You mustn't think like that. It doesn't do you justice. I won't be long.'

Avram walked over to the reception desk. She was deep in thought when she looked up and saw him standing next to her, holding a large key. As the lift moved up six floors, her sense of unreality stopped her from suffering her usual claustrophobia. Once in the room, she resigned herself. She sat on one of the small armchairs by the window, not knowing what else to do, and said, 'I wonder how designers can put so much effort into designing something that looks universally nondescript. Have you ever remembered a hotel room?'

'Perhaps we bring our own baggage with us. We don't come to hotel rooms to feel at home. That doesn't mean that we shouldn't feel comfortable about being here,' he suggested, moving towards her.

'Well, I suppose I'm more than a bit nervous. You see, I haven't had a sexual relationship with Marc for some time, and even when we did, I can't remember exactly what happened.'

Avram looked at her with amusement, and began to undo her blouse. 'Trust me, I'm a doctor.' He smiled. 'Being together is the first step; the rest we should leave to instinct. I'll switch the lights off.'

In the half-light coming up from the street, Avram was aware of Sophie looking at his firm, naked body. 'You see how clever they are? There's just enough light from the street so that you can never forget where you are.' He got into the bed and moved closer to her.

God! What am I doing? she thought.

But he was one step ahead. 'Don't think, just relax,' he said as he moved his hands tenderly over her body, mapping out her slightly rounded tummy and her thighs. Then as she turned towards him, he felt the back of her neck and moved his hand down her back. Her compliance appeared to make him more active. She felt bad about not returning the pleasure he was giving her, but he didn't seem to mind. He took his time, seeming to know how to intensify her pleasure, until she couldn't bear it any longer and, abandoning all thoughts and doubts, responded. An exquisite shudder passed through her.

He put his arm round her, kissed her on her shoulder and whispered, 'You've changed my life.'

Sophie woke from a deep sleep to feel Avram nudging her.

'Oh, I completely forgot where I was.'

'Sophie, it's four o'clock. I've ordered some sandwiches and coffee. Perhaps you ought to get back to the children,' he teased.

Hearing a knock at the door, she leapt out of bed and ran into the bathroom, while Avram opened the door to room service. Lying in the bath, she felt exhilarated. She thought of Marc and compared him to Avram, whom she trusted entirely. He had integrated passion into his being and made her feel like a woman. She stepped out of the bath, dressed and went to sit in the armchair. She gazed at Avram propped up against the pillows, stretching out his muscular arm to take a cup of coffee and a smoked salmon sandwich.

'What happens now?' she asked as a fleeting despondency rekindled her fear of loss.

'You look sad. Don't worry; this isn't a one-night stand. I feel so close to you, it frightens me, but there are so many complications.'

'I know,' she said tentatively.

'Talking of which, as a doctor I was not prepared, and hope that between us we haven't created another complication.'

Pouring herself another cup of coffee, Sophie asked, 'What are you going to say to David?'

Avram smiled fondly. 'Men don't discuss such things.'

'I feel so naive.'

Avram looked at her. 'Why don't you say you feel so normal? I do; we haven't done anything wrong. You mustn't get confused.'

'You're right. We'd better hurry; I must go home,' she said, and stood up, but couldn't help feeling regretful.

As they waited for the car to be brought round, Sophie couldn't bring herself to talk. The crisp night air sharpened her wits and made her anxious.

It wasn't until they drove past Marble Arch and turned into the Edgware Road that Avram asked, 'Sophie, are you all right?'

'I really don't know. I've never done anything like this before; I suppose I'm having some sort of reaction. Does my life proceed normally now, or does this experience become part of a new secret? Or perhaps I should confess all to the family at dinner tonight,' she said, half joking, half guilty.

'It's not altogether funny, although it does have its amusing side. I know what you mean. We are both too analytical to enjoy love for what it is. We must stop asking questions when there are no answers. Let's just continue the best we can. My plane leaves at two o'clock, and I have to be at the airport at twelve to go through El Al security. I have only fought in three wars; how can I be trustworthy?' he added.

She wondered whether Avram was asking her to trust him, as a variety of considerations flooded her thoughts, all leading to the same conclusion. She had acted too quickly. 'Avram, we don't have to do anything. It's probably good that you're going back today. It will give us time to think. We're not children. We can speak on the phone. We have a lot to sort out. I've had an incredible evening. You've restored my confidence, and perhaps it will help me deal with Marc. Please don't laugh, but I must be with my children. After all, their father has just walked out, and my father and my newly discovered brother are coming for dinner in a few hours.'

Suddenly, they arrived outside David's house. 'I won't go into the drive, in case we wake David,' she said, parking in the road. 'I really couldn't face him at the moment.'

'It's enough already, all this guilt.' Avram had his hand on the car door. 'You see, it's better to do all this when you are an adolescent. It's not such fun, but you only have to explain it to your parents. That is, if they catch you.'

Sophie smiled. 'I'm all right, really.'

He leaned towards her, giving her a short hug and a kiss on the cheek, then, standing next to the open door, he saw her glazed eyes. 'I'll phone you from the airport,' he said, and waved until she disappeared around the corner.

THIRTY-NINE

LUCIEN

It was five in the morning when she stepped into the hall. Lucien had left every light on, as if making a point – a point that she conceded. Standing in Marc's empty study conjured possibilities, and her mind raced ahead. She could also change the furniture around in the lounge. It didn't flow, and Marc's ordered arrangement didn't suit the richly coloured and textured Victorian room.

In bed, sleep eluded her. Suffused with Avram's aura, she thought of his intellect, humour and insight; all those qualities she found wanting in Marc. When she dared to recall how he had aroused her, she became light-headed. A quiver shot through her, transporting her back to that ecstatic moment between joy and fear. Exhausted, she fell asleep.

*

Distantly, she heard a muffled voice, and reluctantly opened her eyes to see Hannah standing over her.

'Mum, it's nearly eight o'clock. Are you all right? I'm late for school. I'll be back at about four, and then I'll help with the dinner. I've written out a few suggestions for the menu and left them on the kitchen table. I think you should be able to get all the ingredients locally; if not, just see what's around. By the way, did you have a good time last night?'

'Very. Thanks for waking me. Don't worry, I'll get everything. Goodbye, dear.'

She went into the bathroom and dressed hurriedly; she wanted to be downstairs before Lucien. But when she got there, she was surprised to find him already up.

'Thanks for making the coffee,' she said, helping herself to a cup.

'You look exhausted. You'd better read Hannah's shopping list. When are we going out?'

She caught an undertone of irritation in his manner, but decided to ignore it and read aloud, '"Melon, avocado and tomato salad in a mint dressing; poached salmon and veg; make a cheesecake or a choc mousse plus fresh fruit salad; in brackets, don't worry if you don't have time to make the cheesecake, I'll think of something; don't forget flowers." This looks good, but I can't get started until I get the ingredients.' Daunted by the thought of the tasks ahead, she kept thinking only of Avram's call and worried that she might miss it. 'I was expecting Marc to call, so we'd better wait.' She took a sheet of paper and broke down the menu into shopping, cooking and other tasks as a way of stalling and concentrating her mind. Unbidden thoughts of Avram accompanied by feather-light brushing sensations over her arms made her worry that Lucien would answer the phone and recognise Avram's Israeli accent. 'Lucien, if the phone rings, don't answer it.'

'Don't you want me to talk to Marc?' he said angrily.

'No, it's not that.' She failed to elaborate.

Lucien looked at her suspiciously. 'Whatever you say.'

'So, what do you think of Oska?' Sophie asked.

'He's okay,' said Lucien half-heartedly.

'Lucien, I'm sorry, I'm very tired. I hadn't intended to have such a late night but seeing Avram again after such a long time, we had so much to tell each other and—'

Lucien cut her short. 'I know: you got on so well you couldn't wait for Dad to leave. No wonder he left. You probably caused all this when you were in Israel. I'm not stupid, you know. Yesterday I was sorry for you, but now I can see that you don't care a damn about Dad and us. All you care about is getting rid of us so that you can go off with Avram. Well, that's fine, thanks a lot.' And he got up, knocked over his chair and walked out of the kitchen, slamming the door behind him.

Sophie was mortified. How could he know? Maybe Angelica had been right and it was possible to telepathically convey one's thoughts and feelings. She saw the danger of this, and regarded Lucien's outburst as a warning. It had been a major blunder to imagine that he would tolerate her infatuation with Avram, and she was naive not to have thought of the consequences. She must not repeat the same sort of secrecy to which she had been subjected all her life. Defeated and exhausted, she went to lie on her bed, hoping that Avram would phone.

By ten o'clock she surmised that he wouldn't phone until he got to the airport. Lucien didn't go downstairs; nor did the phone ring. Only the worry of the pressing tasks and the passing time made her get up. She went downstairs to set the table for the family dinner, calculating that by now Avram would be at the airport. Determined to make things better with Lucien, she went upstairs, but before she got to his room, the doorbell rang. Marc stood sheepishly outside.

'Why didn't you use your key?' Sophie asked indignantly.

'I don't know. You look exhausted, Sophie. Have you been crying? I'm sorry it had to be this way.' Marc sounded as if he'd prepared a speech but, in the event, like a frightened child, delivered all the points simultaneously.

'I thought you were going to phone,' Sophie said, demanding a further explanation.

'I've been trying since nine o'clock. The phone must be off the hook; that's why I came round.'

Sophie left Marc in the hall and rushed to the phone. Thankfully, he was right. Avram must also have been trying to phone. Hope returned as she waited for his call.

'How are you?' Marc's concern was momentarily unsettling.

'I was fine until Lucien accused me of being responsible for you leaving, as well as for a lot of other things.' She burst into tears.

'There must be more to it. He promised me that he would look after you until we get things sorted out. He seemed so sensible and mature when we spoke the other day. Shall I go and talk to him?'

'That would be a help. I've got Ernst and Oska coming round for dinner. I've got so much to do and Lucien offered to drive me to the shops. I just feel shattered.'

Welcoming the diversion, Marc went upstairs to see Lucien, while she waited by the phone in the kitchen. She imagined that Lucien would embellish the facts if only to justify his behaviour, and worried that Marc would believe him. Angry with herself for acting like a child who could only see her own point of view, she realised that she should have been like Emma and tailored the facts to suit the situation.

Sitting at the kitchen table, reading Hannah's menu but not taking it in, she heard the phone ring and leapt up. She knew it was Avram when she heard the clicks of a payphone.

'Sophie, I've been trying to get you all morning; your phone has been out of order.'

'I know, I've just found out.'

'You sound depressed. Did you think I'd walked out on you?'

'Sort of, I suppose.'

'That's terrible. Look, I won't go, although I'm already in the departure lounge and the plane leaves in less than an hour.'

'No, don't be silly. I can't talk just now,' she whispered. 'Phone me when you get home; the best time is about midday London time.'

'You're right; I will try and get back to London in a couple of weeks. I must sort out a few things. Please believe me, I love you.' Avram's words slipped out instinctively; a gesture of appeasement. He thought of Yael, his wife, who had been a major in the Israeli Army. Since her death he had felt weak, exposed, hiding behind his role of the comforting physician. He remembered how she had confronted her illness; how even in her last days, when she knew she was dying, she had sought to comfort him. His unexpectedly powerful attraction to Sophie had confused him into believing her to be a strong, assertive woman. He realised now that he had misjudged her, and his thoughts spun into a cul-de-sac. How could he have led her on; how could he hurt her after all she'd been through? Her delicate Englishness seemed to him the antithesis of everything Israeli, and her fragile vulnerability terrified him.

Sophie heard Marc and Lucien coming down the stairs. 'I must go. Thanks for phoning; goodbye.'

She looked up to see Lucien standing next to her. 'Who phoned?' he asked in a tone that reminded both her and Marc that each of them was, in their way, answerable to the others.

She wasn't going to risk another outburst, and surprised herself with her lie. 'David, to say I needn't worry about the car and can take it back tomorrow.'

Offering Marc a coffee had the desired effect on Lucien, who appeared to enjoy seeing her rush around while he and Marc sat at the kitchen table.

'I suppose it's none of my business, but Lucien seems to think that you are involved with Avram the Israeli doctor, and have been for some time.'

Incensed by the hint of alarm in Marc's voice, she wasn't going to explain herself to him, and was astounded by Lucien's perspicacity. Her mind raced ahead. Feigning outrage, she looked defiantly at Lucien. 'Is that it? I'm supposed to be having an affair with Avram – you are absolutely sure about that?'

Lucien didn't answer, sitting with his head down, compelling her to continue.

'Well, if you call David inviting me to his dinner party minutes after I returned from Prague an affair – and remember that it was you and Hannah who persuaded me to go, even though I was reluctant. I can tell you it took some courage to go out after learning that your father had left, which hit me like a bolt from the blue. But I did go, I suppose because David was very supportive and thought it would be nice for me to see Avram again. After all, he was incredible with Angelica in Jerusalem. It was nothing more than an innocent reunion. Then, in the middle of the dinner party, Avram was unexpectedly called to see a patient at the Dorchester – an Israeli woman who's come to London for cancer treatment – so, rather than him wait for a taxi, David asked me to take him. We had intended to return to the party, but stopped to have a drink in the bar and talked all evening about Angelica. So, if you believe that my actions were part of some Machiavellian plan, think again.'

Marc, whose usual stance was to distance himself from emotion, interceded. 'Lucien seems to think that you had an affair with Avram when you went to Israel, and that was the cause of our splitting up.'

'Really? Well, that's extraordinary. We were in Israel for five days. Avram looked after Angelica and supported David. His involvement was amazingly generous, considering that his wife had only recently died of the exact same cancer. He told us that Angelica was dying, and I can assure you that my time with her in Jerusalem was hardly a holiday, whatever you or Lucien may think. So don't try to make me the scapegoat for what happened,' Sophie said, as if washing her hands of the matter.

'I think you owe your mother an apology, Lucien,' Marc demanded.

'Look who's talking,' was Lucien's retort.

Momentarily vindicated, Sophie looked at her watch. It was almost twelve. Careful not to upset Lucien again, she affected an appeal. 'I've got so much to do and we still have to go shopping. We'll have to meet tomorrow, Marc.'

'That's fine, what time?' he said, surprised that everything had gone much better than he had feared.

'I really can't think. Phone me at about ten; I promise the phone won't be off the hook,' she said, looking at Lucien as if to clear up their previous misunderstanding.

Marc got up. Putting his hand on Lucien's shoulder, personifying fatherly love, he said, 'Feeling better?'

'I suppose so,' Lucien grunted.

Marc left, believing he had proved that he was needed, and relieved that Sophie seemed even better than he'd remembered.

Lucien straightened himself up from his hunched position. 'If you like, we could go shopping in St John's Wood and return David's car.'

She was astonished by how he'd intuited another of her lies, leaving her in the dubious position of having to warn David of her lie about the car. Deception added to her exhaustion, forcing her to acknowledge the unpalatable lesson that, at times, lies were preferable to truth, and that she was capable of making her lies sound truthful.

'We haven't got time to go to David's; we'll have to get everything locally. Come on, Lucien, let's get going before Hannah comes back from school.' Feigning composure, she picked up the shopping list.

'I'll get the keys,' Lucien replied, conveying that equanimity had returned.

FORTY

THE FAMILY

By the time Hannah came home from school, Sophie had made the cheesecake and prepared the salmon for poaching. Lucien, in a lighter mood, sat at the kitchen table arranging layers of raspberries, strawberries and blackberries in a glass bowl.

'Lucien! That's fantastic,' Sophie and Hannah exclaimed simultaneously.

'What can I do next?' he asked.

'What about a creative arrangement for the salad?' Sophie suggested, thankful that there hadn't been any further mention of their earlier upset. He even appeared to be working to make amends.

Whilst the frenetic activity helped to ease their hurt feelings, Sophie was near to collapsing with fatigue. It was five o'clock and she hadn't sat down. The pop music on Lucien's hi-fi, essential to his survival, reverberated in her head. Glancing at the fresh-cut lilies wrapped in cellophane lying amongst the dishes in the sink, and Hannah with her attention to detail whipping up some fresh mayonnaise, Sophie wondered how much longer she could last.

'Why don't you go and lie down for an hour? Hannah and I can finish,' Lucien suggested.

'Are you sure?' Sophie asked, amazed not only by his concern but by his timing.

'You look worn out,' Hannah added. 'Lucien and I will clear up. I might make a chocolate mousse.'

'Thanks. The cheesecake should be cool enough to put in the fridge; perhaps Lucien would decorate it?' Sophie suggested.

'Sure,' he replied.

Upstairs, she dropped onto her bed, feeling the circulation return to her aching legs. At last, in the privacy of her bedroom, she phoned David. 'I need you to back me up with a little lie regarding Avram. After last night, Lucien has become so suspicious that I daren't risk upsetting him. I told him that you phoned to say I didn't have to bring the car back today.'

'Sophie, you know I have the greatest respect for Avram as a doctor, but I don't know much more about him. Don't you think you might be rushing it?' David said reproachfully.

'Perhaps you're right; I never learn. I can hear Lucien coming up the stairs; I'd better say goodbye.' She replaced the phone as Lucien came in.

'You look terrible,' he said, placing a tea tray on the bedside table.

'Thanks. I'll be better after a rest,' she replied, anxious for him to leave, and then pulled the duvet over her head to muffle her grief. David's veiled disapproval summoned a rush of self-doubt. She couldn't believe that last night she had felt so exhilarated, yet now she felt so crushed. She had assumed that David would be supportive because he had been part of Avram's scheme, so she couldn't quite understand why she felt she was disloyal to him. Exhaustion sent her mind spinning with suspicion towards Avram, panic over David's unwarranted response, guilt about

Lucien and anger towards Marc, until nature came to the rescue and she fell into a profound sleep.

*

She was startled when she heard Hannah.

'Mum, this is the second time today I've had to wake you. What's wrong with you? It's quarter to seven and Ernst and Oska will be here soon.'

Throwing back the duvet, Sophie jumped out of bed and rushed to get dressed. 'I'll be down, don't worry,' she said, climbing into her trousers. She went into the bathroom and splashed her face with water, spotting her silk blouse, and heard the doorbell as she brushed her hair and put on some make-up. There was no time to put on the necklace.

Downstairs, Oska looked around, taking in the atmosphere as he followed Ernst and Lucien into the lounge. He handed Lucien a brown paper package. 'I thought you might like these.'

Hannah came out of the kitchen and met Sophie at the bottom of the stairs. 'Everything's ready. I've even managed to make a chocolate mousse, but I don't think I have the time or energy to do my homework. Perhaps I should skip school tomorrow.'

'See how you feel in the morning. You've done a great job, Hannah; I'm sorry I've been so useless.'

'I enjoyed it. Let's go and meet the men,' Hannah said, walking ahead.

In the lounge, Lucien was opening a roll of drawings and studying a pencil drawing of a nude. 'Thanks very much; where are they from?' he asked Oska.

'They're mine; I did them at art school when I was your age.'

'I love them, how so few pencil lines can be so expressive! I'll never be able to do anything like this; I might as well give up,' he said, suddenly downcast.

'Lucien, I didn't give them to you to make you feel bad; I wanted you to see them so you would let me help you. Drawing is a skill, a technique you can learn. It's a matter of seeing; there's nothing mysterious about it. I will teach you. A lot of painters today don't worry about drawing, but I believe it's essential. You did say you wanted to go to art school, didn't you? Well, I can help you prepare your portfolio. Of course, we will have to work every day, and I promise that you will produce better drawings than these.'

Lucien seemed ecstatic. Every muscle in his body appeared to come alive; his motivation was almost palpable. 'Mum, Oska is going to teach me – can I use Marc's study as my studio?'

'Of course,' she replied, instantly relinquishing her designs on it. It seemed a small sacrifice considering that Oska would fulfil her fantasy of saving Lucien. Her eyes met Ernst's.

'If you will it, it can happen,' he whispered, and then, noticing Sophie's pallor and the dark rings under her eyes, asked, 'Are you ill? You look exhausted.'

Lucien heard him. 'She came home in the early hours. Parents are such a worry these days.'

Sophie's cheeks flushed, and Ernst and Oska chuckled. Whether or not Lucien was indirectly telling her that there were questions still to be answered, she felt uncomfortable. Any reminder of last night seemed to flood her with memories of Avram. At times, a shudder went through her, or she would break out in goose pimples recalling their intimacy.

Tactfully, Ernst intervened. 'I'm quite hungry, and I am sure we could all do with an early night. Oska, I know we won't be disappointed with the banquet.'

He wrapped his arm round Hannah, which gave Sophie the opportunity to say, 'Hannah did the menu before she went to school and went straight into the kitchen when she came home.'

'I also helped,' Lucien blurted out, still glued to Oska's drawings.

322

Oska surveyed the dining room. 'I like the red tone on the walls; it gives the room a warm glow.'

Lucien beamed. 'Dad spent hours mixing the paint; he even blended three different tones of white for the ceiling and cornices to get the right contrast. I helped him wax the floor. Doesn't it go well with the Victorian walnut table and chairs he found at an antique market?'

'They weren't the bargain we'd thought they were when we paid to have them restored,' Sophie interjected. 'Lucien, would you mind getting the wine from the fridge?' She felt irritated, and couldn't discern whether Lucien's behaviour was due to Marc leaving or to his continuing suspicion.

The ensuing awkward silence between them led Ernst to say, 'This is the best salmon I've tasted; it's so fresh, and I recognise Hannah's home-made mayonnaise. Really excellent.' He looked appreciatively at Hannah, who hurriedly helped him to more.

Sophie made a conscious effort to join the conversation. 'Oska, I'll never forget the lunch you made for us in Prague. Your amazing kitchen with its high ceiling, and that rich mahogany table with our grandparents' antique willow-tree china and Ernst's family silver.'

Oska smiled. 'Yes, it was rather inspirational.'

'Oska, in better times we must take Hannah and Lucien to Czechoslovakia,' Ernst suggested. He then talked about his life in Pilsen and his studies at the Charles University, and about Lotte, reminding Lucien that he was named after his grandmother. Then, becoming quiet and reflective and looking directly at Sophie, he said, 'I know now that it's better to tell the truth.'

As her aching exhaustion took hold, she let Ernst talk, thinking how ironic it was that he had become obsessed with the truth, while she now harboured a lie.

'Ernst, do you regret keeping quiet about Oska?' Lucien asked.

Ernst became thoughtful. 'More than I can ever admit. Oska was always on my mind. I now believe that our thoughts are not isolated from each other. Even if we say nothing, some aspect will seep out when we least expect it. And that can be harmful, even if the reason we kept quiet was to protect others. My timing was wrong. I regret the lost opportunity, the lost years and the suffering my silence caused.'

Sophie's expression was neither reproachful nor condoning. Her deathly pale face and heavy eyes made Ernst stop abruptly and say, 'I think it's time to go home. Sophie needs to go to bed. I'm sure that we couldn't have had a better meal at the Connaught. Oska, I promise to take you there.'

He got up to leave, and Sophie offered him the remainder of the cheesecake to take home.

Lucien leapt up to cut a slice, saying, 'Dad's coming over in the morning and this is one of his favourites.'

Sophie and Ernst shared a silence, letting Oska come to the rescue. 'Really, Sophie, the cheesecake is excellent; even better than the one we had in our cafe in Prague, you remember? I wouldn't mind having the recipe,' he added.

'I can get it for you. We got the recipe from Emma; she's Mum's best friend,' Hannah said.

'Lucien, is it all right for you to drive us back, or shall we get a taxi?' asked Ernst.

'No problem.' Lucien went to get his anorak.

Once they'd left, Sophie and Hannah went into the kitchen and put the leftovers in the fridge. 'Thanks for all your help; it really was a great success. Let's leave the dishes; I'll do them in the morning,' Sophie said.

*

In bed, she cried herself to sleep like an overtired child. It was just past six when she awoke and, desperate for a cup of coffee, went down to the kitchen. Feeling guilty about yesterday's feeble effort, she started piling last night's dishes into the sink. She thought about Avram, deciding that she hadn't done anything wrong. Her feelings for him hadn't changed; she had just been confused by Lucien and David. Sipping her large mug of coffee, she felt certain that Avram loved her, which triggered a brush of feather-light sensations. She planned to talk to him while Lucien was having his art lesson. Oska's arrival had been a blessing. Marc was genuinely contrite and would probably help in getting Lucien and Hannah to accept Avram; after all, he had managed to get them to accept Maureen. Ernst would help in whatever way he could. She had a lot to be grateful for. She decided to phone David and clear up any misunderstanding.

'You're up early.' Hannah, dressed in her school uniform, came into the kitchen.

'I thought I'd start clearing away. I'm sorry I was so grumpy yesterday but I felt so pressured. You're a brilliant cook, Hannah,' Sophie said.

As she helped herself to coffee, Hannah was her old self. 'They really appreciated it, didn't they? The food was excellent, wasn't it?'

'It was amazing and we've got a lot of leftovers, so we can indulge and have an early night. I suspect I'll need it after Marc's visit,' Sophie said, now better prepared to challenge him.

'I blame Maureen,' Hannah said emphatically.

Whilst she resented this, Sophie consoled herself by acknowledging that Hannah's perspective could never be the same as her own. She had learned her lesson from Lucien. Whatever anger she felt towards Marc, he hadn't divorced the children, and they needed him now more than ever.

The phone rang, and Lucien, thumping down the stairs, got to it first. 'That was Dad. He'll be here at ten; he has to go into the office first.'

'Good.' Sophie was thankful that it hadn't been Avram. 'I'll go upstairs and freshen up.'

It was exactly ten o'clock when she heard the doorbell ring

and Lucien go to answer it. When she came down, he and Marc were chatting in the lounge.

'Lucien tells me that you had an amazing evening. I've heard all about your brother; I think it's quite wonderful. He appears to have inspired Lucien, and I must say, his drawings are very impressive. Ernst must be delighted,' said Marc, reminding Sophie of his infinite and selective capacity to ignore the darker side of life.

She sat down on the velvet chaise longue. Marc sat opposite her on a Victorian chair.

'I'll make some fresh coffee,' said Lucien, leaving them to talk.

'I hope his behaviour has improved after yesterday's outburst,' said Marc.

'It's unrecognisable. You should have left three years ago. He might have got brilliant A Levels and be halfway through college by now,' she said.

Marc laughed nervously. 'Well, at least something good has come out of it. I'm really sorry, Sophie. How are you? You look washed out.'

'I'll be all right. Are you happy? I feel obliged to ask,' she said.

'I'm more fulfilled, but of course I miss the family. I still want to be part of it. We can't pretend that we had a passionate relationship, but we respected each other.'

'I don't think cheating and then leaving without talking to me about your relationship is at all respectful.' Sophie pursed her lips.

'I'm very sorry, I never wanted to hurt you. I don't think I would have left if it hadn't been for Maureen insisting that I take responsibility. I am grateful that you referred to my behaviour as a relationship and not an affair. There is a difference, you know. It never was an affair. I have known Maureen for about five years. We just became more involved, and when I realised what had happened, she merely helped me to make a proper decision. You're right, it is unforgivable that I didn't tell you, but I couldn't think of what to say. After twenty years, I just couldn't hurt you face to face. I know it's been far worse for you. Seeing how exhausted you are makes me desperately ashamed.'

She believed him, and was reminded of his gentle side and the way he had uncomplainingly taken care of her. She couldn't argue with him, particularly whilst thinking of Avram.

'I also want to reassure you that I won't be making any claims on the house. Ernst has been more than generous to me over the years, and Maureen has a reasonable flat in Crouch End.'

'I really can't concern myself with those sort of details,' Sophie replied.

Marc looked at her. 'Sophie, you're so naive. I'm very grateful that you have Ernst. I must phone him. I owe him an explanation too.'

'I think he'll appreciate that. After all, it's more than I've had, but then maybe I'm too childish to understand.'

Lucien came in with the coffee and two pieces of cheesecake. 'Mum made this; it's fantastic. We kept some especially for you.' He handed Marc a plate.

Marc took a mouthful and smiled. 'It really is very good, Sophie. Is it one of Emma's recipes? I think you've had some amazing friendships,' he said, to appease her.

'I know.' She wanted him to leave, but he seemed to think he ought to stay. 'I'll be all right; I'm meeting Emma this afternoon for coffee,' she said, hoping that he would take the hint, but he appeared to settle in the armchair. 'Marc, we'll have to talk some other time; I'm awfully tired.'

'Of course, any time that suits you.'

They sat silently. Marc seemed stuck to the chair. Lucien came back into the room and addressed them both as if denying that anything had changed. 'I've just spoken to Oska and I'm going to see him this afternoon to arrange a programme of work. I'll be at home for the next few months, preparing my portfolio.'

'That's wonderful, Lucien; it's an amazing opportunity.' Marc looked at Sophie as if waiting for her acknowledgement.

'We should get ready; I still have a few things to do and I don't want to be late.' She got up.

'Are you sure there isn't anything I can do?' asked Marc, still seated.

'I can't think of anything,' she said offhandedly.

'Here's my address and phone number.' Marc gave her a piece of paper and, without looking at it, she handed it to Lucien. Marc looked around the room. 'I would like to meet Oska sometime.'

'Say when,' enthused Lucien.

Marc paused, and then said, 'Well, maybe when things are a little more settled.' He stood up to leave, and Lucien accompanied him to the door.

'Why do you keep on looking at the phone?' asked Lucien when he returned.

Sophie sighed. 'Actually, I want to make sure it isn't off the hook.' In willing Avram to ring, she hadn't realised that she was compulsively eyeing the phone. As an afterthought she said, 'I'd better phone David to let him know that I'll be bringing back his car.'

Lucien hovered round her, pretending to be busy while David's secretary told her that he was at home. Things were falling into place. Lucien could follow her in his car, then go on to see Oska, giving her time to spend with David. Lucien could pick her up later.

Determined to resolve their misunderstanding, she phoned David at home. 'I'll be bringing back the car about oneish; will you be in?'

'Thanks, just put the keys through the letter box.' David sounded cold and withholding.

It was as if a stone dropped into her stomach. 'Of course,' she mumbled, and replaced the receiver. Trying to conceal her embarrassment, she turned to Lucien. 'I just managed to catch him as he was leaving for the office, so we can drop the car round.'

She had not anticipated David's rejection, and, reeling from the shock, headed upstairs, desperately needing to be alone. Why was he at home? Perhaps something had happened at his office and his behaviour had nothing to do with her. It was inconceivable that he could be so cold towards her. Whilst she saw no reason to explain her relationship with Avram, she had a lingering feeling that she should, and wasn't going to let David's callous response dissuade her.

Lucien watched her slow, heavy movements as she walked upstairs and shouted after her, 'Is anything wrong?'

'No! I just suddenly feel worn out; perhaps we should take the car back later.'

On the landing, she caught sight of herself in the mirror. Her face looked drawn and tired. She went to lie down. At least she would be next to the phone when Avram called, and perhaps she could get him to find out what was bothering David. Calculating that Israel was two hours ahead, she could afford to wait until two o'clock, which would be four o'clock in Israel. That would give her enough time to take the Saab back and be back home for Hannah.

Lucien came into her bedroom. 'Can I get you some tea?'

'That would be wonderful, thanks.' Then she added, 'Lucien, if the phone rings, don't answer it; I'm expecting a call.'

'Who from?' he asked.

'Emma,' she said, then remembered that Emma didn't even know she was at home.

'I suppose you're going to tell her everything as usual,' Lucien said sulkily.

'Lucien, I haven't had a moment since I came back from Prague. I think I'm entitled to tell my best friend that Marc has left and that I have a new brother.'

'I told you, Maureen made him go.' Lucien walked out, returning ten minutes later with a tray of tea. She had to get him out of the house. She couldn't risk his unpredictable intrusions. It was ridiculous that he had turned her into an unthinking jelly.

'Lucien, why don't you get your studio ready? You could put your art materials on the shelves and go and buy some plastic sheeting to cover the floor.'

'Great. Are you sure you don't need me? When are we taking David's car back?'

'It's only midday, we can go at two.'

'I'll measure the floor.' He left without a hint of suspicion.

Within minutes she heard the front door slam and turned onto her side, waiting for Avram's call. It didn't come. She wondered if the phone might be out of order. Why hadn't Avram given her his number? After all, he didn't have anything to conceal; nor did he have Lucien hovering around like a sparrowhawk. If Lucien answered the phone she would have to rely on Avram's quick wit to deflect him, and if she got to the phone first she would ask Avram for his number. Having devised a strategy, she felt better. Then it occurred to her that David must have Avram's number, but she certainly couldn't approach him.

Lucien returned with a roll of plastic and masking tape. 'Can we take the car back to David now? I want to start organising my studio.'

Responding to his new-found enthusiasm, and with a contrived liveliness, she replied, 'I'm ready.'

*

Driving David's Saab behind Lucien in the Volvo, she smiled when he gave her a reassuring wave. As they approached St John's Wood, Sophie felt certain that David would want to see her, persuading herself that his upset might have nothing to do with her. They had always been open with each other. She parked the Saab next to his other car in the drive. He was obviously at home. She rang the bell and waited whilst Lucien sat watching in his car. Standing in front of the closed door, she rang again and then knocked. Feeling the full force of David's rejection, she dropped the keys through the letter box.

'Aren't you going to say hello to David?' Lucien asked as she got into the car.

'I'll phone him later; I don't want to be late for Hannah. After her effort last night, I think we should at least set the table with all the leftovers. And I'm looking forward to seeing how you transform Marc's study into your new studio.'

She felt ashamed of her need to lie, but acknowledged that she was also getting awfully good at it. She thought of how she had been so judgemental about Oska's obsession with secrecy, even to the point of thinking him paranoid, although she knew he had little choice as his survival in a police state had depended on hiding his true identity. She recalled him saying that the real art of diplomacy is measured by survival.

*

At home she busied herself arranging yesterday's leftovers on fresh platters, staying near the phone, ready to pounce with the first ring. Uncertainty about Avram's commitment to her surfaced, but she pushed it aside. She checked the table, wondering if there was enough food, then went rummaging in the fridge, found the bowl with the remnants of the chocolate mousse and, still feeling unsure, grabbed some frozen peas and put them in a pot.

Lucien came into the kitchen. 'Why are you making such a fuss?' he asked.

'I don't know, I suppose I just want to make it up to Hannah,' she said, wondering if Lucien detected her anxiety.

Hannah came in from school, dropping her heavy bag onto the floor. 'What a day! I'm completely wiped out.' Then, noticing the table, she sat down eagerly. 'Gosh, it looks better than yesterday. I'm starving. Can we eat, then I can go to bed? I'll do my homework in the morning.'

'I'll call Lucien.'

Sophie found him covering the study floor in plastic sheeting. An old plastic table, a couple of chairs and his wooden easel and art materials were standing in the hall. 'What do you think?' He stood back, proudly surveying his effort.

'It's wonderful. I can't even remember what it looked like before.'

'When Dad comes, he might have a few ideas about the lighting.'

'Would you come down? Hannah wants to eat, and I could also do with an early night.'

'Okay, I'll do more later.'

The phone rang while they were eating. Sophie felt her throat close as Lucien rushed to answer it.

'She's fine, do you want to talk to her? We're just finishing off yesterday's banquet. I'll tell her.'

She watched Hannah take a second helping of chocolate mousse. She might have been plump before, but now she was definitely fat.

'Ernst says, thank you for a wonderful evening, and he'll phone tomorrow.' Lucien started taking plates off the table, eager to get back to his studio.

'I'll clear up in here,' Sophie offered, wanting to be on her own.

'Thanks,' Lucien said, leaving the kitchen.

'Are you sure?' asked Hannah.

From her bedroom, Sophie heard Lucien moving furniture and banging nails. She turned over to look at the phone, ready for the first ring. The night seemed endless. Tormented by the thought of being utterly alone, she stretched out to feel the empty space in the bed. What if Avram *didn't* love her? Whilst she could resign herself to a future without Marc, she couldn't live with her foolish infatuation. Had she imagined loving Avram? Resolutely, she lay on her side, facing the phone.

*

She opened her eyes to a murky sky and realised it was morning. Her thoughts moved to inventing explanations for Avram's silence. Life in Israel was unpredictable. He could have been called to the army, or the hospital, or there might be some emergency with his children. With daylight breaking, a glimmer of hope returned. She'd been wrong before when the phone had been off the hook.

She couldn't tell how long she'd been staring at her empty coffee mug when Hannah came into the kitchen. 'You appear to be in another world.'

'Sorry, I was just thinking.' Wanting to mask her sadness, Sophie poured herself another cup of coffee.

'Is something wrong, Mum? I mean, more than Dad going. Something else? You seem so preoccupied.'

Disarmed by Hannah's tenderness, Sophie burst into tears. 'I'm just exhausted from my trip to Prague. I suppose I'm suffering from some kind of delayed reaction. I don't know.'

'I'm furious with Dad – how dare he go off like that and not even talk to you about everything, especially with that horrible Maureen? I hate her!' Hannah's outburst added to Sophie's shame.

'It will be okay.' Sophie's eyes filled with tears. 'Things will get better. Don't worry, Hannah; really, it isn't your fault or Lucien's. You've both been magnificent.'

She heard Lucien coming down the stairs and surmised that Hannah had woken him. 'I'll have a bath and get dressed,' she told him before he could say anything.

'Take your time; I'll answer the phone and be around,' Lucien replied.

Lying in the warm bath, she realised that, more than anything, the uncertainty was depleting her. Even Marc's leaving had, at least, had clarity. She needed to speak to Emma, who would understand her predicament.

She heard Hannah outside the bathroom door. 'Are you all right, Mum? I'm off to school, see you later.'

'Fine, Hannah, goodbye,' she replied.

On hearing the phone ring she leapt out of the bath, but Lucien got to it first. It seemed that he was determined to take control, as if nobody could be trusted. She dressed and went downstairs. 'Who phoned?' she asked casually while tidying the kitchen.

'Oh, it was Marc. I told him about the studio, and he also wanted to know how you are.'

'What did you tell him?'

'The truth,' Lucien replied.

Sophie knew that he had told Marc about her sobbing.

FORTY-ONE

RELYING ON EMMA

In need of an adult conversation, once she was out of earshot of Lucien, Sophie phoned Emma.

'When did you get back?' Emma asked. The certainty in her voice highlighted Sophie's own doubt.

'A few days ago. I'd like to see you.'

'You sound terrible, what's wrong?'

'Everything. When are you free?'

'I'm half-day today; I could pop round at about three?'

'No, I'll meet you,' insisted Sophie. 'Can you make it earlier?'

'I could meet you in the coffee shop in St John's Wood, say, about two?'

'I'll be there,' Sophie replied.

Replacing the phone, she spontaneously saw Lucien standing at the end of her bed. 'If you like, I can take you and fetch you home afterwards. I want to see Oska.'

'Thanks,' Sophie replied. It appeared that Lucien was

determined to find out if she was responsible for Marc leaving. At least he would also be out of the house if Avram phoned.

*

The coffee shop had its crowd of elegantly dressed women sipping coffee with their designer-label bags draped around the tables. Spotting an empty table in the corner, Sophie passed the counter of pastries without being tempted. Deep in thought, she waited for Emma, and was taken by surprise when her friend bent over to kiss her and squeezed in next to her on the upholstered bench, saying, 'Sophie, you look washed out. What's been happening?'

Forcing back her tears, Sophie recounted the dramatic events of the past week.

'Dearest, it's all too amazing. I don't know what to say. You seem to have lost a husband and gained a brother. That's if you can call Marc a husband. If you ask me, he's always been more like a house guest or a mother's help. After all, darling, nothing has changed. You still live in the same house with your children. Marc has just left home, but he'll probably visit more often, you'll see. Guilt can make ex-husbands attentive. I know it's tough, but you just have to get on with your life. You've never looked more attractive. Anyway, there are loads of other men; you will just have to go out and find one.'

'I already have,' Sophie interjected.

'I'm impressed, or shocked. But then, darling, why do you look so down?' Emma said, eager to know more.

Sophie told her most of the details, concluding that she couldn't understand why Avram hadn't phoned, and that she didn't know what to do.

'Well, dear, there's nothing you can do until he lets you know what he intends to do. After all, how can you be certain of anything after what you've gone through? But I can tell you that there is a vast difference between an affair and a relationship. My liaison with Aubrey Lewis was definitely an affair; we both knew it and didn't appear to mind. That's why we could end it so easily. But you sound as if Avram is a complete relationship, even with all the complications of him living in Israel. If it's meant to be, you don't have to rush into it, but I must say you seem to have done that already.'

'That's what David said. He implied that I was impulsive and irresponsible.'

'Perhaps he's jealous,' Emma said, wanting to reassure Sophie.

'Don't be ridiculous, Emma, my life is far too complicated for any more jokes.'

'Well, at least Marc is trying, but I hope you are not being stupid about the legal side of things,' Emma insisted.

'What do you mean?'

'Darling, I know I've just started at law college, but common sense tells me that when it comes to divorce, things can get pretty nasty.'

'Marc has agreed not to make any claims on the house.'

'What?! He doesn't want anything?!' Emma exclaimed. 'Well dear, what more proof do you need that he isn't Jewish?'

They both laughed.

'But you must take some legal advice. It's none of my business, but you could prevent problems later on. And go to a woman solicitor when it comes to divorce; they have a different perspective.'

Overwhelmed, Sophie asked, 'How's Alan?'

'I can honestly say we're back together again in every way; in fact, better. I think he still feels quite guilty, and perhaps that helped us get very close again on our holiday. He supports my studies and has even started being helpful at home. I never told him about Aubrey; I decided it wouldn't do anybody any good. It's not a policy I would advocate in principle, but in practice being economical with the truth can be good for one's economy.' Emma spoke convincingly.

'You're probably right. The proof is that you have actually sorted out your life,' Sophie said disconsolately.

Emma placed her hand gently over Sophie's. 'I know you feel rotten at the moment. Believe me, things will change. Be patient, and don't rush into any decisions. Why don't we meet here on my half-day next week? Let's try and make it a regular date,' she suggested.

'I'd really appreciate that.' Sophie looked at her watch. 'Lucien will be here in a few minutes. Can you believe that we've been here for almost two hours?'

FORTY-TWO

LUCIEN'S REVIVAL

Sophie saw Lucien park the car and went to meet him.

'I really think that Oska is one of the nicest guys. He showed me a family album and told me about everybody. Did you know that he only brought one set of clothes? He used up all the space in his luggage for photographs, paintings, old books, family mementos and his paintbrushes. We discussed my programme of work. He's coming over tomorrow to give me my first lesson. Aren't I lucky, Mum, to have private lessons with a real artist?'

'You are, and what's more, Lucien, I really believe in you. I know that you are talented. After all, you've inherited it.' She couldn't remember ever having such a normal conversation with him.

'Do you really think so?' He parked the car outside the house, went round to open the door for her and rushed upstairs to work on his studio.

Hannah was in the kitchen, standing in front of the open fridge, eating.

'Did anybody phone?' Sophie asked with measured disinterest.

'Not since I've been at home.'

'If you don't mind, I'm going to lie down. I'm not hungry and I think there are enough bits and pieces for you and Lucien.'

'That's a good idea. I'll bring you up some Earl Grey tea,' replied Hannah.

*

In the days that followed, Sophie was consumed with the disturbing truth of her folly. Avram's silence could not be more telling. At times she experienced a rush of panic or an overwhelming desolation, reminiscent of those depressing days after Lucien's birth. The connection came to her abruptly. It was then that she had felt so abandoned, so in need of a mother to take care of her, but her mother hadn't wanted to abandon her. Avram's rejection was deliberate. As this revelation took hold, she became incensed with herself. Her self-pity was unproductive. She mustn't be crushed; after all, nothing had been lost. Whatever happened, she had learned a valuable lesson. Avram's silence had shocked her into a desire for independence, and their intimacy had awakened in her something long dormant. The irony was inescapable; her guilt over Lucien was misplaced. He was finding his way, and she must find hers. She would go back to work tomorrow; perhaps even increase her workload to four days a week.

Time dragged by. It was clear that Avram had disappeared from her life, and her preoccupation with the memory of his seduction was slowly fading. Almost out of habit, when she got home, she would ask, 'Has anyone phoned?'

'Who exactly are you expecting to phone, besides Emma, Ernst and Marc? What's happened to David? You haven't heard from him for ages,' Lucien, mindful of his new-found responsibility, asked.

Stirred by that remark, she decided to contact David. It was only a matter of determining the method. She considered writing and then thought that it might create further confusion; it would be better to confront him, even with the risk of rejection. Lucien was having a drawing lesson with Oska. She made herself a cup of tea, took it up to her bedroom and shut the door. When David's secretary put her through, a feeling of inevitability forced her to speak.

'David, I need to talk to you. Can we meet sometime?'

Hearing the tension in her voice, he replied, 'I'm free on Friday; come to the house at two o'clock. Maria is off and Jonathan is away, so we can talk there. Is that all right?'

'That's fine, goodbye.' Sinking back onto the pillows, she sighed with relief. The thought of seeing David excited and unsettled her. His businesslike manner had been unmistakable, but she remained resolute.

She couldn't account for her tiredness. To think that she had contemplated increasing her work hours when she could hardly manage now! Lucien and Hannah were concerned about the way she immediately flopped into bed after dinner. Lucien took it upon himself to talk to Oska, who in turn told Ernst. They all agreed that her exhaustion was a reaction to Marc leaving her.

After her rest, she went into the kitchen to prepare the evening meal. The phone rang.

'I believe my son is with your son,' Ernst announced proudly. 'As it's your day at home, I thought it would be a good idea if we all went out for dinner tonight to celebrate having a united family after all these years. I can get a taxi straight from work and we can go to that nice fish restaurant in Highgate.'

Her first thought was relief at not having to cook dinner. 'That's fine. Oska and Lucien are still busy and I don't want to disturb their lesson. Take it as a yes unless I phone.'

It was a biting cold November evening. She didn't feel like going out but wanted to please Oska, who enjoyed dining out and seeing different parts of London. He had transformed Lucien, which made her forget her previous preoccupation with him. Hannah was on course to do well in her A Levels, but was eating compulsively since Marc left, even though they saw more of him. He phoned every day and visited frequently, although he never used his front-door key. It seemed bizarre how Sophie's family had had to break up in order to come together.

*

Lucien and Oska were still upstairs when Ernst arrived. 'Let them go on a bit; I want to talk to you,' he told her, sitting down in the kitchen. 'Marc has come to see me a few times. We appear to get on better now than when you were together. I'm convinced that he means to do his duty by all of you. As a matter of fact, between us we devised quite a crazy scheme.'

'I'm listening,' Sophie said, wondering what she would have to contend with next.

'You remember a few years ago, Marc drew up some plans to convert the basement? Now that Lucien is so interested in art, I thought we should use the basement for a studio for him, and also a separate studio for Oska. What do you think?'

'I really don't understand why Marc is suddenly taking such an interest in this house. I thought it was my house. Can the Labour Party really spare him? The whole idea feels odd,' she protested.

'I offered to pay him a proper professional fee. He wants to do it. He wants to help Lucien and he feels guilty about you. He has a lot of good in him, you know.'

Sophie burst into tears. 'Really, Ernst, I have no objections; I just feel so stupid, I can't even think properly. I'm sure Lucien will be delighted, and the last thing I want is to stop his amazing progress.'

They heard Lucien and Oska coming down the stairs. Sophie

quickly wiped her eyes. Lucien asked Ernst to come up and see his work and the studio, where the pungent smell of oil paint reminding Ernst of Lotte brought a lump to his throat.

Sophie and Oska talked in the kitchen. 'I'm enjoying teaching him. He's very sensitive and has a natural talent.'

'Good,' she replied. 'And how do you like London?'

'It's quite an adjustment. At the moment, I enjoy wandering around the galleries and museums. I think I would see it differently if I could get back to working again, and also meet some people. In fact, I feel a bit bad about hiding something.'

'Like what?' Sophie said anxiously.

'Well, you remember me telling you about my relationship with Helga and that we'd parted after seven years? Yesterday, I felt so lonely that I phoned her. The odd thing is, she said that at that very moment she was thinking of me too. We both realised that we still love each other, but the situation seems impossible with all the unfinished business from our past. She wants to come over and see me, but I told her it's too soon. I'm getting on very well with Ernst, but I couldn't tell him about Helga. He would never accept me marrying a German, would he?'

'I really don't know what Ernst is capable of accepting or not, nowadays. It must be wrong to judge Helga before meeting her or to blame her personally for murdering the six million. I think you should tell him when you feel he's ready. There's no point in giving information when the other person isn't ready for it. No one thought I was ready to know about my mother; I was kept in the dark. Look at Marc's behaviour: he just assumed I wouldn't understand, so didn't tell me until after the event.'

'You really are grieving over his leaving you,' Oska said sympathetically.

'I suppose so,' she replied resentfully. It seemed to her that she had done nothing to deserve Marc's or Avram's behaviour, or particularly being rebuffed by David. 'You know what I really think, Oska? I think I've been too passive; it's almost a learned laziness. I never had to use my initiative because Ernst, and then Ernst and Marc, were always there to make the decisions. And you know what has helped me to see that? The way you have helped Lucien. I honestly believe that if you hadn't come to London, he would have stayed stuck in his inertia. You enabled him to use his talent, which gave him the confidence to move on. And that's what I have to do. I have no backbone; I must stop having the thoughts and feelings that other people think I should have. I must fight back. And so must you. Tell Ernst about Helga; I'll back you. We have both been victims for too long.'

'Thank you, Sophie, you're absolutely right.' Oska looked at her appreciatively.

They heard Lucien and Ernst coming down. 'His work is fabulous,' enthused Ernst.

'Mum, apparently Marc is going to build me a studio and get me some natural light in the basement – isn't that amazing?' said Lucien, looking at Oska.

'I actually think you should thank Ernst,' Sophie suggested.

'Well, it's going to be two studios. Oska desperately needs somewhere to paint. In the meantime, perhaps we should look for a studio for you to rent,' Ernst suggested.

Hannah came in and dropped her school bag onto the kitchen floor. 'Are we having a party?'

'Sort of – Ernst is taking us out for dinner to celebrate being together as a family,' Lucien announced.

'I'm ready; I'll just go and change,' said Hannah warmly.

'My Hannah, always a smile on her face,' Ernst said, as if reminding Sophie that she should make an effort for the sake of her children.

Lucien drove slowly up the hill, parking the car in a side street. It was a short walk to the restaurant. Sophie tensed against the icy wind cutting through her coat and circling her neck. She could hardly keep up with the others rushing ahead.

In the restaurant they sat at a round table in the bay window. Sophie looked out at the street with its bare trees and haunting forms. She thought wistfully of David, and couldn't understand what had happened to make them estranged. There had been times when she had felt close to him and even entertained the occasional fantasy. His unspoken anger was more upsetting because it made her feel culpable.

'I find the climate here quite gentle compared to Prague,' Oska remarked.

'I don't mind the winter; it's good to live in seasons. Imagine being in one climate throughout the year,' said Lucien.

Hannah prodded Sophie, both remembering when Lucien had spent the best part of the winter in bed. It wasn't so long ago that he'd had to be cajoled into going to a restaurant, and then he could never find anything to eat, controlling everybody with his food fads and unhappiness.

Realising that it was her cheerless mood compelling everybody to talk about the weather, even though she felt worn out and had no appetite, Sophie picked up the menu. 'Let's see what the specials are tonight.' She ordered Dover Sole.

*

At home, Sophie asked Hannah whether she'd thought the fish was all right, as she felt a little nauseous.

'Couldn't have been fresher,' replied Hannah.

In the middle of the night Sophie got out of bed, went to the bathroom and vomited. In the morning she vomited again. She hoped she wasn't getting the flu because she desperately wanted to meet Emma for coffee in the afternoon. But she had no other symptoms, so decided to freshen herself up with a bath.

Relaxing in the warm water, she thought of David.

Something had definitely upset him. It was when she'd told him about Avram. Well, she would have it out with him on Friday. How dare he treat her like this? After all, he was also responsible for going along with Avram's scheme. In the back of her mind she hoped that there had been some terrible misunderstanding which had escalated into this painful rift.

Through the bathwater, she suddenly noticed blue veins traced across her breasts. She sat up instantly. Her heart leapt. She was pregnant. It all made sense: the fatigue, the nausea, and the slight dizziness from time to time. Of course, she had also missed a period. Yesterday, she had resolved to fight back. But now, unimaginably, everything was far worse.

She could hardly wait for the afternoon to see Emma. She stayed in the bath until the water was cold.

FORTY-THREE

AUBREY LEWIS

Sophie sat in a corner of the coffee shop, oblivious to her surroundings.

'Dearest, you look terrible – are you ill?' Emma asked, sitting down next to her.

Threatening tears, Sophie couldn't bring herself to answer.

'What's happened?' whispered Emma.

'I'm pregnant.'

'What?! I don't believe it. Are you sure? Have you had the test?' Emma asked, as if demanding to see the evidence.

'Not exactly.' Sophie related the tell-tale signs, convincing Emma, who noticed that she avoided mentioning Avram.

'Well, you certainly can't go ahead with it, can you?'

'Emma, I really don't know what to do.'

'I'll have to phone Aubrey Lewis; I can't think what else we can do. I'll do it as soon as I get home, I promise. I hope he doesn't think I'm after anything else. I really feel quite embarrassed when I think of our affair, but compared to your problem, darling, it's a joke. I'm sure he'll help. It's probably quite a simple procedure nowadays. But how are you going to explain your disappearance to your family? Even if it's a one-day job, you're bound to be a bit of a wreck. You can't hide anything from Hannah, she's no fool, and Lucien, well, you don't need his brand of sympathy. I know! Tell them that we've decided to go to a health farm for the weekend or something. Don't worry; I'll think of something.'

Emma didn't stop talking, her mind moving ahead through the entire experience while Sophie sat with her head bowed, letting her work the whole thing out.

When she looked up she said, 'Emma, you're being wonderful. I know it can't be easy going back to see Aubrey, but what choice do we have? I'm not very good at all this and I can't cope with any more lies. I can't even remember my last lies without inventing new ones. I feel so deeply ashamed, and you can't imagine how frightened I am. You know, I can't even picture Avram's face. It's as if my mind is purposely shutting him out. It's as if he set out to punish me, or more to the point, I'm being punished for my stupidity. You're the only person I can turn to.'

'Darling, we can't wait. It's too much of a strain. I could try phoning Aubrey now. You never know our luck; he might be in Harley Street and we could go and see him. It's only ten minutes away.' Emma noticed other women looking at them. 'Let's get out of here.' She got up hurriedly, grabbing the bill.

'Are you sure?' Sophie followed her.

'Look, the longer you think about this sort of thing, the worse it gets. It's a blip, that's all, no more. Let's go.'

Sophie had difficulty keeping up with Emma as she walked briskly around the corner towards the public phone box. Leaving Sophie outside watching, Emma dialled Aubrey's number and soon came out to say, 'We're in luck: he can see us in between patients. Anyway, he owes me one. Let's go in my car.'

Driving towards Harley Street, Sophie's silence compelled

Emma to speculate. 'Are you sure that nothing terrible has happened to Avram? After all, in Israel they even send some fifty-year-olds for military duties. From your description of him, his behaviour is totally out of character. I can't believe a doctor would be so callous. There must be something we don't know; I mean, it's six weeks and not a word. Why haven't you tried to contact him? You know the hospital he works at. Sophie, darling, you are far too passive. You really must take the initiative and stop letting everybody walk all over you.'

'You're right. In some bizarre way I feel I've changed places with Lucien. He's gained his confidence and I've lost mine.'

*

The waiting room hadn't changed in twenty years. They looked around at three young women, all in different stages of pregnancy, reading magazines.

'He still seems quite busy,' Sophie whispered nervously.

'I think I'm just as worried as you, for different reasons,' Emma said.

Aubrey came into the waiting room and beckoned to Emma, who followed him while Sophie waited.

'You just have to help her,' Emma told him. 'Poor Sophie, everything in her life appears to have gone wrong. Please don't ask too many questions; she's far too vulnerable. This has to be done with the utmost discretion; I swear she could have another breakdown.'

'Being great in bed doesn't entitle you to tell me how to run my practice,' Aubrey replied, winking, which dissolved any remaining tension between them. 'I used to think of her as "Sad Sophie" when she was in the clinic. She struck me as one of life's victims. I couldn't understand why; she seemed to have a lot going for her. A caring husband, a doting father, good looks, high intelligence. Why is she so lacking in confidence?'

'Really, Aubrey, I know you're a genius in your field, but I don't think you could possibly understand what Sophie's been through. With all her apparent advantages, her life has been a struggle. She lost her mother when she was a baby, she and her father escaped from the Nazis, her family perished in the camps, and a lot more besides. So, with all your good intentions, I don't think you can take Sophie at face value. I know she can be very irritating and sometimes I also feel like shaking her and telling her to get on with it, but she can't, and she really is a brick. You must help her, please.'

'Of course I will. At the risk of making another wrong judgement, I must say that she is very fortunate to have you as a friend. Don't worry, I'll do what is medically possible. I think she ought to come in alone.'

'Thanks, Aubrey. I'm sorry for my outburst, but she's made me feel so responsible for her. I'll go and get her,' said Emma, mildly embarrassed.

Sophie sat down in the chair opposite Aubrey. Her pained and downcast expression reminded him to take Emma's advice.

'How are you feeling, Sophie?' he asked, as she burst into tears. 'Are you quite sure you're pregnant? Have you done a test?'

'No,' she mumbled.

'I'd better examine you to be sure,' he said matter-of-factly, and went out to call his nurse in to chaperone.

Sophie went behind the screen and got herself ready.

He put on his rubber gloves and, without making eye contact, said, 'Just try and relax.'

She felt humiliated as he moved his fingers inside her. It wasn't just the examination but the reason for it that she found so demeaning.

He took off his gloves, saying, 'Get dressed and we'll have a chat.'

She wanted to shout, *Can't you tell me now?*, but remained quiet. She got dressed and went to sit opposite him at the desk.

'Sophie, you are definitely pregnant; only just. So whatever you decide to do, I'll help. We'll also do the test to make absolutely sure, and then we must have another chat before we proceed.' He spoke impassively, which appeared to settle her.

'I know I can't go ahead with another pregnancy. What does it involve?' she asked.

'I can do a termination in one day, but taking your history and the effects of the anaesthetic into account, I would like to keep you in overnight, just to give you a proper rest.'

Her silence had an oppressive quality which kept him talking.

'Correct me if I'm wrong, but I remember that your other two pregnancies weren't planned either.'

She burst into tears again.

He softened his tone. 'Sophie, my dear, you mustn't worry. I'll sort this out. I operate on Mondays and Fridays, so if you can, be at the clinic by eight o'clock next Monday. Don't have anything to eat or drink from ten o'clock the night before, and you'll probably be able to go home Tuesday morning. I'm sure you have good reasons for this decision.'

He hoped that Sophie would confide in him, but she remained silent. He could have forced the issue by saying that he needed to put down a reason for the termination, then decided to put 'Risk of severe depression', which he believed would be accepted by the two other consultants whose endorsement was needed. 'Well, that's all I need to know for the moment,' he said, getting up.

'Thank you.' She wiped her eyes with a tissue. 'I appreciate you not asking any questions.'

Aubrey walked with her to the door. 'Sophie, it's the right decision, whatever the circumstances, and try not to worry. Phone my secretary if you have any queries.'

'Thank you,' she croaked through the lump in her throat.

In the waiting room Emma came towards her, simultaneously signalling goodbye to Aubrey.

'He really is very nice. I can see how any woman could get involved with him,' Sophie said, relieved to be back with her friend.

'Enough of that – what did he say?'

Sophie related all the facts, adding, 'He was really wonderful, and I have you to thank.'

'I'm not so sure I like that connotation.' Emma smiled.

'Oh, Emma, I didn't mean it like that. Really, what do you think I am?'

'I'd prefer not to answer,' said Emma, and they both laughed.

'How am I going to explain a night away from home to the children?' asked Sophie in a lighter mood.

'Say I am going to Oxford to see Daniel on Monday and I asked you to join me. Obviously, it's an opportunity for you to see an old friend. How's that? Then in the evening, say that she or he – on second thoughts, she – invited us to a party and we decided to stay over and come back the next day.' Emma delighted in her impromptu alibi.

'That sounds plausible. You really are a natural, Emma.'

'Well, I am going to be a lawyer.' Emma grinned.

'You know, all these lies are wearing me down. After this episode, I'm going to get back to the boring old truth. I just feel more comfortable with it.'

'You're right, Sophie, but there is always a time in one's life when kindness is more important than truth.'

'Emma, you really are on form today; I knew you were resourceful but today you have surpassed yourself.'

'Darling,' Emma said with an air of satisfaction, 'you'll get past this blip, and things will turn out all right. After all, you never thought Lucien would ever change, and look at him now. The best way to get revenge is to better yourself. That's my motto.'

FORTY-FOUR

TRUTH

Sophie walked around in a trance, forcing herself to concentrate when Lucien or Hannah spoke to her. Their conversation seemed to be sucked into a vacuum; her mind drifted into nothingness. The knowledge that they must never know eclipsed all other considerations; her thoughts were too painful to process. She made her excuses and withdrew to her bed. Her sleep, although brief, was filled with endless dreams, her senses overtaken by turbulent, vivid images, one following the other. If she recognised the people, she couldn't place them, as they merged in space and time. When she awoke, the dreams faded away, leaving bizarre echoes seeping insidiously into her consciousness. The fear that had plagued her in her dreams resurfaced at the thought of seeing David. She couldn't cancel her visit; nor could she recall her previous certainty about the need to see him. She tried to compose herself. Yesterday's consultation with Aubrey had changed everything. It was unthinkable to confront David in her present state. In calmer moments, she clung to Emma's advice, which Aubrey had also inferred: she had to stop being the victim of her own inactivity. In alluding to her previous unplanned pregnancies (Emma more directly), they had been right. She had to take responsibility for her actions.

The time arrived for her to go to David's. Her panic mounted but her determination remained, convinced that she had a right to know the reason for his changed attitude. She dressed in her chocolate gaberdine trousers, cream silk blouse and long, knitted burgundy jacket, made up as best she could to mask her pallor and dull eyes, and arranged her hair into a soft chignon. Then she fastened her grandmother's ruby necklace around her neck and was immediately reminded of her valiant family in Czechoslovakia, whose lives had embodied the futility of self-pity. She would stop hiding from the world. She had no reason to hide from David.

*

At exactly two o'clock, David opened the front door. 'I'm pleased you came. Let's go into the lounge.'

His courteous greeting didn't go unnoticed by either of them. She was making herself comfortable in the Charles Eames chair when an unexpected wave of nausea, accompanied by a dizzy spell, made her put her feet up on the footstool.

'Are you all right, Sophie? You look ill.' Unintentionally, his warmth, reminiscent of their previous friendship, surfaced.

'I could be better,' she said, taking a deep breath.

'Maria has prepared a tray. I'll get the coffee.'

'I don't feel like any coffee, thanks, David.'

He sat down on the settee opposite her. 'You must be ill. I've never known you to refuse coffee.'

'I hate myself,' she said, now past caring.

'I wouldn't be so hard on yourself. It takes two to tango.'

'If you're referring to the night I spent with Avram, I take full responsibility even though I was set up. My naivety is my biggest enemy, ipso facto, I hate myself.'

'I suppose I'm a little responsible. After all, I also got caught up in the adolescent scheme but I never thought...' He fell silent and looked at the floor.

'You never thought I would land up in bed with him.'

'To be honest, no. I thought an evening meal together... I really don't know what I thought. Do you know, I haven't heard from Avram since. Well, it must be over a month. He could have at least written to thank me for his stay, but then, he's Israeli and I shouldn't make a judgement purely on that aspect of his behaviour.'

'It's six weeks, actually! I should know.' Sophie felt her eyes burning and took out a tissue to wipe her tears.

'I'm sorry, it's just that I don't know how a man of his apparent integrity and dedication to his work could behave in this way.'

'I haven't heard from him either.'

His voice softened. 'Oh, Sophie, I thought you were... an item, as they say. And I admit I had more than a twinge of jealousy and went into a bit of a sulk. I also thought that after I had been rather curt on the phone and made those comments about you rushing into it... Well, I thought you were furious with me.'

'David, I really don't understand why you think I would hold something like that against you. I've known you too long. And, in any event, as it turns out, you were quite right. I suppose if anything hurts it's my stupidity. As though a one-night stand isn't bad enough, I'm pregnant!' Sophie choked on the words.

David stood up and paced up and down the room, as if talking to the walls. 'This is all quite dreadful. What's happening with Marc?' he asked, in a way that made Sophie think that he was hoping that someone would take responsibility.

'This is not Marc's baby,' she said. 'Marc is definitely not coming back and nobody knows about this, except for Emma, who, as always, is being wonderful.'

'What are you going to do?' he asked, unable to look her in the eye.

'I'm going to have an abortion on Monday, or perhaps a termination is a kinder description,' she wept.

'Sophie, this is all quite dreadful. What the hell has happened to Avram – why hasn't he made contact? Surely there must be a reason?' David protested.

'Like what – there are no phones in Israel? He has just disappeared. Don't think I haven't thought about it, and I've finally come up with the raw truth: he made a mistake professing his love for me, then felt bad about it and couldn't face telling me. What's new? My father couldn't tell me about our family; Marc couldn't face telling me he was leaving, so he just left. There is obviously something in me that prevents people from telling me the truth.'

David took out his handkerchief and handed it to her. 'Have you tried to contact Avram?' he asked, as if some hard facts might diminish their feelings.

'How could I? I don't have his phone number, and even if I did, I have become resigned to the dignity of silence.'

David stood next to her and, looking down at her tear-stained face, swollen eyes and soft, shapely lips, felt guilty, but also encouraged by knowing what had happened. 'I've got the number. I'll phone him now. Don't worry, I won't say too much.' He walked briskly to his study, reassured that he could do something practical.

Sophie sat back in the chair, the waves of nausea reminding her of the ordeal still to be undertaken, but felt better for having been honest with David.

He returned, appearing more composed, and, sitting opposite her, calmly conveyed his conversation with Avram. 'I managed to get hold of him at the Hadassah Hospital. You're right: he said he wanted to write to you and then thought the letter could get into your husband's or children's hands. He didn't feel comfortable about talking on the phone and, as he resisted each option, the time passed, and then he didn't know what to do. I didn't tell him about the pregnancy. I don't know how I managed to restrain myself. I really feel so angry. All I said was, "It's important to know the truth."'

'What did he say?' she asked, clinging to her last vestiges of hope.

'He said he was sorry, and then annoyed me intensely when he said that at the time, he felt he might have done you some good, and that no real harm was done, and he hoped we would all remain friends.'

'I'm obviously even more naive than I thought. Maybe he *has* done me a favour, although I can't see it, and if that wasn't enough, David, your coldness towards me really hurt,' Sophie choked.

David bent down, putting his hand on her arm to console her. 'At least we know where we stand,' he said, in a tone which sounded inappropriately conclusive.

'*We?!*' exclaimed Sophie.

'Sophie, some awful misunderstanding is occurring. I don't know how to put this, but somehow I've been confused. I've also been a coward. And when I got caught up in Avram's ruse, there must have been a part of me that was vicariously enjoying the possibility. I mean, the truth is that I do honestly care about you, but I was scared to entertain the idea. And when you got together with Avram, I was more than jealous. I really have behaved badly towards you. I'm so very sorry.'

Sophie stopped crying. She felt calm, ushering in a transient sensation of déjà vu. 'David, what are you trying to say? I'm really very unclear, and with my proclivity for getting things wrong, I have to be very cautious.'

David seemed to have grown in stature. His sharp, boyish features took on a concentrated expression. 'I'm trying to say that I think I love you, but have been too stupid to admit it.'

'Oh, David! How can we even think such things without feeling disloyal to Angelica? I don't feel I can trust my own judgement after Avram, let alone anybody else,' she replied.

'I understand. I've been there, remember, and I know how hollow words can sound. All the clichés like "Time heals" and "It's early days", however well meant, were meaningless at the time, but they do encapsulate universal truths. I can wait. I want you to be sure – and, of course, fully recovered from this fiasco. And when you are stronger, could we at least talk about this?' David said compellingly.

A sudden disappearance of her nausea and a return of an inner trembling drew her to face what she had so far hidden from herself. A peculiar sensation swept over her. Somewhere in the recesses of her mind she felt that this event had been destined, and spoke freely. 'David, I feel so ashamed. I could have so easily fallen in love with you, but I would never allow my feelings to develop – I would never have hurt Angelica – but after she died, I felt myself drifting towards you. I suppose I was trying to deny my feelings, and maybe that's how I got involved with Avram. But now, when we are both so entangled in our pasts, how do we know if we can share a future?'

David sat forward on the settee. 'So, who says we have to put the past in front of us?'

'Well, if you're starved of a cliché, that's one that's as clear as mud.' She smiled through her tears. 'David, do you believe in prophetic dreams?'

'I think you should know that, after living with Angelica and going to Jerusalem, I believe in everything,' he said.

Feeling more self-assured, Sophie said, 'I know you were amused by Angelica's "signs", so if I tell you my dream, no sneering or jibing; just listen.'

'I'm all ears. I'm all yours.'

'David, please, I'm serious. Listen. Lucien was in the house. It was on fire. I called Marc, but he was busy in the garden. Hannah and I kept pouring water on the flames, but they got fiercer and fiercer. It was like those trick birthday candles you can't blow out. Then a tramp broke in, grabbed a hat and disappeared. Suddenly I was in a bright house with minimalist furniture. I've forgotten lots of things but that's what I remember.'

'Fascinating – what does it mean? I have often wondered about dreams and the amazing accuracy of Angelica's insight,' David replied. 'It appears to me that, just as in our waking lives it is our pasts that so often determine our future, so too in our dreams do our pasts come together in a different way to shape our future. How do you interpret your dream?'

Worried, yet assured by David's depth and sensitivity, Sophie sat silently for a minute or two before replying. 'I'm not sure what it means, but it was my dream so I must take responsibility for it. I think Marc and the fire that could not be extinguished represent the surprises and upsets of the past few months. Angelica's death, Ernst finally telling me about my mother, finding a brother, Lucien's behaviour, Marc's rejection – they all took their toll and found their expression in the dream. It was, I must face it, Avram who was the intruder, the tramp who behaved badly, for he did not want the valuable thing in the home – me. The minimalistic house I was in just before I woke up stood for you. David, I need to understand what is happening; I need to know the truth.'

'Absolutely riveting, but are you ready to face the truth now?' David asked.

A flush spread across her high cheekbones, and she looked serenely beautiful. 'I think that being honest with each other is the first and most important step. Our silence and hesitation have caused such unnecessary suffering.' She felt herself gaining confidence. 'It all depends; truth can also be harmful.'

He got up and paced the floor. 'I wish I could be more helpful, but it's doubly painful for me. I suppose you know that for years Angelica and I tried to have another child and it never happened. It just seems unfair, in so many ways, that you have to go through this. I'm sorry; I can't quite face it, if I'm being honest.'

'It was foolish of me to tell you. Believe me, it wasn't my intention. The past few weeks I've been naively outspoken. I now value what Ernst always says: "Timing is everything." Emma has arranged everything. She is the most loyal and wonderful friend.'

'I agree, and I regret that I didn't always appreciate how much she helped Angelica.'

'Yesterday, I couldn't have imagined today, and although I am dreading Monday, I can and will face it. You see, it's giving me a chance to grow up and take responsibility for my actions. I feel vindicated knowing that Avram doesn't care. Perhaps it's the perpetual trauma of living in Israel that has hardened him. I suppose he found me when I was ready to make an idiot of myself. But believe me, it mustn't happen again.' She spoke as if warning David.

'The truth is, Sophie, I'm also responsible. You could say it's my fault you are in this predicament.'

Sophie raised her head, and their eyes met. Her eyes glazed over. 'David, there's no absolute truth, just meandering perspectives. I know that now. In a way I feel gripped by a sense of inevitability. I just want to let things evolve.'

David resisted his inclination to touch her delicate, narrow hand resting on the arm of her chair. He looked at her lovingly and smiled. 'Sophie, I respect you too much to lose your friendship, and I will wait for your love. *Paulatim sed firmitur.*'

'Slowly but surely. I haven't forgotten my Latin.' She smiled back. 'I'll let you know.'